MAC

MAC

KEEP A HUMAN TOUCH

DAVE RIGBY

The Book Guild Ltd

First published in Great Britain in 2022 by
The Book Guild Ltd
Unit E2 Airfield Business Park,
Harrison Road, Market Harborough,
Leicestershire. LE16 7UL
Tel: 0116 2792299
www.bookguild.co.uk
Email: info@bookguild.co.uk
Twitter: @bookguild

Typeset in 12pt Adobe Jenson Pro

Printed and bound in the UK by TJ Books LTD, Padstow, Cornwall

ISBN 978 1915122 117

British Library Cataloguing in Publication Data.
A catalogue record for this book is available from the British Library.

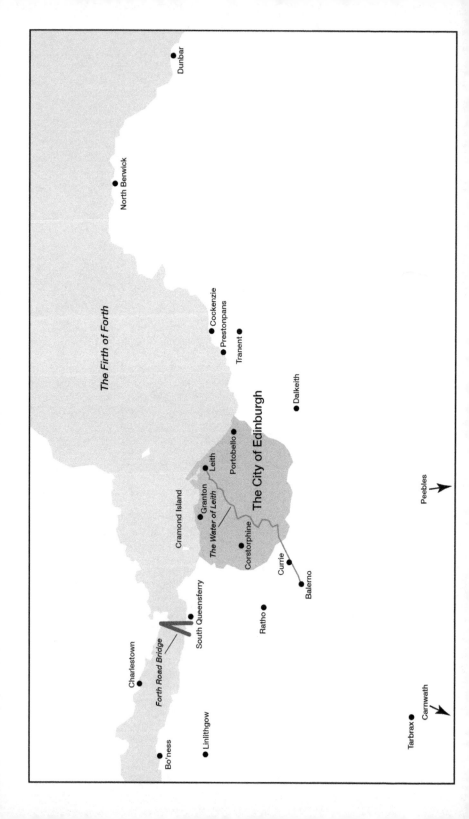

1 MARCH

The surface of the north face of the bing, rough and weathered like the skin of an old elephant, was slowly disappearing under a thin blanket of fresh snow.

A young couple walked along the base of the spoil heap, hoods up, arm in arm, unsurprised by the sudden turn in the weather. After a sudden gust, he huddled even closer to her, their eyes half-closed against the driving snow.

It was the bird in the undergrowth that caught their attention as it squawked through the brambles. Only then did they notice, beyond the briars, something bright red standing out against the whiteness.

Moving closer, eyes suddenly fully open, they took in the red socks, the brown shoes and the rest. Complete stillness. There was no doubt.

Gloves off, she removed the phone from her pocket, and tapped in three digits. A short wait. Police and ambulance required. Another short wait. She reported the body, described the location, gave directions from the main road and added that the last part of the journey would be over rough ground.

The voice, which she imagined to be in the warmth of an office, asked her to stay where she was. Out in the cold.

"An officer will be with you shortly, but with the snow falling, we'll need you there to show him exactly where the body is."

+ + +

It was a welcome day off for Mac. A lie-in, then a walk from the flat to Café Surprise for a first coffee of the day, a copy of *The Herald* on the table in front of him, dying for a cigarette, but not until the white stuff eased.

His phone rang. Work. He'd made the mistake of putting the damn thing in his pocket, which made him far too reachable. And it would be a real stretch to claim he'd already had too much to drink as a way of exempting himself from responding on his day off. The *bevvy waiver* they called it. To be used very sparingly if you wanted to avoid the blacklist.

The call was from PIT HQ. He recognised her voice, a new lass. Couldn't remember her name.

A dead man on a bing down near Tarbrax. He'd passed the road sign often enough, driving away from the city, a right turn off the A70, the 'Lang Whang' as it was known. Back of beyond. West Calder was the local police station, but with cutbacks and reorganisation, all major cases were handled by the PIT – the Peripatetic Investigation Team.

He memorised her directions. Yes, he knew about the snow. Ten minutes and he'd be on his way.

Angelique, who ran the cafe, wrapped a steak and onion pie in a serviette and popped it in a bag for him. No, her mother in Réunion wasn't doing too well. It was a real worry. The only thing to be done was to keep sending the money – until the next trip back to the island.

Mac ran back home for the Jimny. Due to cutbacks, the force no longer provided detectives with cars, just an allowance, which was set at a level everyone moaned about. Mac had never been much bothered about cars and the Jimny was cheap to run.

Driving across the city, the amateurs were out in force, slip-sliding across the roads, making it hard for anyone with a serious journey to make.

The A70 was easier, apart from a few macho speed merchants who'd signed up for the snow challenge. A Lexus up ahead had just failed the test and skidded into a roadside ditch. Mac slowed just long enough to see the driver emerging in one piece. No time to stop – he had higher priorities. His phone rang. A glance at the cradle. It was Roisin. There hadn't been time to think about her suggestion of a weekend away. He let it go to voicemail.

A first bite of the pie, flaky pastry spraying onto the already rubbish-strewn carpet. Two more bites and it was gone. A cigarette was always welcome after a meal. Not wanting to open the window and invite the snow in, he put up with the smoke instead.

He'd not come across any of the West Calder crew for a while. Hopefully they'd send a sergeant. The local squads generally disliked the detective inspectors from the PIT, regarding them as interfering outsiders who thought they knew it all.

Mac saw the sign to his right, just after the satnav's monotone instructed him to turn. His tyres scrunched over proper, pristine snow, no other tracks to be seen. A rare chance to use the Jimny's four-wheel drive. Go through the village and follow your nose to the far side of the bing, he'd been told. The couple who found the body would be waiting for him. Poor buggers would be half-frozen.

Angelique had joked about him getting a transfer to Réunion where it was always warm. But with his inability to speak French, it would be a non-starter.

He peered through the falling snow, trying to locate the couple, eventually spotting them, huddling up against a high stone wall, in the lee of the wind. The two diligent, public-spirited citizens looked in fact to be three-quarters frozen.

He gestured for them to get into the car. She pushed the front passenger seat forward and they both slid awkwardly into the back. Mac turned the heating up to max and shifted in his seat so he could look them in the face. After thanking them for phoning in and hanging around in the cold, he explained he'd come from the city – which was why it had taken a while. As the teeth-chattering from the back seats began to subside, he asked how they'd found the body.

They looked at each other before speaking, as if they were already communicating without actually talking. She gave the first answer, then it was his turn. They'd been having a walk, no, not at all unusual, they liked being outside, even during the winter. They'd seen a bird in the brambles, stopped to try and identify it and only then noticed, a short distance beyond, the partially snow-covered body of a man. Shirt and jacket both unbuttoned, bare chest exposed. Very strange.

No, they hadn't disturbed the body or touched anything, but it was clear just from looking at him that he was dead. The young woman, hesitantly, told Mac of a feeling she might have seen the man before. He asked if she could remember where. No... but maybe it would come back to her.

They lived locally, well, twenty minutes' drive away. Not together, sheepish grins for a second or two. Their car? Why hadn't they waited in its warmth? It was parked about a mile away, wouldn't have been worth walking there and back and besides they'd been told to stand guard.

Mac's phone rang and he struggled to retrieve it from his trouser pocket in the cramped confines of the car. A Detective Sergeant Khan from West Calder had reached the village and wanted to know where the DI was exactly. He looked at the couple. Where was he exactly? She took the phone and spoke to Khan, established his location and gave clear and concise directions. Taking back the mobile, he asked Khan what he already knew. Nothing – just that there was a body. What about the techies? They were out on another case and might be a while. Fucking great!

Mac was pleased about his boots. Normal footwear for him. An urban boy but he'd never been one for urban shoes. The DS arrived. His footwear was less suitable for the conditions, highly polished black lace-ups. About Mac's height, just over six foot, but slimmer, short dark hair. Immediately attentive.

The couple led them to the body which was only just still visible. A good job they'd hung around.

Was there anything else they wanted to say at this stage? There wasn't. Had she remembered where she might have seen the man? She hadn't. It was all a bit hazy.

Not to worry, Mac said. He'd be back later to interview them and would phone with details of where and when. They trudged away through the snow, back to their car, arm in arm once again.

When Mac introduced himself as Detective Inspector Calum Larsen, Khan nodded but didn't say much in response, cautious perhaps, working out the lie of the land.

With much of the body covered in snow, there were no visible clues as to what might have caused the man's death. Mac guessed he was in his thirties or forties, slim bordering on thin, wearing jeans, tartan shirt, light jacket, brown shoes – and those red socks.

Returning to Mac's car to await the arrival of the techies, conversations about football, music and holidays petered out. But then it turned out they were both walkers – when they could get the chance. And both smokers, windows opened just a crack.

The scenes of crime officers finally showed up. Mac knew them, brothers, a pair of jokers, proper Hibs fans like he'd been years ago. He'd worked with them regularly, the last occasion being on a case out near Dunbar. They'd got nowhere on that one.

Suits and gloves went on and tapes were put in place. As usual, Joker One took the lead, taking a swig from a hip flask and offering it to the others. There were no takers. *Suit yourselves!* The two brothers carefully removed the snow from the body.

"Why do you think his shirt and jacket are open?" Mac asked.

"To make a point about the marks on his chest," Joker One replied. "Take a look."

Not wanting to disturb anything, Mac carefully stepped marginally nearer and peered through the falling flakes. He'd seen the distinctive pattern of marks before.

"Poor bugger's been tasered," he said.

"Damn right," Joker Two said. "Don't imagine it'll be the actual cause of death though."

Joker Two took the camera and photographed the body and the wider crime scene from every angle, total concentration on the job. Once the snapping had finished, the brothers began to examine the body, communicating with a series of one-and-two-word grunts which, as usual, Mac failed to make head nor tail of. But when Joker One spoke into his phone to record their findings, he was precise and perfectly understandable.

The brothers talked endlessly as they busied themselves with their remaining tasks. In contrast, conversation between Mac and the DS was intermittent.

Eventually, flashing blue from a distance, siren silent, the ambulance approached, lumbering awkwardly across the uneven snow-covered ground. The brothers greeted the paramedics like long-lost friends. It had been a whole week since their previous meet-up. Cigarettes all round, smoke rising slowly in the cold, still air, football talk in the main, a brief dalliance on the endless saga of independence, a dismissive reference to the virus, before bagging the body and loading it into the ambulance. Corstorphine was the drop point.

Having erected the crime scene tent, the brothers replaced equipment in bags, loaded their own vehicle and followed the ambulance away from the bing.

Two local PCs had arrived to stand guard. The Jokers would be back.

"Anywhere local for a coffee," Mac asked Khan, "before we head off for the big city?"

"Sure. The Saloon should be open by now and if not, they'll make us a brew anyway."

Mac followed the DS's Mazda back to the main road, a right turn further away from the city, followed by another right across a cattle grid and down a bumpy track for half a mile to a large stone building partially hidden by spruce trees, smoke billowing from a chimney in need of a complete rebuild. Mac pulled up alongside the Mazda and a tractor, the only other vehicle in the extensive car park.

The big wooden door was closed and apart from the smoke, the whole place looked deserted. But Khan shoved the door open with his shoulder, Mac followed and did a double-take. Beyond the large lobby was a pair of saloon doors which parted as they made their way into the bar area. Honky-tonk music emerged from a pianola in the far corner. A blazing log fire in a huge grate was an immediate magnet.

A booming voice came from another room.

"What can I get you this fine day, Raj?"

"Two big coffees," he shouted back.

They stood warming themselves in front of the fire, turning now and then so as to cook evenly. Khan threw another log on to the burning heap.

"Bit different, eh?"

It certainly was. The man who brought their drinks on a large silver tray was dressed in full cowboy gear, complete with hat, neckerchief and gunbelt.

"Don't worry, the pistols are fake. I'm Dougie, by the way." He held out a large hand. Mac shook it. "First time here?" Mac nodded. "Hope it won't be your last. Take a look at the events poster over there. One or other of those bands might be up your street. Or you might fancy one of our vintage Western screenings."

As he turned to retreat to the kitchen, the spurs on his boots clicked.

"How come there's a place like this all the way out here?" Mac asked.

"Who knows?" Khan said. "Been going for years. Dougie's father opened it, a complete movie nut by all accounts. No idea how it keeps going."

Chairs were drawn up to the fire, legs stretched out and hands wrapped around mugs as they speculated about the dead man. Mac said that although they didn't know yet whether he'd been killed, the taser marks pointed in that direction.

"Interesting the young woman thought she'd seen the dead man before," Khan said.

"That's what I thought. But she was pretty vague about it. We'll see."

He asked Khan about his experience on murder cases.

The DS told him that since the changes to local stations such as West Calder, inspectors like his boss were responsible for at least three others, which meant sergeants got a wider range of experience more quickly than under the old regime. He'd worked on a murder case and a manslaughter case recently, the first a random attack by a stranger and the other a fight between two drunken lads in Bathgate that had ended badly. But in previous posts he'd been involved with a further five.

Much better than Mac had expected. He glanced at his watch, a present from Freya and more expensive than he'd have wanted. Time to head to Corstorphine.

+ + +

Back in the city limits, Mac checked that the Mazda was still following before turning off the A70 and cutting through a series of side streets to reach the recently built East Caledonia Police HQ in Corstorphine. Mac remembered there'd been an outcry when the cost overrun had finally been revealed. But then, how many developments came in on budget these days? As usual the car park was full and Mac had to park on a side street, two wheels on the pavement, Khan tucked in behind.

"Been here before?" Mac asked.

"A few times. But you PIT guys are based out in Leith, aren't you?" Mac nodded. "So, do you have desk space here as well?" Khan asked.

"We're usually lucky to find a chair. Used to bug the hell out of me when I first started coming but now… well, you get used to things and we're not here that often. Come on. I'll introduce you to Carla."

She was one of those people who kept places functioning. Not only efficient, but welcoming and she knew everything and everybody, probably the only one in the building who met those criteria. Two seats appeared from nowhere, followed by mugs of coffee and even slices of shortbread. Khan looked impressed.

She and Mac had been an item a few years back but it hadn't lasted – par for the course for him. They'd weathered the break-up, with no hard feelings on either side and a post-item friendship had developed.

Mac checked his phone. Nothing yet from the techies. What did he expect? Miracles! There was an email from Khan's boss, full of bureaucratic dos and don'ts. It was a familiar problem for the PIT officers, but such things were generally met with a shrug and then ignored. He slurped his coffee, finished the last piece of shortbread and asked Khan what thoughts he had about the dead man.

"Er… not sure really, Inspector."

"Come on, you must have some ideas!"

"Well, it wasn't natural causes! Those taser marks, the way they were displayed, if not flaunted and something about the positioning of the body. I'm sure he didn't breathe his last out there on the bing. The body was most likely driven there from wherever the killing took place, so there should be tyre tracks to check once the snow's cleared. I doubt that couple will be able to tell us much more. She was alert enough but he looked a bit out of it to me. Do you know when we'll be able to take a proper look at the body?"

Mac glanced at his watch and said, hopefully within the next half hour. The ping of an incoming text on his phone. Freya.

Her face next to Roisin's. He didn't want to think about having to make a choice. Khan didn't seem to notice his temporary distraction.

"What do you know about the bings?" Mac asked. He'd seen a number from a distance, had once walked over the Seven Sisters, near West Calder, with Freya, but had never really understood why they were there.

"Not much really," Khan said. "The oil shale industry was big business. Once they extracted the oil from the shale, the waste had to go somewhere, so they built big hills of the stuff. I reckon they've got a certain attraction."

Mac agreed with him.

"Get yourself down to the fridges," Carla called out. "Just a preliminary with Paula, mind." Mac was surprised but pleased the pathologist had reached this stage so quickly.

He didn't like lifts. They bounded down the three flights to the basement.

Their rapid descent reminded him of life on the top floor of the tenement building, when he and his brother, Erland, would race down the stone steps of the spiral common stair to the bottom before hurtling out of the door and onto the street, glancing at the stopwatch to check whether they'd broken their record. They'd found the little treasure in a box of oddments in the second-hand shop next to the off-licence his father had frequented.

Paula Dubanowski didn't greet them as they entered her domain. She was something of a legend and it was notoriously hard to predict her moods. Sometimes she'd bite your head off, then ten minutes later you could be her best pal. But moods aside, she was professional to the end.

Despite the lack of a greeting, Mac decided from a calmness in her eyes that they'd caught her at a good time. The body was on the table and she walked slowly around it, pointing out relevant details, a birthmark here, a nasty-looking scar – not recent – on his left arm, dirt under the fingernails, roughened hands and, of most interest, the puncture marks on his chest.

Early forties she guessed. Time of death difficult to pin down because the body had been out in the cold, but probably somewhere between twelve and twenty-four hours prior to its discovery. She confirmed Khan's view that the body had been moved from some other location to the bing.

Mac asked if the puncture marks had been caused by a taser.

"Yes indeed," she said.

"Probably not the cause of death though?"

"Too early to tell, but I wouldn't completely rule it out."

Mac reached for a cigarette and placed it in his mouth. Khan looked concerned and was about to say something, but Paula didn't bat an eyelid, having seen the inspector's reflex action often enough before. The cigarette remained unlit, bouncing up and down as Mac asked further questions, took in the replies, but wrote nothing down.

"One more thing," she said. "It looks like he was a user of cocaine."

"Now, that's interesting! A dabbler or longer term?" Mac asked.

"Longer term, I'd say, but I'll need to check further."

"How come our friend was able to jump the queue and get on the table so quickly?" Mac asked.

"When they told me whose case it was, well, I had to give it priority! You can believe that if you want to," she said, turning away from them immediately, "but the truth is I'm so efficient, I'd already cleared the backlog. Now, get out of here. I've got work to do even if you two haven't."

They returned to the main office. Carla pointed to a number of evidence bags in her out tray which contained the contents of the deceased's pockets. There was a note from the Jokers, warning Mac to take great care in handling the bags – as if he needed reminding. They'd be performing their forensic wonders on the objects as soon as possible.

Very little there, really. No wallet, no ID of any kind, no car keys, no phone. Just a door key, an unused handkerchief, a wrapper from a chocolate bar and a receipt for two espressos from a cafe in Linlithgow. A note from Joker One informed them that the key had been hidden in the heel of the dead man's shoe. An amateur job maybe, but good enough for the key to have escaped the attention of whoever might have wanted to get rid of the dead man's identifying possessions.

Mac asked Khan to get onto the coffee shop immediately. The key, which looked to have been newly cut, had a number on one side of the head and a series of letters on the other. A job for the Jokers' resident lock specialist. Mac hoped his expertise would enable them to pinpoint the relevant locksmith. The sight of the chocolate wrapper made him feel hungry. Standing in front of the vending machine, he cursed when it became apparent that none of his pockets held any change. But Carla had coins.

He promised himself that the chocolate bar would be eked out for an hour or so. But after typing only the first two paragraphs of his initial investigation report, laptop balanced on his knee, he found the whole thing had disappeared.

Mac had a habit of sometimes giving an unidentified body in a murder case a working name – not that murder was a certainty as yet. It felt more personal somehow. Mulling over a suitable one, he took himself off to the fire escape to light up. The access door was normally alarmed, but there'd been a fault and the PFI-nominated maintenance firm had yet to show up. It saved Mac having to go all the way down to the ground-floor smoking shelter.

The top of the fire stairs was a good vantage point. Murrayfield stadium one way and the zoo the other. He'd never been one for rugby and had only been to the stadium the once, to please a friend who'd gone on and on about the game and was sure Mac would be an instant convert. As if! The zoo had been visited more often as kids, but his brother had always been keener on the place than he had.

A name for the new body? *Frank* rather than *Frankie*, he decided. *Frankie* had too much baggage.

What had led *Frank* to his death? He gave his imagination free rein. *Frank* was from Glasgow, killed over there, dumped on the bing, gang-related, probably to do with drugs, given he was a user. Or maybe modern slavery – there was a lot of it about.

Reluctantly, Mac brought his fire-escape musings to an end with a decisive rap of his knuckles against the handrail, feeling sufficiently well fed to head off to his car without another visit to the vending machine.

+ + +

Mac phoned the couple who'd found the body and arranged to meet them at her parents' house in Bellsquarry. The snow had stopped which made the drive out there easier than his earlier journey.

The parents were away. Being a little concerned by how young the daughter looked, he wondered whether an appropriate adult would need to be present.

"Sorry to ask, but with your mum and dad not being here, could you just confirm your age?"

"No problem," she said. "I always get asked in pubs."

The passport details surprised him. She was actually twenty-three.

The couple sat close together, holding hands on a sofa which was only slightly better than some Mac had seen dumped on the street awaiting council collection.

"You mentioned before that you might have known the man on the bing," Mac said, hoping that by now she'd be able to remember something about him.

"Look," the young woman said, "sorry about this, but actually I haven't seen him before. He just reminded me of somebody. Everything was a bit flustered in my head… finding the body… you know."

"I appreciate that," Mac said. "Are you sure? Do you need more time to think about it?" he asked, willing her to say yes.

"No… I'm sorry."

"Might this help at all?" he asked, pulling an autopsy photograph of *Frank* from his pocket.

She stared at the picture, shuddered and shook her head.

Mac decided to ask them a few more questions, in the hope that something useful might come out of it.

The two of them followed an unchanging routine in their responses. She'd start to talk and then look at the young man. He'd nod and she'd continue.

But her answers were brief and of no real help in taking the investigation forward.

"Well, that's it really," Mac said. "Would it be OK if you followed me in your car to Police HQ in Corstorphine, so we can get a statement typed up for you to sign?" After glancing at her young man, she said that would be fine.

Sitting in an HQ interview room, Mac still hoped that the process of drawing up the statement would jog a memory in one or other of them. But he was disappointed.

Statement completed, he set off for Leith. A call from Khan.

"The woman at Metro Coffee was very helpful. She remembered the customer because of his foreign accent, somewhere north European she thought, his hat, which she said was like the type the old film stars used to wear and the fact that he didn't look well. The two espressos were downed very quickly and he'd spent the rest of the time, head on his arms, leaning on the counter by the window."

"Remind me of the date when *Frank* was there," Mac said.

"Who?"

Mac apologised and explained about his habit of naming unnamed victims.

"I like the idea," Khan said. "Anyway, the receipt for his coffees was issued at 3.45 on 27 February."

"Ah yes. And how long did he stay?"

"She thought about twenty minutes. But there's more. Just before he left the cafe, he took a call and the cafe woman overheard him saying he'd meet the caller at The Cairn. It's a local pub," Khan said, sounding pleased with himself. "I'm on my way there now."

"That's a helpful lead. Well done," Mac said.

It was always important to have something positive early on in an investigation and the news put Mac in a good mood.

+ + +

The Peripatetic Investigation Team was based in a three-storey converted warehouse, just off Salamander Street, overlooking Leith docks. Although its official name was Kingfisher House, everybody called it the Warehouse.

Whenever he could find the time, Mac escaped to the waterside for a smoke and to gaze at passing boats. He could remember Robbs, the shipyard where his father had worked until its closure in the early eighties. His mother had sent him there once with an urgent message for his dad. The men had taken a shine to him, but he'd found them so difficult to understand, with their yard lingo on top of such broad accents. The 'Wee Norwegian' they'd called him. But he'd never actually lived in the country, born in Edinburgh only months after the family had moved there from the shipbuilding town of Fredrikstad.

Mac took the stairs up to the first floor two at a time, trying to compensate in a very small way for missing yesterday's evening run. Detective Chief Inspector Morag Maeven, his boss, who'd be the senior investigating officer on the new case, was standing just inside the door at the top of the stairs, phone clamped to her ear. Almost as tall as him, an initially forbidding manner, wearing – as most days – a well-cut trouser suit. Like him – a runner. A hand moved, a signal that Mac should wait. Call finished, Maeven told her inspector she needed a word, immediately, in her office. Up another floor.

Where was his final report on the arson case? Twenty-four hours late and the chief superintendent up at Corstorphine was getting restless. Mac was tempted to be argumentative, knowing he'd need as much time as possible to work on the new case. Instead, he bit his tongue, promised the paperwork by the morning and escaped.

Despite the fad for 'agile' working as HR insisted on calling it, they still stretched to a desk each in the Warehouse. Mac had a window in front of his which gave ample scope for distraction. He sifted through a pile of messages and listened to his landline voicemails. Unusually, nothing was urgent, which meant he could move straight on to the arson report.

Maeven had been right of course. The report was late and there was no good reason for it, apart from Mac's need for a life outside the force. His fingers moved rapidly over the keys. He'd never understood why all officers weren't forced to learn how to touch-type. The old two-fingered dinosaurs were so slow. The fire had been in a disused mill in Dalkeith. Mill fires were not exactly unknown and were usually either set by kids or 'insurance' jobs. This one had been neither and as a consequence, it had taken a lot longer to get to the truth.

Just as he reached full reporting flow, Khan arrived. Mac tried not to show his frustration. He was, after all, very keen to hear what the DS had to say.

The landlord of The Cairn had been initially unhelpful until the error of his ways had been pointed out. The DS had spotted several public health infringements in the bar and once these had been brought to the landlord's attention, he was much more compliant. Mac asked where this specialist knowledge had come from. A brief previous life he was told.

It had been maybe a fortnight back. The landlord remembered the man with a foreign accent and a trilby hat – just like his father's. They'd got chatting. Turned out he was a visiting German, well educated, a scientist, something to do with lasers, but with an equal interest in horse racing. Didn't get his name, but he'd been staying temporarily in South Queensferry, somewhere *with a fine view of the bridges*.

With this information, Mac had to revise most of his earlier assumptions about *Frank*.

Khan said he'd drive out there and follow it up. Mac was tempted to join him, but the arson report was a real ball and chain. It was a further two hours before he could email the finished product to the chief inspector.

Who'd know about lasers, he wondered.

Dr Kenneth Macintyre came to mind, his old school pal, who'd decided at the age of seven he was going to become a physicist and had subsequently achieved his childhood ambition. The sort of friend you could go for ages without talking to and then pick up seamlessly at the point you'd left off. How long had it been since their last conversation? A month?

But he'd need to summon up the energy to handle a phone call with Kenny. It might be half an hour before they even got onto the subject of lasers and then… well, who knew how long it might take. Still, if he could make the call from a bar, it would be that much easier to handle.

He phoned Khan, left a message to meet at 8.00 the following morning at the Warehouse and drove home.

+ + +

The estate agent's blurb had described it as the *spacious private parking area* to the rear of the two flats, but there was barely room to squeeze the Jimny in next to his downstairs neighbour's car which, as usual, was taking up a space and a half. A walkway led from the parking area to the front door of Mac's flat.

He stripped down to boxers and T-shirt and lay on the bed, the chug of the central heating a comforting background noise. Turning on the bedside radio was a mistake. A report on the lockdown of the Chinese city of Wuhan sounded like something from a dystopian film. He turned it off.

An hour later, he resurfaced. A pot of tea and a caramel wafer restored him to a reasonably functioning state. He remembered Freya's text message and knew contact should be made, or he'd suffer the consequences – even though they weren't currently seeing each other. Back on the bed, this time fully dressed, he put one pillow on top of the other, adjusted his posture for maximum relaxation and made the call, left arm behind his head.

He and Freya went back a long way. Summer holidays spent at his grandparents' farm not far from Fredrikstad. She'd lived next door. As youngsters, they'd played around the farm and in the fields – allowed to go as far as the stream, but not to cross it – and had spent their carefully eked-out pocket money in the tiny village shop. In the evenings, his grandmother read to the pair of them from the Asbjørnsen and Moe folktales – the bear and the fox stories their particular favourites.

He'd met up with Freya occasionally on holiday visits during his teens, but couldn't remember exactly when he'd started to see her differently, started to dream about her. It was those piercing blue eyes that had first captivated him – and her pixie-like nature, the inquisitiveness, the fun, the unpredictability.

There'd been just the one time, in that late-teen era, when they'd slept together, in the loft of a barn, above the cows, well away from prying eyes. They'd both wanted to, but had both regretted it, unable to regain their comfortable way of being together as friends. For a long while afterwards, he'd associated the smell of cattle with sex.

In their early twenties, they'd got together again. Freya had moved to Scotland, to study at the Edinburgh College of Art and eventually moved in with him. But when things got difficult, she'd moved out. His job had been one of the problems. She'd never understood why he'd joined the police. As a boy, he'd always wanted to work in the shipyard, like his dad. Later, with the yards closed, he'd decided to move back a generation, follow in his other granddad's footsteps and join the force.

Despite their separation, Freya had come to like Scotland and decided to stay. Since then, there'd been apart times and together times.

She now lived on the Fife coast, in Anstruther, one of the picturesque small towns with red pantile roofs. As he waited for her to pick up, Mac pictured Freya in the tiny sea-view cottage, canvases stacked against the living room wall, flecks of paint everywhere.

They talked about nothing very much for a while, before homing in on the big issue.

"What do you reckon then?" she asked him.

He'd been thinking about her suggestion of getting back together without really making any progress, unable to force the idea from the back to the front of his mind. Murder cases tended to suck the life out of the everyday. He didn't tell her that, as it would have sent their conversation off down a previously well-trodden path, leading only to a cul-de-sac. *You never give me enough time.*

The pair of them had been going through an off time for the past three months, long enough for her but he wasn't so sure. Their last period together hadn't ended well, worse for him than her, he felt. And then there was Roisin who he'd only met recently, strangely both lovely and hard work at the same time. He wasn't sure how that could be the case, but didn't want to give her up, not yet anyway.

Mac thought back to his fishing days. Freya was on the hook again, but he was reluctant to reel her in. No sooner had he allowed that particular image into his mind, than he dismissed it. There was no way a woman like Freya would allow herself to be caught or re-caught. It would be more appropriate for him to be the one dancing around the hook.

Surely though, meeting for a drink, one evening after work, could do no harm. After all, there were things he wanted to talk about and when all said and done… he missed her.

"I think we should have a drink together," he said.

She sounded pleased and promised to text with details of time and place. Any meet-up between them was always provisional – that was half the problem. All that was needed was a sudden development in the latest case, whatever it was, or a summons from the boss. Still, if it happened, it happened.

+ + +

Although pleasantly distracted by thoughts of Freya, he managed to haul his mind back to thoughts of Kenny.

Knowing exactly how his friend operated, Mac wanted to control events and decide when he'd had enough. It was much easier to do that by phone than by meeting face to face. And where better to make the call than from the snug confines of The Dunvegan.

Damn – the evening run! He'd missed the last one. Missing two in a row wouldn't be good. He forced himself into T-shirt, joggers and the A trainers – the ones that cost a packet. Despite his frequent tendency to consume unhealthy snacks and meals, he still had a runner's frame. Setting off upstream through Dean Village, he went on towards Murrayfield, before turning back and retracing his steps, relieved that the rise in temperature had got rid of the snow and ice underfoot.

After a shower, he put on jeans, a Fair Isle sweater, the big jacket, the C trainers – the ones he could wear anywhere – and he was off. Out of the door, along the walkway, down the side steps to the river – the Water of Leith – and a right turn downstream towards Stockbridge. After no more than a couple of hundred yards, his legs were telling him that apart from the early morning pie and the vending machine chocolate, his diet for the day had consisted solely of cigarettes and coffee. It sounded like a song title – maybe it was. Not for the first time, Mario's chippy three doors up from The Dunvegan would fill the meal gap nicely.

It was his brother, of all people, who'd introduced him to the Water of Leith. There'd been a brief period of a few months when

Erland had been into walking. For those few months, his interest had been all-consuming. That's how he lived his life, Mac mused, moving from one obsession to another. Erland had been buzzing about the attractions of The Water. *Come with me, man. Meet us at Dean Village and we'll walk all the way to our old tenement in Leith.* Mac hadn't needed a second invitation.

Years later when he'd been looking to buy a place, a flat right by The Water had come up for sale. There'd been no second thoughts about whether to go for it, even though the price had been over his budget. He'd named the flat *Glomma* after the river in Fredrikstad.

The path alongside The Water was lit. There were spates when local youths would indulge in the game of catapult-a-bulb, but the council had recently replaced all the broken ones. The river was full, bubbling and bouncing over rocks, swirling against the banks, driftwood from upstream abandoned in back eddies. Before leaving the path at Stockbridge, he stared into the water and thought about *Frank*. Had he been living and working locally or just visiting from Germany and what might he have done to attract the attention of a killer?

Haddock and chips, a mug of tea and a left-behind evening paper on a tiny red-topped table, the only one free at Mario's. He flicked through the pages. The body hadn't even made the front page. The article on an inside page was brief, which wasn't surprising given the lack of hard information at such an early stage. The haddock, which had been delivered to his table hanging over each end of the plate, gradually disappeared. His normal habit of bolting food was eased by reading while he ate.

On his way out, Mario asked him for the latest. Mac showed him the article. They talked about Catania, Mario's home town which, coincidentally, Mac had visited during his one and only Italian holiday, a volcano walking trip. Apparently, Etna was currently rumbling away nicely, but otherwise behaving itself.

The Dunvegan wasn't busy. A pint of Eighty Bob and a table by one of the front windows with a view of the street. Kenny answered promptly and despite the gap since their last communication, didn't seem surprised to hear who was calling. Mac knew there'd be the usual trivia to get out of the way before he'd be able to move into laser territory. A rant about the government, a recent trip on an old tram, the fortunes of Montrose FC, his home-town club, his mother's latest ailments. Mac could have written the whole script himself – apart, maybe, from the section covering the delights of the tram trip.

Finally, Kenny drew breath and asked about the real purpose of the call. When Mac mentioned lasers, he could almost see Kenny's eyes lighting up. The thing was then to get in as quick as possible and make his pal aware that he didn't want an Open University lecture on the subject, just an outline and the benefit of Kenny's informed speculation about why *Frank* might have been in Edinburgh. His glass empty, Mac wandered over to be served, caught the barman's eye and signalled a top-up. Kenny got into his stride. An idiot's guide to lasers followed and Mac was surprised to find he could follow it. The doctor could be a good communicator when he was in the mood.

And what might have attracted *Frank* to the city? A brief pause at the other end of the line. Well… Midlothian University were into lasers in a big way… maybe the German had been visiting them.

"That's a very useful lead," Mac told him. "Would you be able to find a contact for me in the relevant department up at the uni?"

"No bother. I'll get back to you on that. Just a mo while I top my glass up. All this talking's giving me a thirst."

After the briefest of pauses, Kenny rushed on. Mac sensed it was the start of the lecture, but waited a few minutes before interrupting the monologue, on the off-chance that some additional nugget might be thrown his way. Once it was clear that wasn't going to happen, he terminated the call with the excuse that a colleague had just arrived.

Mac stayed on at The Dunvegan for a third pint, a brief consideration of what Kenny had told him, a chat with the barman about running routes and a few dreamy tunes on the jukebox. The temptation to call Roisin and invite himself around to her place disappeared once it dawned on him that he barely had enough energy left for the walk home. Tomorrow night, maybe.

On the riverside path, a bike hurtling along, no lights, missed him by inches. He swore at the cyclist, knowing it was a complete waste of breath. As he rounded the final bend there was a double-take moment. A light in his flat – and not one he'd left on. There'd been a break-in six months previously and he'd only fitted an alarm following that. And him a copper! First instinct was to catch the bastard in the act this time. But strangely it was quiet, no sound of the alarm – which he'd definitely left on. Then the penny suddenly dropped. When you give someone a key and your alarm code you have to expect that, at some point, they're going to use both to gain access. Maybe he wasn't so tired after all.

2 MARCH

Bursting for a pee, he dragged himself out of bed and swore when the kitchen clock told him it was already 7.15, which gave him only forty-five minutes to get himself sorted out and reach the Warehouse for his catch up with Khan. It crossed his mind to phone and push the meeting back half an hour, but he didn't have such time to waste.

An extremely quick shower, clothes thrown on, no shave, no coffee. Roisin was in full sleepy, early-morning mode. He brushed aside a lock of hair, kissed her on the forehead and told her he had to dash. A mumbled *bye, love* in response. Nothing said about her idea of a weekend away. Traffic was dire as usual, but shortcuts came to his aid and by some fluke, there was a parking space free, close to the back entrance to the office.

Khan was already at his desk, busy at his laptop, as quick over the keys as himself, Mac noted.

The DS had a question about Mac's surname. Scandinavian?

"Yes, Norwegian," Mac said. "And the blonde hair and the blue eyes are a bit of a giveaway!"

"So, how did you get your nickname?"

He was surprised the enquiry hadn't come sooner. Ever since he'd acquired the name Mac, as a twelve-year-old, the question had inevitably raised its head. There'd been five of them in the gang, three from the same class, two a year older. Larsen had met the unwritten entry criteria by virtue of being both the tallest and the most daring. Although the other four happened to have genuine 'Mac' surnames, they had nicknames ranging from Doughnut to Horse. Larsen was awarded the title Mac purely and simply because he wasn't one. And it had stuck. The transition from school to the world of work might have been a time to drop the name, but as one of his fellow gang members had joined him signing up as a police trainee, the name had lived on.

What news did Khan have about where *Frank* might have been staying?

"You remember, the landlord of The Cairn said the German had said he was staying, temporarily, in South Queensferry? *Somewhere with a good view of the bridges*, to quote." Mac nodded. "So I started with an online search for hotels and B&Bs that might have such a view, which threw up a dozen possibles. But the only way to really tell was to drive around and check out the view from each one. Eight of them passed that test. Then I needed to know whether any of them had registered a male German guest recently. After a phone call to the first one and a less than helpful response, I decided it would be easier to call in on the rest of them. That turned out to be a waste of time as none of them had let a room to a German."

"Does that mean no progress?" Mac asked.

"That's what I thought, but driving away from the town, I saw a caravan site – with a view of the bridges – and called in on the off-chance. The owner was very cagey about answering my questions. Guessing it might have something to do with unlicensed letting, I told him I wasn't interested in minor rule breaking, just whether or not there'd been a German staying in any of his vans. He said one recent guest spoke with what might have been a German accent, but he couldn't be sure."

"Did he have a name?"

"Unfortunately not. As the visitor paid two weeks upfront in cash, the site owner didn't bother with any other details. But when I showed him the autopsy picture of *Frank*, he told me it might well have been his guest – and added that he'd worn an old-fashioned hat!"

"Promising," Mac said. "Did you manage to get a look inside the van?"

"The owner wasn't too keen, but eventually let me in. It was spacious and surprisingly well kept... but completely empty. Apparently, our *Frank* cleared off, without a word, a week ago, but as he'd paid in advance the owner wasn't concerned."

"And what kind of car was *Frank* driving?"

"Didn't have a car. Arrived on the number 43 bus from the city centre. There's a stop right outside the site entrance. Presumably he left the same way. But one useful piece of information from the owner. He saw an old green Volvo estate parked outside the van one evening. Claims not to have seen the visitor and of course didn't know the registration number. I'll arrange for CCTV footage to be checked for the Volvo... and for the bus."

"Good work," Mac told him. "I had some luck last night. Spoke to a source of mine and found out that Midlothian Uni is a bit of a hotspot for laser research. It's a longshot at this stage, but maybe our German had some links with them. I'll be following it up."

Mac's phone rang, Maeven wanting to discuss the arson report. It didn't do to keep her waiting. She liked to keep a firm grip on her DIs.

The detective inspectors based at the Warehouse were viewed with suspicion by the local forces. They got parachuted in to head up the big cases wherever they were needed across the eastern side of the Scottish central belt. Local officers moaned like mad about the set-up, but the reality was that after years of cutbacks, it was no longer viable to base senior or specialist staff out in the sticks. So they had no choice but to put up with the PIT. But that meant there were turf wars a-plenty and frequent bushfire outbreaks. DCIs like Morag Maeven had the difficult job of trying to maintain some kind of peace between the warring factions.

It didn't help that the DIs were independently minded, worked on their own initiative, spent most of their time out in the field and frequently ignored the needs of both the local services and the corporate machine.

Standing in front of the boss' over-large desk, Mac prepared himself for a bollocking. The arson report hadn't been his best piece of work. It came as a surprise to be told that the report would do. Praise indeed from Maeven – or was she just softening him up for some dreaded task yet to be revealed?

He summarised progress on the new case and mentioned the possible link to Midlothian. Maeven told him to tread carefully up at the university and reminded him – as if he needed to be told – that the first two days of a murder case were the crucial time. He knew better than to point out that they didn't actually know for certain yet that it was a murder.

Back at his desk, he phoned the pathologist.

There was progress. Paula didn't want to say anything official yet, because more investigation was needed, but it looked as if the taser had triggered a heart attack. Which meant they were probably looking at a murder case or at the very least, manslaughter.

"Anything on the type of taser?" Mac asked. "Hopefully not police issue!"

"Don't know yet, we're working on it. That sort of complication would be the last thing we'd need. There's something else, though.

I mentioned before about him being a cocaine user. Well, I can now confirm that it wasn't just occasional use." It was good to have further solid information, Mac thought, trying hard to avoid the temptation to parcel the case up as yet another drugs-world death.

"I seem to remember reading something about the effects a taser can have on drug abusers," he said.

"Well done," Paula replied. "The cause of death in such circumstances can be down to what's known as 'excited delirium' which can bring on either cardiac or respiratory arrest. Chronic drug abusers are more likely to be prone to it, particularly if they're using a stimulant such as cocaine."

"Brilliant! So, we can tick off cause of death on our progress sheet."

"Not so fast, Inspector!" she said, suddenly stern-voiced. "At this stage, this is my informed opinion, not a final decision. You'll keep it to yourself, understood."

He understood. It didn't do to get on the wrong side of Paula.

Mac knew their mini-team of two would need immediate reinforcement. Khan suggested a colleague from West Calder, an up-and-coming detective constable. Mac phoned Khan's boss who was surprisingly helpful. The DC would be on her way just as soon as she'd finished writing up her report on a recent plague of hole-in-the-wall ram raids.

It was only then that Mac remembered he'd promised to take his mother to a hospital appointment. Why was it seemingly impossible for him to recall anything to do with his private life when he was in work mode? Now it would be a struggle to get her there on time. Having briefed Khan on his priorities for the rest of the day, he set off east along the coast road. His mum had always loved the sea and when, following her husband's death, the chance of a housing association flat had come up in Portobello, she'd jumped at it.

COPD, as the medics referred to it. *Can't catch my breath* was his mum's description. Whichever, it meant regular appointments at the New Royal Infirmary, a constant stream of medication and periodic worrying moments.

Pia Larsen had adapted remarkably well to the family's sudden shift from Fredrikstad to Leith back in 1975. Her English had already been good, far better than her husband's. The baby was born a few months later and the parents decided it would be good for him to have a Scottish first name. Wee Calum it was. Much to her relief, he turned out to be a healthy, easily managed baby, unlike his older brother who'd had a string of ailments and refused to sleep. But with baby Erland she'd had family all around her, helping to take the strain. With Calum she'd been a new mum again, without a support network.

When her husband Per died in 2017 she'd been bereft. The two of them had been very close and his death very sudden. A heart attack. The flat by the seaside had been a godsend.

It was a bad breathing day. Mac helped her into the front seat of the Jimny and made sure the belt was fastened. He felt permanently guilty about not seeing her more often. On their way across the city to Little France, they chatted about relatives back in Norway, this cousin getting divorced and that nephew signing on as a professional footballer with a lower league club, Pia pausing the conversation frequently to catch her breath.

The phone in the cradle rang as they sat in traffic on Niddrie Road. Maeven wanting to know where he was. Mac reminded her about his mother's appointment which he'd flagged up a few days previously. Were there no other relatives who could help, Maeven asked? Had he forgotten that the clock was ticking on a murder case? Mac was tempted to mention overtime hours and untaken leave, but he just sucked it up and said he'd be working late – again. Maeven sighed and ended the call.

His mum apologised for dragging him away from his work, but Mac would have none of it. The problem lay with his boss – not with her.

The display in the waiting area at the Royal showed that clinic appointments were running an hour late. His mum told him not to wait. He was tempted to take advantage of the delay and get across to Corstorphine for a face-to-face with Paula. There were things she didn't reveal in phone calls, as if she was worried someone was listening in. In person, she could be much more open – as could he.

But an hour wouldn't give him sufficient time to be able to do that. He'd have to make do with using the phone. As his mum seemed happy enough with a cup of tea and her book, he rationalised that she'd feel less guilty if he used the hour productively. So he grabbed a coffee from the hospital cafe and retreated to the Jimny.

He was lucky. Paula seemed to be in a good mood and they had a useful speculative discussion about the German.

"Given we've established he was a regular cocaine user," she said, "more than likely he'd have had a local supplier rather than risk bringing a stash with him from Germany."

"Thanks, Paula, that's definitely a line of enquiry worth pursuing. Listen, I was thinking about his hands, the ingrained dirt. My first thought was that he must have had some sort of manual occupation, but we now have information that suggests he might have been involved in working with lasers. Have you any thoughts on this apparent contradiction?"

"One possibility is that the state of his hands could have arisen, not from his occupation, but from being a keen gardener. Some people have skin which soaks up the dirt and no amount of hand-washing is sufficient to get them properly clean. So, there's no reason why he couldn't have had dirty hands and also have played around with lasers."

Mac terminated the call, sipped his coffee slowly and spent the next thirty minutes responding to emails.

When he returned to the clinic waiting area his mother was still sitting there reading her book. The display signalled that appointment delays had increased. His inclination was to return to the car to make some more phone calls, but he felt he owed it to his mother to spend some time with her.

They chatted about her nursing days at the old Royal and the few years she'd worked at the new place following the move there in the mid noughties. Occasionally on her appointment visits there'd be someone she'd recognise and a brief chat about times past.

His mother asked about Freya. She'd never been able to understand why the two of them had danced around each other for so long without ever making a firm commitment. When he claimed things were difficult, she told him it was an excuse. He should face up to the fact that whilst life was often difficult, there was also pleasure to be had in getting on with it. She liked Roisin well enough but worried that the young lass was just another one passing through.

Mac had tried and failed umpteen times to explain about him and Freya. But then he couldn't really explain it to himself. To make matters worse, Erland didn't have that kind of problem. He and Catriona had been together for nearly twenty-five years. Granted there were frequent fallings out, but they'd always kiss and make up.

The hushed-voiced discussion with his mother regarding his love life was brought to a merciful end by Kenny's name appearing on his switched-to-silent phone. A work call, he told his mum. The corridor just outside the clinic area was marginally less public. Mac told him where he was and that the conversation would have to be short.

Kenny had been doing some digging.

"My contact at Midlothian Uni tells me they have a development project relating to drone-mounted laser weapons."

"That's very useful news."

"And that's not all, my friend. This is being carried out jointly with the University of North Rhine-Westphalia!"

It took a few seconds for Mac to latch on to the reason for Kenny's enthusiasm. North Rhine-Westphalia was in Germany. So, had *Frank* been part of the team at NRW and been in Edinburgh working on this collaborative project? He liked the sound of this theory.

"That's unexpectedly helpful. Can you forward your contact's number?"

"Should already be in your inbox, Calum."

Mac thanked Kenny, who amazed him by voluntarily terminating the call. It was a rare event.

He glanced through the clinic door's glazed panel to check his mum was still waiting. She'd disappeared. Shit! One more call and he'd have to go and find her. Khan answered immediately with a *yes, boss.*

Mac told him the gist of what he'd picked up from Kenny, without identifying his source.

"I'll forward details of a contact at the uni. Can you send him a photo of *Frank* and ask him to find out whether anyone working on the joint laser project can identify the dead man? Then find someone to speak to at North Rhine-Westphalia University and repeat the process."

Mac found out which room his mother had been taken to and asked a nurse to let him know when the physical examination and routine tests were completed so that he could be involved in any subsequent discussion. He sat and waited and was about to nod off when a text came in. Roisin. *Can't make tonight. Love R.* Well, that was one less thing to rush around for.

The tests were over sooner than he'd anticipated. The nurse led him to a consulting room. His mum looked worn out. He sat next to her and held her hand, listening carefully to what the consultant was saying. They'd need to up her medication and it might reach the stage where she'd have to access a ventilator from time to time – a series of inpatient visits, in other words. The consultant who was very matter of fact and lacking in empathy, breezed off. Mac answered his mother's questions. She hadn't been able to follow what the doctor had told her. He knew it was down to the immediate stress and that later at home, with a cup of tea, she'd be better able to take it all in. The nurse handed her a booklet about ventilation and had a few comforting words.

Mac checked the time. The day was disappearing fast. There was still the return journey to Portobello and a decent settling-in period with his mum at her flat before he'd be able to shoot off.

+ + +

It was nearly six before he got back to his first-floor office at the Warehouse. No sooner had he made himself a coffee and sat down than Khan walked in, a grease-stained paper bag in his hand.

"My mum's pakoras," he said. "Help yourself."

Apart from two chocolate digestives, Mac hadn't eaten all day. They started on the bag's contents. Khan couldn't wait to give him the good news.

"The German university got back to me. Someone recognised the photo. Our victim is Dieter Hofmann, a specialist in the development of lasers who's been working with colleagues in Edinburgh."

"That's great. Well done!"

"They were a bit cautious about the details of the project and told me it involved some classified activity."

"Ah! That's the sort of complication we could do without," Mac said. "Anything from Midlothian yet?"

"Not initially but I spoke to our contact there and he put me through to a Professor Martin Laing, their head of electrical engineering and computer sciences. I've arranged for us to meet him. He's obviously a busy man, not available until eight tonight. Is that OK for you?"

"That's fine. I must say, it's great to have a name… although I'll be sorry to have to say goodbye to *Frank*," Mac said, taking another bite of pakora. "And thank your mum for these. They're excellent. Any progress on the 43 bus, the one Dieter caught to get to his caravan?"

"I spoke to the site owner again and narrowed down the time frame for Hofmann being on the bus. I let the bus company know and they'll check their CCTV."

"And the visiting green Volvo?"

"The owner said it had been too dark to see anything much when the Volvo arrived and he didn't notice it leave. So we haven't got much to go on. The site itself doesn't have any CCTV but I've arranged for the roadside cameras to be checked."

"It's time for me to update DCI Maeven," Mac said. "I'll check whether she's in."

His call went to voicemail and he left a brief message, with a warning that the investigation might have to move into some sensitive territory.

Khan seemed suddenly awkward. Mac told him to spit it out. A personal matter. He needed an hour, but would still be OK to meet at the uni just before eight. Would that be alright?

He got the go-ahead.

Mac's knowledge of lasers was limited to what Kenny had told him the previous evening. Feeling it would be useful to know a little more, he began trawling the Internet. As ever, the problem was trying to sift through the heaps of information you didn't understand to find some key non-technical, plain-English gems that provided those 'oh I see' moments.

He hopped between research departments, laser forums, press articles and blogs, the wild ones and the saner ones, all the while turning a question over and over in his mind. Could Hofmann's death have been in any way work-related? They could check with the professor what, specifically, Hofmann had been working on. Whether they'd get an answer, would depend on how open the academic was willing to be. It was clear from the details Mac had been able to understand that lasers were big business across a whole range of applications and that it was a fast-moving and highly-competitive world.

His final task before leaving the office was to check the online campus map to locate the prof's office. There was a car park near to the office block, which he assumed would have spaces by the middle of the evening.

As he drove slowly through the still busy streets, he adjusted to the fact that *Frank* had now been replaced by Dieter and conveniently buried the fact that all the details he'd invented for his created character had turned out to be wrong.

Just like his assumption about a half-empty car park. There wasn't a space available – some sort of evening event he presumed. A grass verge came to the rescue. Hopefully the campus traffic wardens wouldn't be working an evening shift.

Khan, who was waiting for him at the entrance door of the undistinguished 1970s block, pressed the intercom buzzer, there was a click and he pushed the door open.

Despite knowing better, Mac had an old-fashioned image of professors, aging, uncontrollable hair, unpredictable, living in their own bubble. The youngish man who bounced down the staircase and greeted them effusively matched none of these stereotypes. Late-thirties maybe, gangling, short and well-groomed hair, gabbling away but using words that were understandable. He led them upstairs and into a spacious office at the front of the building. A red light glowed on a coffee machine in a corner of the room. Three cups were filled and brought across to a round table by the window.

After taking a sip, Mac gave an account of what had happened to Hofmann and expressed his condolences. Laing nodded, was briefly silent and then asked the two policemen what they wanted to know. Mac asked him if he could focus initially on the joint development project and then give them an idea of the specific work the German had been involved in.

"The two universities are working on a joint project, called IntelOper, short for 'intelligent operation'. You'll be familiar with drones – what we refer to as Unmanned Combat Aerial Vehicles, or UCAVs. You're probably also aware that the military use drones which may be equipped with laser weapons. What you may not know is that artificial intelligence can play a part in the deployment of these weapons. Our project is developing the control software to enable this to happen. We're part of a much wider project which will bring in a new generation of laser-armed drones. Are you still with me?"

"Yes. That's a very clear summary," Mac said, looking at Khan, who nodded. "And what was Dieter Hofmann's own area of specialism?"

"The application of artificial intelligence. We were quite lucky to get him on board."

Given the nature of the project, as outlined by the professor, it was clear to Mac that their enquiries would come up against the problem of classified information sooner or later. He hoped it wouldn't prove to be too much of a barrier.

Laing added some further detail regarding the project and Hofmann's role. Mac felt he was one of those natural communicators, able to distil the complexities into something understandable to the layperson, without talking down – or dumbing down.

"Do you mind if I ask what caused his death?" Laing asked.

"We can't say for certain at present," Mac said, wanting to keep away from specifics. "Not long before his death, he was tasered, but whether that was a direct cause of death we don't yet know."

"Tasered! That's awful. So do you think he was killed?"

"We don't know. It's very early days yet. But one area we want to explore with you is whether his death could have been linked in any way to his work." Laing looked suddenly very concerned.

"I can't imagine for a minute that would be the case. It's not that sort of world. Sure, there are disagreements and some people hold very strong views, but these differences play themselves out through the medium of research papers and, these days, blogs and specialist social media sites."

"Thank you, that's helpful," Mac said. "I was wondering whether there would be any vulnerabilities around... how can I put it... trade secrets? Given that the project is involved with highly confidential areas of new development, might hostile parties who are keen to get hold of such information pose a potential threat? To people like Dieter, I mean."

"That's an interesting point you raise," Laing said, "and of course industrial espionage is something we have to try and guard against, but I think it's highly unlikely that his death would have been linked to that."

"Are you aware of anything that may have led to Dieter's death, Professor?"

"I am. It feels bad raising this," Laing said, squirming a little in his seat, "as if I'm trying to blacken his character. But we found out recently that he had a serious problem with cocaine."

"Well, that is a concern," Mac said. "Can you tell us more?"

"Apparently, he'd been using for a long time, but it didn't affect his ability to work and he'd managed to hide the problem. As soon as his addiction was made known to us, we made enquiries.

He'd had problems with his dealer and had run up rather large debts. If you're looking for something which might have led to his death, you might want to start your search in the murky world of drug dealing."

+ + +

"What do you reckon?" Mac asked Khan as they left the building.

"Well, it's clear what Laing thinks. Look no further than the drugs. But I'm not so sure. As you pointed out, Hofmann's work might have taken him into some difficult areas. I think it would be worth probing further."

"I agree," Mac said. "Can you pursue that? Arrange to speak to other people in Dieter's team and see if you can pick up on any tensions, anything that might have got out of hand."

Maeven called just after he'd finally managed to set off for home, wanting to know why his message on such an important issue had been so brief. Mac instantly felt his annoyance gauge swinging round to max, which meant he wasn't really in a fit state to continue driving. He pulled into a gap in a line of parked cars, lifted his phone from the cradle and went into full assertive mode.

He ignored her question and went straight on to tell her about the meeting with Laing and the all-important question of motive. Maeven was big on motive. The prof's view was that Hofmann's death was linked in some way to his drug use – which, interestingly, the uni had already known about. Although Laing had dismissed the idea that it might have been something to do with Hofmann's work, Mac said he and Khan both felt that line of enquiry should also be pursued.

Maeven simmered down.

"Go ahead, Larsen, but watch your step. Given what you've told me, you'll be almost certain to stumble across classified information at some stage. If that happens, don't let the sergeant from the sticks in on that bit of the investigation, unless you can personally vouch for him – and tell me immediately." Mac got the message.

Back home, unable to stop yawning. No sign of Roisin. He'd hoped she might have changed her mind and be waiting for him. A check of the fridge. Two rashers, beyond their best-by date, but they smelt OK and one egg. No milk and only two slices of bread left in the freezer. One for his tea and the other for breakfast. Not wanting to be bothered with going to the shop, a mini fry-up, black coffee and a fag would have to do for his evening meal. He turned his phone off while he ate and watched a reality show with the sound muted, following the exaggerated body language of the participants with amusement. Why on earth were these programmes so popular? He caught the news. The virus was causing havoc in Italy, spreading at a rate of knots. He wondered how long it would be before it started causing similar problems in the UK.

Having digested his snack, he changed into his running gear and set off for a jog, not along The Water this time but through the streets of the New Town, the grandeur of Royal Circus and Moray Place, Queen Street Gardens and back via Stockbridge. Further than he'd planned, but he felt the better for it. After showering, he retraced his steps back to The Dunvegan, book in pocket.

As he walked, the day's events turned over and over in his mind. By the time he reached the bar, the mental spin dryer had worked its magic, leaving him free to concentrate fully on a decent, extremely well-earned pint, a brief chat with the new barman and chapter nine of his political thriller.

He had to watch the drink. The risk of being stopped and tested on the morning commute had increased in recent years. If he had to work the following day, which unfortunately applied to most of his evenings, care had to be taken to keep within his self-imposed limit. Over time he'd trained himself to consume more slowly, enjoy the taste, savour the effect.

And he loved the time spent, hunkered down in some quiet oasis, very little happening, his phone on silent, enclosed in his own small world, a glass close to hand. The problem was he loved these times a bit too much and it was midnight before he said farewell to the bar and meandered home.

3 MARCH

Blinker was used to not sleeping and had a graded set of responses to the almost nightly occurrence. A combination of dressing gown, a cup of tea and the radio was the easiest response and the least distance to travel from bed. Some nights though, it needed more. The tea with an added something and the soporific effect of early morning TV shopping channels usually worked. Some nights he had to go the whole hog, clothes on over his pyjamas, plus coat, hat and scarf during the colder months and out for a dog walk along the foreshore.

It wasn't usually specific worries that kept him awake but a general dread of what might lie just around the corner. Life was tough and making a living even tougher, a bit of this and a bit of that. It was always a struggle.

He'd tried the radio and tea therapy earlier, but it hadn't worked and so, at 6.30 a walk with the dog became a necessity.

His tiny flat above a corner shop was three blocks from the sea. The surrounding streets were nondescript and it was only on hearing the sound of the waves that his spirits lifted. Then it was a choice of left or right. As usual, the dog made the decision –

right towards Cockenzie. The lights of a tanker near the horizon moved slowly across his vision. His spell in the merchant navy had been the best bit of his life and he had no difficulty feeling himself onto the boat and looking back to the twinkling lights of the coast. The dog waited patiently on the worn grass as, despite the cold, his master spent a while resting on a bench, eyes gradually growing accustomed to the half-light.

A tidemark of rubbish lay before him, the inevitable plastic waste, drinks cans, fag packets mixed in with unexpected oddities – a headboard from a bed and a kitchen sink. Had these two items been dumped or washed up?

Just to the right of the headboard was what looked in the gloom like a loose roll of carpet. When sleety rain began to fall, Blinker decided it was time to move. As he drew nearer it became clear that the carpet was not a carpet.

+ + +

Despite the late-night finish, Mac had actually remembered to set his phone alarm, before collapsing into bed. Which meant a relatively civilised start, with time for a black coffee, a piece of toast and a rinse of the crockery. Traffic to Leith was manageable. The phone grabbed his attention. It was Blinker, one of his informants who'd been unusually quiet for a while.

"Thought you should be aware, Inspector. Out walking the dog when I came across this dead man on the beach, Cockenzie end of Prestonpans, you know, above the tideline, so definitely not washed up. His shirt was open and I could see these marks on his chest. Similar, I imagine, to those on the guy I read about in the *Evening News* – your new case, the body on the bing. I'll be in the Mermaid for as long as it takes you to get down here. And I've already called the local boys."

Another open-shirt taser job! What did it signify? Bloody

communications team! One of the problems with releasing specific details about a body too soon was that it risked imitation by other perpetrators. Though it did seem a bit quick for that sort of thing to be happening already. But then maybe this was number two by the same perp, in which case it might give rise to speculation about a serial killer. The shirt thing was odd. Why leave both bodies in this way? He hoped it wasn't a sign of some sort of ritual.

Blinker had known he'd want this case – despite the extra work it would bring. PIT had to wait to be called in by the local chief – that was the protocol. But why wait! There was the taser link. It wouldn't be the first time he'd short-circuited the rules. To be on the safe side, he called the local station, told them he was on his way – and why – and left a message for Maeven, to tell her why he was jumping the gun. His third call was to Khan, telling him their briefing would now take place at the Mermaid Cafe and to bring the new DC along with him.

Mac reached Leith, turned right and drove along the Firth waving metaphorically at his office and then at his mum's flat on the way to Prestonpans. He liked the stretch of coast with its mixture of over and under-development. The cafe was located not far from where the old Cockenzie power station had stood. He still couldn't get used to the huge empty site. There'd been talk of a cruise-liner terminal being built there, but he couldn't see it happening.

He bought a takeaway coffee at the Mermaid, joined Blinker on one of the rickety benches outside and celebrated his first cigarette of the day. His informant ran through the story again. They wandered down to the shore. The tapelines were already in place and the local DS bristled at the sight of Mac. There was the usual warning about territory and waiting for the paperwork to be in place but Mac ignored this, said he'd made the appropriate phone call, asked about the taser marks, mentioned he was already working on the bing case and offered the DS the coffee and a cigarette. The huffiness gradually faded.

Mac told Blinker he'd meet him back at the cafe and poked two twenties into the breast pocket of his old tweed jacket.

He put on a protective suit and studied the body without touching it. The puncture marks were, as near as damn it, identical to Hofmann's. There had to be a link. Maeven called, edging towards a warning, until she heard what Mac had to say. *Don't go throwing your weight around until it's formalised*, her parting shot.

Mac noticed Khan and the DC arriving outside the Mermaid, waved them over and asked the local DS if it would be OK for his two officers to have a quick look around. Yes, they were house-trained – although of course he only had two days' experience of working with Khan and couldn't vouch for the DC at all. An onshore breeze got up, blowing crisp packets, burger wrappers and discarded coffee cups along the pebbly scrub.

Once the three suited figures had completed a preliminary check and with the wind beginning to cut through, Mac told them it was time for a coffee. In the cafe, suits off, Khan did the introductions. DC Wyatt looked keen, perhaps a bit too keen, Mac thought. About five feet, eight inches, he guessed, dark hair in a ponytail, very dark brown eyes and clearly took far more care with her clothes than he did.

He told them there'd be a delay to the start of their investigation, while the right emails were forwarded to the right people confirming PIT involvement and his appointment as the DI on the case. In the meantime, they'd focus on reviewing the Hofmann story to date – just as soon as he'd had a word with the man in the tweed jacket sitting in the corner.

Blinker had been straining to hear every word said at the coppers' table. Mac needed him out of the cafe, but as smoothly and pleasantly as possible. There'd be a next time so it did to keep him sweet. Although sometimes informants disappeared without a word, Blinker had been around for years. Mac squared things off with him, caught up on the latest about his ma and his dog – which very considerately he'd left at home so as not to contaminate the crime scene – and the current state of play amongst the ne'er-do-wells of Prestonpans. Then Blinker was gone.

Mac and Khan chewed over their earlier discussion with the university professor, adding bits of detail so that Wyatt could follow the gist of it. Two lads poked their heads round the cafe door, spotted the polis at ten paces, scowled and left.

Khan's next step would be to speak to members of the Midlothian development team and to find out what they knew about Hofmann. Mac warned him about the risk of coming across classified information.

"If the issue raises its head, let me know immediately," Mac said. "I'll need to clear any further action with the boss. And DC Wyatt, welcome. I'd like you to make enquiries in relation to Hofmann's drug habit. Start with his workmates and see if they've got any useful information. I'll speak to the drugs squad."

As the other two drove off, Mac returned to the beach. Jokers One and Two had arrived. He'd asked for them specifically, so there'd be continuity on the two cases. The likelihood of there being no connection between the two deaths was very low, he thought. Unfortunately, the brothers' humour that morning was noticeable only by its absence – most likely down to a bad investment at the bookies, he guessed.

Even though his formal clearance was still to come through, Mac, suited up again, was allowed into the protective tent that had been thrown up around the body. The dead man, who looked to be about the same age as Hofmann, had a straggly beard and longish hair. A pair of John Lennon glasses was still in place although one of the lenses was missing. His threadbare trousers, socks and shoes were damp, probably from overnight rain rather than seawater, given the location of the body.

Mac tried to avoid jumping to conclusions too soon, but kept coming back to the taser marks. It was surely too early in the cycle for a copy-cat killer to have become active. He hoped that the two investigations would merge into one which would surely increase the chances of usable leads. The dead man's mugshot would be circulated in the hope that he might be recognised.

Mac didn't feel like going straight back to Leith. For one thing it would defer the inevitable grilling from Maeven. For another, the sea air was a magnet, which meant a short beach walk was called for. There was a smattering of dogwalkers out and about, some with their pets closely restrained, others using throwing sticks to hurl balls way ahead for their mutts to chase. One landed near him and he waited for the dog to approach. It was clear that the human's job was to kick the ball. Probably direction wouldn't matter but distance would – the further the better, he guessed. He managed to welly it without losing his balance, back towards Prestonpans. The dog's owner nodded appreciatively as he ambled past.

Mac had been a keen footballer until injury had sidelined him from anything but a kick-around. Back in the late eighties and early nineties, he'd lived and breathed football with almost every weekend in the season taken over by watching Hibs – home or away – on a Saturday and playing on a Sunday.

He stood staring out across the Firth of Forth, breathing in deeply, a brief moment of calm in a day that was only going to get busier and busier, before reluctantly turning back towards the car.

+ + +

Maeven wasn't in when he arrived at the Warehouse. A 'jumping the gun' quizzing would still take place but at least there was now time to give a bit more thought to his response.

He phoned Paula to tell her about the body on the beach, only to be told she was busy cutting someone else open. But at least an autopsy photo had come through the system. It was probably a long shot, but Mac emailed Professor Laing to ask for it to be circulated to the relevant few in a discreet manner. Did anybody know him?

He pondered whether to give the man on the beach a temporary name, a successor to *Frank*. But it seemed too soon to repeat the game. The new body would stay unnamed.

A text from Carla. Corstorphine had been asked by the press for comment on the Prestonpans body. It had been passed to Maeven and she'd said it should be handled by DI Larsen. Mac knew from bitter previous experience that such a call couldn't be delayed, but he was also well aware of his duty to be as bland and non-committal as possible at such an early stage. In other words, don't mention the taser link. Make sure the cases are kept separate. Don't invite any speculation about an emerging serial killer.

He'd dealt with Fraser, the reporter, before and had immediately taken against him – cocky, indiscreet (but what did he expect?), and dismissive of any facts that didn't fit his own speculation. *You don't do this job for as long as I have without ending up knowing more than you lot!* To be fair, Mac knew one or two hacks who could mount a good case along these lines, but Fraser wasn't one of them. Nowhere near!

Despite the usual goading, he managed to keep his cool and give nothing away.

An email from the University of North Rhine-Westphalia pinged into his inbox. Sent by a senior officer in their PR department, it confirmed that Dieter Hofmann had been a member of the development team in their Department of Applied Physics under a Professor Weismann. He'd been on secondment to Midlothian University, their partners on a cutting-edge research and development project. The PR guy said they were deeply saddened to learn of his death in such unfortunate circumstances and expressed their condolences. Details of Hofmann's next of kin were attached.

As these related to a cousin, presumably Hofmann had no partner, no parents, no siblings and no offspring. Mac decided to contact the local German police force about the death and check whether they would have any problem with him speaking to the cousin directly. After a brief online search, he found the relevant number and began to rehearse a few questions dredged from his German Higher memory bank.

Having explained the nature of his enquiry, he was put through to a senior officer in the state police. The woman was very helpful, offered to make the call to the next of kin herself, but said that she would have no objections to Mac phoning if that was his preference. It was. He recalled with dread his first such call. Only his second murder case and a sergeant who believed in throwing rookies in at the deep end. *Sink or swim, laddie.* And it had gone very badly with him crying silently and the bereaved weeping noisily, barely a word said between them. But it was difficult to get the balance right, the need to show sufficient empathy without risking getting sucked into feelings of personal grief. However, the response this time was a first. The cousin showed little interest in the shocking news and asked how come he'd been listed as the next of kin. *Blood relative yes, but Hofmann was a virtual stranger to him. Try Marek, another cousin. At least he'd seen Dieter within the last year.*

Marek Hahn didn't pick up. Message left.

Another call. Mac asked Professor Laing whether someone who'd worked with Dieter Hofmann would be able and willing to identify him. Laing nominated his deputy who was teaching but would be available at 7.00. Did they all work on into the evening, Mac wondered?

"We'll need a photograph of Hofmann to use in pursuing our enquiries. Can you send me one?"

"Certainly. I'll email it straight after this call."

Laing had something else he wanted to talk about.

"I've just had clearance to release some further information about Hofmann. Shortly before he died, we had to terminate his secondment, over a matter of gross misconduct. My apologies for not telling you about this at our meeting, but I'm sure you know what HR people and legal advisors can be like!"

Mac was taken aback by the news. Laing had not so much as hinted that there'd been such a problem.

"Look, Professor, I'll need to know the details. Was the dismissal because of his cocaine use or was it something else?"

"Embezzlement! He was syphoning off funds from one of his budgets in an attempt to clear his debts, which related to his two addictions – drugs and gambling. This just reinforces what I said at our meeting about the need to focus on the drugs world for answers as to why he died."

The news certainly did strengthen that argument, Mac thought.

"One other matter before I go," he said. "Did you by any chance recognise the man in the photograph I sent you?"

"No – sorry. I forwarded it to several colleagues, but they didn't recognise him either. Is the man connected to Dieter in some way?"

"That's what we're trying to find out. Anyway, thanks for your help."

Just as Mac turned to check his laptop, Maeven walked in, looking displeased. He decided not to hold back but to hit her with the latest developments before she had a chance to utter a word. It worked. The frown disappeared and the conversation continued in her office.

+ + +

It was a familiar pattern, a slow start with only a few small pieces of the jigsaw revealing themselves. Early on, it was difficult to place these in any meaningful pattern. Sometimes, that's the way things stayed. But more often the pace of revelation increased and a partial picture began to emerge.

Mac often coped with such information surges by taking himself out, away from the immediacy of the case, into some backwater, human silence, a takeaway coffee and a cigarette his habitual aids. Much of the dock area opposite the Warehouse was out of bounds, either fenced off, or access barred by burly security guards, but Mac knew the parts which had public access or where the gatekeepers would let him through on the proviso that he stayed in sight and behaved himself. He went to one of his regular perches not far from the sewage works, which was downwind – for a while at least. Despite the cold, he felt comfortable there.

A text about a meet-up, as promised, from Freya. She'd be outside the Warehouse at six that evening. Having already had his daily session with Maeven, there was a fair chance of avoiding any last-minute hold-ups.

The boss had actually been quite reasonable. It always worried Mac when she was like this as it usually presaged a later reaction in an equal and opposite direction.

The waves lapping against the Black Rocks, a little distance offshore, were just playing at it, perhaps warming up for a more active performance that night. He hadn't checked the forecast even though it was only a couple of clicks away on his phone, preferring, as usual, to take the weather as it came rather than be forewarned.

Khan had spoken to two people who'd worked with Hofmann on the university development team for Project IntelOper. According to them he was hard-working, extremely knowledgeable within his specialism and a bit of a laugh. Though not always. At times he could be very difficult to work with – dogmatic and argumentative. Apart from the cocaine, which was an open secret, neither of them could throw any light on why he was sacked. As for being killed, they couldn't begin to think why such an awful thing had happened. But Khan had picked up a useful titbit. One of the work colleagues had mentioned a friend of Hofmann's who'd paid a visit to their unit, another German and another AI specialist. He'd been not very subtly sniffing around for the kind of information that any unaccredited visitor would be kept away from. Khan had been given a good description – tall, thin, early thirties, designer stubble, a nose that looked as if it might have been broken, black jeans, leather jacket. Definitely worth pursuing. Unfortunately, nobody had a name for him.

A pair of cormorants on the rocks caught Mac's eye. It seemed as if they were doing the same to him, but no doubt in reality, they were thinking fish. He checked the news on his phone, then wished he hadn't. It was all about the rapid spread of the virus in a number of countries. Lockdowns were being put in place and he wondered how the Brits would cope with a stay-at-home message, once something similar was imposed, as it surely would be.

He drained his cup, thought yet again about buying a reusable one and flicked his cigarette butt into the water. Not straight back to the office but a detour via the kiosk to stock up on cigs, a Cornish pasty, chocolate and a copy of the *Evening News*.

Feeling suddenly chilled to the bone, he stood by an office radiator to thaw out. Unlike the pasty which disappeared within a few minutes, the chocolate was eked out, chunk by chunk, not so much eaten as slowly sucked to death between his tongue and the roof of his mouth.

The front page of the *News* was devoted to a bad car smash on the A1. On page two there was a not-at-all-gripping follow-up article about *The Body on the Bing*, as the case now seemed to be known in media land. Trust Blinker to be ahead of the game. After his phone conversation with the journalist, he guessed tomorrow's front page feature would be headlined *The Body on the Beach*. Sub-editors loved a nice bit of alliteration. Hopefully a catchy headline would be the only connection made between the two cases, at least for a day or two.

But of course, the print version was not the only way the paper released its news. He checked online and sure enough there was the body on the beach headline, a sigh of relief as he scanned the article and saw that it didn't include any reference to tasers. Mac, of course, hadn't breathed a word about the marks on the dead man's chest, but there was always a danger of such detail being leaked.

He thought about Hofmann and how there'd been no belongings of his left in the South Queensferry caravan. But what about his home in Germany? Might the local police find something useful there?

He called the senior officer he'd spoken to about the next of kin. She was again very helpful, would arrange a search of Hofmann's apartment in Dortmund and let him know what they found.

As soon as the call finished, Khan was on the line wanting to tell him about progress at Tarbrax. With the snow gone, the techies had been able to study the newly-revealed tyre tracks on the rough ground adjacent to the bing. Unfortunately, the area was criss-crossed with tracks. Identifying those belonging to the killer's vehicle would be difficult. And if those particular tracks had not impacted on the rough ground, but had melted away along with the snow, it would be impossible.

Khan had led the house-to-house checks in the village. Nobody had noticed an unfamiliar vehicle driving towards the bing. And as it was not possible to see the far side of the bing from the village, nobody would have been able to spot the body being dumped.

However, one of the residents mentioned an alternative access to the spoil heap, which bypassed the village altogether. A private track, developed by the landscaping company who had the maintenance contract for the bing. Access to this was barred by a padlocked gate, but it wouldn't have been a difficult job to remove the lock. The resident had also mentioned a tumbledown barn part way down the track which looked to be abandoned but was in fact inhabited.

"We went down to the track and sure enough the gate lock had been removed," Khan said. "Although the barn really did look a mess, there was indeed an old guy living in it."

"How helpful was he?" Mac asked.

"Very. It didn't take much to get him talking. His dad had worked in the shale oil industry before its collapse so we got a fair old history lesson. After the lecture, he told us about a red Renault van that had been on the track very early morning on 1 March, remembered part of the number plate and gave us a description of the driver and a partial one of his mate. There's no CCTV along the track so we're checking back on to the A70 to see if those cameras show anything."

"That gives us a really good start in trying to trace these men," Mac said. "Talking of cameras – anything yet on Hofmann's 43 bus?"

"Unfortunately not. The company trawled through a lot of footage, some of which was blank – a fault on their system. And no luck with tracing the Volvo either, but then we had so little to go on."

"How's Laura Wyatt shaping up?"

"I've worked with her before and she picks things up very quickly. I'm sure she'll be an asset to the team."

Mac spent a couple of hours tidying up old cases. It was always tempting to put off such work in order to concentrate fully on the demands of the case of the moment. But he'd learned from long experience that you were expected to prioritise both. How you actually managed to achieve this was your problem.

The other distraction was an impending court appearance, one he wasn't at all confident about. There'd been some corner-cutting on the Maxwell armed robbery case and he was worried about being grilled by the defendant's advocate, one of the worst – or best – depending which side you were on. Some revision would be needed – a bit like cramming for an exam – as all the investigative action had taken place months previously. Then there'd be a mock cross-examination, something he and Euan, a fellow PIT man, did for each other, mercilessly exploring the weaknesses and holes that were there to be exposed in almost any case. Euan lived out in the country near Carnwath and they took turns pulling each other apart in the isolation of an old barn at the bottom of his garden. The incentive for reaching the end of the exercise was the sampling of a single malt from Euan's extensive collection.

Mac was jolted from his tedious but necessary tidying-up work by a call from Freya. She was waiting for him outside. Where was he?

How could it be six already? Where had the day gone?

She was leaning against the wall just inside the entrance lobby on the public side of security, her blonde hair newly cut. Reading a book. Naturally! Looking up she gave him one of those smiles that even after all the years, still temporarily disabled essential structural parts of his legs. They kissed as they walked arm in arm to The Dockside. It was full of early-evening, post-work real-alers. One small table was mercifully still free and they squeezed in between a posse of bearded males to grab the seats. The group was on a crawl, one that had started some time ago judging by the content and volume of their conversations.

Unusually it was table service and their pints and crisps eventually arrived courtesy of a man wearing a kilt and a ponytail. They clinked glasses. Mac tore open the first bag of crisps, offering them to her before grabbing a fistful.

"Well, this is very pleasant!" he said, really meaning it.

He looked round the bar, taking in the dark maroon ceiling, ancient, over-wide, uneven floorboards, an open fire in need of a top-up and a forest of handpumps.

"You're right," she said. "It's been too long since we last met, hasn't it? How's Roisin?"

It must have been his mother who'd let that particular cat out of the bag. Maybe Freya didn't mind about Roisin, but he doubted it. There was a temptation to make an issue of it – who'd told her and why was she here if she knew the current set-up? But why bother with the negatives when she was next to him, looking good and with a whole evening ahead of them.

"She's OK, thanks. How are the seascapes?"

He loved her paintings. Great swirls of colour, a bit on the abstract side for him but he could still pick out details – a crumbling cliff, a cluster of rocks, a breaking wave, a rising sun. The canvasses sold well through a few small galleries, but selling didn't come naturally to her, reluctant to blow her own trumpet, if you could say that about a painter.

"I'm just finishing one that's a bit different," she said. "Starting to get a feel for the non-natural elements, you know, like boats, sheds, even some of the older industrial buildings. There are some interestingly mixed places on the north shore of the Forth, maybe a gradual shift in what I'm doing. You must come and see them, Calum."

Unlike most of her artist friends, she never got round to loading photos of her pictures onto her phone. You had to be at her place to see them, or buy one of your own. Mac had six of them, not all on the walls at the same time, which would have been a little overpowering, but a steady rotation. Would he go up and have a look at the new paintings? Maybe it was time. Maybe it depended how the evening went.

The pub-crawl group made a noisy exit arguing about their next port of call. Suddenly there was space and the fire's warmth enveloped them. Mac rose to feed the flames from the log basket, watching the sparks fleeing to the back of the hearth and up the cavernous chimney. The flurry of sparks took him back to holiday midsummer-night bonfires on the farm outside Fredrikstad, with his cousins and Freya, the joy of being out so late with the 'big people' on the biggest night of the year, left by and large to their own devices, fuelled by endless fizzy drinks, apple cakes and whatever meat was on the barbecue. The adults grinning, faces red from the enormous fire, the drink and the dancing, the fiddlers drawing them all inexorably into the ring.

"You OK, Calum?" He turned. When she reached over to brush part of his blonde fringe away from his eyes, it was a reminder of how much he'd missed her touch.

"Just thinking of midsummer on the farm," he said. "The sparks from the fire here set me off. Wouldn't it be nice to dance like that again?"

"Well, you'll be able to if you come up for my ceilidh and help me celebrate the arrival of the big four five."

And in an instant, he knew he would. Freya and parties went together. She had the skill of lining up all the right ingredients, musicians who were part of a local collective, cooks, home brewers and distillers and a nose for the right location. The venue details would be communicated to the party-goers as if it were a late-eighties rave rather than a forty-fifth birthday party.

"Thanks, I wouldn't want to miss that! Is the do on your actual birthday?" She nodded. "Sunday it is then!"

"I know we said let's just meet for a drink, but would you be up for something to eat tonight?" she asked. He was. It would be good to spend more time with her – and to have a proper meal for a change.

He excused himself to visit the toilet, partly because he did actually need the facilities but mainly because he had to check his phone which had vibrated in his pocket a number of times as they'd sat by the fire.

* Paula to say the man from the beach would have to wait.

* Maeven to remind him his monthly stats were overdue.

* The prof's deputy who wanted a lift from the university to the mortuary and back.

The full-blast din of the hand-dryer made it hard to think. It wasn't that he'd actually forgotten about the appointment with the deputy, just that the thought had been temporarily dislodged by Freya's appearance. Still, no harm done. He texted the deputy confirming the availability of a lift. On the way out of the toilets he couldn't help noticing how tired the face in the mirror looked.

"Listen. I've got to take a man to see a body," he told Freya. "Sorry but you know what it's like."

"I know what you're like. How long do you need?"

"About an hour. Then we can eat. Look…" he said, rubbing the back of his neck, his eyes not meeting hers. "I don't think I'm ready for anything else just yet…" He didn't need to spell it out but was unsure how she'd react.

"You mean Roisin's about! Sure, no problem, got to get back to the coast anyway. Where's your meeting?"

"Corstorphine," he said.

"So, does that mean it's Carla, not Roisin, later?"

"Behave!" he said, smiling, pleased that she was in a playful mood. It amazed him how she seemed able to take his other women in her stride at times when the two of them weren't an item. "How about the Olive Branch at eight?"

Freya was more than used to his sudden changes of plan. This one seemed to be working out OK. But it would be wise to text

Roisin saying he'd be working late and that if she was planning another of her spontaneous visits to his flat, he wouldn't be back there until midnight.

Laing's deputy proved to be boringly serious and totally lacking a humour gene. It was also clear not only that he didn't get on with the professor, but also that he resented having to get involved in anything so distasteful as identifying a body – or indeed sitting in the front passenger seat of the Jimny.

Paula, who was still hard at work in her office when Mac and the deputy arrived, led the two of them to the mortuary area, marched across to one of the storage units and paused. She said a few words to the deputy and asked if he felt OK about seeing a dead body and whether there was anything he wanted to ask.

"Let's just get on with it, can we?"

Paula opened the unit door and pulled out a steel stretcher. She unzipped the top of the body bag, sufficient to reveal head and shoulders.

"Yes, that's him, that's Dieter Hofmann. Now, can I go?"

"If you can just sign here, that would be most helpful," she replied, holding out a clipboard with a printed sheet attached. The deputy deposited an illegible scrawl on the page and made to leave. Second thoughts… he had a question.

"Was it the drugs that killed him, some sort of overdose?"

"Why do you say that?" Paula asked.

"Well, that was his big problem, seems the most likely reason for his death. A bright man, I have to say, but what good is such talent if you end up as an addict. He should never have been on the team in the first place, what with his addiction and his damned principles." He turned dismissively towards the door. "I'll make my own way back. Anything to avoid having to travel in your car again, Inspector."

"A charming man!" Paula said, the deputy still within earshot.

He tried to slam the door shut as he left but the closer refused to allow itself to be hurried.

"At least we have a formal identification," Mac said, "and that was actually quite useful – the comments about his 'addiction' and those 'damned principles'. Do you reckon Dieter was addicted?"

"In a sense, probably, yes, but cocaine isn't like heroin. A lot of regular users manage to function very well in highly demanding jobs. Anyway, the thing you need to know is that I can now confirm that the taser was the cause of death. It triggered cardiac arrest, aided and abetted by Hofmann's drug abuse. You have my blessing to spread this information wherever it needs to go. Oh… and it wasn't a police issue taser, thank the Lord! Now, about this other chap, the one who was sunbathing on the beach? I'm afraid I haven't managed to get him on the slab yet, but hopefully first thing in the morning."

+ + +

It was touch and go but Mac managed to push open the door to the Olive Branch just as the church clock opposite struck eight. Freya, sitting at a table in the low-lit rear of the restaurant, was halfway down a glass of house red and studying the menu intently. She stood up and kissed him, as ever for a little too long. He noticed one or two raised eyebrows from adjacent diners. Although she hadn't picked up on their responses, he knew she wouldn't have been the slightest bit bothered by them.

"Risotto with clams," she said.

"Mind reader! I'm going for that as well. No starter though as I'm saving myself for the pud."

"Sounds like a plan," she said. "Do you now have an identified body?" No *sotto voce* for the question, but Mac dropped his voice for the response.

"Yes, we do. What a man – the deputy. Wouldn't last five minutes if he worked for me. Anyway, enough of that. I'm now definitely off duty."

"In as much as you ever are! How's your brother?"

They talked relatives for a while. Freya had a bit of a soft spot for Erland – which was reciprocated. When he'd first picked up on it, years ago, Mac had been annoyed and worried that his brother might be making a move on her. But she'd put him right.

"Will you be going to your dad's grave on Sunday?"

It would be the third anniversary of his death. He hadn't forgotten, but hadn't slotted the visit into his mental calendar either. Did she want to be there as well? She did. Good. He didn't really like Sundays, even when he wasn't working. Something about the underlying atmosphere, even though there were loads of things you could do now on a Sunday, compared with when he'd been a lad. As he'd very little direct experience of any religion, maybe it was part of some weird genetic inheritance from his Lutheran parents. But he liked visiting the grave. He and his mum would take plants – not cut flowers – water the new arrivals and tidy up the old-stagers, huddle together in the shelter of the redbrick wall nearby, eat whatever snacks they'd brought with them and watch the other visitors as they came to pay their respects and carry out their own bits of gardening. And this Sunday there'd be three of them up there, but not a fourth, as Erland wasn't comfortable in graveyards.

Having decided that the Jimny and Freya's Fiesta could stay overnight in the restaurant car-park, they ordered a second carafe of house red. Two ice cream, strawberry and chocolate creations appeared before them thirty minutes after they'd started to digest the risotto. Coffee followed, not the wisest of moves given the late hour.

When Freya went to the ladies, he took the opportunity to look at his phone again. Nothing that couldn't wait. The final text was from Roisin, to say she wouldn't be there at midnight as her mother was unwell.

Despite what he'd said to her earlier, he wondered whether to invite Freya back to the flat. There wasn't long to make up his mind. How had she planned to get back to the coast anyway? Or had she booked a hotel?

Well, maybe the room wouldn't be needed.

4 MARCH

For a second, he couldn't remember who was next to him in the bed. Then he recalled… a brief stop at an all-night shop to stock up on essentials… the late-evening walk back to his flat, his arm around Freya… snuggling up on the sofa with a nightcap… listening to Christian Wallumrod on the piano… tumbling naked into bed. Then… out like a light.

He checked his phone. 6 a.m. Parched, he threw on his dressing gown and stumbled into the kitchen. One glass of water followed by another. Kettle on, spoons of coffee in the cafetière, boiling water added, plunger waiting-time, two mugs poured out, both with milk added, one with a generous spoon of sugar.

Back in bed she stirred, took a mug and stretched lazily.

"Can't take the pace any more then, old man!"

Mac felt sheepish.

"It's early yet and maybe I haven't completely missed the boat."

Coffees were put to one side as they slid back beneath the bedclothes.

Afterwards it was rush, rush, rush. Mac tripping over his running trousers as he tried to put them on, like a character from a French farce, Freya laughing uproariously.

"Shush! You'll wake the dragon in his lair below," Mac heavy-whispered. "See you at the party?"

"Yes, don't forget to keep your phone on for the venue details."

"As if I ever turn it off. Here, you'll need my spare set of keys. And don't forget the alarm – you remember the number?"

"Well, as it's my date of birth, I'm hardly likely to forget! Get off with you now or you'll be blaming me for being late."

All fingers and thumbs trying to tie his trainer laces. A quick check for phone and car keys, closing the front door, breaking into an easy jog. Nothing too strenuous on the route back to the restaurant.

Within five minutes of pulling away from the Olive Branch car park, the traffic had come to a standstill. It wasn't normally as bad as this. What was going on? From the banners and placards held aloft it was clearly an environmental demo, hordes of mainly young people with the message – *get out of your cars, walk, cycle, use public transport.*

It wasn't that he was unsympathetic to the cause, just why did it have to be on his route just now? He phoned Khan, only to find out that he was facing the same problem. And Wyatt had phoned him to say she was also stuck in a queue. Looked like it was a series of spontaneous acts across different parts of the city.

Mac vaguely recalled it was possible to have a three-way phone conversation and asked Khan if he knew how to set it up. Within a minute they were speaking to each other.

"I've got a feeling this is pretty insecure, so let's be careful what we mention. OK, Raj, Laura, what have you got?"

+ + +

By the time they all arrived at the Warehouse, their ad hoc in-car briefing had been completed and they had an action list. Mac showered and changed into a spare set of work clothes he kept in the office. In the mirror he noticed his hair was getting to the stage – just above his shoulders – when it would need a trim. Before the sarky comments started. Just as he was about to start writing up his initial report on the second body, Maeven called, wanting the three of them in her office for her own update.

Mac ran through where they'd got to on the two cases. So far, the only links between them were the tasers and the open shirts. But they were significant links! The body from the beach was due to be examined that morning. At the end of Mac's summary, and after a few questions, she dismissed the other two officers and asked him to stay behind.

"Before you start ruffling any feathers, I need to let you know that Hofmann's death has stirred up interest amongst our spook friends at Oversight Scotland." Mac pulled a face. He didn't particularly like the recently established security overlords. "I share your concerns, Inspector," Maeven said, with a slight smile. "I've sent you a link to the joint protocol between ourselves and Oversight. It's couched in cooperation-speak, warm words about working together to achieve a common purpose. However, an appendix spells out just where the lines are drawn – so far and no further for us common-or-garden plods. You'll be obliged to liaise with one of their officers, a man called Urquhart. No option about this as it's a direct order from the top."

A bloody nuisance, he thought, but really only to be expected. Maeven wasn't finished.

"I wouldn't normally say this, but Oversight are throwing their weight around. There are undoubtedly some issues over which they can legitimately claim exclusivity, but the scope of their list is, in my opinion, far too broad. It's their way of maintaining control. You'll need to tread carefully. If you get close to the edge, tell me before jumping over. Is that clear?"

"Perfectly. Thanks for the heads-up, ma'am."

Back at his desk, Mac took a while to take in what had just happened. It was unusual for a senior officer to make such a comment. Mac felt both pleased that the boss had shown confidence in him and concerned that the need for sound judgement in taking the next steps would be crucial.

Information about the second body was required urgently. So far all they had was the taser. CCTV would have been the obvious starting point, but a quick check had established that the few cameras on the shore road had been out of action for a while. Apparently, it was a popular area for alfresco sex – even, on occasion, in the winter – and participants had a vested interest in making sure their performances weren't filmed. With the lack of footage, it was back to the basics of house-to-house enquiries. The locally recruited team had so far come up with nothing. Although it wasn't one of those areas where people might be scared to talk, nobody had seen or heard a thing. Except surely, Mac thought, it would be difficult, even early on, for a car to drive up and dump a body on the beach and drive off without anyone noticing.

He remembered seeing a single tower block, two streets away from the front. A tenant with a front window and good eyesight might have seen something. He dispatched Wyatt and two of the local uniforms to check the flats out.

+ + +

Mac wanted to speak to Blinker again, but that would have to wait until he'd found out how far Paula had got with the second body. A quick call established that it would be worth him driving over.

She was in a good mood which improved further when she spotted the coffee and cakes he'd brought. They sat on the easy chairs in her office, demolishing the pastries and sipping from the takeaway cups.

Some preliminary conclusions. The second dead man had been a Class A drug user, like Hofmann, but unlike the German, usage had probably only started very recently. And, again unlike the German, it didn't look as if the taser had triggered his death. The actual cause of death was as yet unknown.

"I do have one very interesting piece of information for you, Inspector. Radiation levels! His reading was much higher than the norm. Not sure if you are aware, but because of background radiation, we all have a certain amount inside us. But his reading was about ten times more than usual."

"You're not suggesting that this caused his death, are you?" Mac asked, concerned that this would complicate the twin investigations even further.

"No, it's nowhere near that kind of level. What I am suggesting is that our dead friend is very likely to have worked somewhere where there was a degree of exposure to radiation. Which gives you a lead."

Although it might still involve complications, this was potentially a very positive line of enquiry.

They talked over the likely workplace exposure possibilities.

Medical radiology, possible but the reading might be a bit on the high side for that.

The Faslane-based nuclear-powered subs. Paula thought the guy was probably too unfit to have been an active submariner, but he could have worked on the maintenance side.

Nuclear power generation.

Mac tried to recall how many Scottish plants were still in operation. A quick search on his phone brought up a simple answer. Two. And with one of those currently offline, only

Torness, out near Dunbar, was actually producing energy. It would be a good starting point for his initial enquiries.

Mac thanked Paula for such a useful lead.

Back in the car, he made some calls. The first to fix an appointment at Torness, the second, a voicemail message, to advise Maeven of the possible nuclear connection which could bring with it a new set of political sensitivities, and the third to speak to Roisin. With him and Freya now back together, he knew there'd be a very difficult conversation up ahead. Met with voicemail again, he decided against leaving a message about something so personal.

+ + +

Mac had never been keen on anything nuclear – weapons or power. Chernobyl had happened at a very impressionable age for him and his imagination had run amok. For a few years before his police career took over, he'd been a not-particularly active campaigner for nuclear disarmament and against further development of nuclear power stations.

As his most recent involvement with Dunbar had been on a case that had got nowhere, he didn't have very positive memories of the place. Torness was out of the town right on the coast. He showed his warrant card at the gate and the guard phoned through to verify the appointment.

Colin from HR turned out to be very helpful. Mac showed him a facial shot of the man found on the beach, knowing that such pictures often looked oddly different from the real live individual.

"Not someone I immediately recognise," Colin said. "But then we've well over a thousand staff here. Let's have a look through this little lot."

Within seconds a host of staff photos popped up on the large screen in front of him. With remarkable speed Colin scanned page after page looking for a match for the face in the photo Mac had given him.

"How can you do that so quickly?" he asked.

"Well, I know a lot of them, so I'm just doing a double-check on those I'm not so familiar with. It helps if you've worked here as long as I have."

The sea of faces eventually came to an end.

"Sorry, Inspector, he's not one of ours. I'm afraid you've had a wasted journey."

As Mac was about to leave, Colin held up his hand.

"Just had a thought. Would you like me to check with my oppo at Hunterston? Although they're offline at present there'll still be plenty of staff on site. I could forward the photo of your man and ask them to get back ASAP. Save you a trip to Ayrshire into the bargain. I'll let you know when they get back to me."

Before setting off on the return journey down the A1, he arranged to meet Blinker in the Mermaid and DC Wyatt at the same venue, fifteen minutes later. On the journey to the cafe, he reflected how progress on any investigation often came down to the balance between the two types of people involved, on the one hand those with a willingness to go the extra mile – like Colin – and on the other, those who responded with the stubbornness of a jobsworth. Investigative skills themselves were of course crucial, but they weren't enough on their own.

Taking the Cockenzie turn-off, Mac remembered, for once, the importance of eating during the working day. Fish suppers were a Mermaid speciality.

Just as he was savouring his first mouthful of cod, Blinker arrived at the table sipping a cup of tea. Without asking, he pinched a chip, dipped it in the pool of tomato sauce on the edge of Mac's plate and swallowed it.

"Heard anything new?" Mac asked, shovelling a forkful of fish into his mouth.

"Not much," Blinker replied, pinching another chip and taking a sip of his tea. "Except…" Mac pricked up his ears. This was trademark Blinker. "I'll give you the gen for nothing if you buy me my own chips."

"You're on," Mac said. "You order, I'll pay."

"What have you got?" Mac asked, once Blinker returned with his own plateful.

"That case you were on… about six months ago it must have been. The guy with the speedboat. He's back! Speak to Ed. That's his number."

Mac started re-thieving chips. The information related to a people-trafficking case. He'd pass it on to the DI who'd taken it over.

Wyatt put her head round the cafe door. Mac nodded her towards a free table in the opposite corner. A slice of white bread mopped up the remaining greasy tomato sauce mixture very effectively. He moved across the room to join the DC and asked how the house-to-house enquiries were going, satisfied that their table was far enough away from Blinker's overactive ears.

"Well, we've done the tower block. There was a young feller in one of the sea-facing units, has this telescope set up permanently at the front window. A boat-nut, with a guide to ships of the world – you know, tonnage, flag, capacity, cargo type, that sort of thing. Has these model ships in cases hung from the ceiling. Doesn't have a job and so has lots of time to spend peering through the telescope, watching the shipping world go by. Anyway, the bit you'll want to know is that he saw something!" Mac had been wondering when she'd get to the point. "As the telescope's no use for close-up viewing, he's got binocular backup. We already know about the outdoor sex activity on the beach and I reckon in addition to ship-spotting he's a bit of a perv. Anyway, whatever he was looking for, he spotted something being dumped by two men, 5.05 yesterday morning. Claims he wasn't sure what it was, but it must have been the body."

"Well done, Laura," Mac said. It wasn't anything unusual, just part of the basic grind of enquiry work but Mac had always found that a bit of praise early on, went down well. "How come he's so specific about the time?"

"Told me he has the radio on all day. When he saw the two men, it coincided with one of the time checks."

"And once he had suspicions about a body, why didn't he report what he'd seen?"

"Said he was waiting until we knocked on his door – cheeky bugger. I don't think he gets out much – literally. Gets takeaway food delivered and from the look of the place, he doesn't bother much with slinging the empty boxes out. Gave me an OK description of the driver but didn't see the other man's face clearly – hoodie and scarf got in the way. Looked quite a bit younger than the driver, though. The car was a Skoda estate and, here's the thing, he got the registration number. I sent the details through and just got this back."

She showed him her phone. The vehicle was registered to a garage proprietor in Musselburgh, but wasn't on the stolen vehicles list. It seemed unlikely that the two men who'd delivered the body to the beach would use a vehicle that could be so rapidly traced back to them. So maybe it had been stolen but the owner hadn't yet realised it was missing.

"Let's take a chance," Mac said. "Give the garage a ring and see how the land lies."

It turned out just as Mac had thought. They hadn't missed the vehicle. But the good news was that it was fitted with a tracker. After a few minutes they'd managed to pinpoint its location – Torphin in the Pentland Hills.

"Can you get the techies out there as soon as possible?"

Wyatt made the call, recognised the voice of the woman who answered and persuaded her to let the Skoda jump the queue.

"Just before you go," Mac said, "it would also be useful if you could get Captain Cockenzie to come down to the Warehouse and make a formal statement." She looked reluctant.

"Look, the guy's a bit of an oddball. From that crow's nest he radiates confidence but I'm not sure that would survive outside the confines of his flat. Told me he only goes out for weddings and funerals and has never been invited to a wedding yet! So getting him out of the place could be difficult."

"OK then, do it at his place, get it taped, take another DC with you and somebody from Welfare." She groaned.

"What's the problem?"

"Sorry, but you know what they're like. *Please don't ask my client about that because it might trigger bad memories.* They don't live in the real world."

"Look, the real world says we have to do it or risk the evidence being declared inadmissible and I take it you don't want that!" Not really a flea in her ear, just telling her to get on with it. She was on her way.

Mac thanked Blinker, pinched another of his chips and walked to the Jimny.

+ + +

Back at the Warehouse, Colin from Torness HR called with an update. Body Two wasn't known at Hunterston either. Sod it, Mac thought. Now they'd need to start on the hospitals and the Faslane base. Wyatt could do the radiology departments. He sent her the relevant details and a photo of the dead man.

His own next step would be to find some high-up naval type to talk to about the nuclear sub maintenance squads. Maybe he'd need to check about submariners as well, despite Paula's view that the dead man wouldn't have been fit enough for such a role. But that could wait. This was beginning to get the feel of a case teetering on the edge of something very sticky – treacle, mud, quicksand!

His phone pinged. Freya letting him know that the grid reference for Sunday's birthday party venue would be sent by text, a couple of hours before the start. He'd been to a few raves in the early nineties and could still remember the excitement beforehand – seldom matched by the later reality. But Erland had always told him this disappointment was down to the substances he *hadn't* taken. While his brother had always been more than happy to get off his face, sober Calum would always be there to drive them back to Erland's place in his bright yellow Ford Escort.

But Freya's party wouldn't be anything like that.

Roisin had gone quiet. He wondered if it had been something he'd said and tried to recall their recent conversations. Nothing sprang to mind. And she didn't do huffs. Normally if there was something to say, she'd just come out with it.

Faslane! Of course. There'd been a case maybe five years ago, a series of vehicle thefts, stolen to order as it turned out. Mac had been drafted in because the Greater Glasgow PIT HQ at Bearsden had been short-staffed. He just needed to remember the name of the captain he'd dealt with back then, a helpful down-to-earth guy. It would be in his notebook. When he checked the storage cupboard, the notebooks in there only went back four years. He had a sudden vision of a clear-out, at a time when office storage space was being reduced. Two bin liners full of his stuff. Had he stored the contents at home?

It was better to drive home and check rather than remain sitting in the office, trying to remember. Notebooks were essential to hold onto, even the old ones. Cold cases could become hot ones. And he knew to his cost that his flat was anything but secure.

With his neighbour out somewhere in the car, he had the luxury of a full parking space. It felt strange being in the flat during a working day, a bit less his place in an odd sort of way. Stepladders in position, he eased himself through the trap hatch up into the roof space. It was a tight squeeze and something of a relief to realise that the sizeable feller who'd broken into the flat would never have been able to fit through the gap. His insecure notebooks had not really been at risk.

In theory he'd operated a storage policy of dump first/ sort later. Except 'later' never quite arrived. He pulled the light switch. The floor was covered in cardboard boxes and not a few bin liners. Squatting down, he began sifting through the black bags. And eventually found one full of small black notebooks. Before making his descent, he wondered idly whether, with some roof lights – and a slightly wider access – the space could become a fully usable room.

The dust from the loft had got up his nose and down his throat. A quick wash and a glass of water did the trick.

Back in the kitchen with a cup of tea and, taking advantage of his neighbour's absence, some full-volume Tinariwen, he started with the 2016 notebooks, certain that the Faslane case hadn't been any more recent than that. Working backwards, he eventually found Captain Menzies in a 2014 edition. The name should have been easy for him to remember, as it was the same as his least favourite high school teacher.

His phone rang. It was Torness Colin.

"His name's Alex McGrath, Inspector!"

"Sorry?"

"He's your man." Mac let out a whoop. "I'd forgotten to check the recent leavers list. When they depart, we move them off the main staff database, so I had to search a number of individual HR files, which of course takes longer. Anyway, there he was. I do remember him now, but only met him the once. One of our technicians. He left us two weeks ago."

"Wasn't dismissed by any chance?"

"No – what makes you say that?"

"Well, keep it to yourself, but he had a certain amount of cocaine in his system. I wondered if you'd picked up on a drug problem at your end."

"Absolutely not. I've been through his file. Not a mention. And given that our people are subject to random drug testing – well, it wouldn't have escaped our attention. No, he was on a fixed-term contract which came to an end and we didn't need him anymore, so that was it. His coke use must have started after he left us."

"That's very helpful, Colin. Can you forward any other relevant information you have, contact details, next-of-kin and such like? And a photo of him would be very useful."

Colin's email arrived within minutes.

Two things dawned on Mac. Firstly, now there was an ID, albeit still to be formally confirmed, he wouldn't need the services of Faslane's Captain Menzies after all. And secondly, having brought the notebooks down from the loft, where they shouldn't have been in the first place, he'd need to take them back to the office. They were transferred into his seldom used, large old-fashioned briefcase.

There were calls to make before he set off. The first was to McGrath's next of kin – a frail-sounding mother. Not wanting to break the news over the phone, he confirmed one or two basic facts and asked whether he could visit to talk about her son. She sounded very worried but didn't ask anything and agreed to his request.

Maeven got a voicemail saying that Body Two had been identified.

About to leave the house, he suddenly remembered that he'd sent DC Wyatt off to trawl through the various hospital radiology departments. The relief in her voice when he gave her the good news was clear. Not a task she'd been relishing. Was there anything on the Skoda yet? Yes – it had been dumped in a disused quarry. The scenes of crime officer would be starting work on it shortly.

Mac shoved the briefcase into the back of the car, set off towards Mrs McGrath's house in Ratho and called Khan, telling him to get across to her son's place at Bo'ness, secure it and get the techies in. The mother lived near the Union Canal, her small house in need of a lot of TLC.

It was obvious she'd guessed why he was there, her whole body shaking, face tear-stained, a balled-up handkerchief in her hand. Mac had to clear a pile of magazines from the other seat at the small table before he could sit down. When he gave her the awful news that they had a body matching Alex's description, she sobbed uncontrollably. Unable to console her, he grubbed about in the tiny kitchen and managed to find two mugs, some milk and a caddy. Kettle on, he kept an eye on her as she gradually calmed down and stared blankly out of the backroom window to the yard beyond. After clearing a few dirty crocks from the table, he set down two mugs of tea and asked about her son. The story came out in dribs and drabs.

She seldom saw him and then only when he was on the cadge – not that she had anything much to give. Gambling had been his downfall, just like his father before him. Mac felt bad but knew he had to ask. Any other addictions? He liked a drink but could seldom hold it. She'd never known him take anything else. Would she be able to come with him to identify the body? She didn't answer but simply got up and went to put on her coat and hat.

Mac phoned Paula and headed back down the A8. It proved difficult to get any more out of Mrs McGrath on the journey but she mentioned her sister when asked whether a bit of support might be available.

Paula had to stop the mother from keeling over at the point where she saw her dead son. Afterwards, Mac drove Mrs

McGrath the short distance to the sister's place, just off the Dalry Road and made sure the sibling was at home.

Back at the mortuary he tried to get five minutes with Paula. She was busy, but had authorised his access to McGrath's file. Confirmation that the taser strike had not been the cause of death. But Paula had discovered a single needle mark in his right arm and would be arranging toxicology tests.

+ + +

Needing a moment to gather his thoughts, he went to grab a snack in the Corstorphine canteen. Not much was left behind the plastic hatches. He settled for a doughnut and walked to the end of the line to fill a mug with coffee from a press-button self-service machine, hoping to remove the lingering nasty aftertaste of his earlier cup of tea.

So, what did they have so far?

Body 1, Dieter Hofmann, a German AI expert seconded to work in Edinburgh on a laser weapons development project. Recently sacked, tasered, cocaine in the system, a long-term user, cause of death the combined effect of the taser and the coke on his heart.

Body 2, Alex McGrath, a local, contract as a technician at a nuclear power station recently ended, tasered, coke in the system but no evidence of longer-term use. Cause of death as yet unclear. Needle mark found on the body currently under investigation.

Both had been killed in one location and their bodies later left elsewhere. There were enough similarities to indicate a strong link between the two cases, but nothing conclusive yet.

What exactly had McGrath done at Torness? Colin had referred to him as a technician. What did that involve and could it have included anything which might have had a bearing on his death? Colin wasn't available but Mac left a message and then set off to McGrath's house in Bo'ness.

On the way, he noticed a left turn signed for Linlithgow. So, Hofmann had visited The Cairn pub there and lived temporarily in the caravan at South Queensferry. And McGrath had lived in Bo'ness. All three places no more than a dozen miles apart. Was it possible that the two dead men had known each other?

Khan had already secured the house and managed to get hold of the Jokers. A huge TV screen matched a huge sofa in an otherwise empty living room. A freezer full of ready meals and a microwave in the kitchen. A good stock of booze stored in crates. A few clothes hung randomly in a built-in wardrobe that was missing a door. Mac tried not to assess the man solely on the basis of the contents of the house. There might have been more to him. A gambler, his mother had said. So far, no evidence of that but then he'd have most likely done it online. No trace of a phone or a laptop. It was the same with Hofmann. Might the killers in both cases have removed these items in case they held incriminating evidence?

Besuited, gloved up, overshoes on, Mac did his usual wander about, looking at all the things that didn't seem worth a second glance. A long-dead plant on a windowsill, a biscuit tin containing only a few crumbs, a veg rack under the sink which had probably never seen a vegetable and instead held an assortment of rusting DIY tools. Upstairs, an empty box room at the back of the house, the window giving a view of an industrial building beyond a small garden. He caught sight of the window jambs and guessed they housed a pair of shutters, like the ones they'd had in the old tenement. Sliding a gloved finger into the wooden groove, he pulled. It took some dexterity but gradually the hinged shutter unfolded to cover the right-hand half of the window. In the revealed cavity were sealed packets containing a white substance.

He could hear the voices of previous suspects ringing through his head. *Personal use only, cheaper to buy in bulk.* Could be the case – at a stretch – but every fibre of his instinct told him otherwise. Far more likely that McGrath had been a dealer, maybe to fund his gambling habit. Starting off small-scale perhaps, getting sucked in further, an argument with his supplier that got out of hand? Well, it was a possible scenario.

He shouted for Joker One to get upstairs.

They extended the search and found more packets in two other locations, behind a loose section of skirting and inside a blocked-off coal chute.

Once Wyatt arrived on the scene, the three of them had a briefing in Khan's Mazda which was a lot roomier than the Jimny.

"Could McGrath have supplied Hofmann?" Wyatt asked.

"It's a possibility," Mac replied. "I've spoken to the drugs squad. Given the drug connections in both cases, they need to be involved now."

"As it happens," Wyatt said, "I recently finished a six-month secondment with them and built up some good contacts. Would it be OK if I did the liaison with them?"

"Go for it," Mac told her, "but keep me informed."

Khan suggested they wave a photo of McGrath under the nose of the landlord of The Cairn in Linlithgow. The geographical proximity of a number of their sites had struck him as well. He got the OK from Mac.

The two West Calderites went off in convoy.

Knowing Maeven would want an update on developments, Mac headed back to base. A text came in from Roisin. Damn, how was he going to tell her that it was over? Stopping at a layby overlooking Cramond Island, he read her message. It wasn't going to be an issue. For the first time, he'd been dumped by text!

He's a bit more available than you. It's been nice but you're nearly always somewhere else. Hope you and Freya patch things up.

Relief at not having to make the decision himself, tinged with regret at having to say goodbye to her. But he wanted to try and make things work with Freya and for more than just a few weeks this time. The question was… were either of them mature enough for that?

He was reluctant to leave the view of the island behind, particularly as there was a little warmth in the sun. Sometimes he wondered about alternative lives, that might have happened. Ten years previously there'd been a chance to take up a detective post in Bergen. It would have involved some retraining but nothing too onerous. And being bilingual, there'd have been no language problems. Following two high-profile case failures, things hadn't been going well. An opportunity for a new start – but he hadn't taken it. A difficult decision. He'd always felt somewhat conflicted about his dual-cultural heritage – being Scottish, but feeling Norwegian, even though he'd never lived there. In the end the Scot in him had taken over.

Only when he was back at the Warehouse car park did he remember the briefcase. He'd left the Jimny in two dodgy locations that afternoon, so it was a relief to discover the notebooks were still there, but a worry that he'd forgotten all about them for a few hours.

The update with Maeven went well enough. They mulled over why each man had ended up dead. Her view was that they should focus on the drugs and identify the dealers. Mac didn't disagree but felt that in Hofmann's case, his death could have had something to do with his work.

She asked if he'd arranged to see Urquhart at Oversight.

"Not yet. Haven't managed to get beyond his PA, who's over-protective. I'll try again when we're finished here and push harder."

"Well, don't go barging in. The last thing we need is for him or his boss to get on to the chief super," she said, raising her eyebrows. "By the way, have you checked on the force's intelligence system whether they've got anything on Hofmann or McGrath?"

He told her there was nothing.

Back at his desk, Mac made the Urquhart call. This time even his PA was unavailable. They were pissing him about. He phoned Carla.

"Would you happen to know anyone who has Urquhart's mobile number?" A chuckle.

"Playing hard to get, is he? Why am I not surprised? I'll get back to you. By the way, heard you were out with the lovely Freya the other night. Presumably that means bye-bye Roisin?"

"Anytime you fancy a job as a detective on my team, just let me know, Carla. For your ears only… she beat me to it with her own goodbye."

Thinking ahead to the briefing, Mac felt there was a danger of losing track of the increasing number of threads of the two cases. Normally he wasn't one for the whiteboard approach, displaying the photos of the key dramatis personae, felt-tip lines and text showing the connections between them, a timeline running along the top of the board. In his experience, in the old days of major incident teams, he'd found it could often end up as a distraction or an imagination-limiter. But with annual cutbacks they'd had to get used to working in leaner, meaner teams and now he felt the approach might help. The thing was, he wasn't very good at setting up and maintaining such displays. However, he hoped one of his new team might have a natural talent in this area.

+ + +

It was well after six by the time they gathered for the briefing.

Wyatt was the first to go. She had the statement from the guy in the Cockenzie tower block. As anticipated, it had been a struggle to get the welfare rep to agree the basic rules of the game but they'd got there in the end. The SOCO had started the examination of the Skoda in the quarry and would report her findings direct to Wyatt as soon as possible.

Her drugs squad contacts had led to a DS Colquhoun who'd spoken to an informant of his in Linlithgow. Although he didn't recognise McGrath's photo, the informant said that there were a number of small-time dealers who dipped in and out of the trade and kept a very low profile.

Wyatt and Khan had paid a return visit to The Cairn for another talk with the landlord and had shown him a photo of McGrath. *Never seen him before*, gradually turned into *he'd been in the bar once* and finally into *he'd been talking to Hofmann*.

"When we asked him when this was, he claimed he couldn't remember," Wyatt said. "We pressed him and he finally worked out it was 27 February – the day of his beer delivery. Which of course was the same day that Hofmann went on from the cafe to The Cairn!"

"So, now we know there was a definite link between the pair," Mac said, "we need to find out more about that. How well did they actually know each other? Then we'll need to explore anything that might have made them vulnerable to being targeted. As we've already said, the drugs angle is the obvious starting point and we've made an initial assumption that McGrath might have supplied Hofmann. But who supplied McGrath and how extensive was his dealing? That'll be your focus, Laura, working with DS Colquhoun. Their involvement with both gambling and drugs might well have led both men into problems of debt. Raj is investigating that and has already examined McGrath's card and bank accounts. Anything interesting there?"

"Well, the first thing to say is that he had a big debt problem – his current account was permanently in overdraft and there was a combined limit of £20K on his two credit cards. He was up around that figure often enough." Khan sounded unusually slow and ponderous and Mac thought he looked out of sorts. "There were a lot of outgoing payments to an online betting company, but far fewer credits coming in from them. Some of his monthly repayments were just the minimum amount, whilst others were much larger sums. Maybe his dealing activity was greater than Colquhoun's informant believed and he used that income to subsidise his gambling habit. But then how would he have laundered the drug money into one or other of his accounts? Of course, he may well have carried out much of his dealing and gambling using cash. That activity will be more difficult to probe."

"And what about Hofmann?"

"As far as we know, he didn't have any accounts in this country and we're having problems getting access to his accounts in Germany. There's a lot of red tape involved, exacerbated by Brexit one bank official told us."

"OK, so that covers drugs and debts," Mac said. "The other angle we're following up is Hofmann's work on the development project at Midlothian. Raj has already come up with some useful information from a couple of Dieter's colleagues and I'm due to meet a guy called Urquhart in Oversight Scotland who's been playing hard to get. If there was anything unusual going on within the project, he ought to know about it. How much he'll be willing to tell me is another matter. Now – is there anything else anyone wants to mention?"

Despite being clearly under par, Khan roused himself to give an update on the red Renault seen driving along the private track away from the Tarbrax bing. Although there was no CCTV on the track, or the approach road to the village, the van had been picked up by cameras on the A70, making its way back into Edinburgh. It had been tracked as far as the Haymarket area, where it had been left parked on a side street. Khan had arrived on the scene, a full three days later and been very surprised to find it still there. Normally you could guarantee it would have been nicked during that time. The techies were checking it over.

"Good progress all round then," Mac concluded. "Given we've just had this session, we'll skip tomorrow's 8 a.m. session. And as we've now got two cases and more leads to follow, we're going to need some visuals to help us keep track of progress. So, could you set something up for us, Laura?"

Mac wasn't sure whether she'd take it as a boring admin job or a chance to get a bit creative. But despite a somewhat sour look, she set to straight away gathering up display material.

Walking to the car, he checked his phone. A text from Carla giving him a phone number which he called immediately. Urquhart wasn't best pleased and wanted to know where he'd got the number from.

"I'm a detective. It's my job to find things out. I need to meet you tomorrow. As I've already told your PA several times, it's about a murder investigation. Dieter Hofmann. I'm sure you'll have heard of him. Shall we say 10.00?"

+ + +

Up until their early twenties, the relationship between the two sisters had always been fractious. Although only eighteen months older, Fiona had made it clear from an early age who was in charge. All that was needed to maintain the pecking order was regular low-level, out-of-sight bullying. Their parents hadn't a clue about what went on.

As adults, things had improved, mainly because they no longer lived in the same house. Since the death of their parents, they had taken to texting most days and meeting up once a fortnight alternating between their two houses.

Ailsa felt guilty. There'd been no texts from her sister for over a week. Even though Fiona's job often demanded long anti-social hours, she always texted regularly. Ailsa knew she should have contacted the police before now – hence the guilt – but was also very aware that Fiona wouldn't have thanked her if she alerted them prematurely. Particularly if her current investigation was about to come to fruition.

Ailsa was put through to a sergeant at Lanark Road West, her nearest station. He sounded bored. Having got names and contact details out of the way, he asked why she was concerned about her sister. Even to Ailsa, her response sounded lame. Yes, there had been occasions in the past when Fiona had gone off the radar for a while, but their relationship had improved since then. What were her employers doing about this unexplained absence? Fiona was a freelance journalist. What did she do exactly? She was an investigative journalist.

The sergeant's comment seemed to indicate that he didn't really approve of such activity.

"What's she investigating at the moment?"

Ailsa said she didn't know.

"So, your relationship isn't very close, is it?"

She struggled to respond. They had an arrangement. It wasn't a reflection on the closeness or otherwise of their relationship. It was easier for her not to know because then she couldn't give anything away if ever anyone came snooping around. She weighed up the consequences of saying as much to the police. They would immediately think the worst.

"It's a new investigation, she hasn't had a chance to tell me about it yet."

Lame again. The sergeant asked a few more questions, in a monotone which suggested he was reading from a standard list. Had there been any previous work-related threats to Fiona? There were threats all the time over social media but Ailsa wasn't sure if that counted. But she was not aware of any physical threats to her sister.

The sergeant said they'd monitor the situation and that Ailsa should contact them again in a few days if her sister still hadn't been in touch. When she asked how they would monitor the situation, she found it difficult to pick out anything specific from his response. He rang off.

Although Ailsa felt better for having made the call, she didn't put much trust in the sergeant.

5 MARCH

Khan and Wyatt had been catching up on business back at West Calder. Their inspector, who ran a number of local stations, quizzed them about the murder enquiries and asked their opinion of DI Larsen. They'd both been diplomatic in their responses.

Later, driving to the Warehouse in Wyatt's Golf GTI, it was different.

Neither of them could make him out. Efficient certainly, considerate – up to a point – experienced definitely, reliable maybe but he did seem to disappear from time to time. But their main criticism was his lack of interest in them as people as opposed to them as police officers.

"I mean, has he ever asked you anything about your family?" Wyatt asked. She felt comfortable working with Khan who seemed to have no macho tendencies and no apparent problems about working with women.

"Nothing at all, even when he's had the opportunity. So, for example, I brought in a bag of my mum's pakoras. He scoffed them in a flash but didn't ask anything about her when it would have been a perfect opening. It's as if he's always preoccupied with something else – the job obviously, no problem with that – but maybe also something to do with his personal life. Doesn't seem to have room in his head to take into account any personal needs we might have. Like he's never asked me whether I have any kids. Maybe it's up to me to mention them."

"I disagree. He's the boss so he should take the initiative. Apart from anything else it helps build a team that way. He's the same with me, though. I'm just someone to give work to. It's as if I don't exist outside of work hours. Still, I suppose it's early days with him yet." She took a water bottle from the cupholder and drank from it. "So, what do you reckon happened to the two dead guys? Same killer?"

Khan didn't think so. Yes, they knew each other and yes, they might well have also been linked as user and dealer, but that was as far as it went. There was nothing to show that McGrath had any connection at all to Hofmann's laser world. Khan felt that the German's death was more likely to have been triggered by his work than by his drug use. They urgently needed some intel on the sensitive areas of the joint university development project, but the boss was keeping those particular cards close to his chest. Khan said he was aware of the red lines put in place by Oversight Scotland, but was Larsen doing enough to challenge these? And he hadn't even met with the man at Oversight yet.

In Khan's view, the team would have to get beyond these barriers to stand a chance of finding a motive for the killing. McGrath's death in contrast was more likely to have been down to some drug-dealer row that had got out of hand and was then dressed up to look similar to Hofmann's death.

Although Khan got on well enough with Wyatt, he thought she had a higher opinion of herself than was really justified. Having said that, she'd no doubt make sergeant very soon. He'd met her partner, a high flyer in the audit world, a pleasant enough guy but with a tendency to condescension. Khan found it was a common trait amongst the Oxbridge graduates he'd met, with their assumptions about where everyone else stood in the social order.

He'd had the chance to go to Cambridge himself but had disappointed his parents and most of the rest of the family by opting for Glasgow. Far enough away to justify leaving home in Dundee, which had been his number one aim but near enough to get back quickly if his father's health took a turn for the worse. His original plan had been to become a solicitor, but after graduating in Scots Law, he'd changed direction and gone on to take an MSc in Criminology and Criminal Justice. Joining the force as a constable had its challenges but there'd been a rapid promotion to sergeant. And he had his eye on becoming an inspector. The current case was a chance to get a good look inside the PIT and so far, he liked what he'd seen.

+ + +

John Urquhart sat bolt upright behind his desk and greeted the detective with a curt good morning.

"Detective Inspector Larsen," Mac said, thrusting his hand out towards Urquhart who hesitated before shaking it. They moved to sit either side of a large, highly polished table. "Thank you for agreeing to meet. Obviously, we have a common interest in finding out what happened to Dieter Hofmann. I'll give you a brief outline of what we know so far and then perhaps you can tell me what you know about him."

More hesitation. Mac reckoned the chances of getting a coffee were zero. Not waiting for a response, he gave his summary. At the end of it, he asked Urquhart what he knew.

"You'll have done your homework, Inspector, and given the nature of the IntelOper project, will appreciate that there'll be a limit to what I can tell you. We've had our eye on Hofmann for a while. Midlothian flagged up some initial concerns about him. His cocaine dependency wasn't a direct problem for us, although it made him potentially vulnerable. Given his drug problems, the embezzlement wasn't a surprise, but it was another vulnerability. The issue that really concerned us was the risk of him divulging classified information. We discovered very recently that he had something of a history of whistle-blowing. So, his card was marked and we started to keep a close eye on his activities. The problem with some very intelligent people is that they have little understanding of the demands of the real world. Hofmann was completely enclosed within his own bubble and had a naive commitment to certain principles."

Mac thought that perhaps the same could be said of Urquhart – a security-world bubble in his case.

"Apparently, it was quite a coup for Midlothian to get his expertise on board for the joint project. But it's hard to square his interest in becoming a member of the team with his principled opposition to some of the project's objectives. I wonder exactly what he'd imagined when signing up. That the fruits of his work would not be put to good use in the defence of the realm and the West generally? He started kicking off and raising issues of principle with the IntelOper Monitoring Group. The situation deteriorated when his views began to infect others."

"So, what was your prime interest in all this?" Mac asked.

"To support the university in removing him from his post before things got worse. Easier said than done these days with all the protection staff have. As it happened, he played into their hands. With the cocaine they were halfway there. I understand he'd already been subject to a disciplinary hearing over that. It was the embezzlement and a finding of gross misconduct that finished him off – not literally, I hasten to add, but in relation to his employment."

"That's helpful. Thank you. Tell me, what kind of classified information did Hofmann have access to?"

"Well, by definition, I can't enlighten you on that point… because the information is classified."

"Look! I'm not asking for chapter and verse, just an indication will do."

Urquhart looked hesitant.

"The interface between the use of artificial intelligence and the deployment of laser weapons. It's a complex issue – and not one that non-technicals like ourselves would find it easy to get our heads around."

Mac ignored the condescension in Urquhart's tone.

"And were you worried that Hofmann would go public on this issue?"

"We had concerns in that area and were taking certain steps to remedy that when news of his death broke. An unfortunate business, but when you get involved with drug dealers you have to expect there might be consequences."

Mac picked up no trace of sympathy in Urquhart's comments. But it was interesting that the Oversight man was pushing the same line as Laing. It was all about the drugs.

"So, you don't think Hofmann's death could have had anything to do with his work?"

"I'd say it was extremely unlikely. That kind of storyline might form the basis for a good film, but it doesn't bear any resemblance to reality."

"Point noted. Now, I'd just like to clarify something relating to the use of AI. What is the official policy on whether fully-autonomous laser weapons systems should be deployed on military drones?"

"I see you've done some additional research! But beware of being half-informed. It can lead you into all sorts of blind alleys. Suffice to say that government policy is clear in this area. AI may play a part in the relevant control systems, but full AI control is not sanctioned."

"Thanks. And can I ask whether an American company, Ultimate Intelligence, has any involvement in the joint Midlothian/North Rhine-Westphalia project?"

Mac thought Urquhart's face looked a picture – a struggle between an attempt to maintain composure and a takeover by an angry demon.

"The problem with relying on what a search engine tells you, Inspector, is that you pick up far more dross than pearls of wisdom. The company you mention has an interest in the project, as it does in a wide range of AI-related developments. UI is, after all, a world leader in the application of artificial intelligence, so it's quite natural that they should take an interest."

"Sorry, but you didn't answer my question. The word I used was *involvement*, not *interest*," Mac said, putting his arms on the table and leaning forward.

"I'll need to stop you there. You'll no doubt be familiar with the joint protocol between your service and my own which makes it clear that there are areas of defence-related information that we are unable to comment on. As your question takes us into one of those areas, there's nothing further I'm able to add. You'll be aware that the relevant appendix to the protocol makes it clear that C notice powers control the release of such information."

"In other words, I'm to behave myself and not expect answers to any questions which might actually assist my investigation!"

"On the contrary, my advice is simply to focus on those lines of enquiry that are free from classified information encumbrances. And be careful about trying to access such information via other routes. As I'm sure you're aware, if we feel security has been breached you would be required to attend an in-camera tribunal hearing. Our enquiries about your activity in such circumstances would be both extensive and thorough. So maybe you should spare a thought for your partner. Some of the company she keeps is politically questionable, to say the least. She might not stay popular for long within her radical art world if we had to start probing."

Mac hadn't expected Urquhart would play dirty quite so early in their relationship.

"You know, I'm surprised you'd consider wasting the firm's time on a bunch of Fife artists. They provide about as much of a threat as a Scottish pack on a bad day."

"You hadn't struck me as a rugby man."

"I'm not – football's more my sort of game – but we all need to keep in touch with what's happening in other parts of our world, don't we? If I was you," Mac said, his voice deepening, "I'd be more concerned about the Defence Select Committee's latest report and what it says about your uncle's company – especially if you're considering rejoining them at some point."

It was a reference in the report to the name Urquhart – the said uncle – that had caught Mac's attention during his online wanderings. The report had a number of not very complimentary things to say about Western Reach Defence, mostly on the issue of conflicts of interest. But then, as one of the website commentaries had stated, the well-oiled revolving door between the top echelons of the public and private sectors hardly discouraged this kind of thing.

Mac knew he'd taken a risk making such a pointed reference, but hadn't been able to resist. He'd probably pay for it further down the line. As it was, Urquhart looked as if he was sucking a lemon.

"That comment was completely uncalled for!"

"Tit for tat, I'd say," Mac responded. "Is there anything else you can tell me about Hofmann's activities that may be relevant to my enquiries – anything you're permitted to reveal, that is?"

"No."

"Then I'll take my leave. Thank you for your help."

Urquhart's office was just off the Royal Mile. Despite the driving rain, Mac enjoyed the walk back to his car, with not a tourist in sight. Given how little Urquhart had revealed, updating Maeven wouldn't take long. His own jibe about Western Reach would be unlikely to get a mention.

It was Kenny who'd mentioned Ultimate Intelligence, though he'd picked up no evidence of their involvement in IntelOper. Funded by a pair of right-wing American billionaires, the company was messianic about the application of artificial intelligence across a wide range of fields, but there was precious little detail about its global activity on their bland, superficial website. It did however refer to their commitment to the development of software which would enable super-systems to operate without input from mere people. Their NHR – No Humans Required – logo emphasised their commitment to this approach.

Mac had enjoyed dropping the company name into the conversation and felt that Urquhart's ambivalent response to his question indicated that Ultimate Intelligence probably did have some sort of involvement in the project.

As Mac drove back to the Warehouse, his earlier feeling of bravado began to dissipate. Perhaps it hadn't been wise to antagonise Urquhart. Would the man try and get his revenge?

+ + +

Having reflected on the police sergeant's very low-key reaction to her sister's disappearance, Ailsa decided to take a more active role herself.

Some time back, Fiona had given her a key to the cottage she lived in, out on the edge of North Berwick. Ailsa had always sworn she'd never use it unless it was a matter of life and death.

Well, given Fiona's complete lack of contact recently, maybe this was one such occasion!

Even though most of the journey could be done on main roads, she'd need to put her foot down to get from her home in Balerno to North Berwick and back while it was still light. Driving in the dark was something she tried to avoid. The cottage was a short distance outside the town, along a rutted track. Ailsa drove her Micra with great care, trying to avoid the bigger potholes, filled with snow melt. There was a muddy parking area in front of the cottage.

As the key turned in the lock, she felt almost as guilty as if she was breaking in. The house smelt damp and felt very cold and she immediately turned on a small electric fire that was balanced somewhat precariously in the living room hearth. The heat it gave out was insufficient to persuade her to take off her coat. Through the window there was a fine view of Lamb directly ahead, with two larger islands, North Dog and South Dog – the sheep dogs as they were known locally – off to the left. She always felt the view was the best thing about the cottage. Fiona's earnings fluctuated wildly and there was never enough money to pay for anything other than essential maintenance. Even little improvements seemed to be out of the question.

Ailsa's plan was, room to room, to check shelves, drawers and cupboards for anything that might help in the search for her sister.

Fiona was anything but tidy and methodical and generally her papers and other belongings would be shoved any-old-how into whatever space was available. But as her hunt progressed, Ailsa found very little in the way of paperwork and began to suspect that someone else might have been in the house before her, on their own hunt for information. After an hour, she'd come across precisely nothing relating to her sister's journalism. No mobile, no laptop. But knowing how

Fiona never let those two items out of her sight, that wasn't unexpected.

Ailsa kept half-expecting her sister to burst in through the front door and demand to know what the hell was going on. And she'd find it hard to justify herself. But if only Fiona would come rampaging into the cottage, then this developing nightmare would come to an abrupt and very welcome end.

In the early days she'd had normal, ordinary jobs, working for local papers. But it hadn't taken long for her to build up an interest in investigative, campaigning journalism. She'd taken on commissions from specialist journals, without informing her employer and had a flexible approach to apportioning her time. Effectively the local rags were subsidising her specialist interests. Eventually, this casual approach caught up with her. From then on, she'd gone freelance, financially dependent on small-scale commissions from niche journals. And within that particular specialist area, her reputation had grown.

About to give up on her search, Ailsa found the notebook wedged at the back of one of the drawers in the bedroom. If someone else *had* been searching the place, it wasn't surprising they'd missed it. The notebook was small and only about half the pages had been used. There was a list of some recent items of expenditure, with a few receipts clipped to the inside of the front cover. Other pages contained some random observations on life and a few half-completed 'to do' lists.

The receipts related to two train journeys, one to London, the other to Newcastle, both dated mid-February, an expensive meal at a London restaurant, paid in cash and some film developing carried out by an Edinburgh camera shop, which had also been settled by cash. On the final page of the book, two telephone numbers had been written, the second of which had been underlined three times in red.

This was hard to ignore. Her instinct told her to be cautious but, surely, she'd been far too cautious so far. Some risks had to be taken if progress was to be made. As she made the call, her hands were shaking.

"Law."

Was that his name? Ailsa thought the voice sounded very unwelcoming.

"I haven't got all day!"

"Sorry. I was just wondering if you know someone by the name of Fiona MacMahon." The phone went dead.

Ailsa immediately started worrying about the implications of what had just happened. Was it just a wrong number or something more sinister?

To distract herself, she called the other number. A firm of accountants. She explained the situation. Hesitancy at the other end of the line. In the end they confirmed they acted for her sister but hadn't heard from her in a while.

Perhaps her third and final call – to the Edinburgh camera shop – would be more productive than the first two.

"Image Photography. How can I help?" Such a relief to hear a friendly voice. Ailsa explained who she was and why she was calling. "Well, I've done quite a bit of work for your sister over the years. But there are often gaps when I don't hear from her for a while. Hopefully she'll be in touch with you again soon." She liked the sound of this man, considerate, softly spoken, unhurried and didn't want to end the call without some prospect of being able to find out more.

"Would there be any chance of meeting up, just to have a chat about Fiona? It might help to put my mind at rest." She didn't really think that would be the case, but figured that sounding somewhat vulnerable might make him more likely to agree to meet up.

"No problem. When would be suitable?"

+ + +

Maeven hadn't been surprised to hear about Mac's inability to get anything much out of Urquhart. It turned out that she'd had previous dealings with him and had faced the same problem. Mac confessed to the crime of deliberately annoying the Oversight Scotland man and got away with a light rap over the knuckles.

But the boss had been very interested to learn about Ultimate Intelligence and the possibility that they might have some involvement in the joint university project.

Mac had a feeling that Professor Laing might know more than he was letting on and had arranged a further meeting with the academic. Wanting to check whether there was any further news on what had caused McGrath's death, Mac set off early for his meeting at the university to give himself time to call in at Corstorphine House.

For some reason, Paula didn't want to see him. When the mood took her, she could turn bureaucrat in an instant and everything had to be done by the book. He filled in the requisite form and gave it to the mortuary admin worker who shrugged when Mac asked about the likely timescale for a meeting with the pathologist. And Carla had no idea why Paula had gone off on one, or how long it would take for her to simmer down.

He called Wyatt to find out whether there'd been any progress on the search of the Skoda that had conveyed McGrath to the beach. The SOCO's written report wasn't finished yet but she'd confirmed that McGrath's DNA had been found in the vehicle.

Thinking about one SOCO reminded him of two others. He asked Carla whether the Jokers were in the building. They were and he managed to track them down to the evidence storage and archive room, where they were carefully cataloguing bagged items relating to a serious assault case.

"Well, well, if it isn't our favourite Norwegian DI! What impossible task would you like us to carry out today?"

"I'm here about the door key," Mac replied.

The brothers looked at each other… *I thought you were… no, come on, you said you'd do it!*

"So neither of you has followed it up. That means you both owe me and I never forget debts. Close of play tomorrow at the latest." They swore it would be done.

"Your afternoon not going well then?" Carla said as Mac hung around her desk. Did she fancy a smoke on the fire escape steps? Alarm still out of action. "You're such a romantic, Calum – how can I resist?"

Unusually there was virtually no wind at the top of the steps. The two of them were comfortable together and had no need to try and fill any natural gaps in conversation. She flicked ash off his jacket and asked him if he was getting enough sleep – those bags under his eyes. Surely, he wasn't still trying to burn the candle at both ends – at his age!

They'd always been open with each other. He told her it was a combination of work trouble and woman trouble, as usual, exacerbated by insufficient sleep and a poor diet. When he mentioned his visit to Oversight Scotland and the condescending Mr Urquhart, she responded with a story about seeing him late one evening in a karaoke bar, the worse for wear and singing spectacularly tunelessly, which made him laugh.

"By the way, will you be putting an application in?" she asked, stubbing her cigarette out on the metal railing.

"For what?"

"Vernon's job – he's leaving. It's about time you stepped up to DCI."

Mac hadn't heard anything through the grapevine, but now wasn't a good time to think about that sort of thing. It would be a distraction. Then again, DCI posts didn't come along very often and was there ever a good time to face the hassle of job application and interview preparation? Sometimes he thought he could do with a life manager, someone to prompt him about the less immediate tasks, to ask the right forward-looking questions and carry out the necessary admin. Perhaps he was looking at her.

"When's it advertised?"

"Depends on the room at the top, but my guess would be within a week. Don't forget the Warehouse is already short of one DCI as they never got round to replacing whatshisname. Do you want me to get the papers across to you once they're out?" He nodded. A mind-reader in addition to all her other skills.

Grabbing the railing, he hauled himself up from the metal grating that formed the top step and watched as Carla sprang up unaided. She kissed him on the cheek and he responded in kind. That was as far as they allowed themselves to go.

Colin from the Torness power station had left a voicemail. In his view, Alex McGrath's job as a technician would have had nothing to do with his death.

Mac set off for the university, thinking about what to say later at the press conference. One of his least favourite jobs.

+ + +

Image Photography was in the city centre, just off Nicholson Street, the kind of location Ailsa thought would generate little passing trade. Maybe the business operated mainly online. She pushed open the shop door and smiled as an old-fashioned bell tinkled. A man – early forties maybe – emerged from behind an old-fashioned drawing board.

"Just a little light sketching, a hobby of mine," he said, shaking her hand. "Well, it's obvious you and Fiona are sisters. Take a seat and I'll put a brew on. I'm Lewis, by the way."

English, slightly posh, attractive, she couldn't help thinking. There were framed photos of what looked like Japanese cities all over the walls, daytime shots of soaring high-rise buildings, backstreet wirescapes, blossomed parks full of traditionally costumed visitors and night-time, neon-infused shots, rain slick on the pavements.

"As I mentioned on the phone, I've worked with Fiona – on and off – for years. She comes to me for my discretion," he said, grinning sheepishly. "Given the kind of work she does, it makes sense. The fewer people in the loop the better and she's got to be able to trust them. I last saw her just over a fortnight ago, when she brought a film in for developing, an old-school photographer as you'll know. Mentioned her current commission – bit of a laugh really as she usually commissions herself and then tries to find a buyer for her articles. But she wouldn't give me any details."

"Better that you don't know," Ailsa butted in.

"Exactly. I take it you get the same treatment." She nodded.

"So, what about the roll of film she left with you? Have you developed it?"

"Yes, but I don't think it's got anything to do with her current investigation. Hang on, I'll get the pics."

He disappeared into a back room, sweeping aside a bead curtain as he went. Ailsa wondered whether there was anyone her sister confided in, or did she keep everyone at arm's length.

The bead curtain moved again.

"Here. Take a look. I don't suppose she'd mind, with you being her sister."

Ailsa took the envelope and pulled out a pile of black and white photos. The first few were views from the cottage, very artily shot. The next dozen or so were of a place she didn't recognise, another coastline, rugged, probably not British. Of the remaining photos, two were of Fiona and a man and a woman staring rather seriously at the camera. Friends of Fiona's presumably, but she didn't recognise either of them.

Nothing in any of the photos gave her a clue as to what her sister might have been up to that had led to her self-isolation. Ailsa felt a definite disappointment.

Reluctant to leave on her own she felt suddenly emboldened enough to ask when he shut up shop.

"Round about now," he said, a little nervously. "Would you fancy a coffee somewhere"?

+ + +

Mac asked Professor Laing whether Ultimate Intelligence had any involvement in the IntelOper project.

"Yes – they're advisors. Our software specialists are drawing on their extensive experience in the application of AI to the operation of laser weapons." Mac hadn't really expected such an open response and was suddenly all ears. "It's a minor role. We do this with a number of companies in order to add to the pool of specialist knowledge and skills. Why do you ask?"

"Well, I read about them online and they seem to stir up more than their fair share of controversy. I just wondered whether their activity had become one of Dieter Hofmann's concerns."

"Not to my knowledge. As I said, theirs is a minor involvement."

"And did Dieter have any concerns about your software specialists? Is that provided in-house or have you contracted an external company for that work?"

"It's a company called Blue Star and as far as I'm aware, he had no reservations about them."

Mac didn't feel entirely convinced by the professor's response. Had he been told to play down Ultimate Intelligence's role? *If the inspector starts sniffing around, tell him the bare minimum.* However, he didn't pursue the matter, preferring to leave further questioning until later when he might have more information at his fingertips.

"OK, thank you. Now, I'd like to know a little more about Hofmann's embezzlement. Do you have a summary document

– perhaps something that was used to inform the disciplinary panel about what happened?"

For the first time, Laing looked a little uncertain, Mac thought.

"I'm not sure why you'd need such information, Inspector, given that it can't have had any direct bearing on his death."

"Well, that's for me to assess, isn't it?"

Laing pinched the bridge of his nose and sighed.

"I'm afraid I'd need specific authority to release that kind of document. There might be legal implications."

"I find that hard to believe, but if that's the case, why don't you phone your head of legal services now and I can speak to him?"

Laing picked up the phone… and put it down after a slight hesitation.

"Well, perhaps, given the circumstances, I could let you have a copy of the case summary. If you wait a moment, I'll arrange that."

He left the office and Mac wondered whether the professor had gone to make the phone call in privacy. Minutes passed. Hofmann must have been in a desperate position to risk embezzling money from his employer, Mac thought. Had his supplier been putting the screws on to that extent?

Laing returned and handed over the disciplinary panel document, which Mac scanned through quickly.

"Given this was a criminal offence, did you involve the police at all?"

"No. We handled it all internally," Laing said.

Kept the process well away from any external scrutiny, Mac thought.

Back at the Warehouse, as he'd feared, the press conference didn't go well. Two killings but no progress on identifying the killers. Fraser, the reporter who frequently got up his nose, was dismissive of the police's progress to date. Mac felt that he had a point.

+ + +

They went for a drink, rather than a coffee, at a nearby bar on Cowgate, Bridge Street towering above them. It was all long trestle tables and candles, the sort of place Ailsa loved. Lewis went for a can of craft beer that seemed to her extortionately priced, while she opted for a glass of Pinot Grigio and reminded herself that the car was at the other end of the park and ride. Lewis was good company, a bit of a gift of the gab but not annoyingly so. On his second can, he admitted that at one point, several years ago, he'd asked Fiona out, but she'd turned him down flat.

"I don't know what I was doing really. We're so different. I can see that now. How about you? You seeing anyone?"

Normally she'd have objected to such a question, especially coming as it did, less than an hour after first meeting. But the way he'd asked somehow put her at ease. No one just now, she replied. Truth be told, there hadn't been a man in her life for over a year, as her sister frequently reminded her.

Maybe that was about to change.

+ + +

At the start of their briefing, Mac told Wyatt that she'd done a good job on the whiteboard in Incident Room C and that he was sure it would prove a very useful aid to their discussions.

"So, we have Dieter Hofmann," he said, pointing to the photo in the centre of the board, "a highly intelligent AI and laser specialist, services much sought after, but a bit of a liability, both because of his *principles* and his cocaine use. And now we also know he'd just been dismissed for embezzling university funds.

Then we have Alex McGrath," Mac continued, pointing to a photo to the right of Dieter's. "A technician at the Torness nuclear power station until his contract came to an end a couple of weeks ago, maybe a drug dealer and definitely a very recent drug user. The issue we're considering is what might have triggered each of these deaths? What do you reckon, Raj?"

Khan was clearly ready for the opportunity. He stood up by the side of his chair and without hesitation started his assessment.

"For Hofmann, I think the drugs angle is a deliberate distraction. Yes, drugs were a weakness which would have taken him into risky territory. Yes, according to the university, he had drug – and gambling – debts. But lethal intervention? Apart from any other consideration, that would have meant his creditors having to wave goodbye to their money. I think it's more likely his death has got something to do with his work and him being seen as a threat to the project. Not only is there big money riding on the success – or otherwise – of the project, there's also a key defence objective to be achieved. While, at this stage, his elimination might seem an extreme step, maybe there was more at stake than we're yet aware of. And maybe whoever wanted rid of him decided to distract us from considering any work-related reasons for his death by making it look like it was drugs-related. So, they add in appropriate detail – the taser, the ritual of the open shirt and the moving of the body to display it in a more dramatic location. As far as McGrath's concerned, given the discovery of the coke stash at his place, his death may link to the drug world. But it's early days yet and I wouldn't want to jump to conclusions."

"Good. What are your thoughts, Laura?" Mac asked.

Wyatt walked from her chair to stand in front of the board, demonstrating a sort of proprietorial air. Before addressing the question, she did a quick summary of the display, telling them that it was important to be fully aware of the context before moving on to an analysis of what might have happened. Mac thought it sounded like a dig at Khan who had launched into his analysis without any preamble.

"My thoughts are the exact opposite of my colleague." Interesting she chose that word, Mac thought, rather than 'the sergeant' or 'my boss'. "There's a big risk that we get dragged into conspiracy-theory-land in a case like this. It's much more likely that the reason for these two deaths is drug-related. We know that the actual trigger for Hofmann's death was his long-term cocaine use. If he hadn't used to that extent, he wouldn't have died from the taser hit alone. McGrath was a dealer and became a user following the loss of his job at the power station. My view is that both men upset someone higher up the supply chain in some significant way – over and above whatever debts they had – and that their deaths represent a warning to others not to follow their example. Hence the tasering and the open shirts displaying to all and sundry that this is what you get if you step out of line. I think we should be getting to the local and regional cartels and making use of any relevant informants."

"Another well-argued scenario," Mac said, thinking that the sergeant and the DC could probably have swapped positions and argued each other's case just as strongly. Maybe Wyatt was keen to show her independence and had deliberately chosen not to go along with Khan. But it was good to have them both on the team. "Any other thoughts?" Mac asked, scanning the faces of the other four officers who'd been seconded to the growing group.

"Yes, guv." A DC from Prestonpans. "Perhaps we should focus on gathering more information about how they knew each other. That way we might be more likely to establish why they were killed."

"Well, we've no shortage of suggestions as to how to move forward," Mac said. "Let's keep an open mind at this stage.

DC Wyatt will be following up on the drugs angle, in liaison with DS Colquhoun from the drugs squad and DS Khan will be pursuing the work-related angle. And I may be able to get some background on the links between Hofmann and McGrath when I hear back from Marek, a cousin of Dieter's. Right! I need to update you on my meeting with Urquhart at Oversight Scotland and then I'll run through the list of tasks for tomorrow."

+ + +

Mac met up with his brother every week for a drink or two in the New Town. There'd been a period some years ago when, for a variety of reasons, they'd drifted apart, until Erland, saying he was missing his brother, had made the suggestion of a regular pub meet-up. Mac had resisted at first. Erland could be hard work at times. It was his mother who'd pushed him. *Put your difficulties to one side. Remember that, at the end of the day, you are brothers and if you scrape away all your disagreements, underneath it all, you do get on.*

He'd almost reached their rendezvous when his phone rang. It was Marek. His English was good. He'd been away on a business trip. Mac's message had been left on a landline, so he'd only just listened to it. How could he help?

"Thanks for calling back. I'm afraid I have some bad news about your cousin."

"It's OK. I've already been informed of Dieter's death. It came as a great shock. We were quite close. In fact, he used to confide in me." Mac wondered whether that meant Marek might have information that would be helpful to the murder investigation. "I should have been listed as his next of kin, but typical Dieter, he never got round to changing the details on the relevant forms."

"I'm really sorry for your loss," Mac said.

"Thank you. I'm still coming to terms with it really. If I can help with your enquiries at all, just say the word."

"That's very good of you. We're currently pursuing two main lines of enquiry. The first relates to… sorry if you're not already aware… his use of cocaine."

"Don't worry, I know all about it. We had frequent conversations, with me trying to get him to stop using, but I was never able to make any headway. It was the usual problem. Unless the user themselves wants to quit, you don't get very far."

"Indeed. So, we're following up on some possible drug-world connections locally. Do you happen to know anything about who supplied him in Dortmund?"

"No – sorry. But I'm certain he'd have had a supplier there in Edinburgh. Trying to smuggle coke in from Germany would have been too risky. What's your other line of enquiry?"

"That his death might have been triggered by something to do with his work. We know he wasn't popular with the powers that be, because of his concerns about how artificial intelligence might be used in the operation of laser weapons. But it's a stretch to think that this led to his death."

"It probably is. But I have to say that when he and I last talked things over, he was in a right state. It was to do with some information about the project he'd just discovered. Talked about blowing the whistle, but wouldn't say how he'd go about it. *The fewer people who know about my plans, Marek, the better,* he told me. He has always been a bit like that, saw conspiracies everywhere and was active in the Dortmund branch of a national group, *die Radikalen Wissenschaftler* – a bunch of radical scientists, big on direct action. If anyone at Midlothian University had become aware of his involvement with RW, it would definitely have rung alarm bells. Not to the extent of having the poor man killed, though."

"Thanks, that's very helpful. Is there anything else about Dieter you think I should know?"

"There is. He was gay. Still very much in the closet and he'd only come out to me and a few close friends. Even in these more enlightened days, he was worried that others might find out and use it against him in some way."

"We hadn't picked up on that. It's certainly worth following up. If you think of anything else, perhaps you could phone again."

"Tell you what," Marek said. "As it happens, I'm just about to make another business trip – to the UK this time. I'll be in Glasgow on Saturday. It wouldn't be much out of my way to call in and see you – if that would be helpful."

Mac told him it would be very helpful and arranged a time to meet at the Warehouse.

He'd reached The George, on a quiet side street. It was just the sort of place he and Erland liked, a safe distance away from the Rose Street tourist and day-tripper bars, small, dimly lit, six hand pumps with a range of beers on rotation. A number of conversational topics were out of bounds – anything to do with work, money, or – given their widely differing views – politics.

"You look tired, mate," Erland said as they settled into two corner seats, upholstered in red mock velvet. "Why's that?"

"You know what I'm like, bro, burning the candle at all three ends. The good news is that Freya's back on the scene. I'm always better when she's around."

"Well, that's a matter of debate! How long's it going to last this time?"

"Yeah, I know. Longer than last time I hope, but we'll see… Anyway, how are Catriona and the kids?"

Erland liked talking about his family. His wife was very good for him, kept him grounded, he said, tethered maybe, like a balloon that might otherwise float off into the wide blue yonder, an eternal twenty-one-year-old. The kids were at the awkward age, semi-independent but without the real nous yet to navigate the white waters safely. Mac wondered whether all ages were difficult really. He'd spoken to enough older colleagues with children in their twenties and thirties to know that the concerns and worries about them didn't stop.

"What do you reckon to all this news about the coronavirus?" Mac asked.

"It's a load of hype," his brother replied. "Nothing more than a bad flu. We should just get on with things. The idea that countries should be closed down is nonsense, don't you think?"

"No, I don't." He wasn't at all surprised by Erland's response. "I think it's really serious and only a matter of time before things get shut down here. The government will resist for a while because it won't be a popular move but, in the end, they won't have any choice."

"Well, I hope you're wrong. Anyway, I've been thinking about doing a trip back home. Would you be up for that?"

It was interesting how they both referred to Fredrikstad as 'home', even though Erland had no real memories of living there and Mac had only ever visited the place. His first reaction to the suggestion was to reject it. A weekly evening drink with his brother was fine. He had grown to enjoy it. But three, four, five days together? Would that be wise? On the other hand, it was ages since he'd had a break. He didn't particularly like going away on his own. And the Norwegian cousins, always good company, would help dilute the full impact of Erland-on-holiday.

"Yes – why not? It would be fun," Mac replied.

But he couldn't help thinking that if things worsened with the virus, a trip abroad would probably become a non-starter.

6 MARCH

Though Erland could sometimes be hard work, Mac felt better for the night out with his brother.

His allocation of tasks at the end of the previous evening's briefing session had been received without any audible moans. But he was acutely aware that they'd need to make some concrete progress very soon. It was all very well having plenty of information about the dead men but so far, in the absence of any actual solid evidence, they were still at the stage of throwing around ideas about who might be responsible for their deaths. To date, Maeven, as senior investigating officer, had been unusually patient, but Mac knew it wouldn't last. She'd already dropped hints that the chief superintendent was not happy with the pace of progress... or with the negative media coverage!

But despite these thoughts, such was the state of his early-morning well-being, that he took himself off on a run, beyond Stockbridge and part way to Leith. On his return he was famished, but had forgotten that, yet again, there was nothing left in the fridge. Once he reached the Warehouse, the kiosk on the dockside came to his rescue, not for the first time, with a bacon roll and a coffee.

At his desk by seven thirty, he checked his phone. A message to ring Joker One. Even though it was early, he knew the SOCO would answer.

"You'll be phoning about that key. I've got a result for you, well before your close-of-play deadline. You'll be pleased to know our lock specialist has done a top job. The key is for a double cylinder deadbolt, so whoever it belongs to is keen on security. And the locksmith who cut the key? Well, he's based in North Berwick. I've emailed his details to you. Bit of a relief that he wasn't based in Germany, eh! Oh, and we finally got round to doing a proper search of Hofmann's caravan. Sorry, but apart from his prints and DNA, we found nothing. How was your night, by the way?"

"Surprisingly enjoyable," Mac told him. "My brother was on good form."

The caravan update was disappointing, but not unexpected. The Prestonpans DC was dispatched to the locksmiths.

Switching his attention to McGrath, Mac realised there'd been no news from Paula about the needle mark on the dead man's right arm. Surely the results of the toxicology tests should be available by now.

Although she wasn't known for being an early bird, he was in luck.

"Any news on the McGrath needle mark?" he asked.

"Did I not tell you?"

No, Paula – you fucking well didn't.

"Tell me what?"

"Ah – my apologies. Things have been a bit hectic here. Did you hear about the shooting out at Currie?" He hadn't. "Well, it's all gone a bit mad. Blue-arsed flies and all that. Your mate Euan is the DI on the case. Anyway, back to McGrath. I sent samples through to our forensic toxicologist. She's been overloaded – just like me – so it's taken a while to get the results back. Anyway, you'll be interested to know that her analysis shows he took an injected mixture of cocaine and heroin, known in the trade as a 'speedball'."

"Jesus – that's unexpected," Mac said. "Hasn't that happened to a number of celebs over the years?"

"You're right. It's all a bit complex, but basically, because one's a stimulant and the other's a depressant, a user may misjudge the intake, leading to a risk that they could unwittingly give themselves a fatally high opioid dose. I've done some work on the body since getting this information and can now confirm that the speedball was responsible for his death."

"Right!"

"What we now need to ask is why would a man new to drug use suddenly decide to go for a speedball?"

"Good question – unless of course it wasn't actually his decision," Mac said.

"My thoughts exactly! Proving it might be a little difficult, but good luck!"

What he'd just been told provided weight to the argument that McGrath's death had the hallmarks of a professional hit arising from the world of drugs.

He called DC Wyatt, told her about the speedball and asked her to follow it up with Colquhoun, the drug squad specialist. Could he identify any likely culprits who might have a track record of administering such drug cocktails? She sounded pleased to get the call and said there was already a meeting arranged with the DS so she could add this new development to their agenda.

Khan arrived looking in a bad way – not for the first time, Mac reflected.

"Fancy a trip to the kiosk?" he said. "I could do with another coffee and you look like you could use one."

Allowing for the fact that it was still only early March, the weather was kind, a light breeze and a temperature high enough to risk keeping hands out of pockets. They took the coffees to a battered wrought-iron bench, green paint peeling away.

"Are you OK, Raj? You don't seem your usual self today." The DS looked relieved by the question.

"Sorry, boss, it's my dad. He's been having cancer tests up at the hospital," he said hesitantly.

"I'm sorry to hear that," Mac said, touching the sergeant lightly on the shoulder.

"Thanks. I've gone with him a couple of times – during work time. He finds it hard to take in what he's being told by the medics so I've been there as a second pair of ears. I should have mentioned it earlier. I've made the time up but still, I should have been up front and asked."

"They can be a worry, can't they – parents? My mum has breathing problems and I go with her for some of the appointments. Maeven's usually OK about it. Just let me know in advance. It's not a problem."

"Thanks. That's a weight off my mind. I've been back to the uni again, to try and get a bit more out of the two project workers I spoke to previously. At first neither wanted to add to the little they'd already told me, but eventually I managed to get them to open up a bit. It turned out that Hofmann wasn't the only one on the team to have reservations about the AI angle. But his credibility on this and other issues was undermined by his drug abuse. His colleagues viewed him as unreliable and bad for the project and were therefore reluctant to back him on raising problems with management. Which left him out on a limb."

"Did they think his death had anything to do with his job?"

"No. According to them, skullduggery certainly goes on, but it's a case of undermining reputations and trashing research findings, not physical assaults or worse. I asked them again about the role of Ultimate Intelligence but got no further. However, just as I was getting into my car to drive back here, one of them collared me. *Follow the money*, he told me. Pretty nervous about even telling me this much and unfortunately, I couldn't get any more out of him."

"That's very interesting. My source may be able to help us get a bit further on that issue. In fact, I'd better tell you about Kenny."

At the end of Mac's summary regarding his old schoolfriend, Khan nipped back to the kiosk and bought a second round of coffees and two croissants.

"So, were you born in Scotland, Raj?" Mac asked, once they'd settled back on the bench.

"Yes, like you, I understand." So, he'd been doing some research, Mac thought. "The family's from West Bengal – Kolkata. Dad worked in one of the jute mills there which was owned by a Scottish company. There was very little he didn't know about machine maintenance. When the chance of a job came up with the same firm in Dundee, he jumped at it. The family moved there in the early seventies and I was born a few years afterwards. Despite that and my local accent, I still get asked where I'm from. Do you get that as well?" Mac nodded. "Unfortunately, Dad's mill only lasted another ten years. After it closed, he eventually managed to get a job on the buses. Following his retirement, he and mum moved here to Edinburgh. We live in the same street."

"Well, between us we've got two stories illustrating the decline of Scottish industry, your dad with the jute mill and mine with the shipyard here in Leith. I suppose it's time we headed back."

"Sorry, boss – something I've forgotten to mention. My head's a bit all over the place at the moment. The Renault van spotted up at the bing, the one we traced to the Haymarket area. We talked to local residents there. Nobody noticed it arriving. But one local who'd been away for a day or two has just contacted us – we'd pushed a card through his door. He's given us a good description of the driver, but the angles weren't right for him to get much of a view of the passenger. Something solid to go on and it backs up the driver description we got from the old feller in the tumbledown barn up at Tarbrax. I'll send you the details. I know we did that initial press release about the Renault on Tuesday, but I think we should get another one out today and include an updated photofit of the driver."

"Good idea. Can you arrange that?"

"Yes, I'll sort it out."

"What about CCTV footage?" Mac asked.

"There was a shot of them exiting the vehicle, but it's poor quality – just like the nearest street light! So, we're trying other cameras nearby to see if we can find out where they went next."

"And have we got any further in getting access to Hofmann's accounts in Germany?"

"I'm afraid not. You wouldn't believe the bureaucracy involved. But we'll keep trying."

Mac's phone rang.

"I'd better take this. See you back at the ranch." he said, and watched as Khan crossed the road looking more purposeful and upright than he had before.

"I've been on to them up at Corstorphine and they put me through to you." Male, hoarse, sounding like he smoked too much. "Been reading about the two murders, you know, the taser ones. The thing is, it reminds me of something similar about ten years ago, in Glasgow. I worked over there then."

Mac was growing impatient but knew from plenty of previous experience that sometimes there could be a valuable nugget at the end of a long string of words.

"Caused a bit of a stir, three bodies found over a few months, all with the old taser marks and shirts open – just like your two guys. They reckoned it was a drugs gang behind it. People used to call them the Clyde cartel. There was going to be a trial but it all fell through. That should never have happened. So, you might want to check it out. And that photofit in the paper of the man in the Renault? Well, he looks like one of the guys who was in the gang back then!"

Really, Mac thought.

"It's good of you to phone this in. Could you give me your name please?"

"No way. Don't want any of this getting back to the wrong people."

The man rang off. Mac tried not to get his hopes up too much, but the information might turn out to be extremely helpful. He phoned Wyatt and told her about the call.

"That's very interesting, boss. I'll speak to Colquhoun and get back to you as soon as there's some feedback."

He'd been tempted to speak directly to Colquhoun but felt it was better to allow Wyatt to develop the link with the drugs squad sergeant.

+ + +

The two walkers had left their car in a lay-by and set off on a circular route. A dry day but a strong wind. He checked the GPS which revealed they'd covered just under five miles with about a thousand feet of climb. There were clear views all round. As long as they kept moving, it was a good day for walking.

"Time for a brew," he said. "And maybe a sandwich or two."

After unscrewing the silver metal cup from his flask, steam escaping into the cold air, he filled the cup and the blue plastic one his wife was holding, then topped each one up from a small milk container. They sat together on matching padded picnic mats on one of the big flat rocks and looked out across the valley, not another soul in sight. The burn gurgled past them a few yards away.

"Marvellous, isn't it?" she said. "These Fridays off are a real boon. I've made notes of what we've done each week, otherwise

I might forget the detail. Do you want cheese and tomato or fish paste?"

They both went for fish paste, eating slowly, savouring each mouthful.

"Crisps?"

"No thanks, I'll save mine until later. What do you fancy doing tomorrow?"

They debated whether to join the group walk which started in Jedburgh and so would involve a longer drive, or opt for a garden centre trip to stock up on spring plants. The garden option won out.

"Doesn't do to sit in this wind for long. I'm really cold already," she said. "Can we get going?"

"You're right, it's freezing. Believe it or not there's actually enough space underneath the rock to shelter right out of the wind. A bit cramped but it's doable. I should have thought of it before."

"Really! Show me."

They scrambled to the ground and he led her to an opening big enough to creep into, a rocky roof above. He rummaged in his bag for the torch.

"Look," he said, pointing the beam towards the back of the opening. The torch picked out a figure clad in walking gear, curled up on the rough ground. "Oh! Sorry, I didn't realise there was anyone here. I do apologise." There was no response. "Jesus! I've got a horrible feeling about this. I'm going to check for a pulse."

His wife, looking stunned, didn't say a word.

"Nothing. I'd try CPR but the body's stone cold. Is your phone on?" With a great effort, his wife managed a reply.

"It is… hang on a minute… I've no signal."

He turned his own phone on and waited. Nothing on that one either.

"We're going to have to start walking and hope we pick up a signal. There's no point in us waiting here."

"Are you sure you'll be able to find this place again?" his wife asked, her voice shaky.

"I know it anyway, but I'll also be able to pick it up on the GPS – or the map for that matter." Brisk and businesslike. "Come on, let's get moving."

After twenty minutes walking, his phone suddenly showed two bars. He made the call, explained what they'd found and gave directions for reaching the rocks. When asked, he confirmed the person was dead. As a first-aider at work, it wasn't the first time he'd had to check a pulse.

+ + +

DC Wyatt sipped her espresso. She and Colquhoun were the only customers in The Light and as the barman was out back talking to the chef, they had no need to drop their voices. She was enjoying herself. Perhaps *enjoying* wasn't quite the right word, but she felt a definite buzz. Colquhoun came across as an interesting maverick.

The DS was particularly interested to hear about the speedball and ran through a list of famous names who'd exited the world in the same way as McGrath. He gave her a rundown of the key local drug dealerships. She'd picked up some of it during her recent secondment to the drugs squad, but Colquhoun added a lot more. There was a structure to the trade and although people came and went, several of the entrepreneurs had been around for a while. They didn't like newcomers or anyone who didn't play by the unwritten rules.

Colquhoun had spoken to a couple of dealer contacts and one of his informants about the two dead men. One of them had heard mention of the German. The word was he'd run up debts and was struggling to buy. None of them had come across McGrath and the assumption was that he must have been only a small-time dealer. The common view was that it was unlikely McGrath would have voluntarily chosen the speedball route to death. Someone would have helped him down that particular road. The big question was... what had the two men done that had cost them their lives? Although bad debtors attracted the wrong sort of attention, it was unusual for debts alone to precipitate a killing.

"I've just received some information about a new line of enquiry," Wyatt said. "But before we start on that, shall I get us more coffees?"

"That'd be good."

After calling the barman from the back room and ordering the drinks and a couple of chocolate flapjacks, she told Colquhoun what the anonymous caller had said, without letting on that it was actually her boss who'd taken the call.

"Have you come across this Clyde cartel in your travels?" she asked.

"No. But then I've never worked in Glasgow. However, I've got a mate who's based there. Let me give him a ring."

The sergeant had to make do with leaving a message.

The barman brought their drinks and cakes to the table.

"I'll let you know when I hear from him," Colquhoun said, once the barman had left. "He's one of those guys that picks up all sorts of gen and what's more he remembers stuff from years ago. But, back to what we were talking about, in my experience, it's always advisable to look beyond the obvious. What else may be hiding in the shadows? With Hofmann it's tempting to wonder about his work and whether he upset some powerful interests. But I don't buy it. Those interests might well want to kick him off the job and discredit him, but I can't see why they'd go as far as killing him."

"So, what do you think led to his death?"

"My view is that both deaths are linked. If that's right then we need to be looking at the things the two men had in common. And, from what you've told me, a link to self-activating laser weapons isn't one of those. No, it's much more likely to be something to do with their drug-world connections. That's why your Clyde cartel lead sounds promising. It's not going to be about just dealing. From the sound of it, McGrath was way too small-scale for that. But could they have stumbled across something that put them at risk – an overheard conversation perhaps? Believe me, things can get out of hand very quickly within that world."

"And in your view, would these characters do their own killing or would it be put out to contract?"

"Could be either. There are a few enforcement firms around locally, although most of their business stops short of actual killing. I'll check out what gossip is circulating. Maybe we could have dinner tomorrow and I could update you on the general goss and the cartel."

Wyatt knew she ought to turn down his offer, but the temptation to say yes was too great.

And it just so happened that her partner would be away for the weekend.

+ + +

Although it was most welcome, Ailsa had not expected an actual visit from the police. Detective Sergeant Kershaw had arrived, wanting to talk about Fiona. So at last they were doing something.

Had the other sergeant she'd spoken to given him the relevant details or did she need to go through them again? For a moment, Kershaw looked a little puzzled and then told her a recap would be helpful. She gave him a full account.

He asked what she'd done herself to try and locate Fiona. It felt embarrassing that there was not much to say. She'd checked with a few of her sister's friends and work colleagues and had gone to her house to look for any clues as to her whereabouts. And what had she found? Very little apart from the telephone number of a man called Law. When she'd called, he'd put the phone down on her. Kershaw asked for the number and she gave it to him. She made no mention of Lewis, her new photographer friend. It felt too personal and besides he knew even less than she did.

But she did tell the sergeant about Fiona's two near neighbours. It might be worth him speaking to them. They were both a little strange, in their own different ways, but being a detective, he'd perhaps be able to make more progress with them than she had.

He promised to let her know how things developed.

Lewis arrived not long after the detective had left. The plan was for a drink or two at home, followed by an early dinner at a Polish restaurant she'd recently discovered.

He was pleased to hear about the detective's visit and that, at last, it looked like they were taking her concerns seriously. After the indifference of the officer she'd spoken to originally, it was a positive step forward. Perhaps they'd get somewhere now. She fetched two lagers from the fridge, opened them and passed one to him. They clinked bottles.

"Would you mind if I just checked the news on my phone, before we go out?" Ailsa said. "I'm afraid I've been doing it a lot over the last few days. Obviously, I don't want to actually find anything about Fiona, but somehow, I can't stop myself."

"No problem. It's very understandable," Lewis said.

She scrolled through various screens, pausing now and then to read something in more detail. A headline on the *Edinburgh Evening News* website grabbed her attention. 'Walker's body found near Peebles'. The brief article stated that the walker, a woman, had probably died of hypothermia. There was a photo of a location that was familiar to her, large rock slabs piled high above a fast-flowing burn and felt sure it was somewhere she and Fiona had been to together. Except the scene pictured in the news photo was one of late winter, whereas their walk had been mid-summer, unusually hot, shorts, sunglasses and Factor 50.

This was exactly the kind of story Ailsa hadn't wanted to find. Her hands shook. She dropped her phone and it clattered onto the table.

"What is it?" Lewis asked, looking concerned. At first, she was unable to speak, but gradually her worst fears spilled out. "I can see why you're thinking that," he said, "but it could be anyone. Just because it's a walk Fiona took you on doesn't mean… But I can see you're really worried. Why don't I phone the police in Peebles? They'll be able to tell us enough to know one way or the other."

She looked into his eyes and nodded. He opened his arms and she moved towards him. It was the first physical contact they'd had.

He found it difficult to explain to the duty sergeant. It boiled down to a combination of just a feeling and a photograph of some rocks. In the end he asked whether they could come to the station. The officer agreed.

Ailsa barely said a word on the drive out to Peebles.

By the time they arrived at the police station, the duty officer had changed, so they had to go through their story again. Ailsa found it difficult to hold things together. Lewis suggested that the quickest way of finding out whether or not the walker had been Fiona would be if he was able to view the body. Ailsa shuddered. The officer was hesitant.

"I need a bit more before we go any further. Have you by any chance got a photo of your sister on your phone?" he asked. Ailsa took a moment to absorb the reason for his question.

"Yes, I should have, somewhere. Wait a minute." She flicked through page after page of pictures and was just about to give up when Fiona's face appeared. "Sorry, they're not organised at all."

"That's OK," the sergeant said. "What I'll do now is email the photo to the mortuary which is up at the hospital. We've got no space for one here. I'll ask them to check it against the... er... body. It's a little irregular, but I can tell how important it is to you. Please, have a seat. It may take a while."

+ + +

Mac had heard back from the Prestonpans DC, who'd been out to the locksmith in North Berwick. The key was a copy. He'd also fitted the original lock. The locksmith didn't have the full address, but could remember where the house was and had given the DC the details. The customer, a woman, had paid in cash on both occasions and he had no record of her name.

Mac said he'd meet the DC at the house and set off for North Berwick.

Linking Hofmann's key to a specific house was a good step forward. However, they were still lacking a lot of Hofmann-related detail, including the whereabouts of his phone and laptop. His work email had been accessed, but had thrown up little of interest. So far, they'd been unable to locate either a private email address or any social media accounts.

Thinking about Hofmann's belongings reminded Mac that there'd been no word back from the German police about the search of his Dortmund apartment. Was it two or three days since they'd made the offer? He called the senior officer who'd spoken to him, only to find she was in a briefing about a serious knife attack that had taken place the previous day. A message would be left for her to call him back.

Mac got confused trying to follow the directions he'd been given to access the North Berwick property and had to phone the Prestonpans DC who, it turned out, was already there. Eventually Mac found the right track and pulled up outside the run-down cottage with a striking sea view.

While waiting for him to arrive, the DC had taken the opportunity to speak to the occupants of the two neighbouring properties. Neither really knew anything about the cottage owner. *Keeps herself to herself* they'd both told him.

The DC knocked on the front door of the cottage – just in case there was anyone inside – without response. The two of them put on protective suits, gloves and overshoes as a precaution and used the key to enter the house.

Despite a thorough search, they found nothing that linked back to Hofmann. Perhaps he'd never had a chance to use his key.

"Is it just me," Mac said, "or do you reckon that somebody's beaten us to it searching this place?"

"You could be right," the DC said. "There was no sign of any forced entry at the front, but I'll go and check the rear."

Mac noticed a framed photo on the mantlepiece, two women who looked like sisters. He removed the back of the frame, took out the picture and pocketed it. On the back of one of his business cards he wrote a note for the woman who lived in the cottage, asking her to contact him and stuck it in the corner of the frame.

"You were right," the DC said as he came back into the living room. "Someone's gained entry via the back door. The lock's been damaged. It's poor quality. Surprised she didn't get it changed at the same time as the front one. False economy. There's a couple of bolts on the door which I've slotted back into place. Should stop anyone else trying to get in that way. Anything else just now, guv? Only I'm hoping to meet the girlfriend at seven and need to get home and changed beforehand. Friday night and all that."

"Just one thing," Mac said. "We don't know the name of the occupant yet. One of the clericals checked the electoral roll but there was nobody listed for this address. They must have opted out of the public register. And when we tried the local council, their systems were down. Can you ring BT from here on the landline and ask them for the customer's details? I'm just going to have a quick look round outside."

It had started to rain again. He felt that the Scottish word *dreich* was highly appropriate for the weather out in the small back garden – wet, dark and unpleasant. The shed was unlocked but contained only a few garden tools and a push mower that looked as if it had been a while since it had last cut a blade of grass.

"Customer's name is Fiona MacMahon," the DC said as they stood in the dripping garden together. "I've locked up and I'll be off now if that's alright."

"Yes – have a good night."

Mac's own Friday evening highlight would be the practice cross-examination with DI Forsyth at his house in Carnwath, which was a cross-country journey away from North Berwick.

The last part of the drive was along the A70 and he noticed the Tarbrax turn-off as he sped past, followed shortly afterwards by a sign for *The Saloon*.

Euan welcomed him and they swapped updates on case progress, Hofmann and McGrath on the one hand, the shooting at Currie on the other.

"Did you see today's press article on the Maxwell case?" Euan asked.

"No! Why now? Did they know we'd be rehearsing tonight?"

"Certainly not! I kept that really quiet. But with the court case imminent and the investigation months ago, perhaps they thought some reminders were necessary."

"Well – I suppose we'd better get on with it then!" Mac said.

An old barn at the bottom of the garden provided the venue for the mock drama. Euan, dressed for the part, was wearing a well-cut, double-breasted suit and a bright red tie. He stood on a temporary podium made from wooden pallets so that his questions could be posed to DI Larsen from on high. As a stalwart of the local amateur dramatics group, he knew how to play a part.

"Right – the Maxwell armed robbery case! As the defendant's advocate, I'm about to start tearing you apart."

Euan disappeared in an instant, to be replaced by an arrogant posh-boy silk, whose questions were designed to undermine the detective inspector's competence and credibility. Mac struggled to keep his cool and ignore the personal slurs. All too easily, the weaknesses in the case were exposed and he had difficulty in trying to rebut the accusations of corner-cutting and shoddy workmanship. At one or two points, he came close to committing perjury.

The session lasted an hour, by which time he was completely drained. The advocate departed and Euan returned, the suit replaced by jeans and a Smashing Pumpkins T-shirt. The glasses of Edradour were very welcome.

"Shit! That was hard work. I'm going to have to up my game and plug some of those gaps."

"If you don't, you'll really struggle. But I'm sure you can do it. Maybe you need to be a bit more aggressive. There's always a danger that if you start off on the back foot, you never regain momentum. But enough of that! You mentioned your trip to The Saloon when we spoke on the phone. They've got a blues band on tonight. Do you fancy going after a bite to eat here?"

He did, particularly as it would sweep away the after-effects of the cross-examination. Euan rustled up a frittata, warmed some flatbreads and pulled two bottles of Belhaven from the fridge. They both over-ate, then dozed in front of an open fire until it was time to head for the gig.

"We'll drive down in my car and Jim will pick us up from there, so we can have a drink or two."

It was only a few miles along the Lang Whang.

"Have you heard the story about the UFO?" Euan asked as they drove through the darkness. Mac shook his head. "Back in '92, two guys were driving one evening, out from Edinburgh towards Tarbrax. They were delayed by something and arrived at their destination much later than expected. Months later they went through something called hypnotic regression and claimed to recall that they'd been abducted, examined and communicated with by alien creatures. When you're on this road in the dark, it's not hard to believe something like that might happen!"

"You serious?"

"Aye – just check online. It's all there. Mind you, the other thing you have to watch out for along here, is idiots like that," Euan said, pointing to a Mini Cooper that had suddenly appeared on the wrong side of the road. "They don't cotton on to these hidden dips in the road and forget all about the possibility that there might be other folk on the road. Been a fair few deaths on this stretch over the years."

Mac felt relieved to reach The Saloon in one piece, though there was still the return journey to worry about. In stark contrast to his first visit which had seen a virtually empty car park, the place was heaving. Although the bar inside was surrounded by thirsty punters, Euan managed to catch the barman's eye and signal two pints. They stood to one side, waited a short while and the glasses appeared as if by magic in front of them. Even before the band started playing, it was difficult to make yourself heard.

Mac felt a broad hand slapping him on the back and turned to see Dougie, the owner, who Khan had introduced on that first visit.

"Pleased to see you made it back, but I'd no idea you were acquainted with this reprobate," he said, pointing to Euan. "The band'll be on stage in a few minutes. Enjoy your evening."

Mac reckoned that the members of *Biggar Blues* must all have been at least seventy but they could really belt it out and the singer had a strong rasping voice, bettered only by his harmonica playing. As well as a number of standards, they played their own stuff with lyrics including plenty of local references. It was a good while since Mac had been to any kind of gig. It was so easy to get out of the habit of doing such things. In the toilet, he checked his phone. Work was never that far away, but there was nothing that couldn't wait.

Back in the bar, Euan seemed to have disappeared. He had, but only as far as the dancing area where he'd teamed up with a woman in a denim jacket and long denim skirt. Minutes later, Mac found himself pulled onto the floor for a dance. A woman in her thirties, another long skirt, a cowboy hat which stayed in place despite all the movement and an American accent. A shouted conversation revealed that she was in fact Canadian – with Scottish ancestry – an academic on a European trip that had a few more weeks to go. Mac was always reluctant to reveal what he worked at. The news tended to push ensuing conversations in one of two directions. Either, that's very interesting, tell me what it's really like, or, how can you bring yourself to do a job like that. Instead, he talked about his Norwegian heritage. She'd taken in both Oslo and Bergen on her tour so they had some common ground.

When Euan's son Jim arrived to provide the taxi service, Mac couldn't believe how quickly the evening had gone. Part of him wanted to spend more time with his new Canadian friend, but he knew all too well where that would lead. Not that it stopped him exchanging phone numbers. She'd be in Edinburgh for a few days and it would be nice… you know… to meet up again.

Jim proved to be a fast-talking, wise-cracking entrepreneur – at the ripe old age of twenty-one – full of business plans, some of which were already coming to fruition. Euan said he'd no idea where such enterprise had come from.

Mac's bedroom for the night was in the attic of Euan's house, at the far end of the heating run. Despite throwing on some extra blankets he'd found in the bottom of the wardrobe, it still took an age to warm up. Just as he was beginning to nod off, his phone rang. Surely, he'd left it on silent. A woman's voice. He confirmed he was DI Larsen and asked for her name. She refused to give it.

"What the fuck do you mean by breaking into my house?" Only half awake and still under the influence of the Saloon beers, Mac was at a loss to understand what she was on about – until he remembered the business card he'd left in the North Berwick cottage. Ah, Fiona MacMahon.

"Hold on a moment. That was no break-in. A colleague and I let ourselves in with a key."

"What a bare-faced lie! As if you'd have a key."

"A surprise maybe, but not a lie. What evidence did you find of a break-in?"

"I haven't been there. It wouldn't be safe. A neighbour contacted me, said the two of you had been inside and that your sidekick had spoken to her." One of the two who'd claimed to know nothing about the occupant of the cottage, Mac thought. "She went into my house to check what damage you'd done and found your business card. That's how I got your number. You still haven't told me what you were doing there. You had no right to go in and invade my privacy."

"I was there as part of a murder investigation," Mac said. There was an audible gasp at the other end of the line. It was a while before she responded.

"That's dreadful. Who was the victim?" she asked, managing to keep her voice calm.

"Dieter Hofmann." A much longer silence followed and it was a while before Mac realised she'd rung off. Damn!

Despite trying her number several times, he was unable to

get beyond voicemail. A chance of finding out more about Dieter had disappeared.

And the possibility of sleep seemed also to have vanished.

He thought about his meeting with Marek and wondered whether there'd be any additional news about Dieter. The information about his involvement with RW, the radical scientists' group, had been particularly interesting. Mac found the group's website. They looked to be a bunch of mavericks and there were some fairly wild ideas on their blog. If Dieter had got involved with this group back home, might he also have had some input into a similar organisation locally? If there was one!

His phone screen glowed in the otherwise pitch-black bedroom. Needing more light, and feeling like a cup of tea, he put on socks, trousers and fleece and made his way downstairs to the kitchen, where it was a pleasure to discover the warmth of the range. A large, battered leather armchair right next to the stove provided a much-improved alternative to the cold bedroom. Fetching a blanket, he snuggled into the chair, sipped his tea and continued his online research.

It always amazed him just how many groups of one sort or another were out there, each with their own niche and most of them convinced of their own unique role and contribution. But none of them looked to be the kind of organisation Dieter might have joined. His eyelids felt heavy. The phone fell from his grasp as he slipped into sleep.

+ + +

Ailsa kept reliving the moment when she found out that the woman in the mortuary in Peebles was not her sister. Having virtually convinced herself that Fiona was dead, the wait for news had been agonising. When they'd finally been told that there was no match between the photo and the body, her legs had buckled and Lewis had saved her from falling to the floor.

He'd been brilliant, calming and distracting her, then persuading her that even though they'd be three hours late, a visit to the Polish restaurant would still be a good idea.

After the meal and the journey home, things happened very quickly. Not like her at all. Lewis lay beside her in the single bed. She'd never got round to buying a decent-sized one. He was still asleep. She was too full of jangling emotions to be able to get back to a state of pleasant unconsciousness.

And there was that thought. She knew where her sister wasn't – the Peebles mortuary. But where exactly was she and what kind of risks was she facing?

7 MARCH

The thrill of Saturday morning!

Mac still had that instinctive response to that time of the week, despite the fact that he was more likely to be working than not.

Ignoring his slightly throbbing head and the stiffness arising from sleeping in an armchair, he forced himself out for a run. Although Euan hated the whole idea of running, his son Jim was keen. So keen that Mac struggled to keep up. Very helpfully, every half mile or so, the young man stopped to admire the view, and allow the old man to catch up.

When they got back to the house, Euan the chef was standing, complete with a black and white striped apron, in front of the range, an array of breakfast meats and eggs sizzling in pans on the hotplates, telling Mac to get a move on with his shower, because breakfast was virtually ready.

The run had done him good and given him an appetite. After demolishing two bacon and egg sandwiches, Jim disappeared into the world of his tablet. With Euan pre-occupied preparing for a weekend trip to London to visit his ex-wife, Mac took the opportunity of the unexpected silence to think about the call from Fiona MacMahon. What was the link between her and Dieter – apart from the key? Highly unlikely they'd been in some sort of relationship – unless of course the German had been bisexual. Maybe it was something to do with his work. The problem was, he knew nothing about her apart from her name, phone number and the fact that she had a temper. Still, she obviously felt unsafe being at home. He tried calling her again but it just went through to voicemail. The chances of her calling him again were probably non-existent.

Mac was back on the A70, heading towards the city. UFO tales didn't really resonate against a backdrop of blue sky and sunshine. The original plan had been to drive straight to the Warehouse, but the pull of Café Surprise on a weekend was too strong.

Angelique was on an up. Her mother was feeling better. Although it probably wouldn't last, for the time being, it was one less thing to worry about. After Euan's breakfast, Mac had no need for food – just a coffee. He wondered whether Kenny, who kept unconventional hours, would be up. He wasn't, but he was awake.

There was no difficulty getting his old schoolfriend onto the subject of Ultimate Intelligence.

"I've put out some feelers and discovered that in addition to being advisors to the IntelOper project, they've also stepped in to fill a critical funding gap – not directly, but through a proxy. As it's taken some digging to reveal this link, it's reasonable to assume that the powers that be don't want this information to be widely known. What you need to focus on now is what they'll have got as a quid pro quo for this investment. They won't have taken this step for altruistic reasons."

Mac realised that UI's involvement was more extensive than it had seemed at first sight.

"Thanks, Kenny. While you're on, could I mention something else? There's a company called Blue Star who are fronting the software development on the project. It occurs to me that it might be worth checking if they're clean."

"Sure thing – leave it with me, big man."

Had Raj Khan not been attending an aunt's funeral, Mac would have asked him to make further enquiries about UI. Not wanting to put such a task onto Laura Wyatt's shoulders, he'd need to take it on himself. He already knew Professor Laing worked late into the evenings and it didn't take long to find out that he also worked on Saturday mornings, telling Mac that he was preparing for a seminar on *New Developments in Modern Warfare*. How could he help? Just as Mac finished putting the words finance, joint project, Dieter Hofmann and Ultimate Intelligence into a single sentence, Laing interjected.

"I've already made you aware, Inspector, that UI's role in the project is minor and that their involvement has no bearing on what happened to Hofmann. As for them investing in the project, I have no knowledge of that. But then I'm not a bean counter. If you want to follow this up, I suggest you talk to the university's director of finance. I can give you his number."

On the off chance of catching the head bean counter on a Saturday morning, Mac rang the number and was pleasantly surprised to get an answer. The director responded affably and confirmed that UI had invested in the IntelOper project, not directly but through a proxy. No mystery. Investing via proxies was quite common. Mac was tempted to take the opportunity and ask about Blue Star, but felt it might be better to defer the question until he was armed with whatever information Kenny came up with about the company.

Revived by the combination of the director's response, Kenny's news, the morning run, a good breakfast and his first coffee of the day, Mac resumed his online search for any relevant local activist organisation that Dieter Hofmann might have joined.

An organisation he hadn't noticed during his pre-dawn search activity caught his eye. *Weapons Watch* – the campaign for democratic control over weapons development and deployment. There was an Edinburgh cell, as it was called, and a local convenor with a phone number. Things were continuing to look up. He rang and left a message.

Angelique brought him a fresh coffee and suggested that, as he was her only customer, they could sit outside where there was a little warmth in the sun. She drew on her endless list of Réunion stories, this time with a tale about the restaurant she and her then husband ran in Saint-Denis, the island's capital. Such was its popularity that customers had to queue for a table. And for their traditional maloya music evenings, it was standing room only. Not for the first time, he asked why she'd left the island. Her responses seemed to vary. Sometimes it was a man, a native of Edinburgh who'd enticed her away. On other occasions it had been debt from a failed business that had driven her away. This time she talked animatedly about the lure of adventure in a foreign land.

Erland called. How about agreeing a date for their Norwegian trip? Early May when it might have warmed up a bit. Mac agreed, thinking he could always change his mind further down the line.

"That's if we'll still be allowed to go travelling by then," he added.

"What do you mean?" Erland asked.

"The virus! If it spreads here like it's doing in Italy, they'll impose travel restrictions."

"That won't happen, bro – trust me. Now, just to let you know and to make you jealous I'm on my way to Aberdeen for the Hibs game."

Occasionally, Mac still felt the old pull, that Saturday morning football feeling and the build up to a three o'clock kick-off. Even with home games, the match and everything associated with it filled the whole day. During his first few weeks as a rookie cop, faced with the impossibility of attending a match, he'd missed the buzz like mad.

"And what are the chances of hearing a rousing rendition of *Sunshine on Leith* from the Pittodrie away end this afternoon?" Mac asked.

"Well, I'm feeling positive about the match," Erland replied. "So, there's a good chance."

Always the optimist, Mac thought, and no bad thing. He told his brother to enjoy the trip.

When two customers arrived at the cafe, Mac took it as his cue to leave, calling Maeven on his way to the car to fix up a briefing.

The timing left a gap just long enough for him to head over to North Berwick and drop in on Fiona MacMahon's neighbour, the one who'd checked the cottage after his visit. Maybe she knew more than she'd let on to the Prestonpans DC – like where Fiona was hiding out.

As he drove along the A1, the weather began to turn, the clouds changing from white, to grey, to black. Headlights and wipers on, spray making visibility poor.

By the time Mac reached the cottage, the weather had closed in to the extent that the sea had disappeared and he half-expected to hear the mournful tones of the old foghorn. Not knowing which neighbour had been the link to Fiona, he'd have to try both.

It was impossible to get any sense out of the woman in the left-hand single-storey semi and he left her talking to her cat. The occupant of the other semi was hostile.

"I'm here about Fiona."

"I know nothing about her. She doesn't talk to me!"

"That's strange, because she told me you two had a conversation yesterday." The woman looked confused. "You see, I'm investigating a murder."

"Oh my god! Who is it?"

"This man," he said, showing her a photo of Hofmann. "Do you recognise him?" She shook her head vigorously. "Do you know where Fiona is? We're concerned about her safety."

"So is she! That's why she went away... but I've no idea where... honestly. She said it was better if I didn't know. I've said nothing to either of the other coppers who knocked on my door."

"There's been more than one?"

"Yes. The youngish lad who came with you and then the sergeant who was here... recently... can't exactly remember when."

"What did he look like?"

She gave him a description.

Mac was puzzled. As far as he was aware, nobody else had been out questioning locally. Maybe the woman had got confused.

On the journey back along the coast he called in at the Mermaid for one of their trademark fishfinger sandwiches and a cup of tea. As he started to demolish the sandwich, the cafe proprietor hovered.

"Can I help?" Mac asked, disappointed that his one hundred per cent concentration on the fishfingers had been interrupted.

"You're working on the murder case right, the feller found on the beach?" Mac nodded. "Only Joe, one of my regulars, mentioned something this morning. I was going to phone it in but now you're here, well... I can save the cost of a call. The thing is he saw two men getting into a Skoda estate, parked just over there," he said, pointing to the car park. "This was somewhere around five on the morning the body was found. Says he can give descriptions."

"That's very useful. Do you happen to know where Joe lives?"

Mac made a note of the address.

"And what's his last name?"

"Semple."

"How come he didn't say anything earlier?"

"Well, it's not like he saw the body – just the men and the Skoda. It was only when he read in the paper about the vehicle they'd used, that he put two and two together. Besides, he's had a few bad experiences with you fellers over the years. I had to work hard to get him to agree to say anything if you came knocking."

Mac didn't have time to interview the witness himself as he had to be back in Leith to brief the boss and then meet Marek. However, he managed to catch the Prestonpans DC and asked him to go and talk to Joe Semple.

The briefing went well. Maeven seemed unusually relaxed. He knew little about her. The Corstorphine HQ grapevine buzzed periodically with both compliments and complaints about Morag Maeven, but the underlying feeling was that, still only in her late thirties, she'd go far. Her husband was an advocate. Mac tried to imagine how their dinner discussions might go.

His musings were interrupted by her comment about the chief super.

"I'm not worried... yet... about progress, but you need to be aware that the chief doesn't like the way the media are responding, focusing on the negatives as usual. That reporter you don't like – Fraser, is it – seems to have a hotline to him."

Mac had never liked the chief super, a traditional copper who believed in a strict hierarchy and viewed Mac as too alternative in his views – and his appearance.

As Mac was about to leave, Maeven told him there was another matter. He braced himself. But it wasn't like that.

"The DCI post, presumably you know about it?" Mac said he'd heard. "I think you should consider applying." A conversation like this wasn't at all what he'd expected. Generally, in discussions with superiors, he found it best to be prepared for some kind of bollocking. Then, if for any reason it didn't happen, that was a win. "We need more people like you at this level. One of your pluses is that you're not clubbable." He wasn't sure what she meant by this. It didn't sound like a plus. "You know – the likes of the masons, golf, rugby – as far as I'm aware, you're not signed up to any of them. In the old days that might have been fatal to your chances, but things have improved – at least up to a point. Besides, Calum, you've got the ability and I think you should stretch yourself."

Maybe she was right. He certainly had the experience. Then there was the law degree he'd studied for part-time, evening classes after long days at work, weekends taken up with poring over dry legal textbooks and writing even drier essays. And more recently he'd taken the right kind of courses in leadership, senior management, priorities at a time of scarce resources – all the usual suspects. So, why did he still feel hesitant? Maybe it was all about comfort zone. He'd been a DI for a long time. It had scared the shit out of him at first but he'd grown into the role. Gearing up for a big change would take a lot of effort. But there was more to it. The confidence factor. Did he have it in him? And there was a fear of losing touch with what was happening on the ground.

His phone rang as he left the boss' office. It was the convenor of Weapons Watch returning his call. He decided to jump in with both feet.

"Thanks for calling me back. I'm phoning about Dieter Hofmann."

He'd figured that introducing himself as a detective would have been a sure way of guaranteeing she'd terminate the call. By not revealing his identity immediately, he might at least be able to keep her on the line long enough to tell from her reaction whether or not she knew Hofmann.

"Who are you?" Icy cold – but he sensed immediately that she'd recognised the name.

"I'm Detective Inspector Larsen and I'm trying to find out why he died." A long pause.

"How did he die?" Coldness replaced by uncertainty, perhaps even fear.

He was in.

+ + +

DC Wyatt had been given the task of looking for any potential leads relating to Dieter Hofmann's sexuality. Specifically – did he have a partner locally and might McGrath have been that partner?

Her starting point was The Cairn in Linlithgow where she found the landlord in a particularly unhelpful mood. According to his previous statement he'd seen both Hofmann and McGrath in his pub and said they'd clearly known each other. But he seemed shocked by Wyatt's question about whether they might have been partners and clammed up.

Which took Wyatt on to the interview she'd been hoping to avoid – one with McGrath's mother. She felt uncomfortable at the prospect of asking questions about the son's sexuality, particularly as the old woman would be very vulnerable so soon after learning of his death. When Wyatt had raised these concerns with the boss, he'd responded by saying firstly it was important to make progress on this particular issue and secondly, he was sure Wyatt had the right skills to be able to make such enquiries in a sensitive manner. She'd felt trapped.

The area where Mrs McGrath lived was run-down and reminded Wyatt of the estate she'd lived on as a youngster, when money had been very tight.

It took a while for the mother to answer the door. She'd been having a nap. The poor woman looked extremely worried and completely worn out by life, but still managed to make a cup of tea for them both, though it took a while. Wyatt spent some time talking about anything other than the real reason she was there. Mrs McGrath seemed to have difficulty in concentrating on anything for longer than a minute or two.

Wyatt explained that they were still trying to work out who might have been involved in her son's death and that meant regrettably, she had to ask some awkward questions. She started on safe ground. Would any of her son's friends know about any problems he might have been facing?

His mother spoke in short sentences and left long gaps between them. It became apparent that McGrath had been very much a loner. No close friends, no girlfriends. Wyatt could no longer avoid the question that had to be asked.

"Look, I'm sorry but I need to raise a rather sensitive issue with you. We're aware your son knew a man called Dieter Hofmann, a German who'd been working in Edinburgh for a while. Hofmann was gay and... well... I wondered whether your son might also have been?"

Mrs McGrath stared straight at Wyatt, her mouth open, tears welling up.

"I'd always hoped there'd be a daughter-in-law and maybe a family. But it wasn't to be. Alex never showed any interest in women." She paused. It was clearly an effort talking about it. "For a long while I just assumed that he didn't have any interest in sex at all. After his father died though – they never got on – he finally told me he had relationships with men. It took a lot for him to open up about it. Looking back, I really should have guessed. There were lots of little signs."

Wyatt felt relieved that she'd managed to ask the question and that the old woman had coped well enough with answering it. And Larsen had been right. It was something that had to be raised.

She asked about Hofmann and showed Mrs McGrath a photo of him. Could he have been involved with her son?

"It's possible I suppose, but Alex never mentioned him and I don't recognise the man."

Wyatt picked up on some hesitancy in her response and asked the question again, just to be sure. She received the same answer.

"Do you have any of your son's belongings in the house?"

"Just some of his old school books, a few photo albums, train tickets, souvenirs, that sort of thing. He always travelled light, didn't believe in having much in the way of possessions – well, apart from the car."

"He had a car?"

"Oh, yes," Mrs McGrath replied. "A green one, a Volvo. Cost him a bit to run, but he needed it to get to work what with the power station being a fair distance away and with him on shifts."

"Do you know where he kept it?" Wyatt asked.

"In a garage he rented, not far from his house. I'll get a car key and a garage key for you. He kept spares here. Then I'll explain how to get there."

Wyatt phoned to arrange for a SOCO to meet her at the garage.

+ + +

Marek turned out to be a great bear of a man, wrapped in a huge overcoat. He asked if they could have their discussion somewhere outside, so Mac took him to one of his dockside benches with a detour via the kiosk to pick up two coffees. He offered his condolences and thanked Marek for adding Edinburgh to his already busy British itinerary. The German fingered his moustache, before taking a sip of his coffee.

"I've been thinking a lot about Dieter since your call. He was a man of contrasts, very well organised and meticulous in his professional life, but anything that conflicted with his principles became an immediate problem. Which meant he experienced difficulties with his employers throughout his career. They all wanted to tap into his brilliance but found it hard to deal with his intransigence. No doubt it was the same with Midlothian and I'm not surprised to hear he was fired. But, that said, I still think it's unlikely issues arising from his work led to his death."

"And what about his personal life?" Mac asked.

"It was something of a contrast to his working life! He was disorganised, impetuous and a risk-taker, but you couldn't help liking him. Well, I couldn't anyway. To give you an example of his impetuosity, I've just found out about problems he created with his cocaine dealer in Dortmund – complaining about quality and refusing to pay – which led to his supply being cut off. Once the dealer put the word out, other suppliers refused to fill the gap. Maybe he had similar problems over here. An issue worth pursuing, I'd say."

"That's very helpful, Marek. Is there anything else you can tell me about his private life that might have some relevance to our investigation?"

"There is. Quite a sensitive matter, which is the reason I wanted to talk to you in person about it. Dieter suffered from depression and sometimes it took him over. I wouldn't rule out the possibility that he deliberately put himself in harm's way and this could have had some bearing on his death."

Marek expanded on some of the problems Dieter had faced.

"I appreciate your openness," Mac said. "That's helped me to get a more rounded picture of him. The other matter you mentioned on the phone was that Dieter was gay. Are you aware whether he was involved in a relationship in Edinburgh?"

"I found out that he and his partner in Dortmund split up last year, so I'd say it was quite likely. But even though he confided in me about his sexuality, he didn't keep me up to date with new partners, so I'm afraid I can't help you on that."

"Now, is there anything you'd like to ask me?"

"Well, there may be a limit to what you can tell me, but I'd like to know something about how he died and whether you're close to finding out who was responsible?"

Mac ended up being more open in his response than he'd intended, feeling that Marek was owed a degree of frankness.

Marek had a final question.

"When can my cousin's body be released?"

"Right away," Mac replied. "I'll give you the relevant details."

"That's good," Marek said. "I'll make arrangements for the body to be flown to Dortmund."

+ + +

The pathologist phoned the Peebles police station to give the duty officer his preliminary findings about the woman found at the rocks. His best estimate was that the woman had died sometime during the thirty-six hours leading up to the morning of 29 February. Her death hadn't just been down to hypothermia. Sure, that had been the actual cause, but there'd been something else going on beforehand. The woman was a type 1 diabetic, which meant it was essential she took insulin regularly. For some reason, she'd failed to do so. Hypoglycemia had set in, which led to unconsciousness, so, being unable to move, there'd have been no way of avoiding hypothermia if she'd been out in low temperatures overnight.

The duty officer told the pathologist that with just one man and not even a dog at the station, he'd have to refer the details on to HQ.

+ + +

Mac was revising, trying to strengthen his arguments in the areas of weakness that Euan's cross-examination over the

Maxwell case had exposed. But even though the real court hearing was only just over a week away, his heart wasn't in it, not helped by the fact that his ear pods were distracting him with a commentary on the first half of the match at Aberdeen. Hibs were leading 0-1. Erland's earlier call had whetted his appetite for the game.

His short conversation with the Edinburgh convenor of Weapons Watch had been difficult but he'd eventually managed to prise out of her an admission that she'd known Dieter Hofmann and had arranged to meet her after the weekend.

The Prestonpans DC called. It had taken time, but he'd extracted a witness statement from a clearly unwilling Joe Semple. He had been parked up, waiting for the newsagents to open – for his usual fix of papers and cigarettes – just after five on the morning Alex McGrath's body was found. Two men, who'd come from the beach, got into a Skoda estate in the car park by the Mermaid Café. It had still been dark, but the car-park lights had been working, so he'd got a good view and was able to give descriptions of the two of them. A big, middle-aged guy, with a goatee and longish hair and a younger man, tall, short blond hair, stylishly dressed.

Mac arranged for revised photofits, based on the new descriptions, to be circulated and coordinated the preparation of an updated press release. Within minutes of being issued, Fraser the reporter was on the phone. Mac's response that he had nothing further to add to the release didn't go down well.

Hibs had been reduced to ten men. Aberdeen equalised. He groaned. A feeling of inevitable approaching defeat crept over him.

His phone rang again. DC Wyatt to say she'd spoken to Mrs McGrath who had confirmed her son was gay. But she hadn't recognised the picture of Hofmann. The other news was that Alex McGrath owned a green Volvo!

"Two very useful pieces of information, Laura. That's good. Have you been able to arrange an inspection of the vehicle?"

"Yes. I went up to McGrath's garage with a SOCO and he found three sets of prints since confirmed as McGrath's, Hofmann's and one unknown. Significant evidence of the link between the two men. But there were no traces of cocaine, or any other drugs in the vehicle."

Mac remembered Torness Colin telling him how strict they were about drug abuse at the power station. Maybe McGrath had felt it would be too much of a risk to use his car as a delivery vehicle.

Mac told Wyatt about the new descriptions of the two men who'd delivered Alex's body to the beach. Things were looking up. Had she been able to speak to Colquhoun about the taser deaths in Glasgow ten years ago? She had and he was checking it out. They'd be meeting again that evening when the DS would report back.

Two more home goals at Pittodrie and it was all over. Hey ho!

Mac had run out of steam. It happened sometimes, usually when he'd worked seven days or more on the trot, a gradual shut down and an inability to think straight. The only cure was to leave the workplace as soon as possible – wherever he happened to be at the time – and immerse his mind in something that had nothing at all to do with work. A game of chess could do it for him. There'd been a time when he'd thought about little else. Not that he'd ever been anywhere near a Magnus Carlsen, the Norwegian grandmaster, but he had made it to the dizzy heights of under-14 schools area chess champion. There was a good chance that someone would be up for a game at The Dunvegan.

The drive home felt like being on automatic pilot, him going through all the motions but taking in nothing else. A quick change of clothes and he headed off to Mario's for a pre-chess pie and chips.

+ + +

Arriving at the restaurant, DC Wyatt was at a loss to understand why she'd ever agreed to a dinner invitation from DS Colquhoun. It had seemed like a bit of harmless fun at the time and a good chance to get some valuable information on the drug issues swirling around the two murder cases. The fact that her partner was away for the weekend had also been a factor. And both offer and acceptance had been made in a jokey sort of way – or so she'd thought. So, it was a shock when Colquhoun turned up suited and booted and with serious intent. She played it cool, didn't respond to his cheesy personal compliments about her own appearance and managed to move the conversation quickly into work territory.

The question she'd been itching to ask – had he heard back from his mate in Glasgow? He smiled and tapped the side of his nose.

"I have indeed. Rollo has been very helpful."

The DS had the knack of being able to eat and talk simultaneously, without food falling from his mouth, but at this point he put down his knife and fork and ran fingers through his well-trimmed beard as if wanting to make the most of his big announcement.

"He's spoken to a Glasgow DI who was involved in the case against the guys in the Clyde cartel. They didn't use that name themselves by the way. It's just what the press called them. Apparently, there were three killings over a six-month period. All the victims were tasered prior to death and the taser marks were openly displayed on each body – just like with McGrath and Hofmann. It was assumed this was done as a warning. *Mess with us and this is what you'll get!* Word on the street was that responsibility lay with a bunch of drug dealers who were operating as a cartel with the aim of squeezing out all opposition.

But inevitably they had a big falling out and within a year it all collapsed. Unfortunately, the case against the dealers collapsed as well – and nobody was ever convicted of the killings."

"That's really very helpful," Wyatt said. "Does the DI have a view on whether there might be a link between what happened then and our case?"

"Rollo said he's got an open mind on that. Several ex-cartel men are still active in the drug trade and some have enforcement experience. He's going to put some feelers out and find out what these guys are up to now."

"Thanks very much, Sergeant. I can't wait to feed back this information."

"It's a pleasure and now that's out of the way, perhaps we can get a bit more personal," he said, with a smile that was not quite a leer.

She couldn't dance around the issue any longer. A decisive intervention had become a necessity.

"Look, Sergeant," she said, ignoring his earlier suggestion that they should use first names, "it's very good of you to have taken the time to meet me tonight, but this was never meant to be a date." She hadn't expected this comment to be the equivalent of lighting the blue touchpaper.

"You've been leading me on! Agreeing to have dinner with a man on a Saturday night is bloody obviously agreeing to a date. Not only will I be paying for the meal, but I've already given you valuable information. So effectively I'll be paying twice – and getting nothing back in return."

She wasn't going to stand for this.

"I don't remember anything being said about who'd be paying for the meal. My natural assumption was that we'd go Dutch. After all, we're colleagues – nothing more! And since when did the provision of information by a male officer to a female officer on a case have to be reciprocated by the offer of a night in bed?

So, if you can just drop your oh-so-predictable macho approach, then we can carry on and enjoy the rest of the meal."

At that moment his phone rang and, as he grabbed for it, his half-full beer glass went flying. She tensed. Would he lose it completely?

"Guess what," he said to the phone, "I've just knocked over my bloody beer glass – again – just like last week. You're a jinx! Anyway, can't talk now as I'm at a critical point in an argument with a young lady and she'll be waiting on my every word. Ring you back." A grudging smile flickered. "Perfect timing, eh, stopping me from acting like a complete pillock. OK, what about a pudding?"

+ + +

Sure enough Tam was in The Dunvegan when Mac arrived, a better chess player, but prone to the occasional careless mistake which meant they were fairly evenly matched. Tam set the pieces up and opened with his trademark knight move, keeping his finger on top of the piece for a moment as if he really needed to think hard about the consequences of that very first move. Mac went pawn to king 4, *his* usual first move. He and Tam still used the traditional way of describing chess moves, rather than the not-so-new alternatives and both preferred the pub's chess clock, an old analogue model, to the flashy modern digital alternatives. Over time, they'd trained the landlord to keep an eye on their glasses and replenish them as and when, with the tab settled at the end – so as not to break their concentration. The game followed a familiar pattern of good early progress by Tam, followed by stout rearguard action from Mac. But this time Tam edged it. They sometimes went for a rematch, but Saturday was quiz night, so instead the pair of them teamed up with two other chess regulars to form the Checkmates.

As quizmaster, the landlord brought his own style to the job, his voice rising and falling randomly, reminding contestants that it was phones in pockets and hands on the table at all times. They worked through sections on geography, sport, politics, soaps and a specialist area which changed each week. This week it was food with an emphasis on celebrity chefs. The Checkmates finished second, pipped, not for the first time, by the Also Rans.

The therapy had been effective. Not a thought about work all evening. As Mac walked home alongside the river, nearing the flat, there was the sound of an incoming text. *Do you fancy a nightcap? Kath.*

Trying hard to think who this was, a woman's voice with a Canadian accent suddenly sprang into his head. Earlier in the evening, before the beers, his answer would have been a definite *no thanks.* But what harm could one more drink do? As he pressed the reply key, he had a sudden awareness of not being alone.

A fist came out of nowhere and he fell, his phone flying from his hand into the undergrowth. A man was suddenly down at his level, young, muscular, stinking of after-shave, mouthing off some kind of warning. As the man stood up, Mac managed to grab his ankle and send him sprawling. But his attacker was up again within seconds, feet lashing out. Mac, unable to get up, curled into a ball, trying to protect himself. Sudden shouts from two passers-by, accents so strong he could barely take in what they were saying. Which worried him, until he realised they were on his side. His attacker fled. The teenagers checked Mac was OK and saw him to his front door.

Collapsing onto the bed, he fell asleep instantly.

8 MARCH

Ailsa couldn't get back to sleep. In bed by eleven, asleep within minutes, deep sleep until five and then... wide awake.

It had been such a relief to find out the dead walker was not Fiona. And the visit by the detective had been a positive step forward. But there was no getting away from her original worry that her sister hadn't been in contact for two weeks. Lewis had gently pushed her into phoning Law again but there'd been no response.

Should she try yet again? Her instinct was to leave it until later. But the worst that could happen was another flea in her ear.

It rang and rang but eventually someone picked up.

"Who on earth is ringing at this ungodly hour?"

"It's Fiona's sister. Please don't put the phone down, I'm really worried about her."

"And what makes you think I know anyone called Fiona?"

"Well, your name and telephone number were in her notebook."

"And how do I know you're not just making this up? Tell me something personal about this Fiona that only a sister would be likely to know." A little bit of interest had crept into his voice.

Ailsa thought for a while. It was critical to get this right.

"Well, she has a birthmark at the top of her left thigh."

That was it. He'd gone. Had that information been a bit too personal? Still, she was pleased about getting further with him this time. Would he call back?

All of a sudden, she felt sleepy and was desperate to stay awake in case he did. But her eyelids were so heavy and she couldn't resist the pull of sleep.

+ + +

Mac's head hurt like hell.

A glance in the bathroom mirror revealed there was some tidying up to do, blood to swab away, but nothing too serious revealed beneath. His ribs were extremely sore, but, thankfully, still intact.

He tried to work out why it had happened. Random attacks were not unknown in the neighbourhood, but he had a feeling this one had been planned. The man had been waiting for him. What was it he'd said? Some sort of warning!

Fuck! What about his phone? He'd forgotten all about it… and it was his work phone which contained all sorts of confidential information. He hobbled down to The Water and began his search in the bushes, near to where he'd fallen – or as near as he could remember. At least most of the shrubs were not yet in leaf which made things easier. No sign of his phone but there was something of interest under a laurel bush – a car key. Was that where his assailant had fallen? Might it be his key?

As he continued to poke about for his phone, a dog walker stopped and asked what he was looking for. Taking in the damage to Mac's face, he offered to help – two pairs of hands and all that. The dog waited patiently at the side of the path watching the two men scrabbling about in the undergrowth. After a minute or two, the dog walker suddenly stood up.

"What's your phone number, mate?" Mac, not really with it, couldn't understand the point of the question. "If you give it to me, I can use my phone to locate yours!" The penny dropped. Within a few seconds Mac's phone rang out from a clump of nettles. He thanked the man, retrieved the phone and made his way slowly back to the flat. Apart from needing a recharge, the mobile seemed none the worse for its adventure.

Mac stayed in the shower for a good ten minutes. Slowly he began to feel a little more human. Things began drifting back to him. The quiz, the chess game, the text from the Canadian woman. Had he actually sent a reply and if so, what had he said? A quick check and much relief – he hadn't replied. He couldn't remember whether he'd been tempted to accept her invitation for a nightcap.

It was supposed to be his day off, but as he slowly drank a cup of tea, wincing at the pain each time his jaw moved, he knew there were two things he needed to do. The first was to report the attack – which should really have been done before now. The second was to ask Khan to check out the car key. Reluctantly, he decided it would be necessary to call into the Warehouse to hand the key over and while he was there it would be better to report what had happened directly to Maeven rather than do it over the phone. Only then did he latch on to the fact that it was Sunday morning – the graveyard visit morning! A glance at his watch. He just about had time to fit in a Warehouse pit stop. And was he fit to drive? Well… fit enough.

The phone continued to charge in the car. Calls to both his mum and Freya to pre-warn them about his altered appearance, playing down the attack. A call to Khan, who was already at the Warehouse, to explain about his assailant and the car key. It occurred to him that the car might even still be around, parked somewhere near his flat. Khan said he'd investigate the possibility. A final call to check Maeven would be in her office.

On arrival, Mac handed the car key over to Khan, who was very concerned about the attack and the damage to Mac's face and keen to make the follow-up enquiries.

"Just one thing to mention while you're here, boss. We finally got something more back on the CCTV not far from where the Renault was abandoned. It's a better shot of the driver – not brilliant but an improvement. I've arranged for the photofit to be adjusted accordingly."

"Thanks, Raj. I'll see you tomorrow."

In contrast to Khan's obvious concern, Maeven seemed distracted. She told him he was needed out at Peebles. A body had been found in the hills nearby. The case would be allocated to DI Forsyth, but very inconveniently, he was away in London for the weekend.

"So I need you to go out there this morning," she said glancing at him and only then taking in the damage to his face. "What have you been up to, Calum?" Mac held his head. Apart from the pain, he already had two murders on his hands. And it was supposed to be a rare day off.

When he told her about the attack, her previous distraction disappeared and she was immediately sympathetic.

"Sorry about not noticing your injuries sooner. It all seems to be happening at once. Cases keep coming in, Forsyth's away, a couple of officers are off sick. Still, forget about Peebles. I'll find somebody else to go."

"That would really be appreciated. Look, you'll probably want another DI to take this on until Euan's back, but Sergeant Khan would certainly be able to pick it up and hold the fort until then."

"I suppose that's a possibility." Some reluctance there. "Have you reported the attack?"

"Well, I really wasn't in a fit state to do anything last night, so this is the first chance I've had. Not sure I'm quite up to completing a B7 though." A wry smile from her.

"OK – this is what we'll do. I'll ask Khan to drive out to Peebles and do the necessary. As for the B7, just run through the details of the attack with me again and I'll fill it in."

As Mac retold the story, he suddenly recalled what his attacker had said.

"Look, my mind's been a bit fuzzy since the attack and I've only just remembered what the bastard actually said. *Be very careful what you say about Maxwell, or next time will be a lot worse.* I can only assume he read that press article about the case. The attack was all about getting me to change my story at the trial."

"That is worrying," Maeven said. "Straight intimidation. We'll need to get onto it immediately – high priority."

Mac told her about the car key and Khan's involvement.

"He can prioritise that first thing and then get out to Peebles," Maeven said. "What about you? Do you need to get checked out at A&E?"

"No, apart from a sore head I'm fine. I didn't lose consciousness at all." That was as far as he was aware.

"OK. We'll arrange some observation on your home. I know you won't want it, but you haven't got any choice in the matter. Don't worry – it'll be unobtrusive."

Mac didn't want it, but knew better than to argue the toss.

"As I'm here, do you want an update on progress?" She nodded.

He ran through the recent developments. She homed in on Weapons Watch and Hofmann's link with the group.

"You'll need to take care dealing with that kind of organisation. And watch your step because it's possible Oversight might have someone in there undercover. Keep me posted. Overall, the team's making good progress, but we're still short of specifics on the killers. What have you got on for the rest of the day?"

Mac told her it was supposed to be a day off.

"I'd forgotten. Another good reason you weren't keen to drive out to Peebles, eh! In that case, I suggest you get out of here and take some recovery time."

As he left the building, Mac wondered whether attending a wild birthday party would count as recovery time.

After the Warehouse delays, he drove on to Portobello. His mother was ready and waiting and her breathing was steady, but she was most upset by the marks on her son's face. He dismissed her concerns, telling her he'd broken up a fight outside his local. She got quite emotional about their graveyard visits at the best of times and the sight of his injuries certainly didn't help. Traffic was light on the journey to the cemetery which was close to the Water of Leith and only a short walk away from the shipyard where Per Larsen had worked. Mother and son liked the thought that he had a view of his old workplace.

Mac parked up behind Freya's Fiesta and carried his mother's bag which was loaded with plants, pots, trowel, fork and gloves. Freya was already at the graveside. He repeated the fabricated story about his damaged face. Freya, looking both concerned and sceptical, didn't pursue the matter. After hugs all round, they set to removing the old annuals in the grave and planting up the new. This was both the best and the worst time for Pia, feeling so close to her husband and yet so far apart. Once the gardening was finished, Mac returned to the car, brought out the picnic basket full of sandwiches, cake and a flask of coffee and the three of them sat on a bench with a view towards the sea.

Mac surprised himself by managing a couple of sandwiches and a piece of jam sponge, despite the difficulty of eating. It was their habit at graveyard gatherings to take it in turns relating stories about Per. Freya chose a tale about him and her own father, late teens, a trip to a visiting funfair, going mad on the dodgems. Pia told them her favourite, a trip to Bergen on their honeymoon and Mac talked about going with his father to watch his first proper football match. It had been at the old Fredrikstad stadium. Since then, a new stadium had been built – in the former shipyard where his father had worked!

The sun emerged from behind a bank of clouds. A thrush began to sing, a hint of spring in the air.

+ + +

Having waved Freya off after a whispered conversation about the real nature of the attack, he took his mother home and stayed with her for a while. Something was bothering her, over and above his injuries and the visit to her husband's grave. It didn't take long to winkle out the problem – the coronavirus again. She'd watched a programme on TV about it and worked herself up into a state about catching the virus and how bad it would be given her breathing problems. Mac did his best to reassure her, but in truth he had exactly the same concerns. When he told her that in some other countries, people with underlying health conditions had been specially protected, that calmed her a little. But he made no mention of the likelihood that she wouldn't be able to have any visitors. Having made her a meal and set up one of her DVDs, he said goodbye, feeling even worse than usual about having to leave.

His phone rang as he walked to his car. It was the German police officer, who'd promised to get back to him about searching Hofmann's Dortmund apartment. Finally!

"I must apologise for the delay," she said, "but we've had a high-profile fatal stabbing to deal with and the place has gone mad. However, I carried out the search myself with two other officers last night. I'm afraid we didn't find much. I've emailed a summary to you which includes a few photographs that might have some relevance. We were pretty thorough, but if you feel you want to come over and look for yourself, just let me know."

He thanked her for carrying out the search, said it would be unlikely he'd be flying over and wished her well with her own murder case.

Before setting off in the car, he read her email which included a list of documents, none of which had a direct bearing on the case and as she'd mentioned, a few photographs. He flicked through them quickly, noting one that showed Hofmann, garden fork in hand, standing in the middle of an allotment. So, he had been a gardener with dirty hands. He stopped abruptly at the last image. There was Dieter, with his arm around Alex McGrath's shoulder, a view of Edinburgh Castle in the background. Not conclusive proof, but it looked very much like the two of them were in a relationship. A note in the email mentioned that the photo had been displayed in a frame on a bookshelf in Hofmann's apartment and had a date written on the back. November 2019. It looked like they'd been together for at least a few months.

Mac phoned DC Wyatt to let her know. He asked her to speak again to Mrs McGrath, and try and get confirmation of the relationship.

+ + +

Khan was used to juggling priorities. His boss in West Calder was keen on delegation – as long as he thought the officer could handle it. Maeven had made it clear that although he was needed, pronto, at the hospital mortuary in Peebles, that didn't mean he wasn't also required to carry out the follow-up on the car key and pursue whatever leads he was currently responsible for on the Hofmann/McGrath case.

It hadn't taken long to establish that the key was for a BMW X4. As a search of the streets around the boss' flat had revealed no cars of this type, attention was switched to checking local CCTV. Leaving a couple of DCs sifting through footage, Khan drove out to Peebles, picking out one or two familiar walking landmarks en route.

At the hospital, he was taken to the pathologist, who asked if he'd received any briefing information from the Peebles-based officer about the woman's death.

"I'm afraid not, but unfortunately it's not unusual for information to get stuck in the system. Could you give me a rundown?" The pathologist sighed.

"OK, well, initially I thought it was a straightforward case of hypothermia. Then I discovered she was a type 1 diabetic. She'd failed to take her insulin – which is an essential requirement for a type 1. The combination of a lack of meds and overnight cold makes it difficult to pin down exactly when she died – but I estimate it would have been sometime between late evening on 27 February and early morning on the 29th."

"And where was she found?"

"So, your colleague didn't pass that information on either! Well, it was out near Hart Hill. Do you know the area?" Khan nodded. "The body was under some large flat rocks, by the side of a burn. She must have tried to shelter from the worst of the weather, poor lass."

"I know the rocks. It would have been a very cold night out there!"

"Yes, particularly as she wasn't wearing sufficient clothing for the conditions, although her waterproof and boots were of good quality. There was some food in her rucksack, a map and two insulin pens. But crucially they were both empty. In my experience, it's very unusual for diabetics to expose themselves to such risks."

"Talk to the mountain rescue boys, though," Khan said, "and they'll tell plenty of tales of walkers going out completely unprepared, for the terrain or changes in the weather. But you're right. The lack of insulin does seem strange. Was there anything else in the rucksack or her pockets?"

"Some cash, but no purse, wallet or keys. However, there was a bus ticket in her trouser pocket – a return for the Edinburgh to Peebles route. Here, have a look. I'm still waiting for your colleagues to collect this."

Khan peered at the ticket inside a small plastic evidence bag. Dated 28 February, time of issue twelve noon. It was a good starting point. Khan had used that bus route on one occasion – for an afternoon walk with his wife. So where had the dead woman disembarked, he wondered? Eddleston maybe, with the intention of catching a return bus from somewhere near Peebles?

He put the evidence bag into his pocket.

The pathologist took him to view the body. The woman looked to be in her early thirties, had short dark hair and, according to the information on the clipboard, was five feet, nine inches tall and weighed nearly ten stone. He thought she had the sort of face it was difficult to recall, with no real distinguishing features.

Khan's first steps would be to contact the bus company to arrange to speak to the driver of that noon bus and to get a photofit picture prepared for circulation as part of a media release. And he'd check with the Missing Persons Unit, just in case they had a possible match. There'd been nothing with either Hofmann or McGrath, but it was worth a shot.

+ + +

Although they'd parted on good terms and there'd been no suggestion from him about going on somewhere else, Wyatt had found Colquhoun's initial outburst unexpected and out of order. She was used to old school, unreformed cops and could give as good as she got. But the sergeant was an odd mix of old and new.

The boss had phoned and asked her to visit Mrs McGrath again and get her to confirm that Dieter and Alex had been in a relationship. All in good time, she told herself, knowing that she was really just delaying an awkward conversation.

She was back in Alex McGrath's house, propelled there by a lingering feeling that the team might have missed something in their previous searches of the place. It was not a house with any warmth. Obviously, there was no heating on, but it wasn't just that. Very few personal belongings, walls painted off-white, curtains – where they existed – dark green, no ornaments, picture, photos. She walked slowly from room to room. There was a knock at the front door. The next-door neighbour, with two items of mis-delivered post to hand over. The woman hovered on the doorstep.

"You're from the police, right?" Wyatt nodded. "I was sorry to hear about Alex. Our paths didn't cross much but he helped me out once or twice. Did you know there was a man staying with him for a few days, just before he disappeared?"

"No, I didn't. Did you tell one of my colleagues about this when they were doing the house-to-house?"

"I've been away, looking after an elderly uncle. Just got back. That's why I came round when I spotted you."

"Was it this man, by any chance?" Wyatt asked holding up a photo of Hofmann on her phone.

"Hang on a minute… yes, it certainly looks like him. They left the place together. I was tidying the garden up – after the winter you know – the day before I went away, which would have made it the Thursday… the 27th. I overheard Alex saying they could stay at his mother's place. They went off in his car."

"Did they speak to you?"

"I don't think they saw me. I was behind the hedge – which is a bit on the large side."

"Thank you, that's very helpful. Is there anything else you can think of which might be relevant?"

"No, I don't think so."

Wyatt was surprised to hear they'd gone to stay at Mrs McGrath's. The mother obviously knew a lot more than she'd let on. The visit couldn't be put off any longer.

This time she wasn't offered the preliminary of a cup of barely drinkable tea. When Wyatt started talking about her son's movements immediately prior to his death, Mrs McGrath looked very nervous. Wyatt managed to tease out the story from her gradually. Yes, she'd known Hofmann. He'd been living in a hotel in Edinburgh. When he lost his job, he could no longer afford it and moved to the caravan site. But he got worried. There was a man hanging around the site, someone he'd had a big argument with. So, he'd moved in with Alex.

"I have to ask, Mrs McGrath. Were they in a relationship?"

"They were, lassie. I'm sorry, I should have told you before."

"That's OK. What happened then?"

"Well, a few days later Dieter spotted the *someone* again. I told Alex they should come to my house – just for a night or two. They came round in his car. He didn't want to leave it outside where it might have been spotted, so he took it to the garage and came back here by bus. There was some talk about them hiding out at a friend's house in North Berwick. Dieter even had a spare key for it. But they never got the chance to go there." Wyatt made a note to let the boss know about the key. "In the next breath though, he was on about going to America – important business he said. Some pals out there were going to pay his airfare. With Dieter – I was never quite sure what he'd say next!"

"Do you know why he was on the run?"

"He wouldn't say at first but then told me he had information which could be very damaging to… how did he put it… *certain interests.*"

"Why didn't you tell me any of this before, Mrs McGrath?" Wyatt asked.

"I'm really sorry, but I was far too scared by the men who came to get my son and Dieter."

"Which men?"

"Alex and Dieter had only been here for one night." Mrs McGrath started to cry and was unable to continue for a while. Wyatt explained that she needed to know as much as possible to help in the search for whoever had killed Alex and Dieter.

"In the afternoon of the second day," Mrs McGrath said, still trying to stifle her sobbing, "I heard this vehicle pull up outside and then a hammering on the front door. Two men, both middle-aged, I think, but one of them had a hoodie on and a scarf wrapped round the lower part of his face – so I couldn't be sure. They were really threatening, pushed past me and dragged my son and Dieter from the living room. They were both terrified, poor things. Do you think I could have a glass of water?"

After a search in the untidy kitchen, she eventually found a glass, filled it and took it in to Mrs McGrath, who sipped the water slowly. Wyatt tried to be patient. Nearly there, she told herself.

"One of the men – definitely the boss – demanded their laptops and phones, but Dieter refused to say where they were. The man started hitting him, but Dieter still wouldn't tell him. He and my boy were taken out and shoved in the van and they drove off. I don't know how I got through the rest of the day. But to make things even worse, the boss man came back in the evening, ransacked the house and found the laptops and phones. Then he gave me a warning – had this horrible smile as he spoke. Told me not to tell anybody what had happened or Alex would suffer… and so would I. It was terrifying."

"That must have been dreadful for you," Wyatt said.

"It was – and it's why I've said nothing before. I was too scared. But now, well I've got past caring what they might do to me. I want to give you something." She rummaged in one of the sideboard drawers, pulled out a piece of paper and handed it to Wyatt. "I hope it helps you catch those evil men."

Written on the note were the registration number of the vehicle – a grey Transit van – and descriptions of the two men. Wyatt read them, then scrolled back on her phone to find the email attachment which had details of the two men seen driving away from the beach at Cockenzie, shortly before Alex McGrath's body was found. The descriptions of the driver were virtually identical, but those of the other man didn't match.

Wyatt had another very difficult question for Mrs McGrath which she worked up to gradually. Had her son been a drug dealer? Already completely drained, the shock at being asked such a question was obvious.

"No! No! No!"

A mother probably would say that, Wyatt thought. But it had come from the heart.

+ + +

Khan's media release included a description of the dead woman found at the rocks, a photofit picture, reference to her diabetes and details of the clothes she'd been wearing. He reflected that in the old days it had been a question of waiting for the next edition of the relevant newspapers to be printed, but now it was so quick. Online headlines could appear within minutes of a release being issued.

There'd been nothing from the Missing Persons Unit in response to his previous enquiry.

The bus company had got back to him with the name of the driver of the noon bus from Edinburgh to Peebles on 28 February. It turned out it was his day off and he was playing golf on a course in Musselburgh. Khan tracked him down at the ninth hole. His fellow golfers were not best pleased at the interruption to their game.

Khan handed the bus driver both the photofit of the dead woman and a head and shoulders autopsy photograph. Each could be misleading when it came to a comparison with a real person, but he figured that being able to view both might be helpful for the driver. He explained she was a walker who might have been on her own and had probably got off the bus part way along the route.

The driver put his putter down on the green and rubbed his chin as he took a long hard look at both pictures.

"I don't recognise her. In fact, I don't remember a female walker being on my bus on that particular trip. You see, I usually make a point of having a quick word with the walking brigade, you know, ask them where they're off to, what they've got in their sandwiches, that sort of thing."

"Are you sure?"

"I am. Sorry I can't help."

Disappointed, Khan thanked the driver and watched as the golfers resumed their game. Assuming the driver was right, why would the woman have had the ticket in her pocket if she hadn't been on his bus? Then there was the issue of the empty insulin pens.

Khan began to wonder whether somebody else had been involved in the woman's death.

+ + +

The weekend gave Ailsa too much time to sit, think and worry.

It was lovely being with Lewis but he'd gone to Dundee – a photographic commission. Law hadn't called her back. What was going on there and who was he? And the detective hadn't been in touch either. He hadn't given her a contact phone number. But she ought to be able to find him through her local station.

She asked for Detective Sergeant Kershaw and was told to hold. After a few minutes, someone said the detective wasn't based with them, but they'd make further enquiries and get back to her.

+ + +

The last thing Mac felt like doing was attending a birthday party. But Freya would really take it to heart if he didn't turn up. At least, having been told by the boss to leave the office, he'd had time to head home, take a rest, soak in the bath, change his clothes and force himself to eat. He'd suffered from the party-empty-stomach-problem too often in the past. Her text arrived with details of the location. He checked the grid reference. A barn near Arncroach, not far from where she lived. It would be a late finish for him, followed by an early start – another 8.00. briefing at the Warehouse. The thought of trying to catch a few hours' sleep on the floor of a barn was not one he relished. After loading a change of clothes, his sleeping bag and Freya's birthday present into the Jimny, he set off.

The warning from his attacker was on continual replay in his head. *Be very careful what you say about Maxwell, or next time will be a lot worse.* The armed robbery court hearing would be starting all too soon. Had Maxwell really paid someone to persuade him to change his evidence? The man was a headcase, but a professional one. The attack had been carried out by an amateur. Still, they'd find him and in the meantime Mac's flat was under discreet observation.

As he drove north, his work mind gradually switched off, assisted by the combined effects of a full-on week, a punch to the head and a lack of good sleep. Maybe a descent into party mode was just what he needed.

The switching-off process was interrupted by a call from Kenny, who was quite obviously on a high following Montrose's 4-1 victory. But he moved on rapidly to news about Ultimate Intelligence.

"Blue Star – the software specialists you asked me about. My finance man has just got back to me. He found a trail via various offshore companies and guess what – they're one hundred per cent owned by Ultimate Intelligence. Maybe your man Hofmann became aware of that fact and wasn't too happy as a result!"

So Laing's description of UI's involvement in the IntelOper project as *minor* was getting more and more threadbare! And UI seemed to make a habit of hiding their true colours.

Lights twinkled on the far shore as he crossed the Forth. The coast road through Kirkcaldy and Methil took him eventually to the minor road leading uphill to Arncroach.

A minibus and around twenty cars were already parked on the muddy field. The yard in front of the stone barn was lit with fire torches hung from the walls as if lighting the way to some medieval jousting contest. Inside there were already at least fifty people, three large trestle tables, one laden with glasses, two barrels and a host of bottles, long-flexed lanterns hanging down from the rafters, casting a subdued light over the proceedings and a DJ on a raised platform, head bent over a pair of old-school double decks, dispensing early-party ambient sounds on a low volume.

He could hear Freya talking to the DJ, giving him instructions about what to play. In Mac's experience most DJs ignored other people's playlists – even the host's. As soon as Freya saw him, she leapt down from the platform and ran to greet him. Mac loved the dress, one she'd made herself, long and flowing with a delicate flower pattern. They kissed and he wished her happy birthday.

"I was worried that, with your injuries, you might not make it, although I have to say the bruising does give you something of an air of mystery. So, a big thank you," she said, kissing him again. "Here, come and get a drink." She led him across to the table, filled a glass from the barrel and handed it to him. "One of Barney's brews. You remember him?" He nodded. "How are the injuries, love?"

"I'll survive. Look, can I just ask? Will we be kipping here tonight?"

"No, no. I got a lift here so I could drive you back to my place in the Jimny and you'll be good to go straight off to work in the morning. The party's likely to go on for hours and I figured you wouldn't want to see it through to the end."

Relieved at not having to spend a very late night on a very hard floor, he relaxed. Freya grabbed an orange juice – she didn't like to drink at all if she was driving – and introduced him to the other guests. Some he knew, some he didn't. They seemed a pleasant bunch, but he was aware that the hardcore party people would still be getting tanked up in a local hostelry or two.

Mac was familiar with the strange way time passed at parties, slowly at first but with every succeeding hour flying past quicker and quicker until that moment when you wonder how the dim light outside could really be the dawn.

He spent most of the time, whatever speed it happened to be moving at, dancing with Freya. It was clear from his selections that the DJ was ignoring her instructions. But after a second, much firmer set of orders from the birthday girl, this was rectified. Highly danceable eighties and nineties tracks pounded from enormous speakers, Human League, New Order, Depeche Mode and on to Nirvana, Soundgarden and The Lemonheads.

The two vacant trestle tables magically filled with Indian street food which equally magically disappeared at speed.

By the time the ceilidh band, complete with caller, came on, the hardcore punters had arrived, throwing themselves into the dancefloor fray with abandon. Dancers lost themselves in an orgy of whirling and spinning and the barn seemed to expand to accommodate the newcomers.

Mac kept up the pace until exhaustion suddenly set in, as if someone had switched his motor off. Freya picked up on the change, led him outside and bundled him into the Jimny. She was gone for maybe ten minutes saying her thanks and farewells, before returning to drive him to her home.

Stretched out on her bed, having downed three glasses of water, Mac felt revived. She set her alarm for six thirty and slid under the duvet beside him. He thanked her for the party. Two nights dancing in one weekend. Could he take the pace? Freya opened his present, a pair of jet earrings. They kissed and then lay together, arms around each other.

"So, how would you fancy becoming a dad, Calum?"

After taking in his puzzled look, she repeated her question. Was she proposing that they try and start a family, Mac wondered? The subject had never reared its head before and he'd never really thought about the possibility. Surely, they'd be ill suited to becoming parents – with all their breaking up and getting back together!

"Are you saying you'd like a baby?" he asked in such a way that it sounded like you could just pop down to the supermarket and buy one.

"No, you fool, I'm telling you I'm pregnant – three months." He couldn't stop himself doing an instant calculation. When had they last been together? Before Christmas definitely, early December maybe. And that was what… three months ago? So maybe it was his. But had anyone else been on the scene just beforehand… or just afterwards? He hoped not. A response was required and he had to get it just right.

"That's fantastic. I can't believe it, but in a good way. Do you think I can do it – you know, be a dad?"

"I think you'll be as good a dad as I'll be a mum." Said with a straight face. Of course, there were two ways of interpreting such a statement. The serious look melted away, replaced by a wry grin. "Who the fuck knows how we'll manage, but I'm up for it."

"Me too," he said, hugging her tight. "Is it still OK to… you know?"

"Oh, we should be alright. Just this once, mind!"

9 MARCH

Mac had been dreading the early morning drive into Edinburgh, but felt better than expected. He'd managed coffee and toast and the traffic was tolerable.

He was trying to get his head around Freya's small item of news. How would it all work? Could it all work? Entirely voluntarily, she'd confirmed he was the father. There'd been no other man on the scene for a year or so. Whereas his own recent sex life had of course been somewhat different. Still, now was the time to change that. Roisin had already given him the push and the late-night attack on the river path had prevented him from making the wrong move with the Canadian.

To his own surprise, he felt elated at the idea of becoming a father and he had no doubt that Freya would make a loving mother. But she was wedded to her paintings and could get lost for hours in her work and he wasn't exactly known for spending a lot of time at home. So they'd have to work at it.

He buried himself in his work, partly because he found it difficult to tear himself away but partly, he feared, because there was nothing else that consumed him in the same kind of way. What difference might a baby make?

Then there was the question of where this cosy little threesome would live? Although Freya's place would be far too small, it was difficult to imagine her not being there, with the artistic inspiration of the sea on her doorstep. His flat was more practical and had the advantage of two bedrooms, but how would his prickly downstairs neighbour react to a wailing baby above? Or could there be a third option, a new property that offered the triple advantages of more space, no too-close neighbours and maybe a beach nearby? At least they had time to consider all the alternatives.

Freya had mentioned her first scan in a week's time and asked whether he'd go with her. *Of course*, he'd replied.

In the end it was touch and go whether he'd arrive at the Warehouse before eight o'clock. Having squeaked in with less than a minute to spare, he started off the discussion by explaining why his appearance had changed over the weekend.

"The attack was work-related," he said, "and nothing to do with me brawling outside my local," managing a rueful grin. There were murmured expressions of concern. "My attacker made it clear it was a warning – to do with the Maxwell case that some of you will know about. Anyway, the attack is being investigated, so let's leave it at that for this morning – apart from mentioning the car key I found which Raj will tell us about later." Mac paused and took a sip of water. "Laura, can you start us off with a résumé of what we've got so far?"

Part of his mind was focusing on what she was telling the team. But he was also planning what to say later. His intention had been to spend the drive to the city mulling this over, but thoughts of babies, and places to live had taken over.

As he'd come to expect, Wyatt was both comprehensive and concise. Thanks to information from Hofmann's cousin and McGrath's mother they had been able to piece together quite a detailed account of Dieter's and Alex's last few days. They had the registration number of the Transit van used in the abduction and details of the two abductors – who they knew were also in possession of the dead men's phones and laptops. Mrs McGrath's description of the Transit driver was consistent with the details they already had for the driver of the Skoda and the Renault. They were confident it had been the same man driving all three vehicles and the search for him was now a high priority. But her description of the 'other man' in the Transit didn't match those they had for the 'other man' in the Renault and the Skoda.

Wyatt continued.

"There's been an unexpected development, an anonymous call referring to details of three killings that took place in Glasgow a decade ago where a taser trademark was also used." She paused for effect and to let the murmurings die down. "It was suspected but never proved that they'd been carried out by a drugs cartel, long since defunct. Greater Glasgow PIT have asked a DI who'd worked on the original case to review it and check out whether there might be any links between what happened ten years ago and the deaths of Hofmann and McGrath."

She fielded a number of questions and added that the news strengthened the view that the drug connection was paramount in the case. Mac wondered whether she was point-scoring over Khan, a known supporter of the alternative view that the deaths were in some way related to Hofmann's work.

The sergeant was up next. He didn't make any comment on Wyatt's presentation but went straight on to tell them about the car key Mac had found.

"Although the attack relates to the Maxwell case, and not this case, we thought it appropriate to give a quick update. Yesterday morning, the key was identified as being for a BMW X4. I made a search of the streets immediately adjacent to the boss' flat to check whether any such vehicle was parked nearby – without success. But CCTV footage we checked later was very helpful.

It picked up a young man matching the assailant's description getting into a BMW parked only about 200 yards from the flat, very early yesterday morning. As this happened less than two hours after the attack, we figure he must have spent that time getting hold of his spare key. We were able to track the vehicle, using CCTV and automatic number plate recognition cameras, as far as the entrance to an industrial estate. There's no footage of it leaving. Unfortunately, as the private camera network on the estate isn't working, we'll have to foot-slog our way around to try and find the exact current location of the BMW."

After some questions from members of the team, there was a brief lull.

Maeven strode into the room… closely followed by DI Euan Forsyth. Mac wondered why on earth he was present. Maeven had a quick word with Khan and moved to the front of the room.

"Just before DI Larsen takes over, Sergeant Khan has some important news… which will explain DI Forsyth's presence here this morning."

Mac couldn't imagine what the reason for this might be. Having seen Euan as recently as Saturday morning, what had happened in the short time since then to warrant his involvement in the case? He wondered for a moment whether Maeven had roped Forsyth in behind his back, in a bid to boost progress. But if that was true, Euan would have tipped him off – wouldn't he?

Khan started speaking.

He'd stepped in temporarily for DI Forsyth, who'd been away in London over the weekend, on a new case involving a woman who'd died of hypothermia – except that it had turned out to be more complicated than that. He told the team about the diabetes, the hypoglycemia, her seeming ill-preparedness for the walk, the bus ticket and the comments of the bus driver.

"We did a media release yesterday afternoon and I got a call late last night from the woman's father, who as you can imagine, was in a very bad way. Her name's Maxine Kilcline. The father identified the body first thing this morning. But when I told him how his daughter died, he was insistent that she would never have gone out walking without being properly equipped. And as for not taking enough insulin with her, it was unthinkable. That rang alarm bells."

Mac was struggling to work out why this update was being given at *his* team meeting. Khan continued.

"I began to explore the possibility that there might be something suspicious about her death. When I asked Mr Kilcline about this, he initially dismissed the idea, but then went on to tell me that Maxine had previously been in the military and had since taken a particular interest in issues around weapons control. Very recently she'd been researching something to do with laser weapons." There were mutterings from team members. "Yes, it surprised me as well. Given the subject matter, could she have come across Dieter Hofmann? If that was the case, it could mean there's a link between their deaths which would add a lot of weight to the theory that Dieter's death was connected to his work. I'll be briefing DI Forsyth after this meeting."

"Why hadn't the father already reported Maxine as missing?" one of the DCs asked.

"Well, I picked up that contact between them tends to be intermittent. I don't think he exactly approves of what she's been involved in since leaving the army."

"Thank you, Sergeant Khan," Maeven said. "Over to you, DI Larsen."

Mac had been caught on the hop. Why hadn't somebody told him about Kilcline and the possible link to Hofmann? Now he had to address the team having had no chance to digest the implications. Still – that was the reality. He just had to get on with it!

He told the team about his meeting with Marek and how the cousin felt that Dieter's death was unlikely to have been caused by issues arising from his work.

"Following my conversation with Marek and other recent developments we now have five further lines of enquiry to pursue. Firstly, Dieter had an argument with his coke dealer in Dortmund which resulted in his supply being cut off. We've speculated that McGrath might have been his dealer recently, but if that wasn't the case, might Hofmann have had similar problems with whoever his supplier was here? DC Wyatt will be following this up with the drugs squad. Secondly, Marek felt that Dieter was a risk taker and might have deliberately put himself in harm's way. So, what more can we find out about his actions over the last few days of his life? And thirdly, we already knew from Marek that Dieter was gay and would probably have had a partner locally. DC Wyatt was able to establish yesterday that he was in a relationship with Alex McGrath!"

This revelation sparked a series of mini-conversations which Mac brought to a halt by holding up his hand and starting to talk again.

"Number four is that in addition to having links to a group of radical scientists back in Germany, which Marek told me about, I've discovered that Hofmann was also involved here in the local branch of an organisation called Weapons Watch. I'll be meeting the convenor later today to find out more. She's hard work and, to say the least, doesn't have a high opinion of us, so progress may be slow. And finally – last but by no means least – there's Sergeant Khan's news about Maxine Kilcline and the issue of whether there might be a link between her and Dieter Hofmann."

"Anything further on Ultimate Intelligence?" Wyatt asked.

"Yes. We now know that in addition to their advisory role, they've also put money into the project, not directly, but through a proxy. The question is, what are they getting for their money?

And we've just learnt that Blue Star, the company developing the new software for IntelOper, is one hundred per cent owned by UI! Laing has consistently sought to play down their role, but it's clearly a lot more extensive than we've been led to believe. So, there'll be more discussions with the professor."

Pausing to answer questions about these new developments, Mac tried to keep a lid on his annoyance at being left out of the loop regarding Kilcline. At the end of the questioning, it suddenly dawned on him that, with Freya's baby news distracting him on his early morning commute, he hadn't bothered to check his phone. Maybe Khan or Maeven *had* tried to contact him.

Regardless, he needed to seize the moment, respond decisively and capitalise on the stimulus provided by the morning's positive news.

+ + +

It turned out that Khan had indeed left him a message about Kilcline – which would teach him not to make unfounded assumptions.

Mac was driving out to the Tranent area of the city to interview the Weapons Watch convenor in her home. She'd been most insistent that the meeting should not take place in a police station.

DI Forsyth was in the Jimny's front passenger seat. Maeven had made it clear that he'd be in charge of the Kilcline investigation and if it turned out that her case was linked to the other two then all three enquiries would be merged. Mac was happy enough with the arrangement. There was a limit to what his small team could take on and if it came to it, working jointly with his friend wouldn't be a problem.

He asked Euan about the shooting at Currie. How was the investigation going?

"Badly," he said. "We're getting nowhere fast. And the DCI's nowhere near as good as Morag Maeven. Still, I'm due a change of fortune, so I just need to look on the bright side."

When they stood on the convenor's doorstep and presented their warrant cards, she asked immediately why it was necessary for two DIs to interview her. Wasn't this just harassment of a legitimate organisation whose work had been praised by a number of political leaders and university researchers alike?

Mac stopped her in full flow.

"There are two of us here, because we're both involved in the investigation regarding Dieter Hofmann's death."

"I see. It's dreadful what happened to him." She seemed unsteady and had to hold onto the door frame for support.

"We'd like to ask you some questions."

"Why me?"

"Because you confirmed over the phone that you knew him. Was he involved with Weapons Watch?"

"Yes, but…"

"Look, may we come in? It's not ideal trying to hold a conversation on the doorstep."

It was with some reluctance that she led them into a small kitchen. The detectives perched on two high stools at a breakfast bar while she remained standing. As Mac outlined briefly what had happened to Hofmann, her legs began to shake and she collapsed into an easy chair in the corner of the room.

"I'm sorry to have to pursue this now. What was the nature of his involvement in Weapons Watch?" She roused herself and sat upright in the chair.

"That's not the kind of information I'm able to reveal."

Mac tried hard to control his frustration but felt instinctively that confrontation would not be a profitable way forward.

"Look, we appreciate this is difficult for you. But we're trying to find out how Dieter died – to be blunt, who killed him. Can you help us in any way?"

A sudden coughing fit took her over. Mac asked if she wanted a glass of water but she shook her head.

"We know Dieter was working on a weapons development project at Midlothian University," Mac continued, "and believe he was planning to blow the whistle on aspects of the project he was uncomfortable about. Do you know anything about this – anything that might help us to find his killer?"

The convenor looked from one officer to the other, seemingly uncertain how to respond. Eventually she started speaking.

"Look, I'll probably regret saying anything to you, but given what's happened to Dieter, maybe it's right that I tell you what I know." Her facial contortions suggested that the process of doing this would be about as painful as pulling teeth. "He first made contact with the group about a month ago." She paused and took a deep breath. "It really is hard to believe what's happened to him."

Mac hoped such a show of emotion might mean she'd open up a bit further.

"We couldn't believe it when he came to us to tell his story – the drones, the lasers, the use of artificial intelligence to control their deployment. I mean we knew about the basics but he had so much more than that."

"And why did he come to the group?"

"He wanted some support and also advice about how to get his story out, without using mainstream media, which he didn't trust."

"And were you able to help?"

"We have some good contacts in the alternative media and, as it happens, a new member who joined us recently, with a lot of relevant knowledge – and an ability to communicate, which Dieter didn't really have. They teamed up and prepared a draft article."

"Who was this other new member?" Euan asked.

"Look! I'm willing to answer questions that relate directly to Dieter but I'm not prepared to identify other members. I have a duty of confidentiality."

"This is really important," Euan said. "Was her name Maxine Kildine by any chance?"

The convenor stood up abruptly, her face reddening.

"How on earth did you know that? Jesus, have you lot been spying on us?"

"Absolutely not!" Euan said. "But I have to break the awful news to you that Maxine is also dead and that we've had to set up a second murder enquiry."

The convenor was unable to hold things together any longer and wept openly, her body shuddering. It was a while before she regained any semblance of composure.

"It's incredibly worrying and... no wonder that I've been unable to contact her. Do you have any information on who might have been responsible for these deaths?"

"Not yet," Mac said. "We were hoping you might have some idea."

"Me! Look, we're not the most popular organisation around. We get an awful lot of online abuse and harassment, which is only to be expected these days. And then there's the dirty tricks brigade, basically the militarists who are opposed in principle to what we do. But we've never had any serious intimidation in person. However, we've never had people like Max and Dieter involved with the group before. That might be the difference."

"Do you have a copy of their article?" Mac asked.

"No. Dieter and Max became as thick as thieves, but they wouldn't let me or anyone else see their draft. For security reasons, they said. As far as I know they had the only copies. But I do remember Max saying – it must have been during the last conversation we had – that they were virtually ready to send it to her buddy to be finalised and published. They'd decided not to use any of our media contacts."

"I don't suppose you know the buddy's name?" Euan said.

"No, but whoever it was, it sounded like they had ultimate control over its release."

"You asked just now about whether we've been spying on the group," Mac said. "Well, we certainly haven't been, but it occurs to me that somebody from an organisation opposed to your aims might have infiltrated. Do you think that could have happened?" She bristled immediately.

"Certainly not!" she said with vehemence. "We'd know straight away if anyone tried that sort of thing."

"Well, such people can be very adept at covering their tracks. The reason I ask, is that whoever was involved in the deaths of Dieter and Maxine must have got vital information from somewhere about their very recent activities. Your group would have been the ideal place to try and do that. Are you certain there's no one who might have been snooping on your activities?"

"I'm certain."

"OK, we'll leave it at that. There is one more thing I need to ask just now. Have you seen this man before?" Mac asked, holding up his phone. At first, he thought she was going to ignore his question completely. But then there was a brief glance at the photo.

"No."

"Thank you for agreeing to talk to us. There are some more detailed questions we'd like to ask and we'll need a statement from you as well. We can do this either later today or tomorrow."

She rolled her eyes and sighed, but eventually agreed a time to meet the following day.

+ + +

As it wasn't far from Tranent to Cockenzie, Mac decided to treat Euan to a coffee and a fishfinger sandwich at the Mermaid. The TV was on when they arrived, a news report about the spread of the virus in Italy. Euan mentioned that a friend of his had just returned from a skiing holiday in the north of the country, had felt unwell and been told to self-isolate. The TV was telling them that around 150 people in Italy had already died from the virus. Mac hoped his mother wasn't watching the news.

They mulled things over. The convenor hadn't recognised the photo of Alex McGrath. But then just because he'd been in a relationship with Hofmann didn't necessarily mean the two of them would have had shared acquaintances.

Everything else they'd picked up from the interview had been positively helpful – confirmation of a very strong link between Maxine and Dieter, the existence of a controversial draft article and the news that somebody else had a controlling role in the publication process.

Euan squeezed tomato ketchup onto his fishfingers, replaced the top layer of bread and took an enormous mouthful. The two words he managed to utter sounded like *very good*. His phone rang and he had to swallow rapidly in order to answer it. *Mr Kilcline*, he mouthed to Mac. The conversation lasted a few minutes.

"An update on Maxine," he said, taking another bite from his sandwich. "Her father has just recalled something. Poor feller actually apologised for not having remembered sooner! He got a rare text from his daughter on the morning of 27 February, telling him she was about to go into a meeting and expecting to be given – in her own words – *some crucial, hush-hush information*."

"Wow. That could be very important," Mac said. "Does he know anything about this meeting?"

"Nothing about who it was with or what the information might be about – typical Maxine according to her father, very secretive. But she mentioned in the text that her meeting happened to be in a building next door but one to his favourite shop – a model railway specialist. He's given me the location."

"That's really useful."

"I'll be checking it out as soon as we're finished here. But given the date of the meeting, I'm wondering whether something happened there that led directly to her death. Attending that meeting might have been the last thing she did."

"If you're right," Mac said, "that would certainly explain why the driver didn't see her on his bus on the 28th. So, thinking that through, maybe someone made sure that bus ticket was in her pocket, to make it look as if she'd travelled by bus to reach the start of her walk. Whereas, in reality, whoever was involved in her death must have transported her out there, either once she'd died or perhaps, perish the thought, as she was dying."

"That's been my line of thinking. Raj phoned at the crack of dawn this morning to brief me on the case, I decided to take advantage of that early start and drive out to the rocks where Maxine's body was found. It's not far from my place. The thing is there's only one way to get there, a tiny road, more of a track really, which ends at the rocks. No public CCTV out there in the wilds of course, but I've asked for cameras on the nearest main road turn-off to be checked for the period in question. And bearing in mind the problems of thefts and rustling these days, there's a chance that one of the farms bordering the road might have its own cameras."

"That would be very handy," Mac said. "There's another question bugging me. If our theory's right and she wasn't out there walking, how come she was dressed and at least partially equipped for it?"

"Ah!" Euan said. "I think I can answer that. Maxine's text to her father mentioned that she'd be off walking straight after the meeting. So, she probably turned up at the meeting already dressed for it."

"So, what do we actually *know* so far?" Mac asked. "Number One. Maxine was invited to a meeting, enticed by the prospect of getting her hands on crucial, secret information which she could then use for her article. Number Two. She was dead within forty-eight hours of this meeting. And what can we reasonably assume? That they – whoever *they* are – gave her some juicy bits of information to start with, to draw her in and then maybe asked her what she already knew, offering the bait of further information if she were to confide in them. Their aim would probably have been to establish just how much of a danger she was to them. So far, so logical. But what's difficult to get a handle on is, what was the trigger that led to her death?"

"Maybe something she said really spooked them," Euan suggested. "Or perhaps her death wasn't intentional. They'd have searched her bag for sure and would have come across the insulin pens. Perhaps they thought she'd be likely to tell them more if they deprived her of the medication and after that, it all got out of hand."

"Well, no doubt, Sherlock, you'll be able to replace such speculation with hard fact very soon!" Mac said.

"Naturally! How are you getting on with Hofmann?"

Mac told him about Oversight Scotland's interest in the German.

"Do you think *they* might have infiltrated Weapons Watch?"

"Highly likely, I reckon. But, much as I dislike Oversight, it's hard to believe they'd have been involved in any way with the deaths."

With the sandwiches demolished, they ordered a second round of coffees.

"What about the woman – Fiona, is it – who phoned and accused you of breaking in to her house? Have you found out any more about her?"

"No, she won't return my calls. I spoke to one of her neighbours who claimed to know very little about her."

"Didn't Dieter have a key to Fiona's place?" Euan asked.

"He did. Mrs McGrath told Wyatt that he and Alex had thought about hiding out there but they never got the chance. We've no idea how he knew Fiona or whether she might be connected in some way to the case."

"So, she's a bit of a mystery. What did she sound like the one time you did manage to speak to her?"

"Paranoid." As Mac took another sip of coffee, his eyes lit up. "Wait a minute though, something's just occurred to me. Who in this jigsaw puzzle might react like that if they found out that Dieter was dead?" Euan thought for a moment.

"The 'buddy'!"

"Exactly."

They agreed that when Euan returned to take a formal statement from the convenor, he'd probe further about the buddy.

Mac was tempted to tell Euan about Freya's news, but felt it would be premature. So instead, he let him know they were back together as an item.

"Well, I'm pleased to hear that. You're getting on you know, mate. Why don't you try and make it really work this time? This yo-yo business is no good. Not that my relationship advice can be trusted! Anyway, pass on my best wishes. Tell you what though, that sandwich was top notch. I'll have to add this place to my list of lunch spots. Look – you might have time to hang around here, but I've got a murder case to be getting on with. That's my DC outside, come to give me a lift. Must dash!"

Mac did hang around and indulged in a cup of tea and a slice of apple pie, sitting at an outdoor table, watching the lazy ebb and flow of the waves. All the crime scene paraphernalia had been cleared away and it was now hard to believe that McGrath's body had so recently been left on the beach.

He reflected on the three cases. Euan had told him about Maxine Kilcline being found under some rocks, by a burn. And then there'd been Hofmann on the bing. Could all three deaths have been the work of some alliteration addict – bing, beach and burn? Given they'd already picked up on the first two 'b's', he was certain it wouldn't be long before the media would add a third.

For the first time, he worried about the possibility of a fourth death. Maxine's buddy suddenly seemed very vulnerable.

+ + +

Over the phone, Urquhart had been reluctant to agree to a further meeting, claiming that he didn't have the time and that, in any event, there was nothing further to discuss.

Mention of Weapons Watch had changed his response.

Mac arrived at the Oversight office and was made to wait in reception. After ten minutes he waved his warrant card at the receptionist and demanded to be taken through to Urquhart who looked less than pleased that the policeman had gate-crashed his office.

"Look, I don't appreciate your stupid games," Mac said. "Let's try and behave like adults, shall we? And a coffee would be welcome – particularly as I wasn't offered one at reception."

Urquhart responded by phoning for drinks.

"Now – Weapons Watch. I assume you were keeping tabs on Hofmann's involvement."

"Of course," Urquhart replied. "Just because they're a bunch of ineffectual troublemakers, student types who've never grown up and are generally impotent, doesn't mean that they're incapable of causing us real problems. We've had a man in there for a while now, bored out of his mind until Hofmann arrived on the scene."

"What about Maxine Kilcline? Were you watching her as well?"

"Yes."

"And you didn't think to mention these facts when we met previously?"

"We were concerned with issues of state security, not a murder investigation."

"How do you know they're not connected?"

"As I told you before, it's pretty clear Hofmann's death is related to his drug activity – not his work for Midlothian. And as for the woman, I understand she died from hypothermia."

Mac was about to tear into Urquhart, to attack his utter complacency and complete lack of cooperation. But he realised it would be a waste of breath – and valuable time. Instead, he asked what UI's undercover man had found out.

"Well, Hofmann teamed up with Kilcline, who was ex-forces, to cobble together a dangerously misleading article on the IntelOper project. They were using classified information and making fabricated claims. But being amateurs, they had no idea our man was watching."

"So was the fact that Hofmann was playing fast and loose with the Official Secrets Act the real reason he was kicked off the project – rather than his embezzlement activity?" Mac asked.

"We were not involved in his dismissal. You'd have to ask Midlothian about such matters. Our job was to make sure their story never saw the light of day. The fact that the two of them were using classified information gave us the power to seize their phones and laptops."

"What! Why on earth didn't you tell me about this immediately it happened?"

"They've only recently come into our possession and as you'll understand, we had a duty to remove all information covered by the Official Secrets Act. We'll hand the devices on to you once that process has been completed," Urquhart said, shrugging his shoulders as if the issue was just some minor detail.

"For as long as you have them, you'll be effectively withholding evidence relating to a series of murder enquiries. I'll expect handover by tomorrow at the latest."

There was a brief pause while coffee was served from a trolley wheeled in by a uniformed young man. The interview continued once he'd left the room.

"We should be able to comply with that timescale," Urquhart said. "For the sake of completeness, I should inform you that, having become aware that McGrath had been told the full story by Hofmann, we're also in possession of his phone and laptop as well. You presumably know they were in a relationship?" Mac nodded, struggled to control his mounting anger but managed to concentrate on asking his next question.

"How did you get hold of their devices?"

Urquhart hesitated before replying, perhaps uncertain whether to reveal anything further.

"It's really none of your business, Larsen. Suffice to say that we managed to obtain information regarding their whereabouts."

"That's very interesting – and of great concern. We know for a fact that the phones and laptops belonging to Hofmann and McGrath were taken by two men we want to speak to in connection with their deaths. So, how did your organisation obtain them?" During the pause which followed this comment, Urquhart looked thrown. "You don't know, do you?"

"Of course I know! However, I'm not at liberty to reveal such detail."

"Well, there's a surprise!" Urquhart ignored the jibe.

"We're confident that the rot stops with those three individuals," he said, "and that there are no other copies of their draft article in existence. But in the very unlikely event their material resurfaces, we have the necessary information ready to go which will completely discredit their falsified version of events."

"And what about the fact that three people ended up dead?" Mac asked. "What can you tell me about that?"

"Naturally, their deaths were a great shock to us and we trust that your investigations will bear fruit as quickly as possible. But we have no information about who was involved in their deaths."

"Well, we won't know for sure what led to any of the deaths – will we – until our investigations are complete?" Mac said. "And progress towards that end isn't helped by your people holding on to vital evidence! You used the phrase *the rot stops with those three.* Which begs the question, what about the fourth person, the one who was arranging for the final article to be published?"

"Ah, so you know about Fiona MacMahon." Mac hadn't expected Urquhart to let slip a name. So, Fiona was the buddy! "Something of an enigma, gone to ground, waiting in vain for a copy of the final article so she could publish it on whatever grubby little online site was willing to take the risk of handling classified information. I don't think she remains a credible threat."

"You may be right. But she's very much at risk of becoming yet another victim of whoever is behind these killings. What steps are you taking to locate and protect her?"

"I can't imagine there's any credible threat against her. But in any event, that would be a matter for the police, Larsen, not Oversight Scotland. I trust the force will assess the risks and respond accordingly."

Mac was about react to such complete, unfeeling detachment, but knew it would be pointless.

"That brings me to my final question," he continued. "How confident are you about your undercover man? Might he have been involved in a dubious trade-off with someone who has a strong interest in silencing Hofmann and the others?"

"You need to be careful, Larsen," Urquhart said, his face darkening. "That's a very serious allegation and one which I utterly reject. Our operatives are very thoroughly vetted, entirely trustworthy and loyal to Oversight's values. To suggest otherwise is preposterous. And to imply that we might have had any kind of connection with the deaths of these three unfortunate individuals is outrageous. I think your judgement has been warped by reading too many of the wilder online conspiracy theories."

"You don't need to be a conspiracy theorist to suggest that at least one organisation has an awful lot to lose if Hofmann's article ever sees the light of day. All I'm asking is that you check that your undercover man hasn't been leaking information."

"There is no need for that. We monitor our operatives' activities very closely. I would remind you again of the joint protocol. Your attitude at our meetings has been such that I have no alternative but to submit a report to the review panel who will then contact your superiors."

Mac knew this was no empty threat. But maybe there was also an element of bluster, in Urquhart's reaction, to obscure the fact that he was hiding something. How had Oversight obtained the victims' phones and laptops? And who might their undercover officer be in contact with?

+ + +

On his return to the Warehouse, he emailed Euan to tell him that Oversight was in possession of Maxine Kilcline's phone and laptop and that they were due to be handed over.

He managed to catch Maeven in her office. After giving his update, they discussed whether the embezzlement charge against Hofmann might have been a fabrication. Maeven proposed involving the force's forensic finance team, one of the specialist groups based at Corstorphine House, to go through the relevant paperwork held by the university. If the fabrication was substantiated that would leave Laing and his team with some very difficult questions to answer.

There was then the issue of how Oversight had managed to get hold of all three victims' phones and laptops. Had they gone as far as establishing a link with whoever was involved in the deaths? That seemed highly implausible. But what about their mole? What role might he have played in recovering those devices? The boss said that, despite the organisational sensitivities, Mac should investigate both issues.

Mac told her of his concerns for the safety of Fiona MacMahon who Urquhart had identified as the person who had been going to arrange for the publication of the Hofmann/Kilcline article. Maeven shared his concern and his frustration at being unable to contact her.

Back at his desk, he felt further frustration about the team's lack of progress in identifying the killers of Hofmann and McGrath. Knowing more hard information was needed, he thought it might be useful to have another look at the email sent by the German police officer which detailed what they'd found in Hofmann's apartment in Dortmund. He reread it slowly. It was disappointing that there was little of interest in the apartment – no laptop and no written documentation relevant to the case.

Mac looked through each of the attached photos again. One was of Hofmann standing next to a man in his thirties, a very wide river in the background. Although it was hard to be certain, they looked more like friends than partners. He hadn't really given this picture much attention first time around, but studying it more carefully this time, he felt there was something about the man that seemed familiar. Not that he'd actually seen the man before but… that was it… he matched the description of the friend of Hofmann's who had visited the Midlothian development project and asked inappropriate questions. Khan had been given the description by one of Hofmann's work colleagues.

Flicking back in his notebook Mac found the details – *early thirties, tall, thin, designer stubble, broken nose, black jeans, leather jacket.* The man in the photo ticked all those boxes. Although wearing the same clothes on two different and random occasions hundreds of miles apart might seem unlikely, Mac reflected that some of his own friends wore pretty much the same uniform every day – Kenny being a prime example. He checked the email to see if there was a note about this photo. There was. It was dated six months previously, they'd been on the bank of the Rhine, near Cologne and the man's name was Bernie. Unfortunately, there was no surname.

Although none of the Midlothian staff Khan had spoken to had known the name of the visiting friend, there might be someone else in the development team who did. Or perhaps someone at North Rhine-Westphalia. Mac sent off emails with photo attachments to both universities. As an afterthought he emailed Marek. *Could he identify Dieter's friend?*

Having expected an update from DC Wyatt about the 2010 Glaswegian taser deaths, Mac was surprised to get a call directly from DS Colquhoun and unsettled when the DS said he had a few concerns about Wyatt – which could be summarised as unprofessional behaviour. Not that he was asking for action to be taken against her, but he thought the inspector should be made aware.

It wasn't the first time Mac had received unofficial complaints of this type from an officer who wanted a colleague's card marked for some perceived slight.

The DS attempted to move straight on to talk about the Glasgow killings, but Mac pulled him up short.

"Look, Sergeant. You can't just make that kind of accusation, then blithely continue as if nothing has happened. I want the full details from you. In what way did she behave unprofessionally and when did this happen?"

Colquhoun stuttered in his response.

"I just wanted to make you aware, Inspector, you know, man to man. Perhaps we should just forget about it."

"What is 'man to man' supposed to mean, Colquhoun? Did she turn you down? Complaints need to be on the record or they don't exist. Are you going on the record or not?"

The DS backed down. Mac was sorely tempted to put the screws on him. In his experience too much of this sort of thing went on, informal hints about a more junior officer, often down to some minor personal issue or petty squabble, but remembered and passed around amongst those of like mind.

"Right, instead of trying to report directly to me, you need to speak to DC Wyatt immediately about Glasgow progress and she'll update me. Is that clear?" The sergeant said it was, but sounded far from happy.

Mac had wanted the update there and then, but that wouldn't have been fair on Wyatt.

The call from the DC came half an hour later.

"Only five of the dealers involved with the former cartel are still alive," she said. "The business must have a high casualty rate! The Glasgow DI has managed to trace and question four of them."

"That was quick work!" Mac said.

"Indeed. Apparently, he's a bit of a Rottweiler when it comes to the cartel. Hates the fact that they got away with it ten years ago. He's trying to find the fifth man. Word is he's changed his name which is making it difficult. But he does have a photo and I've just been sent a copy. And here's the thing. As your anonymous caller indicated, the guy does resemble the description of our driver – Transit, Renault and Skoda estate man!"

"That makes it all the more imperative we find him. And if Glasgow are also looking for him that improves our chances of success. Well done, Wyatt."

+ + +

The police had been back in contact with Ailsa with news that made her feel dreadful. Detective Sergeant Kershaw didn't exist. They asked her for a detailed description of him. What had he asked her? Had she noticed his car?

The description was the easy bit. She was observant. A bit hazier on the questions he'd asked. She'd spoken to a few policemen recently, found it difficult to recall the detail of each conversation and as a result risked getting the conversations muddled up. The car? Yes, she'd seen the detective drive away in it. But she wasn't very knowledgeable about cars. Black, an 18 plate, medium sized.

They asked her to come to the station to help get a photofit prepared.

Afterwards she phoned Lewis and poured her heart out. Who could the fake policeman have been? Was she in danger? After a brief hesitation, he told her she'd be welcome to stay at his place if that would help.

Her... going to live with a man... could she manage that... and would it not be imposing on him? She said none of this. Just thanked him and asked when it would be OK to drive around and, by the way, where did he live? He gave her the details and said to come just as soon as she liked.

"By the way," Lewis said, "did you see on the news that the walker found under those rocks has been identified? Her name's Maxine Kilcline."

"Sorry, could you just repeat that?"

"Yes, she was called Maxine Kilcline."

"Oh no! Fiona has a friend called Maxine and it's an unusual name. God – I hope it's not her."

"Why don't you phone that man Law again? Maybe he could find out for you."

"I will. Thank you. I'll let you know what he says."

She dialled Law's number and wondered why he hadn't already been back in touch.

"I was about to call," he said. "You checked out OK with Fiona. I'm her solicitor, by the way. She's fine, and sends her love." Ailsa was so pleased to hear those three words. "But she's in hiding and unable to speak to you just now. I hope you'll understand why this conversation needs to be a short one."

"Of course, but, sorry, just before you go, there are two important things I need to say." Ailsa really hoped he wouldn't hang up abruptly again. "She has a friend called Maxine. Do you happen to know her last name?"

"Er… yes… it's Kilcline. I take it you know what's happened to her?"

"Unfortunately, yes, I've just found out. It's awful."

"Terrible news and one of the main reasons why Fiona will stay in hiding."

"The other thing you need to know," Ailsa continued, "is that I reported Fiona as missing. They sent a police sergeant to interview me about it. I wasn't able to tell him much – because I don't really know anything! But I've just found out he's a fake. It's really worrying me and I thought you should know about it."

Law immediately wanted to know more; what did the man look like? What exactly did he ask? She told him.

"I'm afraid I gave him your phone number," she said, fearful of Law's response.

"Not to worry," he said. "This particular phone is hard to track."

"All of this has scared me out of my wits, so I'm not going to stay at home. Let me know if anything happens… if you can… and please pass my love on to Fiona."

Ailsa felt both better and worse for having spoken to Law. Better because he'd said Fiona was fine, but worse because everything else he'd said had just reinforced her own rapidly escalating worries.

It was a while since she'd been away anywhere and her packing was slow and not very methodical. How much should she take? Would she be away for a day or two or longer? Best take a bit more to be on the safe side.

After a goodbye to the house, she drove to Lewis' place.

+ + +

Although nobody at either university knew anything about 'Bernie', Marek came to the rescue. Bernie Schroeder had been a friend of Dieter's for many years, based at a university in Berlin and a fellow expert on artificial intelligence. Armed with this information, Mac searched various online sites, found his man and managed to catch him between lectures.

Schroeder was initially cagey, but once Mac explained the background to the call, the conversation opened up. Schroeder shared Dieter's concerns about the morality of allowing artificial intelligence to be in complete control of weapons systems. When Mac asked about Ultimate Intelligence, the floodgates opened. Schroeder had been tracking the company's development for a dozen years, from its humble beginnings as a start-up in the founder's garage, to its current status as a large shadowy global organisation.

"So what aspect of their activities was Dieter so concerned about?"

"Do you know about their money?" Schroeder asked.

"We picked up that they've invested indirectly in the project."

"Ah, good. But there's more to it. Dieter found out that their contribution, which filled a crucial funding gap, was only made available on condition that a company called Blue Star was awarded the contract for the development of the software package that will control the operation of the new laser weapons system. Note, I used the word *awarded*. There was no competitive process. They were handed it on a plate."

"That's a very significant piece of information," Mac said. "Did you know that Blue Star is effectively owned by UI?"

"No! I was aware there was a close link between the two, but not that it amounted to outright ownership. That makes things even worse. When Dieter asked Midlothian about the contract award, they told him it was justified because no other potential tenderers met the required conditions. He was convinced this wasn't the case and was trying to piece the evidence together. Tell me, do you have anything yet that indicates who killed Dieter and his friend?"

Mac told him they were following a number of leads and were hopeful of an imminent breakthrough.

"So, you have nothing certain," Schroeder said. Mac didn't contradict him. "One area you might want to focus on is the role played by the head of department at Midlothian, Professor… Damn! I've forgotten his name."

"Laing," Mac offered.

"Yes, Laing. I know for a fact that Dieter went to see him – just days before his death as it turned out. He'd always got on OK with the professor and felt safe confiding in him. However, when he started to question the terms on which the contract had been awarded, Laing became very confrontational and demanded to know what evidence Dieter had. In my book, this puts the professor under some suspicion. Don't get me wrong. I'm not accusing him of murder, but that kind of reaction shows he was probably trying to hide something. Worth pursuing, I think, particularly in light of your revelation that UI owns Blue Star."

+ + +

Stuck in traffic on the drive back home, Mac recalled that Khan had mentioned some new CCTV footage of the driver of the Renault van that had been used to take Hofmann's body to the bing. Not having yet had a chance to view the clip, he texted Khan and asked him to forward it.

When he spotted Freya's Fiesta parked on the road by his flat, it dawned on him that he hadn't been in contact with her. Day one of knowing about the baby and he hadn't remembered to phone or text her. It wasn't a good start.

The aroma hit him as soon as he opened the front door. Lapskaus, a thick Norwegian stew and a particular favourite of his. How had she known when he'd get back home? Maybe an educated guess that with three late nights on the trot and a sore head, it was unlikely to be a late finish. And the stew could have stayed simmering on the hob for as long as it took.

He held her in his arms for a good while. As usual he'd only snacked during the day and it was only after two big bowls of the stew and several slices of wholemeal bread that he felt restored. No booze, just a jug of water.

"Don't think that you're going to get this sort of treatment every evening once we're together. I just thought you needed building up. I would ask how your day was, but I don't really want to know and anyway you should have a break from it. But what about your injuries? Are they still painful?"

Mac put on his best injured soldier impression and limped across the room to refill the jug.

"Better than expected, actually. Must be tougher than I look. What about you? Are you doing OK, with morning sickness and stuff?"

"Alright so far. I was a bit worried about my age – you know, for being a first-time mum – but I had a helpful chat with my GP."

"That's good. Anything specific to be concerned about?"

"Well, a few things to keep an eye on and if difficulties develop, I'll be straight round to the surgery. But it was reassuring when she told me there's a lot of us mid-forties expectant mums about these days!"

They forgot about the washing up and cuddled up on the sofa, Esbjorn Svensson's *Seven Days of Falling* providing the soundtrack.

"What would you think about us living here?" he asked.

"Well, I've always liked your flat... but where would I paint? And you know the way I leave stuff around, the mess that trails in my wake. Not sure you'd be able to put up with that. On the other hand, my place is definitely too small for three. Barely big enough for one!"

"Maybe you could rent space somewhere round here to use as a studio. Perhaps you could start looking now. Before long you'll be too big to get around!"

"Cheeky sod. I plan to keep moving... and painting... until the very last moment. But it's a good idea. The one thing I am worried about though is my muse."

"Your what?"

"Muse – you know the thing that inspires me. The sea and the shore. How would that work if the sea wasn't right on my doorstep?" she said, a sudden faraway look in her eyes. "Still, as I'm beginning to take an interest in non-natural elements, maybe that could change."

The Swedish jazz came to an end. When Mac put on Shooglenifty's *A Whisky Kiss*, neither of them could sit still. They danced around the living room trying to avoid the furniture until he banged his knee against a low table.

"Do you think this can work then?" she asked as they tumbled back onto the sofa.

Mac knew that although he hadn't thought about it consciously during the day, some cognitive processes must have been at work, because he felt a definite confidence about becoming a family together.

"Yes, I do," he said emphatically.

"Really? You're not just saying that?"

"Look, if we don't do it now, with the baby and everything, we'll never do it and that would be such a waste, don't you think?"

"You're right," she said. "I worry about whether we're mature enough. I mean we haven't got a good track record, have we? Wouldn't win any prizes as couple of the year. But we've got more pluses than minuses, so that gives me hope. How do you think you'll cope with not having a place just to yourself?"

"Living by yourself has its advantages – as you'll know. But it also has big downsides, not the least of which is that by definition you are very frequently on your own. Maybe I get too much of my own company. And I love having you around. Of course, there's also a very practical consideration. If we live together, we won't have to lug the baby and all the baby stuff backwards and forwards from your place to mine!"

"Ever the romantic! Well, while we're both feeling so positive, I'll start looking for a studio tomorrow, first thing after breakfast… and yoga. Will you be running?" He nodded. "That man's not going to come back, is he?" She fingered his bruised face and looked worried.

Surprised the subject hadn't reared its head before, he reassured her it had been a one-off and reminded her that they were getting some discreet protection. If he was honest, it was a concern. But it didn't do to give in to such worries.

And it wasn't going to stop them enjoying an early night.

10 MARCH

It was the first time Mac had been back on the river path since the attack. The image of his assailant's face was gradually fading. And the likelihood of the man making a return visit? Hopefully very low, given that he'd taken enough risks already, no face covering, no backup, losing his car key. Surely, he wouldn't be daft enough to try again.

Mac's early-morning run took him down to Stockbridge and then on a circular route, returning via Comely Bank and Dean Village. Stopping for a breather he checked his phone and noticed that Khan had sent the new CCTV footage of the Renault van. It gave a much clearer picture of the driver, but he'd need to check it out on the bigger screen of his laptop.

Freya was just finishing her yoga session when he got back. Breakfast was porridge with berries on top, followed by potato cakes cooked on the griddle. For once he could leave for work with a proper meal inside him. And she'd be there when he got home, whenever that might be.

Before setting off, he used his laptop to study the clip of the Renault driver. He went through it frame by frame. For a fleeting moment there was a view of the driver's neck. Just enough time for Mac to be able to spot a mark on it, before it was covered up with a repositioned scarf. In the previous footage, the neck had been permanently covered by the scarf. After staring at it again, he was convinced the mark was a tattoo. A possible lead. He phoned Khan to ask him to look on the big screen in the office and check whether the tattoo was in any way distinctive.

On the drive in, he mentally ticked off agenda items for the briefing. There were some updates to do, but he wanted to spend the best part of the session asking the team to speculate on who might have been responsible for the three deaths. They'd gathered so much information about other aspects of the case that there was a danger of drowning in a sea of facts. But so far, they had very little that might help to answer the biggest question of all.

Maeven phoned to tell him she'd be putting the pressure on at the briefing. Media coverage had continued to be negative because of lack of progress in identifying the killers. And the chief superintendent shared that view. Mac wasn't surprised. He'd expected such a reaction sooner.

Khan was waiting for him on his arrival at the Warehouse.

"You're right, guv. It is a tattoo on the driver's neck. Managed to blow up the image without losing too much clarity and it's quite distinctive. Come and have a look."

Mac stared at the two crossed axes and realised he'd seen that particular design before.

+ + +

Ailsa felt so much better being with Lewis. The thought of the fake detective making a return visit to her house terrified her. But of course, he'd really been after Fiona. Her fervent hope was that her sister would be able to stay hidden away.

When she got a call from a man claiming to be a Detective Inspector Forsyth, all her anxieties flooded back. How had he got her number? From the police in Peebles, he told her. Having already been visited and interviewed by one fake officer, how could she be sure Forsyth wasn't another?

"Look, I know you went to the Peebles station because you were very worried that the dead woman found by the burn might have been your sister, Fiona. If you're concerned about whether I'm genuine, please call Peebles and they'll be able to reassure you. If I provide you with some personal information about me, you'll be able to ask them whether it tallies with my official record."

He sounded like a policeman. But then Kershaw had also sounded genuine. It was so hard to tell. Not wanting to take any chances she phoned Peebles. The call took a while, but she got confirmation of Forsyth's details. She rang him back.

"You may already be aware from media reports that the dead woman was called Maxine Kilcline," he said. "We know she had links with an investigative journalist and have reason to believe that person is your sister. Do you think that's likely to be the case?"

Ailsa said that the two women had been friends and that her sister was indeed an investigative journalist.

"I understand you've not been able to contact Fiona recently but would you be able to tell me a little about her, what she's been working on recently and where she might be living now? A description and a photograph would also be very useful."

"I'm afraid I can't really help you with her work. She never gives me any details of her assignments. And I've really no idea where she might be hiding out. But I'll give you a phone number for a Mr Law – a solicitor – who's in touch with her."

"And could you email a photo of her?"

"I'll do that right away. Will the search for her now become a high priority?"

"It already is."

Given what had happened to Maxine, Ailsa was even more worried that her sister would be under threat from the fake detective. And the police had still not found him.

"I'll give you my number," the DI said. "If there are any developments or you think of anything else that might be useful, please give me a call at any time." He rang off.

Ailsa had a sudden thought. She pulled up a photo of Maxine from a news site on her phone and then picked out one of Fiona's black and white photos from the roll that Lewis had developed. A trio: her sister, another woman who she now knew was Maxine and a man. Once she found a photo of Dieter Hofmann on another news site, she knew who the third member of the trio was. And only one of them was still alive!

Lewis was there with a cup of tea. He'd been so supportive. They sat holding hands. She wanted more than anything for her sister to be beside her as well.

+ + +

DC Wyatt had rearranged the whiteboard. It now included details relating to Maxine Kilcline's death, updated information regarding the three vehicles used to transport Hofmann and McGrath and the descriptions of two men seen by witnesses in the vehicles.

Wyatt summarised this for the benefit of the team.

A grey Transit van, not yet traced, but registration known, seen by Mrs McGrath on 28 February, used to abduct her son and Hofmann from her house. She'd given a detailed description of the driver and a partial one of his sidekick.

A red Renault van seen driving away from the Tarbrax bing, by the old man in the derelict barn, very early on the morning of 1 March. The same vehicle identified by a resident in the

Haymarket area of the city, after it had been dumped. No prints found, but traces of Hofmann's DNA found in the back of the vehicle and unidentified DNA found in the passenger-seat area. The old man had given a description of the driver and a partial one of the passenger. CCTV footage of the van and of the driver making his exit and walking along the street.

A Skoda estate seen by the witness in the Cockenzie tower block, who'd observed two men from the vehicle, leaving what he thought was probably a body on the beach at about 5 a.m. on 3 March. Skoda found abandoned in a quarry. Again, no prints found, but traces of McGrath's DNA in the vehicle. The witness in the tower block had given partial descriptions of both men. A second witness, Joe Semple, had provided more detailed descriptions of them.

The team had already agreed that the descriptions of the driver all tallied and that the same man must have driven all three vehicles. But because the descriptions of the non-driver varied and were only partial, there was still uncertainty about whether it had been the same man on each occasion.

"And hot off the press," Wyatt added, "we have reason to believe that our driver may have been involved with the defunct drug cartel over in Glasgow."

The news created a real buzz. Those members of the investigation team who'd pinned their colours to the theory that killers were from the drug world looked reinvigorated. Although the discovery of Maxine Kilcline's body had moved the balance of probability towards work-related reasons for the killings, if a cartel connection was confirmed, then that might shift things back in their favour. Mac reined in the discussion once it became too speculative.

"We're pursuing our efforts to identify the driver," Wyatt added, "and Glasgow PIT are doing likewise in relation to the missing cartel man. Hopefully he'll turn out to be one and the same. I'm sure that between us, we'll find him."

Khan said he had something to add to the discussion about the driver and revealed the news about the distinctive tattoo.

"We don't yet know what the symbol relates to, but we've contacted an expert and expect to hear back from him soon."

DI Forsyth reported on progress regarding Maxine Kilcline. She'd texted her father on 27 February to tell him she'd been about to go into a meeting in Edinburgh, expecting to pick up *some crucial hush-hush information*. The meeting had been in a building which by chance happened to be next door but one to her father's favourite shop, a specialist dealer in model railways.

Euan had traced the building's owner. He had no idea his vacant property had been misused and had arranged for Euan to be able to access the building straight after the briefing. Euan's other news was about tracing the vehicle it was assumed had been used to transport Maxine's body to the rocks by the burn. As he'd hoped, it turned out that one of the farms close to the narrow track leading to the rocks had cameras fitted as part of a farm-watch scheme. The pathologist had defined a timeslot during which the body would have been left at the rocks. The footage during and immediately either side of that period showed only three vehicles – a pickup, a tractor and an ex-ambulance – making a journey both ways along the track. It was after all a lonely, isolated route that led nowhere. Work to trace these vehicles was proceeding.

Mac told them the news about Oversight being in possession of the phones and laptops belonging to Dieter, Alex and Maxine and gave details about Hofmann's friend Schroeder and his in-depth knowledge of Ultimate Intelligence.

Maeven started to turn the screw. It was ten days since Hofmann's body had been found. The top floor at Corstorphine House was rumbling, the chief superintendent was breathing down her neck and media coverage was relentlessly negative.

"It's essential progress is made on identifying the killers," she said. "I've asked DI Larsen to submit an action plan on how the team is going to get from where we are now to a successful outcome."

Although Mac knew the boss' comments were justified, he felt it was important to balance her message with a boost to morale and his end-of-meeting summary focused on the positives.

"Let's keep our momentum going," he said in his closing remarks. "What we need in addition to all our hard work is a little good fortune and I'm convinced that's due."

+ + +

Although it didn't relate to the murder cases, the call from Khan was the kind of positive news Mac had been hoping for. The sergeant and two uniformed officers had searched several of the empty units on the industrial estate and had managed to locate the BMW used by Mac's attacker. The vehicle had false plates, so as yet the owner was unknown. But the Joker brothers were at the scene examining both the vehicle and the empty building.

"One other thing while I'm on, boss. We finally got details of Hofmann's German bank and card accounts. Disappointing, though. After all that waiting, there was nothing interesting or unusual about them."

"That's a bit of a downer. Anything on the tattoo yet?"

"No, not yet. What about you? There was something familiar about it you said."

"Still working on that particular memory! I'm just about to set off for our interview with Laing, so I'll see you there."

Mac, who had long ago given up expecting that Hofmann's accounts would provide anything useful, grabbed a coffee from the dock-front kiosk and headed for the university in the Jimny.

+ + +

As he and Khan were welcomed into the professor's office, Mac felt that Laing had less of a spring in his step. Perhaps he was getting concerned about the frequency of their meetings and the growing extent of the enquiry.

Khan asked what his relationship had been with Hofmann. Looking puzzled, the professor said they'd met a few times, but it hadn't really gone any further than that.

"The reason I ask is that we now know that he came to confide in you, only a few days before his death. He was concerned about the extent of Ultimate Intelligence's involvement in the project. What can you tell us about that?"

Laing sighed and shifted slightly in his seat.

"Yes – that was one of the few occasions we did meet. He'd found out about the money they'd put in and asked why they'd been allowed to invest, clearly convinced something sinister was going on. But let me make it clear. Firstly, as I've already told you, as UI are acknowledged experts in this particular area of software development, their advisory role is perfectly justified. And secondly, they were willing to step into the breach to fill a funding gap. What Hofmann seemed incapable of grasping was that without their money, the whole project would have been threatened. I think his reaction was a reflection of his overall naivety."

"So, what did UI get for their money?" Khan asked.

"I'm not sure what you mean."

"Well, presumably they weren't motivated by altruism!"

"They stood to benefit in the longer term from the work of the project. It's an area of development they're very keen on. Not all companies are after an immediate return, Sergeant."

"What about the immediate return of a juicy contract being awarded, without any competition, to Blue Star, a company wholly owned by Ultimate Intelligence?" Mac asked.

Laing got up, walked across to the window and looked calmly out to the campus below.

"Blue Star has very considerable expertise and experience in the development of software for weapons projects involving the use of artificial intelligence. The contract award was entirely consistent with our procedures. No other companies were able to clear our pre-tender vetting hurdle."

"How usual is that?" Khan asked.

"It happens more frequently than you might think."

"And what about the fact that UI owns Blue Star?"

"That is of no relevance. We made the assessment of Blue Star on the basis of *their* experience."

"And how concerned were UI that Dieter Hofmann was asking awkward questions about Blue Star and the way the contract was awarded?"

"They had no direct concerns about the award, as the procedures we used complied with all the rules. Their worries, which I shared, were in relation to Hofmann's behaviour, his constant undermining of the project and the effect this had on other members of the team." When Laing turned to face the room, Mac noticed how cool he seemed. "As far as his dismissal was concerned, the key factors were his drug abuse and the embezzlement. His approach to the project didn't help matters but that was not the decisive factor. And I must stress that the decision to dismiss was made by the university. UI had no input into the process."

"I'm puzzled," Mac said. "From our discussions with members of the project team, we were led to believe that his cocaine use was an open secret. And we have a suspicion that the embezzlement charge was cooked up to provide a useful pretext to sack him."

"I resent the implications of such a claim. Nothing was *cooked up* as you put it!"

"But surely it was Hofmann's behaviour that was the real worry for both the university and UI and a fear that he was about to blow the whistle on the project."

"I'm not sure what you mean by 'blowing the whistle," Laing said.

"Well, we know that he and a woman called Maxine Kilcline – who is also dead – were writing an article on IntelOper, for imminent publication, with the aim of exposing certain – what shall we call them – irregularities? At this stage, we don't know the full extent of these. But our concern is that the revelations in their article might have been sufficiently serious to have driven someone to take steps to eliminate the authors."

Mac picked up on the professor's response – a look of sympathy and concern.

"Although I've not heard of this lady, I'm very sorry to learn of her death. Based on the information available to you, your analysis is understandable. However, if you are implying that the 'someone' is Ultimate Intelligence, you're making a big mistake. I don't know where your information is coming from but it would appear that your source is – like Hofmann – motivated by a vendetta against Ultimate Intelligence. It sounds to me as if you have a prejudged answer as to what led to Hofmann's death and are now trying to arrange a sequence of events to back up that assumption. The truth, Inspector, is much simpler. Dieter Hofmann lost his job because he wasn't fit – in any sense of the word – to continue. And I believe he lost his life as a result, directly or indirectly, of his drug activity."

Mac felt that Laing put forward a persuasive case. There was this continuing, nagging doubt that UI would have felt sufficiently threatened to kill three people. He'd need to talk to them directly, in order to get an idea of what made them tick.

"You may be right, Professor. It would help if we could speak to someone from UI."

"By all means. I'm sure they'd welcome an opportunity for a discussion. I'll give you a name – unless, that is, you want to make your own contact."

"No, that would be helpful. After we've spoken to them, we'll probably want to talk to you again."

Although Mac was tempted to push the professor further there and then, he decided it would be better to have the conversation with UI first.

+ + +

As Khan was about to drive away from the faculty car park, an image popped into Mac's head. An image of two crossed axes. A tattoo he remembered seeing on a biker's arm on one of his trips to Fredrikstad. He called out to the sergeant.

"It's a biker image – the crossed axes, I mean. Popular in Scandinavia for sure, but maybe it's used here as well. Worth checking out. Remind me to tell you sometime about the Great Nordic Biker War!"

Once Khan had driven off, Mac walked across to one of the campus snackbars, bought a ham and tomato sandwich and returned to the Jimny to eat it.

It was difficult trying to keep up with developments across all three cases that the team now had responsibility for. And there was also Fiona MacMahon to think about.

Giving up on the struggle to fish out stray bits of tomato that had fallen into the gap between the two front seats, he called Euan for an update on the two sisters. Ailsa and Fiona were chalk and cheese, it seemed, one a nervous worrier, very concerned about her sibling but with no idea where she might be, the other an inveterate risk-taker who seemed to have very successfully gone to ground.

Euan had unexpected news.

"A detective who interviewed Ailsa about her missing sister has turned out to be an imposter. He's clearly on Fiona's trail. Given the known link between Fiona and Maxine, I reckon he might have been involved in Maxine's death in some way. Ailsa's been very helpful in providing a detailed description and we've now been able to circulate a photofit."

"Good progress then," Mac said. "Anything further on Maxine's case?"

"Not really. We haven't been able to find any social media accounts of hers. We searched her flat but found nothing useful and there was no trace of her phone or laptop. Of course, your email about our friend Urquhart now being in possession of them changes the picture! Do I take it he also has the devices belonging to Dieter and Alex?"

"He does indeed. Most annoyingly, he refused to say how Oversight got hold of them and didn't seem at all bothered that they've effectively been withholding vital evidence from our investigation. Just kept playing the Official Secrets card. What a surprise! Which reminds me, he's due to hand over all the devices today and there's no sign of them yet. Hold on a sec." He put Euan on hold and left a message for Urquhart demanding immediate action.

"Good, that's done," Mac said.

"Let me tell you about your favourite, friendly convenor," Euan said.

"The woman at Weapons Watch?"

"She's the one. I went back to get her statement. Then we got chatting. Remember how much of a chatterbox she is! Anyway, you'll recall when you asked her yesterday whether someone might have infiltrated the organisation, she nearly blew her top. Having had time to reflect, she'd changed her tune. Hadn't wanted to admit to the likely presence of a mole, as it felt like a failure. But there's a group member who's been a concern – linked to a number of incidents. I got a name out of her – which is bound to be false – and even a photo which was a real bonus. Just sent you a copy. She was at pains to point out that they're not in the habit of photographing members. It was a still taken from one of their online gatherings."

"How on earth did you manage to sweet-talk her into that?"

"Either you've got it, Calum, or you haven't. Need I say more?" Euan said, chuckling. "Seriously though, I was surprised by the extent of her cooperation. She made it plain that she was only responding in that way because of her feelings for Dieter and Maxine and her desire for their killers to be caught. I take it you'll be asking Urquhart about the mole?"

"You bet. I'll send him the mugshot and then speak to him."

"Have fun with that!"

"As if! That man's a real barrel of laughs. Did the convenor have anything to say about the *buddy* – the person who was supposed to be coordinating the article – who we now know is Fiona MacMahon?"

"She was very cagey. When I dropped Fiona's name into the conversation, she visibly flinched. Maxine had warned her off asking any questions about Fiona – which makes sense, knowing how paranoid she is. And the convenor had no idea where she might be hiding out."

"Damn. So we're no nearer to finding Fiona. By the way, have you cracked the Currie shooting case yet?"

"Naturally – with my skills, what else would you expect? Helped by a huge slice of luck, I have to say. Must be off."

It wasn't far from Midlothian University to Corstorphine HQ, and Mac felt like talking to Carla. But it took him ten minutes to find somewhere to park and another ten waiting for her to finish a difficult phone call.

But then he had her undivided attention and they retreated to their no-smoking balcony, Mac lighting up immediately.

"Have you seen it then?" she asked.

"Seen what?"

"The email I sent you – about the chief inspector vacancy – like I promised, remember?"

Mac checked his phone. There it was. Since Carla had first mentioned the job – when had that been, last Thursday maybe? – he hadn't given the matter much thought. Not surprising perhaps as his mind had been full of murder cases and concerns about impending fatherhood.

"I can tell from that look. You've pushed it to the back of your mind! Well, my opinion, for what it's worth, is that you'd be a fool not to go for it. Has Maeven said anything?"

He told her about their brief conversation.

"There you go then. If she and I are both pushing it, you haven't got any choice in the matter."

"Well, you see, there's a complication. It looks like I'm going to become a father." He regretted it as soon as the words were out of his mouth. He'd promised Freya not to say a word to anyone… apart from his mother. Still, at least Carla was the soul of discretion, when she wanted to be.

"Did I hear you right?" He nodded. "Well, that's fantastic." She threw her arms around his neck and kissed him on the cheek. "But it makes it even more of a nailed-on certainty that you should apply for the job. Apart from anything else you'll need the extra money. Please tell me that Freya is the lucky woman!"

He nodded and asked Carla not to say anything to anyone, particularly as nobody else knew yet – not even his mother.

"And having been more or less single for all these years, how do you feel about the idea of becoming a family man?"

"Well, for the first thirty seconds I was terrified. Then this calm seemed to descend and I began to think it could work. But all that and becoming a chief inspector… I'm not sure I could handle it."

"Of course you could. Don't forget, over the years I've seen men – and women – without half your skill, take on the job and most have made a decent fist of it. What does Freya think?" Mac looked sheepish. "So, you've not told her! Come on, Mac, things are changing. You need to be sharing."

She was right. And the job? Becoming a father would be a big enough challenge. Could he face that and take on a new position higher up the chain, full of political challenges?

+ + +

Two incoming calls. The first was from Kenny who rambled on about climate change targets until Mac told him to get to the point.

"Have a little patience, my friend. It's worth the wait," Kenny said, not at all fazed by the interruption.

He'd picked up news of an enquiry report issued by a committee of the US House of Representatives which included some very critical comments about Ultimate Intelligence and the business methods they used. Mac asked for a link.

When he enquired about the latest breaking news, Kenny told him to stand by for virus lockdown, predicting it would be imposed within two weeks at most. Would it really happen that soon, Mac wondered?

The second call was from Freya. She'd visited his mum and brought her back to Glomma to eat with them and stay the night. Although this was a considerate thing to do, Mac felt a little resentful that he'd not been asked about it beforehand. But now wasn't the time to raise such petty issues. And it would give him the chance to tell his mother about the baby... except... of course... Freya would probably already have given her the news. More resentment. Why did he react in this way? Maybe this kind of thing was at the root of the problem between him and Freya, an inability to give each other a bit of leeway. Could he really change? Could she?

An email from Khan. The guy who'd been driving the BMW – the man who'd clobbered him – had been identified. The prints found in the car were those of a Robbie Toner, aged twenty-five. He'd been arrested two years previously and charged with drunk driving – a charge which an expensive advocate had managed to get dismissed. But his prints had still been on file. The surname seemed vaguely familiar to Mac, some association with a case from years back.

When he told Maeven the news, she ordered him not to go and pick up Toner.

"You're too personally involved," she told him "and there's a danger you'd do something that would fuck up the case against him."

Mac knew she was right. Khan would go, with the necessary backup.

The name Toner was bugging him. The Internet came to his rescue. It didn't take long to find what he was looking for. Ah, Craig Toner, the man who owned the site security firm. Might he be related to Robbie? A quick check. Yes, they shared the same address.

Then it came back to him. That feeling of resentment. A case from maybe a dozen years ago in which he'd had a minor role. A developer putting a site together, stopped in his tracks by a couple of elderly owners who refused to sell. Craig Toner brought in to 'encourage' the owners to see sense. Late-night harassment, followed by physical assaults. Witnesses intimidated. The owners had given in and sold up. In the end they'd been unable to pin anything on Toner and it had rankled.

From the details on his company website, it was clear that over recent years, Toner had presided over a rapid period of growth and consolidation. Worth a bob or two then. An online photo of the Toner residence confirmed that assessment. Mac phoned Khan to warn him. A man like that would have connections and the resources to defend his son.

The thought uncoiled slowly. Given Craig Toner's actions in the case from a dozen years ago and the son's very recent attempt at intimidation, would it be worth finding out more about the father's track record? After phoning a couple of colleagues it was apparent that although rumours had swirled around the activities of Toner senior for years, he possessed an uncanny knack of not being in the wrong place at the wrong time – unlike his son. One of Mac's colleagues mentioned a retired former detective inspector by the name of Angus, an obsessive who'd spent a considerable time towards the end of his career, trying to pin something serious on Toner – without success. Just like the Glasgow DI and his obsession with the Clyde cartel, Mac thought.

He called Angus.

Since retirement, with plenty of spare time available between rounds of golf and birdwatching trips, Angus had continued his research, off and on, and built up a dossier of accusations against Craig Toner. But there'd never been enough hard evidence to warrant charges being brought. Wondering whether the information in the dossier might be enough to at least justify putting a watch on Craig Toner, Mac told Angus he'd ring him back and called Maeven.

But she blocked the idea. Too much hunch and not enough solid fact to justify such a step at this stage.

"If, as you suspect, it turns out that Toner does have some well-connected friends, the last thing I want is for any investigation of him to go off half-cock and for the chief super then to come hammering on my door talking of witch hunts. By the way, talking of the chief, have you done that action plan yet?"

"Just finished it. I'll send it to you."

"Good. Now listen. If you can find something recent and solid against Craig Toner, or better still something that links him to this case, I'll back you all the way."

With the official avenue closed off, at least for the time being, Mac toyed with the idea of arranging some unofficial observation.

Urquhart from Oversight Scotland called, sounding most unlike his usual superior self. Mac confirmed the phones and laptops belonging to the three victims had arrived. Relief at getting their hands on them after such a long wait had been short-lived. A preliminary check revealed almost nothing that wasn't already known. All the significant content must have been previously removed by Oversight.

"Look, this is rather awkward," Urquhart said. "That photo you sent me. I wouldn't normally reveal anything about one of our undercover operatives, but we have a problem and I could do with your help." Mac hadn't anticipated such a response and wondered what was going on. "The information I'm about to share with you is in the strictest confidence. In his Weapons Watch role he operates under the name Mallory. We have some concerns about him and suspect he's got rather too close to Ultimate Intelligence. Any evidence you could provide in this respect would be most welcome – and your assistance would not be forgotten."

In the spirit of this unexpected *entente cordiale*, Mac said he'd see what could be done.

Being cooped up in the Warehouse was getting to him. A brisk walk around the block was in order – long enough to make a phone call to Hedley Baxter, the UI name that Laing had provided.

When he answered, Baxter was eating, so noisily, that Mac had some difficulty in following what he was saying.

"How did you get my number?" Undisguised annoyance at the interruption of his meal. Mac explained about Laing.

"OK. What do you want?" Mac asked him whether he knew about Dieter Hofmann.

"Yeah, I know all about him, a damn nuisance, who threatened to foul up what has all the potential to be a very promising enterprise. He sure as hell had it in for us. What with his constant undermining of the project, his damn principles and his drug abuse – not to mention his thieving – it's no wonder he was kicked off the job. Sure, it was a bummer to find out he was dead but you know, to be honest, that's always a risk when you seriously mess with drugs." Even less sympathy than Urquhart had displayed, Mac thought.

"Your company has a lot invested in this project, doesn't it?" he said.

"We have interests in a whole range of developments that take forward the cause of AI. And we're happy to provide an advisory role."

"But there's more to it than that, isn't there? I'm aware that your company has put money into the project and that, in return for this investment, Blue Star, which you just happen to own, was awarded the contract for the development of the software for IntelOper – without any competition."

"Look, buddy, you know damn all. Repeat that kind of garbage in public and you'll be looking a lawsuit in the face before you can turn around."

"Oh, I'm not sure you'd want UI's involvement in this matter discussed in open court. Especially after the revelations in that House of Representatives report. But my concerns go further than Hofmann. I take it you've also come across Maxine Kilcline?"

"Never heard the name before. Now if you'll excuse me, I was rather enjoying this burger until you butted in. So, if that's all, I'll bid you farewell."

"Not quite all. Her body has been found – and it wasn't natural causes. She knew a lot about your company but unfortunately wasn't able to finish writing up her account, before her untimely death. However, what I've seen makes very interesting reading."

"You're getting into serious shit here with such wild comments. My advice would be to watch your back."

"That's an interesting choice of phrase, Baxter. UI has a chequered history, to say the least, and according to what I've read, an established track record of eliminating opposition. That's one of the reasons we're rather concerned about your company. Thanks for your time."

He felt all the better for having made the call. No doubt UI would be straight on to Oversight Scotland who'd be straight on to the chief superintendent – or someone higher. But the House of Representatives report had used that exact phrase – *an established track record of eliminating opposition* – so he felt on safe ground. And the word 'eliminating' was conveniently ambiguous!

But why had Baxter responded so pugnaciously? He was a complete contrast to Laing, who throughout their meetings had remained calm and measured. If UI had been involved in anything underhand, why would he draw attention to himself in such an obvious way? Maybe it was just down to Baxter's character.

Finishing his walk via Leith Links, Mac found that on his return to the Warehouse the place was buzzing.

Robbie Toner had been charged with assault and was being questioned. He'd arrived with a fancy lawyer in tow who'd already made noises about a bail application. Mac would be required to ID the young man as his attacker.

He was suddenly worried. The attack had taken place in the dark and his memory of the exact details was still a little hazy. What would happen if he failed to recognise Toner?

Khan arrived at Mac's desk with a question.

"You weren't a biker were you, boss?"

"Me! Not likely. Cycling was as far as I got on two wheels. No, I just remember that particular crossed axes tattoo, which at the time I thought was pretty cool."

"Well, our expert has come up trumps. The image is used not only in Scandinavia, but also by some bikers here. He's narrowed it down to a couple of groups. With a combination of this info and the photofit, we might get somewhere. I'm arranging for a team to do a trawl of the groups."

"That's excellent. I'd no idea the image was also used in Scotland."

"And what about the Great Nordic Biker War you mentioned?"

"It was actually pretty violent stuff, back in the eighties and nineties. Maybe when we've got a bit more time, I'll give you the low-down."

+ + +

By the time Mac reached home he was exhausted and would have liked nothing better than to crawl into bed.

His mother was trying to hide the fact she already knew about the new grandchild. But the broad smile and lengthy hug gave her away. He did his best to bury the thought that Freya had jumped the gun and that he'd been deprived of the opportunity to announce the news himself.

However, as soon as the enticing aroma of roast duck in a rich sauce, which he knew would be spiced with juniper berries, wafted in from the kitchen, his irritation drifted away.

He sat down at the table next to his mother. She was full of it. Who would ever have thought it… after all these years… and wasn't it just the best news? Had they decided where to live? And if they needed someone to look after the baby from time to time, they knew where to come!

Freya said they were thinking that she should move into Glomma and talked about her hunt earlier in the day for studio space. There'd been two possibles, one down in Dean Village, the other in Haymarket. Although a bit on the pricey side, each provided the kind of space she could feel at home in. Her excitement at the prospect was evident.

Mac opened a bottle of Zinfandel and put on Ketil Bjornstad's *Life in Leipzig*. The meal had come at just the right time. Left to himself, cocooned on the sofa, he'd have nodded off. Freya and Pia talked about the baby with Mac throwing in the occasional comment. Eventually the conversation moved on to respective relatives back home.

His mother reminisced about previous holidays, excursions to the countryside and to Oslo and the coastal cruise that she and Per had enjoyed for her seventieth birthday. It was a fair time since her last visit to Norway and she'd love to go again. Mac said they ought to plan a trip for her next birthday.

Later, after Pia had retired to the spare bedroom, Mac and Freya snuggled up together on the sofa listening to Jan Garbarek's *Remember Me, My Dear*. Realising that he still hadn't said anything about it, he mentioned the DCI vacancy. There were plenty of questions, some of which he couldn't answer. She said he should go for it.

When the conversation drifted on to the events of his day, he inadvertently let slip that he'd told Carla about the baby. Freya, never quite convinced that their relationship was completely over, was immediately prickly.

"Why did you have to tell her, of all people, when we hadn't agreed who to tell and when?"

"Well, exactly," he said, rolling his eyes. "It would have been nice if I'd had the chance to tell Mum about it first." So much for self-control, he thought, immediately regretting his outburst.

Freya disentangled herself and shifted across to the far end of the sofa. When Mac said that because his day had been so tiring, he was off to bed, she turned on the TV and pretended to be engrossed in a gardening programme. He gave her a peck on the cheek and left the room.

Lying awake in the middle of the night, Freya curled up far away from him, Mac wondered whether there was any way they'd ever be able to break out of their cycle of endless, repeated bickering. After all, did it really matter who'd told who about the baby? In an attempt to distract himself, he started to weigh up the pros and cons of applying for the chief inspector job. Another mistake as, veering repeatedly from yes to no, sleep continued to elude him. The one time he did manage to nod off, there was a familiar dream, him back as a police trainee wandering endlessly around Tulliallan Castle in the dark, trying to find the right lecture room.

Giving up on the struggle, he climbed quietly out of bed, grabbed his dressing gown and headed for the kitchen and a cup of tea. It was nearly impossible to think about nothing, but the tea helped and he gradually slumped backwards in his chair on the verge of sleep until he felt Freya's soothing hands on his forehead. She led him back to bed.

+ + +

Four in the morning staring at the dying embers, still a little heat to be found, Thomas Rook drank his tea slowly and cursed the way things had fallen apart.

The boss should never have taken on the job in the first place. Success in their line of work was dependent on proper planning and there hadn't been enough time for that. The client had interfered, corners had been cut and actions taken without thought for the consequences.

He didn't really want to think about what had gone on in that vacant building – where a little knowledge really had been a dangerous thing. *Deprive her of insulin*, he'd been instructed, *then she'll tell you everything.* But she hadn't. Instead, she'd lost consciousness. They'd left her overnight, thinking she'd come round. But the next morning she was dead. Hypothermia had probably finished her off.

At least the delivery, late that evening, had been carried out properly – but then he'd been in total control of that.

Rook thought back to the journey.

Snow falling, heater on the blink, the cold penetrating their bones. Like something out of a dream, the black edge of the narrow road intermittently disappearing into a white blur. He gripped the steering wheel at ten to two, like a learner driver, following the headlights down the white tunnel of snowflakes.

Ash was in a real mood, had been going that way for some time. Kitted out with a baseball cap, a tightly-wound scarf and a pair of motorcycle gauntlets, he strained forward against the seat belt, in an attempt to get a clearer view through the windscreen, cursing the foul weather and asking why they didn't just dump their load at the side of the narrow road and get the hell out of it.

Rook had to remind him that the whole point of taking the body to the rocks was to delay its discovery.

It seemed to take an age to reach the gate across the road. Ash refused to get out and open it. There was an argument but, in the end, he gave in. Once through the gate, Rook was tempted to put his foot down and leave the bad-tempered bastard at the roadside, but knew only too well that it would be a two-man job to get the body into position.

The snow stopped as suddenly as it had started, just as ink-black clouds parted to reveal a pale moon, illuminating the burn to their left. Once the vehicle stopped, he savoured the moment, not the slightest sound apart from the ticking of the cooling engine. It seemed like the middle of nowhere.

They let down the tailgate, lifted the tarpaulin and dragged the canvas-covered package along the bed of the pickup, before hoisting it onto their shoulders. The trickiest part of their journey was the descent to the rocks and the nearby burn, the snow slippery and at a couple of points Rook, leading the way, almost lost his footing.

The huge stones were just as he remembered them. With a series of awkward movements, they lowered the canvas bag onto the snow. Not requiring any further assistance, he sent Ash back to the vehicle.

His gloves skin-tight, Rook unzipped the bag, rolled the body over the snow to the rocks, curled it into the back of the rocky recess and placed the rucksack beside her.

They'd removed her laptop and phone from the bag during the interrogation. The insulin pens had been taken out, emptied, and put back. She'd volunteered the information about going for a walk in the hills after their meeting. That had been during the earlier, friendly part of the discussion, before things had got serious. It seemed somehow appropriate for her to end up being left in peace by the burn.

Back in the pickup, Ash asked about their footprints. Rook had checked the forecast. They'd disappear with the snow the following day. The journey back was uneventful until a blazing row developed out of nothing. Back in the city, Ash jumped out while they were waiting for a red light to change and stormed off into the night, shouting insults to the rooftops.

He hadn't heard from Ash since.

But the problems had kept coming. The interrogation of Kilcline had revealed MacMahon's role. The client had panicked and instructions were hastily issued. It didn't do to be rushed.

The journalist went to ground.

The boss, no longer listening, was playing the fucking hard man, telling him he'd be off the job. He wasn't going to put up with that!

Poking at the remains of the fire, he finished his tea.

It was essential to concentrate. His only option now was to pay another visit to the sister and apply the necessary pressure.

And he'd just found out where she was.

11 MARCH

Craig Toner had the use of a friend's slipway on the north bank of the Forth, a short drive from his house near Charlestown.

Easing the single scull onto the water, he manoeuvred his way onto the seat and pushed off with an oar, loving the peace of the dawn. Upstream first, a tough work-out, followed by a hard row against the incoming tide, his mind focusing solely on the rhythm and the water.

Back home, after a shower and a well-earned early breakfast, he allowed himself the luxury of spending some time in the large garden shed, oiling shears and secateurs, checking over the large ride-on mower ready for the first cut of the season and rearranging the garden tools. Normally his wife would have been out there doing some garden spring cleaning, but she was in one of her moods. She'd been asking awkward questions again. Despite the money, the clothes, the car, her whole lifestyle in fact – all paid for by him – she was never satisfied.

With his garden-shed work completed, he should have set off straight away to his site security depot at Granton. But it was still early, and rather than an immediate commute to work he felt like taking the Honda out to clear his head. There was this feeling, one he was unfamiliar with, that events were beginning to spin out of his control.

The deadline for completion of the latest job had passed. He'd have to negotiate extra time with the client, kick Rook off the job and put in a replacement.

And as if that wasn't bad enough, his own son had taken it upon himself to intimidate a detective inspector and was in custody. Craig Toner hadn't the slightest idea why this had happened. Robbie would, of course, get the best advice and would hopefully be seen – accurately as it happened – as a young hothead and therefore not to be taken as a serious threat.

The Nighthawk 750 cruised through the back lanes, hugging the corners and taking him away from negative thoughts. The temptation was to keep going, head for the mountains and leave everything else behind. But an appointment with his lawyer was looming.

Stopping at the top of a rise, he looked down to Loch Leven. Maybe it was time to change his approach to life and to leave its risky underbelly behind. But he feared that would emasculate him. Reluctantly he put his helmet back on and headed for home.

His brief had first acted for him thirty years ago when, a young hothead himself then, there'd been that first brush with the law. The lawyer, only in his twenties, had impressed with his command of detail and powerfully persuasive arguments.

Now it felt different. His legal man was unusually worried, with talk of loose threads leading to unravelling garments. Whilst confident that the consequences of Robbie's offence itself could be minimised, the lawyer was concerned about the risk of a wider police enquiry which might lead to a much more dangerous place.

+ + +

Over a shared pre-run, early morning cup of tea, Mac felt he'd managed to regain the ground lost with Freya over his ill-chosen, late-evening words.

The run along the streets of the New Town lifted his spirits. He crossed Princes Street, passed Waverley Station and headed up Advocates Close to High Street. Still early, there were very few people around. A fine view out to the Forth.

At yesterday's line-up, despite his previous uncertainties, Mac had been able to pick out Robbie Toner as the young man who'd slugged him. After two lengthy interview sessions, DS Khan had managed to get Toner to talk – despite the advice from his solicitor to stay silent. One of Maxwell's sidekicks had paid him to carry out the attack on DI Larsen.

Khan had briefed Mac after the interviews. They'd agreed Toner's claim didn't stack up. Why would Maxwell, a seasoned pro, allow a rookie like Toner to play the intimidator?

Mac's breathing seemed better than usual, which he put down to a drop in his intake of cigarette smoke. Running around the back of the castle, he headed down King's Stables Road, recrossed Princes Street and wound his way back home through the New Town.

At breakfast, Freya was back to her usual self. With a good night's sleep behind her, his mother was also on good form. After porridge, followed by eggs Benedict, he left them to it. Freya would take Pia home and then drive back to the Fife coast. He'd have the place to himself again. The thought gave him more pleasure than it should have done. There'd be a need to adapt in due course to having someone else around in the flat. Two someones, in fact.

Erland phoned, bright and early for him, to check that Mac was OK for their usual Thursday evening meet-up. His brother liked to have advance warning of a no-show so that he could arrange alternative entertainment. Mac told him that with the way work was going, Friday would be a better bet. Although Erland made it sound like changing days was a big deal, in the end he agreed.

His brother's call was quickly followed by one from Carla. Had he made a decision yet? Given that it was less than twenty-four hours since they'd last spoken about the DCI job, his answer was no! How come everybody else – Freya, Carla, Maeven, Euan – all seemed to be far more interested in the job than he was?

But it wasn't lack of interest, was it? Just lack of time – and head space. He'd have to create some of each.

The team briefing session was longer than usual, the whiteboard fuller and it was a record attendance of ten. Morag Maeven sat at the back, hovering, Mac thought, like a potentially disruptive school pupil.

The big news was that the driver of the Transit van, the red Renault and the Skoda, the main suspect in the deaths of Hofmann and McGrath, had just been identified as an Eamonn Gallagher. The tattoo had led to a biker group which had led to a current member with a long-held grudge against a former member – Gallagher. As yet they didn't have an address for him but enquiries were being made as a matter of urgency.

The team was really spurred on by the news.

There'd been no progress in identifying the fake detective suspected of involvement in the death of Maxine Kilcline and of posing a very real current threat to Fiona MacMahon.

Khan confirmed his scepticism regarding Robbie Toner's evidence. A further interview would take place that morning. But a bail application was anticipated.

Mac told the team about his conversation with Baxter, the Ultimate Intelligence man and the company's track record in dealing with people who got in their way, stressing that – so far – there was no evidence to suggest that this extended to killing them.

While answering questions, Mac reflected that Maeven hadn't intervened during the update. Perhaps there'd been no new orders sent down from the top floor of Corstorphine House.

It turned out his assumption was wrong. After the briefing, she spoke to him in her office and showed him an email from the chief super and the attachment from the attorney acting for Ultimate Intelligence. The company was after Mac's blood, demanding he be taken off the case. The chief's initial reaction had been to consider meeting the spirit of the demand – without admitting anything – by bringing in Yates, a longer-serving DI above both Larsen and Forsyth. Maeven had persuaded him otherwise. But results had to come quickly. Mac was grateful for her show of confidence – particularly as he and Yates had history.

"I need more dirt on UI from you, to pass on to the chief and keep him… well, not exactly happy… but off your back! What have you got and where's it coming from?"

"Two sources," Mac said. "The first is Bernie Schroeder, the friend of Hofmann's who I referred to at yesterday's briefing. He's been tracking UI's activity since their early days. As you know, they recently invested in the IntelOper project, not directly but through a proxy. That money filled a crucial gap in the project finances and Schroeder's discovered that the money had strings attached. It was made available on condition that a company called Blue Star was awarded the contract for the development of the operational software, without the need to go through the usual competitive process. And as I mentioned before, it just so happens that Blue Star is owned by UI – although the ownership trail is shrouded in secrecy. And Schroeder thinks the company might have imposed other conditions."

"Interesting," Maeven said. "Good work, but of course it'll be essential to find solid evidence to back up these claims."

"Schroeder may be able to come up with more and we'll be pursuing these areas with Laing as well. Despite our questioning, he seems to be able to stay as cool as a cucumber, but I'm not convinced we're getting the full story from him. So, I'm going to speak to one of the senior guys at Midlothian to find out what he has to say."

"Who's that then?"

"He's got a bit of a long-winded title – the Pro-Vice-Chancellor for Research and Development!"

"Mind how you go with him," Maeven said. "From what I hear, he's got a lot of clout. Who's your other source?"

Mac had never before placed information provided by his mate Kenny on official record. However, he felt now was the right time to introduce Dr Kenneth Macintyre as a serious player, not in his capacity as a friend, but as a theoretical physicist with a reputation for out-of-the-box thinking and a highly sensitive ear to the ground in respect of new developments.

"He was the first to suggest that Ultimate Intelligence might have an involvement in the joint university project and he's provided some very helpful information about how the company operates. Such as allegations of them using illegal payments to secure approval of a contract for the application of artificial intelligence in the US long-distance road haulage business. A prosecution was lined up, but following several alleged acts of witness intimidation, in the end, the case didn't proceed. And he also told us about a highly critical US House of Representatives report on UI's business methods which is very revealing. Here, take a look," Mac said, handing over his phone. Maeven scrolled through the executive summary, eyebrows raised. "And it was Dr Macintyre who unearthed the fact that Blue Star is owned by UI!"

Maeven said she'd ensure that the chief was made fully aware of the details.

+ + +

Robbie Toner had been bailed – to his parents' house. His fancy lawyer had pulled some fancy tricks to get him out. What had played well in the bail application was the claim that he spent much of his time when not at work caring for his mother who suffered from a chronic condition. That and his age. He'd only recently turned twenty-five.

Mac was seething. Although knowing nothing of the nature of Mrs Toner's illness, he was certain that her husband would be able to afford a whole team of carers to fill any gap left by Robbie. And as far as Mac was concerned, Robbie's caring side had so far been notably absent.

To distract himself from his annoyance and frustration, Mac speculated again as to why Toner junior would ever have got himself involved in an attack on a police officer. It didn't make any sense. The father had kept himself out of police hands his whole working life. Why would the son have taken such a big risk? Unless … could it be… that his violent activity extended further than one isolated attack on a copper?

Leaving his office, he made his way down to the room they used for the briefings, stood in front of the whiteboard and scrutinised the descriptions of Gallagher's sidekick in the Transit, the Renault van and the Skoda. Although Mrs McGrath had given a good description of the driver of the Transit – the man now identified as Gallagher – she hadn't been able to say much about his accomplice who'd been wearing a hoodie and had a scarf covering most of his face. But she'd guessed both men were middle-aged. Well, not a promising start for his new theory!

The old man who lived close to the bing at Tarbrax had also seen the driver clearly enough. While only having a partial view of the passenger, he'd stated it was a younger man. 1-1. That was better. What about Joe Semple's description of the 'other' man? He'd got a good view, helpfully illuminated by the car park streetlight. Another young man, mid-twenties maybe, well built. Which was identical to Mac's own description of Robbie Toner. 2-1, the clincher? So maybe Gallagher had used someone else for the trip in the Transit when he'd picked up Hofmann and McGrath and subsequently taken on Robbie to assist with everything that happened afterwards. It was certainly an idea worth pursuing. He called Joker One and asked him to check whether the unidentified DNA found in the cab of the Renault was by any chance Robbie Toner's. And could he also check whether there was any trace of his prints or DNA in the vacant unit.

The threat of DI Yates being sent in by the chief superintendent to take over the investigation drove Mac on. Although the identification of Gallagher was a really big step forward and might buy him some time, he couldn't afford to let up. A colleague, who was well plugged into the force's gossip network, had told him the chief was in for a promotion and wanted the murder cases wrapped up before his interview.

Having bought a coffee and a haggis pie from the dockside kiosk – neglecting yet again to ask exactly what was inside the pastry – he sat on a bench and gazed out to sea. The islands, the waves and the birds were all in his vision, but he didn't really take any of them in, focused as he was on the demands of the chief's timetable.

His phone rang, a Cameron Law, dour, slight hint of a Geordie accent. Did he know the man? Then it dawned. Euan had mentioned the name – Fiona MacMahon's solicitor. Mac was briefly distracted wondering whether Law's choice of career had been down to nominative determinism.

"Look, I've got an urgent request but haven't been able to contact DI Forsyth. That's why I'm calling you. Fiona's just had a very worrying phone call from one of Ailsa's neighbours. Her sister has been badly injured by a car, which mounted the pavement. We're on our way to the hospital now, but naturally Fiona's really concerned about the risks of being back in Edinburgh. So, I need to ask whether it would be possible – given what's happened to Dieter Hofmann and Maxine Kilcline – to provide her with some form of police protection at the hospital?"

Mac said he'd set it up and would also meet them there. As a precaution, they should phone him once they were close and he'd escort them into the building.

This could be just an accident, Mac thought. But what if it wasn't? Vehicles didn't hit pedestrians on pavements very often. Could it have been a deliberate attack, carried out with the purpose of enticing Fiona into the open? Might the fake detective be behind this? If that was the case, it would mean he – or one of his men – would also have to come out into the open.

Phone calls to make. Maeven first. She shared his concern about the 'accident' and authorised the presence of armed officers at the hospital and the arming of himself and DI Forsyth.

Next call to Euan, to tell him about Ailsa's accident… was it really an accident? … Fiona's impending visit to the hospital… the armed backup… and guns for the two of them.

"See you there," Mac said.

"On my way," Euan replied. "While you're on, you'll be pleased to hear that the SOCO picked up several sets of prints in the building where Maxine was. Hers, but no matches for any of the others yet. Could be interesting though!"

Mac set off. A call from Kenny.

"A bit more information for you, pal, free gratis!"

Mac could never quite match the academic written prose of Kenneth the scientist with the strongly accented spoken word of Kenny the Montrose supporter.

"A wee birdie let slip a rumour about Blue Star – or shall we just call them Ultimate Intelligence! The new software for the operation of drone-mounted lasers is being configured in such a way that it prevents full AI control. The United Nations, amongst others, are against systems that give free rein to AI. There must always be an element of human control. That is also official UK government policy. The rumour is about Blue Star developing a *secret back door* – sorry to use such a highly technical term – in their software which will allow the system to function with full AI control. Of course, our esteemed government wouldn't dream of taking advantage of this option, but it seems there is a demand from some governments – and some criminal conglomerates – who would have no such moral qualms. My hunch is that Herr Hofmann found out about this and ended up paying the price."

This was a gem, Mac thought, as he texted Maeven about Kenny's snippet of news. But hard evidence would be needed. It wouldn't be sufficient to cite a 'wee birdie' in court. Not that there was time to make follow-up enquiries immediately. The priority task was to get to the hospital.

+ + +

DS Khan was outside the house where Eamonn Gallagher lived. Some solid, basic policework had led them to the property.

Given their well-founded suspicions about the man, Khan had arranged, via Maeven, for an armed squad to be in attendance for the raid on the house.

It turned out to be an anti-climax. All they found in the property was a young man, still in his bed, who turned out to be Gallagher's son, and an elderly dog unable to raise the energy for even a token bark. The youngster was stroppy and under the influence of some substance or other. When he reacted aggressively, Khan had no hesitation in handcuffing him. His phone was confiscated to remove the temptation of a warning call to his dad.

An observation van was left parked nearby and the son was carted off to the Warehouse. Khan, heading for the same destination, had reached the end of the street and been about to turn onto the main road, when he noticed an Audi turning in the opposite direction. The driver was definitely Gallagher.

Khan phoned the observation van to warn them and U-turned back up the side road.

As he rounded the bend, he saw the van slewed across the road blocking the Audi's way forward and he pulled up right behind the car. Knowing the game was up, Gallagher slumped over the steering wheel, the horn sounding plaintively across the suburban street.

+ + +

DC Wyatt hadn't expected to be back in the old woman's kitchen, drinking yet another cup of tea. Her task this time was to show Mrs McGrath a photo of the newly-detained suspect Gallagher. Wyatt, who'd been reinvigorated by the news of his capture, needed to ask the mother whether she'd be willing to take a look at Gallagher and confirm he was the man who'd abducted her son and Hofmann. Given how she'd been threatened by him, Wyatt felt this was something of an unfair ask, particularly as there were other witnesses who'd also provided descriptions. But, to her surprise, the old woman agreed, saying if it helped to put the man behind bars, then she'd grit her teeth and do it.

Wyatt helped her into the Golf. On the journey to the Warehouse, Mrs McGrath asked when her son's body would be released. The funeral was preying on her mind. Wyatt said it would be very soon and promised to set the wheels in motion.

A two-way mirror meant that Gallagher couldn't see Mrs McGrath as she stood there shaking, but adamant that he was the man who'd taken her Alex. Wyatt suggested a cup of coffee at a cafe just around the corner from the Warehouse. As the shaking gradually eased, Mrs McGrath began talking about her

son, the hopes she'd had for him early on, followed by a gradual
realisation that he was going to struggle throughout his life. Only
half-concentrating, Wyatt almost missed her comment about a
notebook. But then she was all ears.

Dieter had given it to her for safekeeping – called it his
journal. Worried that 'they' might search the house again, she'd
taken it to her mother's and asked her to hide it. Wyatt thought
she must have misheard. Mrs McGrath's mother was still living!
How old must she be?

There'd be no problem going there straight away to pick
up the journal. The reason Mrs McGrath hadn't mentioned it
before was fear. Fear that the awful man who'd taken her son to
his death, would find out about the journal and return to ransack
the house and punish her. But now he was in custody she could
leave that particular fear behind.

Alex's grandmother turned out to be a sprightly ninety-five
and still fully independent. She wanted to know about progress
on the case and made Wyatt promise to do all she could to help
get Gallagher convicted. The journal was handed over. Leaving
mother and daughter together, Wyatt sat in the car and turned to
the first page. Unfortunately, she couldn't understand a word of it.

Driving back to the Warehouse, Colquhoun phoned with an
update.

"The Glasgow DI has found the missing surviving member
of the Clyde cartel. He now operates under the name of Rory
Dalziel. They'll be interviewing him up at Glasgow PIT HQ to
see if he's had any connection with recent deaths on our patch.
I'll let you know what they find out."

Although very pleased to hear that the man had been tracked
down, Wyatt also felt strangely disappointed to find out that it
wasn't Gallagher.

"We've just picked up a suspect by the name of Gallagher,"
she said. "We'd been led to believe he might have been the

missing cartel man. Apparently very similar facially. Presumably what you've just told me about Dalziel, means that Gallagher didn't have any connection with the cartel."

"I'd assume not. But that doesn't necessarily mean that Dalziel has had nothing to do with the recent taser deaths."

Despite the importance of this news, Colquhoun sounded subdued. His spark – which she'd found instantly attractive – had gone. Half-tempted to raise it with him, she decided against it. A personal discussion like that might run the risk of reigniting the problems she'd experienced at the restaurant. The sergeant was an unnecessary distraction.

Wyatt needed an urgent discussion with DI Larsen about Dalziel – and about Hofmann's journal.

+ + +

Mac had imagined Fiona to be small, thin as a whippet, short-haired and sharp-tongued. But as was so often the case with such imaginings, the reality was far different. Tall, long-haired, no resemblance to a whippet and quite reserved.

He walked with her and Law into the hospital, past reception and on to Ailsa's ward. Once made aware of the security issues, the staff had moved her to a single room – without disclosing why. Her injuries were serious but not life-threatening. Mac waited outside the room so that the sisters could have a proper reunion. He couldn't stop himself from scanning the corridor every few minutes, looking for doctors, nurses, cleaners or porters who didn't quite look the part. But no doubt the armed, uniformed officers stationed just around the corner would pick up on any problems before they reached him.

Euan appeared and said he'd wait in the cafe by the hospital entrance and keep an eye on things outside.

DC Wyatt called.

"It's good news." She told him that the missing Clyde cartel man had been identified as Rory Dalziel.

"So, it's not Gallagher after all," Mac said. "Do they think this guy might have some connection to our murders?"

"Well, Glasgow PIT will be interviewing him about that shortly. Do you think we need someone in on it?"

"Yes," Mac said, "and I think it should be you."

She'd hoped for, but not expected, such a response.

"Thanks, boss. I'll shoot across there now and keep you posted. The other piece of good news is that – thanks to Mrs McGrath – I now have a journal kept by Dieter Hofmann. I'm sure it'll be useful but as it's written in German, I can't make head nor tail of it."

"Well, I'm sure my schoolboy German won't be up to it! Have a word with Carla up at Corstorphine and ask her to arrange for a translator to be sent to the Warehouse. Leave the journal with admin."

Mac took a few moments to digest the two new developments and tried to keep his newfound feelgood factor under control.

But Joker One's call only enhanced the feeling.

"The boy who floored you!" he said with a chuckle. "Just for you, I did the necessary in record time. Don't forget that."

"And what?" Mac asked, trying to ignore the SOCO's smugness.

"Although there were no traces left by Robbie in the Skoda, we identified the DNA sample we already had from the Renault as his. He'd been snacking in there and left the remains tucked under the seat. And his dabs were also in the vacant unit, but that's not surprising given he took the Beamer there."

Had he not been at the other end of a phone, Mac would have kissed Joker One.

"There's more. Three other sets in the unit, Hofmann's, McGrath's and… you'll be pleased with this one… the feller who's just been brought in, Gallagher. Looks like him and Robbie were up to no good in there."

So, the vacant industrial unit must have effectively been their murder HQ. Mac got little chance to take in the full significance of all this, because just at that moment he got the signal to go into Ailsa's room. She seemed to be putting a brave face on things. Had she seen the driver of the vehicle that knocked her over? No… and the car had driven off immediately. That being the case, he saw no point in raising his suspicions about the fake detective's involvement in the accident just yet. Better to make an assumption it was him and act accordingly. He'd arrange for the armed presence at the hospital to be retained, for enquiries to be made at the scene of the 'accident' and for someone to interview Ailsa later on.

Back out in the corridor, Fiona told him she and Law intended to stay in the city for a night, hoping that her sister would be well enough to travel with them the following day, to an undisclosed location. Mac offered to provide a safe place for her and Law to stay but they declined. They already had somewhere lined up. Were they absolutely sure? Yes, it was better that nobody else, not even the police, knew where it was. They did however agree to Mac's suggestion that a plain-clothes officer in an unmarked car should escort them, discreetly, for the first three miles of their journey, just to check they weren't being followed from the hospital.

Mac phoned Euan to ask him to tail Law's Jaguar.

"I agreed you'd follow them for the first three miles, but you might want to go a bit further than that. Maeven has authorised armed support in two unmarked vehicles as backup. Can you sort out a plan with them? Meantime I'm going to have a word with Fiona. I'll let you know when she and Law are due to leave the hospital."

The ward sister managed to find them a vacant room for their discussion. Fiona was initially very reticent, but Mac gradually managed to coax her into telling him what she knew.

"Given what's happened to both Dieter and Maxine, I find all this very difficult," she said. "It started when my cottage was broken into. Foolishly I'd kept a hard copy of part of Dieter's article in the place and of course that disappeared. I left the cottage right after that. It was obvious they'd be after me next. Cameron found me somewhere to stay in the north-east of England."

Had the break-in been carried out by the fake detective, Mac wondered? He recalled Fiona's taciturn neighbour saying something about a visit from a second detective – in addition to the Prestonpans DC. Perhaps that had been the fake detective, hoping to pick up useful information about Fiona.

"And what about Dieter and Maxine's article?" he asked.

"They each worked on separate parts of it. I was responsible for the third part and overall editing. For security reasons, we wanted to leave the assembly of the complete article until the last moment – just prior to publication. They were due to send me their sections at the end of last month, but I never received them. I've tried to pull something together from what I already have, but there are too many vital gaps. It's so very disappointing that their story won't be told."

"Unfortunately, the killers took their laptops and phones," Mac said, "which would have been the reason why Dieter and Maxine were unable to forward anything to you. We've only just managed to get hold of their devices, but all the important information has already been wiped. I need to ask whether you have any idea who might be responsible for their deaths? We now have two suspects in custody, but so far we've been unable to get much out of them."

"We think it's likely that the prime movers were Ultimate Intelligence," Fiona said. "The trouble is we've no solid evidence of that and – even for them – it seems an extreme step to take. But Professor Laing clearly knows an awful lot about what went on so it might be worth focusing your enquiries on him."

"Interesting!" Mac said. "You're not the first person to have told me that. One other thing I need to raise. Presumably you know about Blue Star."

"Sure. They were brought on board by IntelOper to develop the software which will control the deployment of the new generation of laser weapons."

"Did you know they're totally owned by UI?"

"You're joking!"

"Unfortunately not. But there's more. I've been told about a rumour that they're secretly developing a 'back door' in their software system, that will enable laser weapons to be fully controlled by artificial intelligence. You'll know more about this than I do, but I understand that the United Nations, amongst others, are very much against such systems, believing that there should always be human input into the process. Have you picked up anything about this?"

"No, I haven't, but it doesn't surprise me and, if true, would be very, very worrying," Fiona said. "The problem is this area of development – *killer robots* as the press calls them – is riddled with claims and counterclaims. But it occurs to me that if Dieter got to know about this… it might explain why he ended up dead!"

"I share that concern."

"Look, if I find out anything that might help to substantiate this rumour, I'll let you know."

Mac thanked Fiona for her help. She met up with Law and they returned briefly to Ailsa's bedside.

Having told Euan to stand by, as the couple would be leaving the hospital shortly, Mac phoned the local Weapons Watch convenor. She continued to be surprisingly cooperative and agreed to his request to set up a video meeting involving herself, himself posing as a keen new member of the group – and Mallory, the Oversight undercover officer.

He had a feeling that her continuing cooperation stemmed from the fact that she had as much to gain from the exercise as he did.

+ + +

Thomas Rook was pleased with the success of his plan to use Ailsa MacMahon as bait to flush out the sister.

Posing as a detective again, he'd spoken to her neighbours and found out that Ailsa was temporarily away from home. It was helpful that people were so trusting and gullible. As he'd hoped, one of them had CCTV cameras. It was clear from his conversation with the neighbour that the man used them as much for spying on others as protecting his own property, justified, naturally, by his prominent role in the local neighbourhood watch. The cameras had picked up on a male visitor who'd recently started visiting Miss MacMahon's property and had stayed late on more than one occasion. The film quality was good enough to be able to pick out the registration number of the visitor's car.

That was all Rook needed. A contact of his, with access to the right kind of database, had provided him with the address of the car's registered owner. On checking the property, he'd found that Ailsa was now living there and spent some time observing her movements. It hadn't been difficult to find the right moment. Following her in the car as she walked on her own towards the local shops, he'd mounted the pavement, and inflicted a glancing blow. At well below 20mph, there'd been no danger of killing her. After all, he wasn't being paid for that.

Following the incident, he'd phoned Law, using the number Ailsa MacMahon had so conveniently given him and, posing as a helpful neighbour, had passed on the news of Ailsa's accident and her subsequent ambulance journey.

Parked near the hospital entrance, he'd watched the couple arrive. Fiona, who he recognised from a photograph in her cottage and a man he presumed was Law, flanked by another man, too obviously a real detective. It gave him something of a thrill that after all his recent problems, she was now within reach. He considered calling Toner to shout down the phone that he should have shown a bit more loyalty. But maybe it was better to wait until the job was completed so he'd be able to tell Toner what he really thought of him.

An hour later, the couple emerged from the hospital and he followed their car out onto the main road.

+ + +

There'd been some delay in pulling the heavy squad together but they were now ready to pick up Robbie Toner for a second time, from his father's house. Mac, who was being driven out to Charlestown by DS Khan, kept his fingers crossed that the young man had not already high-tailed it.

The black vehicle convoy of armed officers, Khan's Mazda bringing up the rear, swept up the drive of the expensive, architecturally-designed palace of glass and blocked off the exit route for either the new Mercedes or the 750 Nighthawk that stood on the forecourt. Robbie's BMW was, of course, still in custody.

Having secured front, side and rear entrances to the house, the lead officer hammered on the front door. There were no dramatics. Craig Toner opened the front door, hands held high, grinning sardonically.

"What's he done now?"

Having introduced himself, Mac told him and the grin turned instantly to a look of incredulity.

"What are you doing fitting him up like this?"

Mac explained that they'd found Robbie's DNA in one of the suspect vehicles and his prints in a vacant industrial unit where two men, both now dead, had been held.

"At some point I think you're going to need a heart-to-heart with your son, Mr Toner."

Without another word, the father withdrew into the hallway, shouted for his son to get himself down the stairs and stood back to allow the armed officers to take up their positions. For a moment, as his son was led away, Toner looked a broken man.

The remaining officers searched the house to check whether anyone else was present. They found two occupants, Mrs Toner and a friend who provided caring support.

Mac told Craig Toner they needed a discussion. Where would be a convenient place to talk? They took seats around an enormous dining table, Khan to Mac's left, Toner sitting opposite.

"Do I need my lawyer?" Toner asked, his poise returned.

"Not at this stage," Mac replied. "We'd like to talk to you about your son and two other men. Sergeant Khan will take you through it. If at any stage you feel you want your solicitor present, please tell me. We can adjourn and reconvene at my place of work."

"Can I get coffees for us all?" Toner asked, as if his visitors were making a social call.

Mac said that would be good. Toner ordered their drinks by text.

Khan started things off. He and Mac had discussed their approach on the drive over. As they had no evidence of Craig Toner's involvement in the murder cases, they'd need to treat the visit as more of a fishing expedition. Given what they already knew about him and aware of the rumours about the dubious nature of some of his business activities, they felt it might be instructive to drop one or two names into the pool and watch how far the ripples went.

Discussion stopped as Mrs Toner brought in the drinks. Mac wondered whether the husband usually treated her in this way, ordering drinks by text and completely ignoring her presence in the room? She didn't look to be in need of caring support, he thought, but then maybe her condition wasn't immediately obvious. Once she'd left the room, the interview continued.

Toner knew nothing about his son's alleged involvement in the deaths of Dieter Hofmann and Alex McGrath. Any charges subsequently brought against him would be resolutely defended.

As for Gallagher, the name meant nothing to him.

His business was one hundred per cent legitimate and despite what they might have heard, the company was not involved in what they'd termed enforcement activity. As he'd made enemies over the years and there was jealousy over his success, it was no surprise that such accusations were put about.

Khan suddenly switched tack and asked if he knew anything about a now defunct group of Glasgow drug dealers that had been known as the Clyde cartel. Toner thought for a moment, before saying that as far as he could remember they'd tried – but failed – to take control of the drug trade in the city several years ago.

Did he remember anything about allegations of their involvement in a number of deaths where the victims had been tasered?

"Ah, let me stop you there. I can see where you're going with this, trying to link me in some way firstly to this group and secondly to the killings you're blaming Robbie for, just because tasers were used in both cases. It's not going to work. How many times do I need to tell you that I run a site security business not a criminal enterprise!"

"OK," Khan said. "What about a company called Ultimate Intelligence? Have you ever carried out work for them?"

"No. I've never heard of them, but with a name like that, they're probably not building contractors. And that's who I carry out work for. Look, I've been good enough to agree to talk to you," Toner said, getting to his feet, "but so far, you've come up with nothing that would warrant further questioning. And as you'll be aware, I do have a business to run. So, unless there's anything specific you want to raise…"

"As a matter of fact – there is," Mac said. "Please sit down for a few more minutes. We've been checking back in the records and your name cropped up in the Ross case some years ago, a death in suspicious circumstances. There was a fair bit of evidence linking you to that, but somehow, one by one, the key witnesses withdrew their testimonies. Maybe just coincidence… who knows? Would you like to comment on that?"

"I think you're really scraping the barrel now," Toner said, staring hard at Mac. "It's not unusual for cases to be dropped because of lack of evidence. Frequently that's because there is no evidence to find. What starts off as a police hunch, finishes as a police failure. Time to see you out, I think."

Mac pulled his phone out of a trouser pocket.

"Well, that was good timing. According to this text we now have Eamonn Gallagher in custody." Although he'd actually been picked up some hours earlier, Mac had been keen to paint a more immediately dramatic picture. "We'll see what he has to say about Robbie and who knows, he might even have something to say about you. You may be interested to know that we're also hot on the trail of a man who we think was involved in the death of Maxine Kilcline. A man who likes to pose as a detective. You wouldn't know his name by any chance?"

The only reaction from Toner was a shake of the head.

"And talking of Gallagher, you didn't know about Robbie teaming up with him, did you? It must be a big shock. Perhaps working for your site security business wasn't enough for the young lad and he wanted more excitement. Maybe you deliberately kept him away from the more contentious parts of your business empire – knowing that he lacked the right temperament? He certainly lost control when he attacked me!"

"He shouldn't have done that. I apologise."

Completely taken aback by Toner's unexpected words, Mac brought the discussion to an end. There was, as yet, no justification for bringing Toner in for further questioning. Mac was worried about the risk of flight, but maybe that would be unlikely for as long as his son was in custody.

As they left in Khan's vehicle, Mac saw Toner watching them from an upstairs window, phone to his ear. Who was he calling? His lawyer, perhaps, or maybe someone connected with the killings. That was wishful thinking though. Craig Toner had given nothing away. It was very possible that the father was not linked in any way to the son's activities. But Mac's bones told him otherwise.

+ + +

Driving along the dual carriageway, DI Forsyth kept one eye on Law's Jaguar, which was two cars ahead and the other on the rear-view mirror that showed the two unmarked police vehicles following at a distance, a pair of plain-clothes armed officers in each. Officially he was supposed to follow the Jaguar for no more than three miles, but his guess was that they wouldn't object to him tailing them a little further.

A mile further on, a blue Citroen caught his attention as it moved smoothly into a space immediately behind him. Without being too obvious, he managed to get sight of the driver through his mirror. The man looked very much like the fake detective's photofit. Euan called up the other two cars on his body-worn radio and told them about the Citroen.

He watched as they slotted in behind the blue car. In response to his order *positions*, the first of the unmarked cars pulled out to overtake the Citroen, then stayed alongside preventing it from pulling into the outside lane, while the second moved up right behind its bumper and Euan slowed gradually to a crawl. Boxed in, blues and twos suddenly flashing, the Citroen tried but failed to create a gap by ramming the car on its right to one side. The Citroen screeched to a halt.

The driver leapt from the vehicle brandishing a gun.

+ + +

The interview rooms were on the ground floor of the Warehouse. The windows on the external walls had opaque lower sections and clear upper panes which gave a view of little but the tops of a few trees and the sky.

In interview room 1, Gallagher, who'd been cautioned previously, sat on one side of the table, next to an empty chair. No need for a solicitor, he'd declared. Mac and Khan sat on the opposite side. A uniformed officer stood to one side of the doorway. Khan set the tape running and gave the date and time and the names of those involved in the interview.

Each question Mac asked was followed by a brusque *no comment*. He decided to change tack.

"Sergeant Khan has just had a very useful conversation with your assistant Robbie Toner. It's clear you're able to do a good imitation of a Trappist monk, but poor Robbie doesn't really have your level of experience, does he?" No response. "What puzzles us is why you took him on. He wasn't with you when you picked up Hofmann and McGrath, was he? What happened to the man who helped you drag them into the Transit?" No response. "Big mistake taking on Robbie though, wasn't it? Especially when he went completely off script and attacked me! It wasn't hard for us to find him after putting himself in the limelight like that."

Silence.

"Look, Mr Gallagher, as we've already explained, you'll be facing two charges of murder," Khan said, taking over. "We've told you what evidence we have against the pair of you. It's serious for Robbie, but he's only young, is pleading ignorance about most of what you were up to and is adamant he had nothing to do with the tasering or the speedball. Claims they were both down to you. His job was just to help dispose of the bodies. Was that the case?"

Silence. Khan continued.

"Things look bleak, unless you decide to do yourself a favour by telling us exactly what happened. And you could also let us know what Craig Toner's involvement has been in all this. Interestingly he denies any involvement in these deaths, or indeed any knowledge of you. Now that's only to be expected. But the danger from your point of view is that he'll continue with that line, we'll fail to get any evidence to implicate him and you'll be left standing on your own taking the full weight of two murder charges. So, perhaps you could start off by telling us how the set-up works."

"You've got nothing on me," Gallagher said. Mac felt it was a sign of progress – however small. Anything was an improvement on yet more silence.

"We'd be very interested to know who hired you to carry out this work," Mac said. "We've a suspicion it might be Toner. What do you say to that?" Silence. "We're wondering whether Robbie might have let anything slip about his dad. After all, you must have spent a fair bit of time together in the Renault and the Skoda."

"You must realise the boy's an idiot!"

"Would you like to tell us a bit more about that?"

Silence.

"If you weren't hired by Craig Toner, who were you working for?"

Despite their continued probing and goading, Gallagher refused to reveal anything. Mac felt that, as getting a confession from him would prove difficult, they'd either have to rely on Robbie breaking down or try and gather further evidence. And the time available for doing that was running out.

+ + +

Mac was in the middle of briefing Maeven when her phone rang.

"Forsyth," she mouthed to him, her face drawn, body tensed.

"Yes, I understand… so, is he dead? Christ… that's a relief. And our boy is OK? Thank goodness for that. Is this your first time? Right … so you may be better able to cope with it all. Could you please tell me the exact sequence of events?"

Mac watched as she scribbled down notes, brows knitted, intense concentration.

"I appreciate you might not be in the best state of mind just now, Inspector, but can you send an email confirming what you've just told me. You'll be aware that any discharge of a firearm triggers a full investigation, so it's best to get your thoughts in order while things are still fresh in your mind. I'll arrange for you to get appropriate psychological support. And well done, Euan. It sounds as if you handled a highly challenging situation very professionally."

She sat silently for a moment, looking drained, shoulders slumped.

"They've got the fake detective. His name's Thomas Rook. He pulled a gun and fired it at one of the armed response team, hitting him in the leg. Forsyth did what he's been trained to do and removed the threat by shooting Rook in the arm, causing him to drop his weapon. Both injured men have been taken to hospital, but hopefully it won't be long before you can start interviewing Rook. So, we've now got three suspects. And Fiona MacMahon is safe."

"Well, that's such a relief," Mac said. "I'm really sorry to hear about the injury to one of our officers. Is it bad?"

"No, just a flesh wound, thank goodness. You might want to speak to your pal though. It sounds like he could do with some peer support. Are you off to see the professor now?"

"A couple of things to do first, then I'll be across to the university and after that it'll be down to the hospital to try and get an audience with the injured Mr Rook."

"Good. Look, before you go, I need to tell you the chief's been on the warpath again. And he won't like the news about the shootings! Bad publicity. Although he knows you have my full confidence, I'm not sure now how long he'll hold off before bringing Yates in."

Mac made a detour to the dockside kiosk, to stock up on unhealthy food. Breakfast had been hours ago. Back at his desk, he ate quickly – far too quickly. The chief was a pain in the backside. Mac sensed they were close to a final breakthrough. The last thing the case needed was a change in management!

The thought of making a surprise evening trip to the Fife coast popped into his head and a text was on its way to Freya before he could change his mind.

Euan was pleased to get Mac's call and seemed OK, saying it was such a relief both that the bullet he'd fired had hit its intended target – Rook's arm – and that his colleague's injury was only minor. When Mac told him to go home, he didn't argue. The only thing Euan really wanted to do was to grill Rook, but was well aware that Maeven wouldn't allow him anywhere near the suspect. On hearing about the chief super being on the warpath, he said it was no surprise.

"I've had problems with him as well. We'll just have to crack on and hope we get to the finishing line before his patience runs out."

It was time for Mac's video meeting with the unsuspecting Mallory and the Weapons Watch convenor. He found an empty room and locked the door. The last thing he wanted was someone bursting in with *a message for you, Inspector*. After checking that the background for the call was set to blank, he thought himself into his temporary role as a weapons control activist, activated the recording mechanism and clicked on the link. With the convenor oiling the wheels, the conversation went well and Mallory agreed to meet up in person with him to pursue some of the issues raised.

"Seven thirty tomorrow suit you? I'm an early morning man," Mallory said. They agreed the time and a location.

There was something about Mallory's voice, a slight lisp, that reminded Mac of another he'd heard recently. But the memory was elusive. And he was well aware that virtual conversations often suffered from distortion.

Wyatt called as Mac was driving over to the university.

"I'm nearly back in Edinburgh. The interview was shorter than we thought! Dalziel was sullen, stroppy and once his solicitor arrived, completely silent. But the trip wasn't a complete waste of time. The Glasgow DI confirmed Dalziel's involvement in a range of enforcement activities, not only in the city, but across the central belt. So, there could be a link to the Hofmann and McGrath cases. They've got grounds to hold him, but only for a further twenty-four hours."

"And they'll keep us informed of any relevant developments?" Mac asked.

"Absolutely."

"Good. Meet me in Laing's office. I'm on my way there now. Have you had a chance to look at the translation of the first part of Dieter's journal?" She had. "Excellent. Let's talk now about how we're going to play it with Laing."

Once the call was finished, Mac continued to think about the professor. At the end of their previous discussion, he'd felt the man had little more to reveal and that they'd have to focus instead on Ultimate Intelligence. Now it was apparent from the first part of the translated journal that Laing had been a much more active player in the whole Hofmann story. His underlying character was clearly very different from the persona he presented publicly.

+ + +

In interview room 2, Robbie Toner again ignored his lawyer's advice and started to talk.

"Look, me and Eamonn Gallagher used to work together in Dad's security company, until he went freelance a year or so back." So Craig Toner was lying when he denied knowing Gallagher, Khan thought. "Gally calls me up. The guy who'd been working for him went down with the fucking virus, and he needed a replacement that day. Gally already knew I wanted to get into his line of work. I mean the site security stuff's OK, but boring as hell. I jumped at the chance. The job sounded straightforward, two guys, both lightweights, with information they shouldn't have had. All we had to do was track them down, apply some pressure, find out what they knew and get hold of their laptops and phones. Gally found them OK but then they didn't want to talk."

"What did you do to persuade them?" Khan asked.

"That's when the problems started. Gally's alright, but talk about a short fuse! I could see he was losing it when all we needed was a bit of patience. Basically, those guys were soft as shite and would've talked soon enough. But Gally doesn't do patience. Suddenly pulls out this taser and fires it at the German guy – full on at his chest. Next second, he's down on the floor and turns this weird colour. His breathing goes to pot and then just stops. I almost threw up. The job hadn't been about killing anyone."

"Did you know Gallagher had a taser?"

"No way! Our job was to get them to talk and... yeah, if

it came to breaking a few bones, we'd have done it. But using a weapon like that on them? Absolutely not."

"And what about Alex McGrath? What part did you play in his death?"

"With the German already dead, there was no way Gally was going to keep the other one alive. I mean he'd seen everything. He was only useful to tell us where their gear was – the computers and mobiles. Once we'd got that information out of him, Gally had no more use for McGrath. He fired the taser again and followed up with the speedball thing. When I tried to bail out, he turned proper nasty, said I was in it up to my neck and had to stay on board until the job was finished."

"So, you confirm your involvement in getting rid of the bodies?"

"Yes – but only under... what do you call it?"

"Duress?"

"Exactly."

"But you're telling me you had no involvement in the actual killings?"

"That's right. I was just gobsmacked by it all. After the taser business, I just did as I was told. That night, we left McGrath in the unit, under the influence of the speedball. We drove in the Renault out to the spoil heap at Tarbrax. Gally said we had to make Hofmann look like he'd been the victim of some sort of ritual drug-related killing, you know, with his shirt and jacket open so that the taser marks were obvious and in some dramatic location like one of the bings. He went on and on about bings – seemed obsessed with them. After dumping the body, we abandoned the van somewhere in Haymarket. Don't ask me where! I was out of it by then."

"And what about McGrath?" Khan asked.

"The following morning, we went back to the unit. He was still alive but looked fucking dreadful. He pegged out that afternoon. Gally said we had to wait until early the next morning to get rid of the body. We put it into the Skoda, which Gally had nicked, drove to Cockenzie and left McGrath on the beach. Same drill with the open shirt. Gallagher told me he'd chosen that beach because he'd happy memories of the place as a kid. He's more than a bit weird."

"How come both bodies were left in places where they'd be found quickly?"

"Well, they were meant to be warnings. From what Gally said, this guy from Falkirk wanted it done because Hofmann and McGrath had been muscling in on *his* dealing scene."

"Really? They'd been into dealing in a big way then?"

"So I was told."

"And that's why they were killed?"

"Yes."

"And who was paying Gallagher?"

"The guy from Falkirk."

"And how do you feel about it all now?"

"I've been a fucking naive idiot. If it was possible to turn back the clock, I'd do it in a flash."

"One last question for the time being," Khan said, taking out the pin before lobbing the grenade. "What's your dad's role been in all this?"

The remorseful facade crumbled instantly. Robbie Toner bristled and his face flushed.

"What the fuck do you mean by that?"

"Well, it's hard to believe, what with your involvement and Gallagher being an ex-employee of his, that your dad didn't at least know what was going on."

As Robbie jumped to his feet and lunged across the table towards Khan, the officer on guard leapt to intercept him. The young man slumped back into his seat.

Despite this outburst, Khan could imagine Robbie Toner's

defence working and that a good advocate – which he'd be sure to get – would be able to sway a jury. Young, naive, suggestible – and so remorseful!

But at least Robbie had given them plenty to throw at Gallagher.

+ + +

They'd agreed a plan. Wyatt would start by requestioning Laing about everything he'd already told them and then follow this up with some new questions based on information recently received. The professor seemed untroubled by the need to repeat the information he'd provided previously. Stretched back in his seat, he continued to exude confidence.

Mac thought Wyatt responded with equal confidence, calm and firm as she reeled off her questions. Having finished the recap, she started on the new queries.

"Do you regret not taking Dieter Hofmann's concerns more seriously?"

"I regret very much what happened to Dieter. It was dreadful – but had nothing to do with his work for us. And you need to understand that a lot of his claims were inaccurate and, in some cases… totally fabricated. I learned to treat much of what he said with a great degree of scepticism. The project stakeholders wouldn't have thanked me for muddying the waters by pursuing baseless claims."

"And would Ultimate Intelligence be one of the stakeholders?" Mac asked.

"Yes, both as advisors and funders."

"But UI's involvement goes much further than money and advice," Wyatt said. "Blue Star is *their* company, although they go to great lengths to obscure the paper trail that links the two. And as you've already stated, they were appointed as developers of the new software system, without the need to go through any competitive process. Supposedly this was because they were the only contractors with the capability and capacity to carry out this work."

"There's no *supposedly* about it. It's a fact! I really don't see where any of this is getting us!"

"Ah, but is it a fact? We have an email from Bernie Schroeder, stating that two other potential firms were identified, but were never invited to submit a tender."

"Schroeder's even more of a fantasist than Hofmann." Laing almost spat the words out. Mac felt that, for the first time, their questioning was beginning to get to the professor. "I'm sorry. That came out more strongly than I intended. But Schroeder is something of a militant, a member of a group of so-called radical scientists who constantly harass those involved in the development of legitimate defence systems. What he claims in relation to the tender for the new software is simply incorrect. The two firms you referred to were disqualified from tendering because they failed to meet our requirements. And this was reported at the time."

"We're aware of that," Wyatt said. "We have a copy of the tender report, which confirms what you've just told us." Laing looked puzzled.

"I don't follow you, Detective Constable. If that's the case, why are you giving Hofmann's claims any credence?"

"Because we also have a copy of this document," Wyatt responded. "It provides information about the two disqualified firms, that differs from the details included in the official tender report. Both of them met the necessary tender conditions. Here, have a look."

Laing took the document. As he read through it, his face hardened. Mac exchanged a brief conspiratorial look with his DC.

"Where did you get this?" Laing asked.

"Your pro-vice-chancellor for research and development gave it to us. Although we had to tell him where to find it," Mac said.

"And how on earth did you find out about this fabrication?"

"Dieter referred to the document in his journal… and gave details of where a copy could be located on the Midlothian system. I understand it was very well hidden."

Laing's composure finally deserted him. But only for a moment.

"So, he kept a record of his false claims and imaginings. I can't say I'm surprised."

"You called it a fabrication," Wyatt said. "We don't think it is, but more importantly, nor does the pro-vice-chancellor."

Laing was momentarily lost for words.

"Look, I'm sure there's a simple explanation to all this. Wires have got crossed somewhere. I can assure you that the tender arrangements were signed off by the relevant committee. And surely you need to be focusing on the bigger picture here. You see, Hofmann wasn't what he seemed on the surface. I strongly suspect that he only took on the IntelOper role with us in order to sabotage the project. Like Schroeder, he was involved with the Radical Scientists group, which has a strong antipathy towards large multinational companies such as UI."

"Did you know he was also involved with a local activist group called Weapons Watch?" Mac asked.

"No, I didn't, but it fits in with his general approach. Right from the start, his aim was to undermine the development and, as you are well aware, to leak information, including classified details, to the media. Whether all the official pieces of paper relating to the project were in the right place at the right time is really a trivial matter in comparison to what Hofmann was up to!"

"That's a very interesting perspective, Professor," Mac said, "although I don't think it would be one your pro-vice-chancellor shares. And it's not just doctored tender information that's a problem here. There's also the question of whether UI effectively 'bought' the tender for Blue Star, with their financial injection into the project, which as you've said yourself, wasn't substantial."

Laing, his self-confidence resurfaced, smiled sardonically.

"You really have taken the Hofmann propaganda on board! Blue Star was uniquely qualified to carry out this work and, unlike the other two companies, was able to start work on the contract immediately."

"Let's move on, shall we?" Wyatt said. "The embezzlement. Are you confident that all the information used to prove Hofmann's guilt was accurate?"

"Naturally. We wouldn't have used such information if there'd been any question about its accuracy. Why do you ask?"

"Because we arranged with the pro-vice-chancellor for our forensic finance team to examine the paperwork and to talk to the staff who prepared the information for the disciplinary hearing." Mac noticed small beads of sweat on Laing's forehead. "Our team found, based on that information, that the claims against Hofmann could not be substantiated."

"But..." For the first time, Laing seemed lost for words. "I would need to examine their report in detail."

"The pro-vice-chancellor has already done that and he found no fault with the findings of our team. It looks to us as if the embezzlement charges were fabricated in order to provide a convenient way of being able to dismiss Hofmann. Sure, his drug use might have been a way of doing that, but there was considerable evidence that it had been known about for a while without any action being taken."

Laing didn't respond.

"One final question," Mac said. "I'm afraid it's about an even more serious matter. Hofmann's journal refers to threats of physical violence. Made by you, Professor. Would you like to comment on that?"

"As I've already emphasised," Laing said, stuttering in his response, "this kind of accusation is trademark Hofmann. There's no way you can substantiate this."

"Not yet. But other claims made in his journal are turning out to be surprisingly accurate. Maybe it's just a question of time before we're able to obtain proof. Regardless, we'd like you to come with us for further questioning," Mac said. "And we'll speak to the pro-vice-chancellor in order to clarify any inconsistencies between his views on these matters and yours. To be clear, although you are not so far under arrest, I'd like you to give us your phone and laptop. Do you have any objections to that?"

Without a word Laing handed the devices over to Wyatt.

+ + +

Back at the Warehouse, coffee mug in hand and with fifteen minutes to go before he was due to restart interviewing Laing, Mac suddenly remembered where he'd heard Mallory's voice before. That slight lisp. It was the anonymous caller who'd told him about the Clyde cartel!

There was just enough time before the Laing interview restarted for him to find the recording of that call on his phone, retrieve the recording he'd made of the video meet-up with Mallory and forward both to the forensic voice service for comparison.

+ + +

It would take about an hour to drive from the city to Anstruther.

Mac's head was buzzing. After the frenetic action of the day, it was impossible to switch off. Having made good progress with Robbie Toner, Khan had used his statement to start trying to open up Gallagher. The suspect's endless response of 'no comment' had gradually been punctuated, initially with a few one-sentence responses and later with a series of counter accusations against Toner, *a vicious little thug who completely lost his head when he attacked Larsen.*

The hope was that a night in the cells and the positive news that his son had been released from custody, might encourage Gallagher to say more.

Traffic on the Forth Bridge was light. Mac was making good time.

The call to the university pro-vice-chancellor had not gone well for Laing. An internal enquiry would be set up to investigate the professor's recent actions, in particular the withholding of crucial information regarding other potential tenderers, forged approvals of relevant documentation and the engineering of Hofmann's dismissal on the grounds of embezzlement. Mac would be pursuing the relevant criminal charges.

Despite the reference to physical threats in Hofmann's journal, Laing was sticking resolutely to a line that he'd had no involvement in any such thing.

Mac had visited the hospital and spoken briefly to Rook, who was under police guard and claiming that the effects of the painkillers were making it impossible for him to think straight. Mac had been advised by the medical staff to return in the morning.

The news about the former Clyde cartel man, Dalziel, was intriguing. Had he been involved in the two recent 'taser' deaths? Did he have a link with Gallagher... or Rook? It was hugely frustrating that he could only be held for one more day and that his solicitor was advising him to keep his trap firmly shut. But that was no surprise.

At the sound of an incoming text, Mac pulled onto the verge to check. It was from his mother. Could he call in to see her sometime tomorrow? Whatever it was about, he'd have to somehow make time available.

Before he could restart his journey, Angus phoned to give his end-of-day report. The retired DI had jumped at the chance to carry out some unofficial observation of Craig Toner and had been doing alternate watches on the security boss' house with an old mate, another ex-copper. Angus had relished being back on observation duty, a flask of coffee and a plastic box of his wife's sandwiches on the passenger seat. As so often the case with any watching brief, things had been quiet. The only action of any interest had been the appearance, early in the afternoon, of a Range Rover which had pulled up on Toner's driveway. Angus had binoculars and camera at the ready. A casually-dressed man, forty-ish, had emerged from the car. Toner had answered the door and greeted his visitor as someone he knew. A good snap of the two of them together on the doorstep, as the driver turned to activate the car's locking mechanism with his key.

The binoculars had given Angus a clear view of the two men in the living room. Both had looked concerned from the off and after a brief, heated discussion, the visitor had left hurriedly.

Angus said he'd just forwarded a copy of the photograph.

Still parked up on the roadside verge, Mac checked his emails and opened the photo attachment. He recognised Toner, of course, but was amazed to find he also recognised his visitor.

Professor Martin Laing!

Ten minutes later, the soft light from the living room window welcomed him to Freya's tiny cottage. She kissed him and said how good it made her feel that, despite being up to his neck with work, he'd taken the time to come and see her. After a quick cup of tea, he set off on a pre-dinner run along the front to the harbour, where he stopped to phone Maeven and left a message about Laing's visit to Toner's house.

There was an earlier text from her. The chief superintendent had given him forty-eight hours to have the relevant charges in place. Otherwise, he'd be effectively demoted. There was no point wasting time thinking about it.

Looping along side streets back to the cottage, he tried to let all thoughts about work drain away.

Dinner was *fiskesuppe*, a warming stew with three types of fish – whatever had been left over in the fridge, Freya said – and a mix of vegetables served from a seemingly bottomless pan. When she asked him about the case, he told her the work part of his mind had been temporarily closed off and asked whether there'd been any progress on her hunt for a studio. The one in Dean Village was definitely too expensive, she said, but the Haymarket option looked quite promising.

There might be an alternative, he told her. The roof space above his flat, already floored out, had plenty of room and if they put in some roof-lights and enlarged the access it could be just the job. Freya was very interested in the idea. Part of her liked the thought of going out to a studio, walking there, using the time to think painterly thoughts. But with the baby, it would make an awful lot of sense to have a workspace in the flat.

Curled up together on the sofa, Bugge Wesseltoft's *Yellow is the Colour* on the stereo, glasses of Pinot Noir close to hand, they rambled on about the past and the future.

"And are you sure you'll be OK living in the big city?" he asked. "It'll be quite a change for you."

"I'm coming round to the idea, especially if there's a chance of having an artist's garret in your attic. If I need to see the sea, it'll only be a matter of me and the little one in the pushchair following The Water down to Leith and getting a lift back home from a detective I know down there," she said, a cheeky glimmer in her eyes.

"That sounds good, apart from the fact he can't be relied

upon to finish work on time." A knowing smile. "And that might get worse if he got the new job."

"Ah! Have you decided whether to apply for it?"

"No… I'm still mulling it over."

She asked him all the questions he should already have asked himself. Perhaps the clincher was how would he feel the day after the closing date if he hadn't submitted an application. Not good, he thought.

Her latest painting was on the easel. Normally she didn't like him looking at unfinished work, but this time felt more relaxed. A dusk view of a tumbledown shack just above the shoreline, old wooden crates piled against a leaning gable, a big sea beyond, something slightly worrying about the scene. He loved it.

He kissed her. They finished off the wine bottle and tumbled into bed – *don't forget your alarm* her final words before they wrapped around each other.

12 MARCH

Rising extra early, Mac beat the traffic over the Forth Bridge and arrived in Leith in good time for his seven thirty appointment with Mallory. There was no need for him to dress down for the 'undercover' meeting. He dressed down most days.

The venue was a bench near the lighthouse at the other end of the docks from the Warehouse.

Mac arrived armed with two coffees. His plan had been to find out how much Mallory would reveal about Ultimate Intelligence. But following receipt of an early-morning text from the forensic voice service, he'd decided that the subject of UI could wait.

After a brief chat about the weather, Mac launched off.

"What about the old Clyde drugs cartel? Do you reckon one of them might have had something to do with Dieter Hofmann's death?" Mallory looked completely thrown.

"I don't really know anything about them," he said, "apart from what's been in the media."

"That's not what you told me before," Mac said.

"I'm sorry, you've completely lost me. We've never had a conversation about this."

"Ah, but we have!" Mac said. Taking his phone from a pocket. He started to play a recording and simultaneously waved a hand in the air.

As he heard his own voice talking about the former cartel, Mallory turned to face Mac.

"What the hell is this? Who are you?" He stood up, but two hands placed firmly on his shoulders from behind pushed him back down onto the bench. Urquhart, who'd been alerted by Mac's hand signal, took his place next to Mallory, effectively hemming him in.

"Let's go through the whole story, shall we?" Mac said. "We already have some very useful information about you in a journal kept by Dieter Hofmann." Mallory's whole body seemed to shrink.

"And I know enough already to be able to tell you that your career with us is over," Urquhart added. "Beyond that, it's a question of what criminal charges you might face. But if you're able to assist Inspector Larsen with his enquiries that would be taken into account."

The interview took place back at the Warehouse.

Afterwards, when Urquhart thanked Mac for his cooperation, it sounded heartfelt.

As Mac climbed the stairs up to the boss' office, his phone rang. A man called Ash. He had some information about Thomas Rook.

+ + +

Mac hadn't expected to see Euan in Maeven's office. It turned out that he'd managed to persuade the boss that half a day out of action was more than enough for him. They discussed the news about Laing's meeting with Craig Toner. Maeven didn't ask Mac how he'd got hold of the photograph of the pair of them and he didn't volunteer the information. As it wouldn't be used as evidence, it didn't matter. They'd wait until after the next interview session with Laing before bringing Craig Toner in for questioning. Hopefully that session would provide additional detail to assist in interrogating Toner.

Mac updated them about Rory Dalziel and said he was expecting further information from Glasgow, later that morning.

Then he told them about Mallory.

"I'm pleased to be able to report on some effective joint working between ourselves and Oversight Scotland," he said, with a wry smile. "Urquhart and I interviewed Mallory just now. We have some very useful evidence from him and, in addition, corroboration of some of the detail in Hofmann's journal. As we suspected, in his undercover role, Mallory passed information he'd gathered about the activities of Hofmann and Kilcline directly to Ultimate Intelligence – in return for substantial backhanders. When UI judged matters had reached a critical stage, they ordered Mallory to entice Maxine Kilcline to the vacant office building, with the prospect of some juicy inside information about UI. He claimed that once the fateful meeting became an interrogation, he was told to leave and therefore knows nothing about what happened subsequently."

"Did he say who else was there?" Maeven asked.

"Yes. Laing – who he already knew – and another man he'd not seen before. When I waved a photo of Thomas Rook under his nose, he confirmed it was him."

"That's excellent news," Maeven said. "And it's come just in time. The chief super told me to remind you of his forty-eight-hour deadline – which is now more like thirty-six hours. And, as you can see, despite the arrests we have made, this morning's papers are as critical as ever about our perceived lack of progress." Mac glanced at the headlines of the two papers on her desk. "So, how close are we to having the necessary charges in place?"

"We're pretty confident of being able to nail Robbie Toner," Mac said, "and with a lot of effort, Gallagher could go the same way. Euan?"

"Yes – there's already sufficient evidence to charge Rook with impersonating a police officer, causing serious injury by dangerous driving – in the attack on Ailsa MacMahon – and the attempted murder of a police officer. And given the new evidence you mentioned from Mallory, we can now place Rook in the same room as Maxine Kilcline, which is a good start in the process of linking him to her death. I'm expecting more information shortly, which hopefully will tie him in further."

"What about Craig Toner?" Maeven asked.

"Well, his involvement is still speculation at the moment," Mac said. "But the link between him and Laing is very interesting. I look forward to quizzing him about that. But, even if we are able to establish a connection between him and the case, he'll be a difficult nut to crack. I'm sure he will have insulated himself from what happened on the ground. Mallory claims to have no knowledge of him. But my gut feeling is that Craig Toner is involved."

"OK. I'll tell the chief. Let's hope that's enough to keep him happy, at least for today! And I'll prepare a media release, to try and get a more balanced response from them. Anything else?"

"Yes," Mac said. "Hofmann's journal. The translator completed the first half of the document yesterday and DC Wyatt and I used it to good effect interviewing Laing soon afterwards. Now the second half is finished. She must have been up half the night working on it! There's confirmation that Dieter *did* find out that Blue Star is secretly developing a back door in their software to allow full AI control of the laser weapon system."

"That's real progress," Euan said.

"More than I expected. But as there's no reference to a technical analysis in the journal to support his claim, I've asked the pro-vice-chancellor at Midlothian whether one of his experts could come up with the necessary. We can hit Laing with the back-door news now, but I think we'd need that technical data before raising it with UI, or they'd just blow us out of the water."

"Excellent," Maeven said. "Fingers crossed that one of the Midlothian boffins can come up with the necessary details and then we can confront UI. Now, we'd better get to the briefing."

It was kept deliberately short because of the pressure of their interviewing schedule, and Mac was happy to leave most of the updating to Forsyth, Khan and Wyatt. When they'd finished, he added the important news about Laing and about Mallory. With key suspects now in custody, the mood of the meeting was one of optimism. Overall, good progress had been made. Mac didn't want to risk damaging this positive mood, but he threw in just enough cold water to keep them on their toes and Maeven from intervening, as she lurked in her usual seat at the back of the room.

+ + +

The plan for the first part of the morning was for Mac and a DC to visit the hospital to check whether Rook was in a fit state to be discharged and brought to the Warehouse for questioning; for Khan and Wyatt to try and break through Gallagher's continuing resistance and Robbie Toner's claims of innocence as far as the deaths were concerned; and for Forsyth to put pressure on Professor Laing.

Maeven would keep a watchful eye over all the proceedings.

At the hospital, they were informed that Rook was still in considerable pain. Allowed only five minutes questioning by the medics, Mac asked him about Maxine Kilcline. Could he tell them what had happened on 27 February?

No response.

"We spoke to a man called Ash."

A spasm, but it could have been Rook in genuine pain.

"Doesn't do to double-cross a partner, Mr Rook. He sounded quite upset, even claimed you still haven't paid him for the last job – whatever that was. My guess is that it would have been the killing of Maxine and the disposal of her body. Am I right?"

No response.

"Anyway, he told us you were driving a Toyota pickup that evening. Was that the case?"

No response.

"You might be interested to know that it was *he* who phoned *us*. Must have thought that we wouldn't be able to trace him – you know, using a pay-as-you-go mobile and giving us just a nickname. But when we find him, he may well give us some more dirt."

"I haven't the slightest fucking idea who this man is. Now if you'll excuse me, I'd like to get the nurse back in here to sort this goddam pain out."

As the DC drove him back to the Warehouse, Mac thought about Mallory. Who had told him to make the anonymous phone call about the Clyde cartel? Someone who wanted to reinforce the message that the deaths of Hofmann and McGrath were about drug-related issues… not Hofmann's work-related issues? Laing possibly, but more likely somebody at Ultimate Intelligence.

+ + +

The two sisters grasped hands tightly. Cameron Law had gone down to the hospital cafe to get a late breakfast. Ailsa knew that being with Fiona at long last was helping her to cope with the pain from her injuries, with a little extra help from the injection the nurse had given her first thing. There was so much catching up she wanted to do.

Had the fake detective really been caught and were they both safe now? Yes, Fiona told her. He was under police guard in hospital – not this one, she added hastily – and would then be taken into custody. After that he'd be charged and would have no chance of getting bail.

"And, what about Cameron? Is he a bit more than just your solicitor?"

"Yes!" Fiona responded, blushing a little. "He's also my partner. Sorry for not telling you before."

"Well, sorry he and I didn't get off to a very good start," Ailsa said. "But he seems very nice. And where have you been hiding?"

"Don't breathe a word to anyone else, but I've been with Cameron in Newcastle, out of harm's way."

"Well, I need to tell you about Lewis. He was here last night."

Ailsa found that once she started talking about him, it was difficult to stop.

+ + +

Khan was trying to prise answers out of Gallagher in interview room 1. Next door, Wyatt was attempting to get beyond Robbie Toner's 'naive young man' defence. Periodically, the two officers would take time out to swap information, compare notes and check progress. Each was facing a range of responses from their interviewees with periods of sullen-teenager-style silence suddenly replaced by no-holds-barred rants about the accused in the next room.

The officers had the benefit of a new SOCO report on the empty industrial unit that Robbie Toner had led them to. Prints of both suspects and both victims had been found there, together with traces of Hofmann's and McGrath's DNA. Although it was apparent an attempt had been made to clean the place, the job had been nowhere near thorough enough.

Based on the SOCO evidence and the interviews to date, it was clear that the two victims had been taken in the Transit from Mrs McGrath's house to the unit, interrogated and eventually killed there. All the adjacent units were also empty – the whole row awaiting demolition – and the CCTV had not been operational. So, Gallagher and Toner had been able to carry out their gruesome work without being disturbed for the whole period, including the time it took for the speedball to have its effect on McGrath.

Although Gallagher was still refusing to answer questions, his slumped shoulders and sarcastic asides indicated that the double whammy of his prints being found in the industrial unit and information drip-fed to him about Robbie's constant accusations was beginning to take its toll.

Robbie Toner's solicitor consistently denied his client's culpability for the two deaths. Robbie had been completely out of his depth, had thought that the job consisted of inflicting one or two broken limbs at worst and had greatly assisted the police by providing evidence which could be used against Gallagher.

Both Khan and Wyatt felt it would be hard work to get beyond this defence.

+ + +

On his return from the hospital, Mac was surprised to find Forsyth and Maeven on their way up to her office. Why weren't they in interview room 5 with Laing?

"Got the prof's confession already?"

"You wish!" Maeven said. "We're just letting him have five minutes with his solicitor. He's admitted wanting rid of Hofmann, but only in the sense of getting him off the project and claims he had no part in what happened following his dismissal."

They reached Maeven's office.

"What do you think Laing's role has really been in all this?" she asked as they walked across the room to the meeting table.

"Sorry – would you mind if I just grabbed a coffee? Anybody else want one?" Mac asked. He needed time to think through his answer to the boss' question. Euan used the opportunity to take a toilet break.

"Never turns off, does she?" he said as they walked down the corridor together.

"Do any of us?" Mac replied, stopping in front of the drinks vending machine. "What do you reckon then? Were Hofmann and McGrath's deaths planned from the start or were they down to a cock-up, the unintended consequences of the taser strike on Dieter?"

"I think the jury's going to be out on that one for some time," Euan said, calling back down the corridor as he headed for the toilet. "And you could ask the same kind of question about Maxine's death. Did they know what the effects would be of depriving her of insulin?"

Feeding coins into the slot, Mac tried hard to concentrate on the job in hand. But thoughts about babies and artists' studios kept blocking out serious consideration of such things as the extent of Laing's control over events.

Carrying three over-flexible plastic cups back to the boss' office was not an easy task, but he managed it without spilling a drop. A shaft of sunlight penetrating a gap in the office blind lifted his spirits and it felt suddenly as if his mental clouds had also parted.

"Perhaps, initially, Laing was the string-puller," Mac said, "instrumental in getting UI to save the IntelOper project financially and involved directly in negotiating and agreeing the contract with Blue Star. But as soon as Ultimate Intelligence realised the extent of the threat posed by Hofmann, it's more than likely they'd have taken control. A powerful multi-national company versus a university professor out on a limb is an unfair contest. And perhaps the more Laing was sucked in, the more he had to do for them – including any necessary dirty work."

"You may well be right," Maeven said.

"The trouble is," Mac said, "he's a very hard man to read."

+ + +

Maeven sat in on the interview.

Laing duly surprised them. He wanted to cut a deal. Mac told him they didn't do deals. But if he had useful information, that could be taken into account further down the line.

The professor decided to talk.

It was no surprise to get confirmation that Laing had indeed personally engineered the initial involvement of Ultimate Intelligence in the project, got them to commit financially and facilitated Blue Star's appointment as the software development contractors – without going through a competitive tendering process. That had put him, initially, in a position of strength. But his knowledge of and responsibility for the missing information about other potential tenderers created a vulnerability which UI had been more than happy to exploit. Further down the line, realising the weakness of his position, he'd contemplated blowing the whistle on them, but already compromised, that would effectively have ended his career.

"So, you saw no way of escaping," Mac said

"That's right."

"Talk us through what happened after Hofmann's dismissal."

"Well, UI had already been pretty spooked by his open opposition. When they found out about his involvement with the local cell of Weapons Watch, that rang real alarm bells," Laing said.

"You told us before you didn't know about that," Mac said.

"I'm sorry. I must have got confused. Baxter told me about it."

"And how did he find out?"

"He was being fed information by Oversight's undercover man in Weapons Watch."

"So, you already knew about Mallory, but you didn't think to tell us," Euan said.

"Well, I'm telling you now."

"Were you aware that Hofmann was in contact with the Weapons Watch cell in UI's home town?" Mac asked. It was one of the little gems in Dieter's journal. "In fact he'd been about to fly out there."

"No! I had no idea," Laing said, banging his fist on the table in frustration. "But no doubt Baxter knew and that's the kind of thing that could have tipped them over the edge. UI are paranoid about compromising information being spread between their opponents in different parts of the world."

At last, Mac thought, Laing was starting to open up about UI.

"Given that level of paranoia," he said, "how did Baxter react when he found out about the tell-all article that Hofmann and Kilcline were finalising?"

"That's when the gloves came off. We had to find out exactly what they were up to, in order to limit the damage. Baxter decided to start with Kilcline who he saw as the weak link. Ironic, really. As I understand it, she turned out to be the toughest of the three."

"So, were you involved in her interrogation?"

"No. I refused to take part in any of the interrogations."

"Really! Didn't Baxter want you involved with Hofmann — given you'd probably had more to do with him than anyone else?"

"He did, but I refused."

"What about Alex McGrath?"

"I didn't come across him at all," Laing said. "Apparently he was caught in the net because he knew too much. Hofmann had told him everything."

"Are you certain about having no direct contact with Kilcline?" Euan asked.

"I've already told you that!"

"That's not what Mallory said," Euan said.

"What do you mean?"

"Well, he told us you were there when she was brought in, just before her interrogation started."

"You can't trust the word of a paid informant, surely!"

"We'll have to see whether we get any supporting evidence of your presence there... won't we? So why did Mallory get involved with UI?" Mac asked.

"Money. He didn't have the best of relationships with Oversight and UI offered him a lot of cash. It was him who told UI about MacMahon's role as the coordinator of the article and the route to publication. And that triggered UI's decision to go after her as well."

"You referred just now to *the gloves coming off*. Who was responsible for that?"

"Baxter. He talked about bringing in a contractor. That's when I made the decision to pull out – regardless of the consequences."

"And do you know who the contractor was?"

"Not sure, but I overheard Baxter mentioning an operator called Craig Toner."

Maeven signalled it was time for a break.

Back in her office, they were elated about now having sufficient justification for bringing Toner in for questioning. Maeven told them that she'd accompany the armed units to Toner's house, Mac would lead the first interview and Euan would continue with the interrogation of Laing.

Which meant Mac had time for a few tasks.

His first priority was a phone call to Angus, to tell him the watching was over and that it wouldn't be a good idea to be hanging around once armed officers swooped on Toner's place.

Next was the lure of a fishfinger sandwich from the dockside kiosk, almost as good as the Mermaid Cafe version and consumed in record time.

And finally, he had to respond to the message his mother had left the previous evening. He apologised for not calling in on her and explained about being away at Freya's house. It turned out she was worried about Erland, that he and his wife seemed to be going through another difficult patch. Mac said he hadn't picked up any such vibes and she managed a little laugh and said – *well, you wouldn't, would you?* Which was fair comment.

Friday evening's meet-up with his brother would give him a chance to do a little subtle probing, he told her, hoping that particular skill would be in his locker. Just as he was about to finish the call, she told him how worried she was about the virus. The prime minister had been giving a press conference on the TV, telling everyone that it was now a global pandemic and warning that the disease was particularly dangerous for older people. What should she do? How would she be able to get hold of food if the time came when people like her had to stay at home?

Mac did his best to reassure her that between them, he and Erland would be able to arrange online deliveries of food and medication, if they became necessary. It took a while to calm her down.

+ + +

On arrival at Craig Toner's house, Maeven told him about Laing's claim. That he'd been the contractor involved in putting the frighteners on Dieter Hofmann, Alex McGrath and Maxine Kilcline – actions which ultimately had led to their deaths.

They would need to question him about this. Toner was surprisingly cooperative.

Having checked that the carer would be able to stay on at the house, with his wife, he was as good as gold about accompanying the officers back to the Warehouse. There was no fuss about handing over his phone and two laptops, and only limited objections raised to their application for a warrant to search his security company's office. There was no problem with having his fingerprints taken. He even waived his right to have a solicitor present – for the time being.

In interview room 7, having gone through the preliminaries, Mac looked straight at Craig Toner.

"Let's start with an easy question. How do you know Professor Laing?"

"He's my brother-in-law."

Mac groaned inwardly and an awful sinking feeling swept over him. How could they have missed the connection? Any contact there'd been between the pair could be explained away as just family business. And as for Laing's claims about Toner? Well, they would be dismissed as the accusations of a desperate man.

He poured himself a glass of water, one for Toner and another for the DC in attendance. Buying a little time, hoping to counter that sinking feeling.

"Your wife's brother?" Toner nodded.

"We never got on. He doesn't approve of me, doesn't like the fact that I grew up on a council estate and now earn a damn sight more than he does. By the way, have you checked his bank account yet? You could do worse than ask him how he supplements his meagre salary as a university professor and how he can afford that splendid house of his without a little extra coming in from somewhere?"

Mac, struggling to keep on top of things, began to think he might have got it completely wrong and that Laing had been the real string-puller all along. Or was Toner very effectively pulling *his* strings?

"But Laing's accusation still stands. What's your response to it?"

"It's just his way of causing trouble. Does he have any evidence?"

"We're working on that," Mac said, knowing it was a feeble response. "Why would he make such a claim if there was no truth to it? After all – he's family."

"Which is exactly why he likes to stir things. He's never forgiven me for marrying his sister."

"So, were you the contractor?"

"As I've already told you, Inspector, my business is completely legitimate!"

"OK, let's focus on Eamonn Gallagher. According to your son, he used to work for you."

"That's correct."

"Really!" Mac said, pleased that some progress was being made. "You denied knowing him when we asked the same question at your house."

"That's because he's in the past as far as I'm concerned. I got rid of him once I found out about his drug connections. If he was involved with the deaths of the people you mention, that's his business and has absolutely nothing to do with me."

"And what about Robbie? Were you aware he was working with Gallagher and was involved in actions that led to those deaths?"

"Knowing my son, he wouldn't have been involved in any activity of that kind voluntarily." Toner placed his hands flat on the table. "Maybe he got carried away with the prospect of being able to throw his weight around – like with the attack on you. But take it from me, he's not a killer. Whereas Gallagher... he's certainly capable of it. Now, just to be clear, apart from Laing's accusations you don't have anything else against me – do you?"

Mac had to restrain himself. Toner certainly knew how to wind people up!

"First of all, I wouldn't be quite so quick to dismiss the statement your brother-in-law has made. And secondly, you'll be disappointed to hear that we do actually have other evidence against you. We'll come onto that, once I've spoken to Laing again. In the meantime, just let the DC know if you want to speak to a solicitor. Oh, I nearly forgot to mention. In case you're interested, we've arrested Thomas Rook."

Out in the corridor, Mac took a few deep breaths. It was important to keep level-headed. If Craig Toner had been involved, he'd have isolated himself from the action. The team wouldn't find his prints or DNA at any of the crime scenes, or in any of the vehicles. A SOCO would check – just in case – but it would be a fruitless task. Mac was doubtful whether either Gallagher or Rook would sell the boss – if that's what he turned out to be – down the river and there was no mention of Craig Toner in Hofmann's journal. It looked very much as if they'd be almost completely dependent on Laing's evidence and that didn't feel like a good position to be in.

Still, Mac did have one other piece of evidence up his sleeve.

He put his head round the door of interview room 5 and signalled to Euan that he needed a word. Leaning up against one wall of the narrow corridor, they had to squeeze in to let anyone else pass.

Mac told him about the family link between Laing and Toner.

"That's a complication we could have done without!" Euan said.

"And, according to Toner, they hate each other's guts, so we could be in for all sorts of mud-slinging which won't help either," Mac said. "How's it going with Laing?"

"I can't make my mind up about him," Euan said. "One minute I'm almost feeling sorry for him about the way he got dragged further and further into the mire and the next, I'm thinking what a manipulative bastard."

"Well, we really need something more from him that will allow us to keep Toner in the building."

"OK. Maybe I can help with that. Laing talked about a recording he has which contains compromising detail about Toner. Referred to it as his *get out of jail free card*. Asked if he could go and pick it up from his home."

"Why does *he* need to go?"

"Apparently it's in his safe and he's worried about security!"

"Maybe it's clutching at straws but we've nothing to lose," Mac said. "Do you want to go there with the escorting officers? The SOCOs should already be in the house, so you could get the latest from them while you're at it. In the meantime, I'll have to stall Toner."

Mac paid a visit to the vending machine for a bottle of water and a packet of crisps. Outside interview room 1, he caught Khan's attention through the door's glazed panel. The DS joined him in the corridor. The salty snack was shared.

"Any sign of Gallagher cracking under the strain yet?"

"Plenty of signs of him wanting to land one on Robbie – if only he could reach him next door! Can't fathom how he thought they'd ever be able to work together. But he's not cracking yet. Clearly fancies himself as a hard man. What is getting under his skin though, is me mentioning the Clyde cartel. I'm exploring the line that one of the ex-members might have been involved with him in the killings and he's not happy. And according to Laura's latest update, Robbie's leaving most of his responses to the solicitor who's selling the *poor little exploited boy* story for all it's worth."

"OK, thanks. I'll let you get back in there."

Mac didn't really want to return to his own interview. How long could he leave Craig Toner stewing, before the man demanded to be let out?

+ + +

While two escorting officers stood guard, Euan entered the house with Laing and wondered just how much professors were paid. Detached, in a leafy suburb, garden of at least an acre, complete with swimming pool. Perhaps his wife had money… or perhaps as Toner had indicated, Laing had a second income. They'd already set the wheels in motion to access his bank account, but Euan was tempted to try a shortcut to get the necessary information more quickly.

If Laing agreed to volunteer the information… there and then in the house… it would count in his favour.

The professor agreed. Surprisingly he had an old-school file full of paper statements. Euan scanned the detail. One monthly credit was clearly his university salary. But there was another substantial monthly payment into the account. He asked Laing about this, not expecting to get a clear answer.

"It's a retainer paid to me by Ultimate Intelligence for consultancy work I do for them directly – seminars for their staff on accelerated development modules. They pay well – but I earn it and to be honest, I deserve it. We academics are the ones who come up with all the original ideas, and what do we get for it? Exploited, that's what!"

Euan thought the response revealed Laing in his true colours. It was certainly an extraordinarily generous payment for giving a few seminars. Surely there had to be more to it than that.

"Let's retrieve that recording and we can get back to the Warehouse."

Euan and one of the escorting officers followed Laing up to the master bedroom, where he removed an attractive watercolour from its position at one side of the bed to reveal the wall safe. Why did someone like Laing need a safe, Euan wondered? After a few rapid twists of the dial, Laing opened the door, took out a manilla envelope and handed it to the inspector.

"Take care – it's the only copy there is."

While the professor was led back to the police vehicle, Euan took the opportunity to ask the SOCOs about progress searching the house. Limited so far, but they did have some information about Maxine Kilcline that he'd definitely be interested in.

+ + +

The tape began to play.

A phone call, Laing's voice to start with, then a woman's, a Western Isles accent, Mac thought. Very concerned, but very assertive.

"You should never have got involved with Craig on anything like this. You're totally out of your depth. I know I'm a fine one to talk – been out of my depth for years. If only you'd spoken to me first. With them involved, Lord knows what might happen to the German now! You need to get out, before it's too late. I beg you, Martin."

Mac's annoyance that they hadn't known sooner about the relationship, was outweighed by his relief that the recording would give them justification to hold Toner for a longer period.

"Your sister?" Euan asked. Laing nodded.

"It's a pity she doesn't actually name Ultimate Intelligence," Laing continued, "but I can assure you, that's who she's referring to with the word *them*. UI set things up with Craig Toner. His job was to use whatever threats were necessary to extract the information needed from Hofmann and McGrath, but it was made clear that didn't extend to killing them. At least, that's what I was told. It was thanks to my sister's warning that I managed to get out before it all went haywire."

"Your story has changed yet again," Mac said, almost shouting. "Not long ago you claimed to know nothing about all this, then you gave us the contractor's name and now it's clear you were up to your neck in the arrangements. And precisely when were you planning to tell us that Craig Toner is married to your sister?"

"That really is of no relevance."

"Of course it's relevant!" Mac exploded. "Apart from anything else, it brings into question who selected Toner as the contractor in the first place. You've maintained that UI were responsible but it's hardly credible to claim that they picked out a contractor who just happened to be your brother-in-law. We'll come back to these issues, but right now, we need to bring your sister in for interview and to do a test recording in order to confirm that it's her voice on the tape."

"I understand," Laing said, "but you'd better hurry. I'm pretty certain she'll use the opportunity of her husband being held here to pack her bags and leave. He's kept her very much under his thumb over the last few years. Coercive control I think they call it these days. In fact, she may already have left."

"Right. I'll phone the house now to check. I may need you to speak to her," Mac said.

It rang and rang. Eventually a woman answered, sounding breathless.

"I was just leaving when I heard the phone."

Mac asked to speak to Mrs Toner.

"I'm one of her carers. I'm afraid she left a while ago, didn't say where she was going, but took two bags with her."

Mac asked Laing for his sister's mobile number. When he made the call, it went to voicemail. Laing gave him details of his sister's car and three possible places she might have gone – all within the city. Mac left interview room 5 to make arrangements for the car's details to be circulated and each of the locations to be checked.

His phone rang. It was Angus.

"You know you told me to leave Toner's place before the cavalry arrived – well, I didn't leave completely. It was more of a temporary tactical withdrawal. I'd nothing better to do. Well, good job I returned to my post, because I spotted his missus doing a runner with a couple of wheelies." Mac sighed. "So I followed her." Angus was a star. "She's just gone into a house near Warriston Cemetery. This is the address."

It wasn't one of those on Laing's list. Angus really was a star.

Mac and a DC drove the short distance to Warriston to pick her up. It would have been difficult to have chosen anywhere much nearer to the Warehouse as a bolt hole. It turned out to be a friend's house.

Back at PIT HQ, they recorded her voice, which sounded identical to the professor's recording. The two were sent off to be checked by the forensic voice service – both for speaker identification and to detect whether the original recording had been subject to any tampering.

Afterwards, Mac found an empty interview room and asked Mrs Toner about her husband. What could she tell him about Craig Toner's less publicised activities?

"I don't know. He's always kept his business activities to himself. I'm sorry, but I can't really help."

Mac felt she was struggling, perhaps torn between a desire to say more and some vestige of attachment to her husband which was preventing her from talking. Or, bearing in mind her brother's comments about Craig Toner, maybe it was fear that was holding her back.

But might she be able to persuade her brother to say more? He felt it was worth a try and offered the pair the use of the interview room for a private conversation. They agreed. A uniformed officer stood guard outside.

+ + +

Craig Toner's solicitor took his seat in interview room 7, oozing experience and superiority. The message was loud and clear. *I've got clients out of deeper holes than this before.* Mac was encouraged that Toner now felt he needed his solicitor present.

After Laing's tape was played, the whole dynamic with Toner changed. It was not as if the suspect suddenly went onto the defensive – far from it. A previously unseen belligerence emerged. No, the real change was in Mac himself, a rejuvenation and a confidence that they were really getting somewhere.

"Can you explain why your wife should have made these accusations against you?" Mac asked.

"As you'll be aware, Inspector Larsen, she's not a well woman. Although it's primarily a physical illness, there's also a psychological side to it. Over the years she's developed some mental problems and occasionally gets deluded, particularly under stress. And recently, with her brother's increasingly unpredictable behaviour, there's been a lot of that."

Mac should have expected such a forthright response.

"And is she now displaying further delusional behaviour, as you describe it, by taking the chance to leave home while you are our guest?" If Toner was surprised by the news it didn't show.

"Not at all. She doesn't like being in the house overnight when I'm not there and as I had no idea how long I'd be detained by you gentlemen, it's a natural thing for her to do."

"So – do you know where she'll have gone?"

"To one or other of her friends."

"Very well. Now I'd like to ask you something about Eamonn Gallagher?"

"I'd prefer to forget about him, given how he's exploited my son. But what do you want to know?"

"You mentioned before that he has connections with the drug world?"

"That's the reason I got rid of him. I found out he had a long track record of involvement, which meant he was a liability and no longer of any use to me. And from what I've read about the Hofmann case… and the other feller who died… it's clear Gallagher's still operating in that world. I'm completely unable to understand why Robbie agreed to help him out. But I can assure you he'll have learned his lesson."

Clever, Mac thought, emphasising the drug-world link and steering suspicion away from Hofmann's world of work. He was effectively dropping his former employee in it, then standing back to watch the fun.

"At the end of our last session I mentioned Thomas Rook. Is that name familiar to you?"

"No. Why should it be?"

"Well, he's a man who has very recently been involved in some extremely violent behaviour. Remember I mentioned we had some other evidence against you – someone who can put you and Rook in the same place at the same time? Not that long ago as it happens."

The solicitor whispered something to Toner.

"And who might that be?"

"Someone by the name of Ash."

"I don't know anyone of that name either."

"Maybe Rook didn't tell you what his assistant was called, although I don't suppose it's his real name. The two of them are suspected of involvement in the death of a woman called Maxine Kildine. You might have read about her in the media. Anyway, they've since had a serious falling out. Which turns out not to be good news for you."

"As I don't know the guy, this can hardly be bad news." Despite the comment, Mac thought he detected the first glimmers of concern in Toner's eyes.

"He saw you talking to Rook in his car almost two weeks ago."

"Whoever this man is, he's mistaken."

"Granted, we can't necessarily rely on someone like Ash to tell the truth, especially as he has a grudge against Rook and maybe one against you as well. But a CCTV camera might be a more reliable guide to what did or didn't happen on a particular street, on a particular day. We thought you'd like to see the clip."

Mac explained what the footage was and that it might be used for evidential purposes at a later date.

The picture on the screen was reasonably clear. *A silver Honda pulls up... a man on the pavement opens the passenger door... face seen only in profile... As the vehicle moves off, towards the camera... two faces can be seen beyond the windscreen... one looking remarkably like Craig Toner... the other bears a close resemblance to Rook.*

"Now, I'd expect you and your solicitor to challenge this footage. We can't say one hundred per cent that the passenger is you, Mr Toner, although it looks very much like you. However, if we follow the Honda on its short journey, we can see in this clip the passenger stepping out of the car and very conveniently – or inconveniently depending on your point of view – he looks almost directly at the camera. I think you'll agree that there's no doubt this time who this is. So, what was your conversation in Rook's car all about?"

The solicitor whispered to Toner again and then requested some time alone with his client.

+ + +

Maeven took a seat in interview room 1.

Just as Khan finished describing Robbie Toner's latest claims about the events that had taken place in the empty industrial unit, Gallagher suddenly leapt to his feet.

"This is complete nonsense. Let me get my hands on the little fucker!" he shouted. Two uniformed officers moved rapidly to restrain him.

The episode triggered a rethink on Gallagher's part. With a

face like thunder, he admitted his involvement in the disposal of the bodies of Hofmann and McGrath, but vehemently denied responsibility for their deaths. Khan tried not to show his relief at getting such a breakthrough.

"Forget the lies he's told you! Robbie was the one who fired the taser – both times. It was his weapon. He bragged about buying it on the Internet and was itching to use the thing. It was never part of the plan to use a weapon of any kind. There was no fucking need! And it was him who injected McGrath with the speedball. From the look on his face, he took a sadistic pleasure in it."

"This is very hard to believe," Khan said. "You're the experienced one. Robbie's a total beginner. Are you really telling me he ran rings round you in this way?"

"I'm telling you what happened. The lad's a psycho."

At that point, Maeven called a temporary halt to the interview.

She'd been dipping in and out of all the interrogations and now summoned the full interview team to her office.

"We're making good progress. Let's recap on Gallagher and Toner junior first. With their confessions and other evidence, we now have more than enough to prove they were both involved in the disposal of the two bodies. But each is trying to lay the blame on the other for the actual killings. We need something to help us break this logjam. One option would be to go down the route of joint criminal enterprise – collective liability. Now the court won't necessarily look favourably on such an approach, but it might be our best bet. And before we actually reach court, we may be able to gather further evidence which puts one or other of them firmly in the frame. Let's start by lining up Gallagher, older and more experienced, as the principal and Toner as the naive accessory. We'd need to show he'd provided an act of assistance or encouragement. You OK with that, DS Khan?"

"Yes, Ma'am. I'm familiar with the law in that area."

"Good. Have you mentioned Rory Dalziel's name to him yet?"

"Yes, just before you joined the interview. It really threw him so I'll be pursuing that in the next round of questioning."

"Right. Craig Toner. The techies have found nothing of interest so far on his phone and the two laptops. They'll keep searching and also check out the devices from the company's office. We have his wife's evidence on tape that he was the contractor and we have Laing's accusations. But neither is sufficient in itself to make a conspiracy to murder charge stick. We'll need corroboration from elsewhere about his role. It's a good start that we now know he and Gallagher were acquainted and we should probe further about that relationship. What evidence can we find of more recent links between them? Toner claims there isn't any current link – that he cut his ties with Gallagher when he sacked him. But if he was involved with the contract to deal with Hofmann – as his wife stated – how would Gallagher feel now about being left out on a limb by his boss? Not too happy, I'd guess. Let's see what we can do to exploit this."

"We also need additional evidence that ties Toner in to Rook," Mac said. "We've got the CCTV footage which is very helpful but we could do with more than that. Is there any up-to-date news on Rook's condition?"

"Yes, the hospital has been in touch," Maeven said, "and we'll finally get the chance to interview him properly later today."

Mac said that after all the delays, he couldn't wait to begin.

"Which leaves the unfathomable Professor Laing," Maeven continued. "We need to know more about the relationship between him and Craig Toner and who was responsible for what. Let's try playing one off against the other. Now, given that we've been at it almost non-stop so far today, let's take a short break and grab something to eat."

Mac felt the intervention by the boss had been helpful. She

had the advantage of hovering above them in the helicopter, able to see the bigger picture.

There was just enough time for him to get across to the kiosk, before resuming the interviewing marathon. Waiting for his two sausage rolls to be heated up, he sipped his coffee.

A call from Fiona MacMahon. For a brief moment he was worried something bad might have happened. But she sounded uncharacteristically upbeat.

"I take it you won't be a regular reader of *Arc Light*, Inspector."

"No, I've never heard of it."

"It's an online journal on an obscure weapons control site, which now features an article called *Keep a Human Touch* by our late friends, Dieter Hofmann and Maxine Kilcline."

"How on earth can that be?" Mac said. "And why now?"

"Well, it's a long story but I'll give you the edited version. I told you before that because of the very sensitive nature of the story, we'd agreed to keep it in three separate parts until it was finalised and ready to be published. By some quirk of fate, Maxine managed to send her part to Dieter's solicitor just prior to her abduction on 27 February. Maybe she had a premonition! It was sent by post to avoid leaving an email trail. Her captors may well have found a version of the document on her phone or laptop, but because it would only have been part of the story, it wouldn't have been that much use to them on its own."

"And what about Dieter's section?" Mac asked.

"Well, according to a note sent to his solicitor, Dieter had arranged to meet up with Maxine on the evening of the 27th. She didn't show, he was unable to contact her by phone and got worried. On top of that, he was by then concerned about his own safety and decided to send his part of the article to the solicitor – again by post. This was on the morning of the 28th." Only hours before his abductors arrived at Mrs McGrath's house, Mac thought. "The lawyer was instructed to hold on to these documents for a fortnight. If there was no word from either Dieter or Maxine by the end of that period, he was to contact Cameron, my lawyer."

"So, when did you hear from him?"

"Late yesterday. It was completely unexpected. To be honest, I'd given up on the idea that the article would ever see the light of day. I worked through the night to add my section to theirs, edit the whole document and send it to *Arc Light*. And hey presto, it's online. I've just forwarded you a link."

"Thanks very much for all this. Is there anything in it that's new, anything which might be relevant to our enquiries?"

"Nothing new as far as I'm aware, but some of the content should provide corroboration of evidence you already have. And you'll be interested to know that the article makes a feature of the claim that Blue Star is developing a back door to allow full AI control of laser weapons!"

"Wow. So, *Arc Light* are really sticking their necks out!" Mac said.

"They are, particularly as that part of the story is based solely on Dieter's claims."

"Isn't that a dangerous step to take, given how litigious UI are known to be?" Mac asked.

"That's what I asked *Arc Light*. Their answer was that they expect UI to deny the story but then quietly drop the development of the back door. They'll be too worried about mud sticking, even in the absence of any supporting technical detail."

"Well, we may be able to help turn Dieter's claim into hard fact," Mac said. He told Fiona about the discovery of the journal and Dieter's confirmation of the back door. "I've asked the university whether they can provide a technical analysis that verifies Dieter's claim and will let you know how we get on."

"It would be brilliant if they could come up with that," Fiona said. "What's really worrying though is that if Dieter kept anything about this discovery on his personal laptop, which I'm sure would have been the case…"

"… that could have been what triggered the three deaths," Mac said.

"Exactly. It's dreadful to think about."

"One thing that Laing claimed was that Dieter had been out to sabotage the IntelOper project from the start, because of Ultimate Intelligence's involvement. Do you think that might have been the case?"

"Well, if he was still with us, I'd have declined to comment on that. But given we've lost him, I can confirm that was the only reason he took the job. He really was very single-minded."

"I gathered that! How about you and Ailsa? Are you both OK?"

"Yes thanks, Inspector. Ailsa doesn't look it, but she's a tough nut. Look, can I belatedly apologise for my rudeness during that first conversation we had? I was so stressed out about everything that it all came out wrong."

"Don't worry, I've been known to react like that on occasion. Thanks for your help since then. I wish you and Ailsa all the best."

Mac clicked on the *Arc Light* link, glanced at the article's key points and forwarded it to Maeven. Fiona was right. The article contained valuable corroborative evidence. With his coffee half-finished and his break-time rapidly disappearing, he ran back to the Warehouse and upstairs to Maeven's office, trying to keep the remains of his coffee from spilling, the two sausage rolls warming his jacket pocket.

The boss didn't seem to notice the appearance of his small picnic on her desk, distracted as she was by speed-reading the *Arc Light* article. Having finished, she turned to Mac and asked whether there was any chance of a sausage roll. It was duly handed over.

"I didn't imagine Laing would be so central to this dark tale," she said. "He comes across so plausibly – butter wouldn't melt and all that. Yet, he was clearly hand in glove with UI. What I still can't get my head around, is how they ended up with three people dead."

"We can only assume that it was because both parties had so much to lose," Mac said. "The extra detail in the article on UI is just what we need, but it's a real pity that there's nothing in there about Toner. We still need something to link him directly to the three deaths. I'm going to talk to his wife again. She must know more, but it'll be a question of whether she's willing to tell me."

"That'll be a good move," Maeven said. "Look, there's something else I need to mention. I briefed the chief super about the back-door issue and your request to Midlothian to try and come up with the technical supporting evidence. He wasn't too happy, felt it wasn't our job to get involved in the issue – despite the fact that it could turn out to be a critical factor in what led to the deaths. I explained that although we can attribute motive to UI, we've currently got no basis on which to charge them. Which is why you're making further enquiries about them."

"Let's hope we get some hard, technical information back from the university. Of course, the other issue is Mallory. In addition to boosting his income by leaking confidential information to UI, we suspect he was instructed to acquire stolen property from the killers – namely the victims' phones and laptops. Given how Urquhart reacted to the news, he clearly wasn't aware of this. Which means UI must have arranged it directly with Mallory."

"If we can prove that, it would be real progress. But given the sensitivity of these issues we'll have to tread carefully. Now let's get back to interviewing."

"If it's OK with you," Mac said, "I'll team up with DI Forsyth to break the *Arc Light* news to Laing and see what else he might give us and then get back to Craig Toner. By the time that's been done, Rook should have been brought down here and we can start on him."

"You're going to burn out if you're not careful. My suggestion would be that you and Euan continue to focus on Laing and Toner and I'll make a start on Rook."

It was actually something of a relief to Mac. Not that burn-out was a worry, but there were only so many plates he could keep spinning at any one time. On the way back to the interview room, Freya called.

"How's it going, love?" It was a real pleasure to hear her voice.

"Relentless, but we're getting there."

"I was thinking of coming over this evening."

"That would be great," he told her.

"I'll arrange a takeaway. Text me when you're done. Doesn't matter what time it is."

Euan stopped Mac just before they went into interview room 5.

"The SOCO report on the empty office building where they held Maxine," he said handing over a file, a broad grin on his face. "We've now got corroboration that Mallory, Laing and Rook were all there! And the Toyota pickup – the vehicle we spotted later on the farmer's CCTV – was caught on camera just around the corner from the building."

"Terrific!"

"Incidentally, no sign of Ash in any of this. Probably explains why he felt so confident about shopping the boss."

+ + +

"Did you find the conversation with your sister helpful?" Mac asked Laing.

"I did. Thank you for the opportunity. However, there's very little more I can help you with. Isla thinks I know a lot more than I do."

The professor's reaction was disappointing, but not really surprising. However, they could always return later to the issue of precisely how much he knew.

Mac watched the colour draining from Laing's face, as he read the *Arc Light* article. Hofmann and Kilcline's revelations made it clear that Laing had known exactly what was going on, had participated in some of the actions and acquiesced in others. Of course, he'd had so much to lose… job, career and a substantial second income from UI, which had subsidised his expensive lifestyle.

When Euan hit him with the revelations in the latest SOCO report, he lost control, slumped forward and banged his head against the tabletop.

Eventually the story came out, slowly and painfully, of what had happened to Maxine Kilcline.

"We used this vacant building, empty properties either side – so we wouldn't be attracting anyone's attention. Mallory had arranged it. I was there with him. He was the bait, knew Kilcline through his undercover involvement in Weapons Watch. She arrived, full of anticipation, dressed in outdoor gear and talking about catching the Peebles bus after the meeting to go off walking. Seemed very excited by the idea of picking up some new dirt on Ultimate Intelligence. Mallory kept the pretence going for a while, feeding her chunks of new information about UI and then gradually getting her to talk about the article she and Hofmann were writing. We were surprised how open and over-trustful she was."

"When did that approach change?"

"When we asked to see a copy of her part of the article. She refused. So, at that point, the pretence was dropped, Mallory left and Thomas Rook was brought in – a nasty piece of work. He seized her phone and laptop which she'd been foolish enough to bring along and found a draft of her part of the article. But it was clearly only part of the story. The interrogation which followed was aimed at finding out exactly what else she knew. That's when we found out about Fiona MacMahon's role as the coordinator and publisher of the final article."

"What do you know about the insulin?"

Laing looked puzzled.

"What insulin?"

Euan explained.

"I know nothing about that. It must all have happened after Rook told me to leave."

It was time to let Laing sit and fester for a while.

"Do you believe him about the insulin?" Euan asked.

"No more than I believe that headbanging was genuine," Mac said. "I reckon he could have had an alternative career on the stage."

They switched to interview room 7. In contrast to Laing, Craig Toner still looked calm and collected, a wry smile on his face. The solicitor demanded a bail hearing for his client. The only evidence they had was the CCTV footage showing Toner meeting Rook in a car, which was hardly a hanging offence. The audio recording of Mrs Toner proved absolutely nothing on its own and Laing's evidence couldn't be trusted, because he himself was the guilty party.

Mac said he'd have to speak to his boss about a hearing. But instead of going back upstairs straightaway, he stopped outside interview room 1 where Khan and Wyatt were questioning Gallagher and indicated through the door's glass panel for the sergeant to join him in the corridor.

"How's it going?" he asked hoping there might be something – anything – that he'd be able to use to keep Craig Toner in the building.

"Not good… at first. I told you about Gallagher's reaction to the name Rory Dalziel. Naturally I assumed it was because of some common link to the old drug cartel. But it turns out that

Dalziel had taken enforcement action against Gallagher years ago, over a drug debt, which had nothing at all to do with the cartel."

"That's a downer," Mac said, "particularly given the amount of time we've spent diverted by that particular line of enquiry. I've been wondering whether UI instructed Mallory to make the call, in order to lead us off the main trail. Anyway, you said *not good… at first.* Does that mean there's some better news?"

"Indeed there is!" Khan said. "Gallagher's really got it in for both the Toners. I don't think he meant to come out with it, just got totally carried away. To quote – *what's the betting fucking Craig Toner tried to tar me with the drug cartel brush?* Ironic really given what you just said about Mallory and UI. But it's a very promising development."

Mac knew it would be enough to kill the idea of a bail application. He texted Euan, asked him to relay the good news to Craig Toner and his solicitor and told him he might want to leave the pair sweating for a while.

"Gallagher's also talked about Robbie's attack on you," Khan continued.

"Oh yes – anything interesting?" Mac asked, instinctively rubbing his face which was still a little sore.

"Well, despite what he yelled at you, it had nothing to do with the Maxwell case and everything to do with your progress on the Hofmann investigation. With the naivety of youth, he thought disabling you would derail the whole case."

Khan went back into the interview room.

Sidling along to the other end of the corridor, Mac peered into interview room 8. Rook was in there with his solicitor, Maeven and a DC. The suspect didn't look well.

Mac managed to catch his boss' attention and she came out into the corridor.

"Sorry to interrupt. Is he talking?"

"Slowly but surely. He certainly is a tough one. Claims that depriving Maxine of her insulin was nothing to do with him. Somebody else gave the instructions for that, but we've not found out who yet. And one really distressing piece of news. He told us earlier that she died of hypothermia, overnight, in the vacant building. I managed to contact the pathologist out at Peebles Hospital. His view was it wouldn't have been cold enough for that to have happened inside the building. He felt it was much more likely it was the cold outside, under those rocks, that killed her."

"Which would mean that she wasn't actually dead when she was driven out there. That's awful," Mac said.

"Dreadful," Maeven said.

+ + +

"A feller called Gav worked with me for a while, a good lad," Gallagher told Wyatt. "He was with me in the Transit when we took Hofmann and McGrath from the mother's house. He'd been feeling dreadful for a while, reckoned he had the virus and once we reached the empty industrial unit, he took himself off to hospital. That meant I needed a replacement straight away to get the job finished. I knew Robbie from the site security work. We'd got on OK. He was always going on about wanting to get into something more exciting. That's why I gave him the chance. And he was immediately available! But it turned out to be the worst decision of my life. You think you know someone, but... Turns out he's a real headcase, no self-control and not a clue about sticking to a plan. I've already told you about the taser. He hadn't been in the building ten minutes, when it was out of his pocket, there was this weird, cracking, fizzing sound and wham, the feller was on the ground, dead to the world as it turned out. Still, even Robbie couldn't have known it would be fatal."

"Couldn't you have stopped him?" Wyatt asked.

"No chance! He was so quick, must have had it in mind all along, like zapping someone in one of those computer games."

"What about McGrath?"

"Well, I was bent over Hofmann trying to see what the damage was and Robbie goes and does the same bloody thing to McGrath. So that's two of them on the ground, McGrath screaming, the German quiet as a mouse, not moving a muscle. It felt bad. I mean the job was supposed to be at most a battering, not a fucking death sentence. I was trying to revive him and not really paying any attention to Robbie. Before I knew it, he'd shoved this syringe into McGrath's arm – the *speedball*. So, fair enough I own up to abducting the two of them in the first place and then dumping their bodies, but I'd nothing at all to do with the killings. That was all down to psycho Robbie."

"And what about his attack on Inspector Larsen?"

"Well, that just proves the point I'm trying to make. I mean, what possessed him? If it hadn't been for that, you'd never have caught us."

"And if Gav hadn't got the virus… you'd never have taken on Robbie in the first place," Khan said musing on the way fate worked out.

"I only found out later. A real bloody irony! He never had the virus. It was some other nasty bug."

"So, who did you get your instructions from, for this job?" Khan asked not expecting to get an answer.

"From fucking Craig Toner as you'll have guessed already." Khan tried very hard to keep the smile off his face.

"And how did that work?"

"Minimal contact between us, nothing on the phone or online, just a verbal agreement. He told me who the targets were and what punishment level to apply and it was up to me how that was carried out."

"So, you don't have anything at all in writing from Toner," Khan said.

"Well … there was one text." A pinched smile. "A big mistake on his part. I took a screenshot before deleting it. Insurance you could say. You've got my phone, so no doubt your techies will be able to retrieve the original. I'll tell you what it was about."

Khan listened and then texted his boss about the information Gallagher had just given him. The questioning continued.

"And why was McGrath caught up in this punishment?"

"Well, he knew everything, didn't he? Hofmann had told him the lot, all the stuff about laser weapons."

"So, it wasn't anything to do with their drug-world connections?"

"No. It was to do with Hofmann's job. But apparently the client wanted it to look like those two were real druggies. With Hofmann it was easy – because he was one. With McGrath we had to make it look like he was a dealer so I made sure some stuff was left, badly hidden, in his house, which no doubt you lot have already found."

+ + +

Mac entered interview room 7 in a good mood. Khan's text was just the boost he'd needed. He took a while filling glasses with water, adjusting the recording equipment and generally fussing around, in no hurry to get started. He asked Toner whether he had anything to say before the interview resumed. The answer was no.

"So, no bail for you – at least for the time being – and on top of that, Gallagher's got it in for you. Thinks it was you who made sure we found out about his drug-world connections and the activities of the Clyde cartel. I can see he has a point. A good way of taking the heat off your son. As a matter of fact, I did get an anonymous phone call telling me about the cartel. Not from you, but maybe you knew it was going to happen. Not that it really matters to you or me now. Matters to Gallagher though, which is why he's started talking about you."

Mac ran through Gallagher's evidence.

Toner had another whispered conversation with his solicitor, a pained expression having replaced the previous glow of confidence.

"What other lies has he come out with?"

"Well, so far he's told us fewer lies than you have. Basically, he said you've been the boss in all this. We're inclined to believe him, partly because it fits in with what Laing and your wife have told us and partly because he's given us some details which could only have come from you. Like that text you sent him! I thought you would have avoided such direct communication but then, I suppose, you had an emergency. Having already kicked Rook off the job, you instructed Gallagher to find and deal with Fiona MacMahon."

"It's not that difficult to fake a text," the solicitor said.

"And, for an expert, it's not that difficult to tell fake from genuine," Mac replied. "But it gets worse. This man Rook seems to know quite a lot about you. Not the first time you've worked together. Apparently, you've done something to piss *him* off – as well as Gallagher. And with you and Robbie at loggerheads, it's not exactly happy families time – is it? There are still some gaps to fill in, but we're getting there. Oh, and you'll be pleased to know that all your efforts have been in vain because the all-revealing article your client wanted suppressed has just been published. Or perhaps you weren't made aware of that part of the story. I'm afraid the news hasn't made Professor Laing's day."

Mac smiled as he left the room.

Laing seemed to have shrunk and closed in on himself during

the short time Mac had been away. The combined effects of a night in the cells and the continuing interrogations were taking their toll.

"I'm wondering if you'd had a chance to think any more about the conversation with your sister and whether there's anything additional you might want to tell us," Mac said.

Laing seemed to be uncertain as to where he was and it took him a while to focus on the room and its occupants.

"The crux of my problem," Mac continued, "is the need to find out who ordered the deaths of your colleague Dieter, his friend Alex and his fellow author, Maxine. I did consider that it was you, Professor." A sudden look of horror on Laing's face. "You have constantly surprised and disappointed us. But, somehow, I think that, even for you, it would have been a step too far." The haunted look was still there, as though it was impossible to remove. "My second suspect was Craig Toner. Did something happen which led him, unilaterally, to take the decision to kill?"

"No, no," Laing blurted out.

"In that case, I think there's only one candidate left. Hedley Baxter… or possibly someone higher up in his organisation."

Mac left the sentence hanging.

Laing squirmed in his seat and ran his fingers repeatedly through his hair.

"What would your sister want you to do, Martin?"

"She'd want me to be honest – for the first time in a long while."

+ + +

It was a tradition to celebrate successes in The Dockside. Not that there was a precise definition of what constituted success.

As Mac had told the chief superintendent, there were still gaps in the story – and in the evidence – but they'd gathered enough to bring the relevant charges and there was confidence that they could be made to stick. The chief had backed off.

Exact responsibilities remained to be clarified. Gallagher and Toner junior had been charged with joint criminal enterprise in the murders of Dieter Hofmann and Alex McGrath.

Evidence from Ash and Laing, CCTV footage in two locations, fingerprints and traces of his DNA found in the vacant office building, had all effectively tied Thomas Rook into the killing of Maxine Kilcline. A charge of murder would be added to the many others against him that were already being processed.

Gallagher and Rook, both keen to exact revenge for being effectively disowned by Craig Toner, had provided enough detail to show that he'd put out two contracts, one in relation to Hofmann and McGrath, the other for Kilcline and MacMahon.

Laing had eventually admitted he'd advised Hedley Baxter to recruit Craig Toner as the contractor. But he was insistent that the job had initially been limited to inflicting only such punishment as was required to extract the necessary information. After Kilcline's death however, Hedley Baxter had instructed Craig Toner to arrange the killings of the other three. But as Mac had no corroborative evidence of this, it remained a big hole to fill in the case.

Although the exact extent of their respective responsibilities remained unclear, there was sufficient evidence to show that both Laing and Craig Toner had participated in a course of action that had resulted in unlawful killing. Charges of conspiracy to murder were pending. And both were competing furiously in the race to distance themselves from the role of being the key link to Ultimate Intelligence. An interview with a senior UI representative had been arranged for the following day and it was hoped this would generate further evidence not only to help resolve this issue, but also to expose the extent of UI's own culpability.

Mac had received a call from the Midlothian pro-vice-chancellor for research and development. One of their software experts had managed to replicate Dieter's work and demonstrate conclusively that Blue Star's software did indeed include a back door which would have enabled full control by artificial intelligence of the laser weapons system. The university would carry out an urgent review of the IntelOper project. But Mac could imagine them closing ranks in order to minimise the institutional damage. No doubt Laing would be portrayed as the proverbial bad apple.

Maeven, Mac and Euan had between them put sufficient money behind the bar to keep the evening going. Her impromptu speech thanking them all for their hard work went down well. The Joker brothers had prepared a series of awards... most inventive interview question... most unusual fingerprint... best recall of suspect vehicle number plates... best impersonation of DI Larsen... best excuse for avoiding compulsory overtime.

Maeven left after the awards ceremony, whispering to Mac not to forget about applying for the vacant DCI post. The realisation dawned on him that it would be easier just to get the bloody application done rather than waste any more time thinking about whether to apply.

As the psychological after-effects of the shooting were beginning to take their toll, Euan departed at the same time, ferried home by his son, Jim.

Mac stayed for a while longer, but eventually left the rest of the team to enjoy themselves without having to continue watching their p's and q's in front of the DI.

A seat overlooking the docks, a cigarette. The first for a while. He was definitely cutting down. His mind drifted off as he looked out across the swell.

Having kept off the alcohol, he was fine to drive home. The Jimny took a diversion via an address in Warriston. He'd arranged the appointment prior to the visit to The Dockside.

Isla Toner offered him a cup of tea.

"When we spoke earlier, you didn't want to tell me anything about your husband which was understandable. But since then, you've had a conversation with your brother and I've interviewed him again. He told me that it was a man called Hedley Baxter who ordered the victims' deaths. That takes us a long way forward, but unfortunately, not far enough. So, I'm here to make an appeal to you," he said, blowing on his tea to cool it. "There are two areas where we need help. Firstly, we need someone to corroborate what Martin has just told us about Baxter. And secondly, more difficult for you, we need further evidence against your husband."

Mrs Toner sipped her tea. For the first time Mac noticed a subtle resemblance to her brother, something to do with the way she held herself.

"I had a feeling you'd come after me," she said. "I've been thinking a lot about our previous conversation. My conscience won't leave me alone. There's not the slightest bit of peace to be had. I've also been thinking about where I go with my life from here. You may not know that I have a younger son." Mac hadn't picked up anything about a second child. "Ally left home as soon as he could and… oh, how I wish I'd left with him. You always think you can change people. But Craig wouldn't change, of course. Anyway, I've decided to join Ally in Stornoway. Some of my family still live there."

"That's good to hear," Mac said. "I was worried for you. Can I ask how you are going to respond to your troubled conscience?"

There was a long silence broken only by the sound of a blackbird singing in the garden. Mac continued.

"On the recording your brother made, you said, if I remember rightly, that *with them involved, Lord knows what might happen to the German now.* I'm interested in *them.* Ultimate Intelligence?"

She nodded. "And this man in particular?" Mac brought up a photo of Hedley Baxter on his phone. She nodded again.

"A reptile," she said. "He came to the house on the morning of 28 February." A critical date, Mac realised. "I shall never forget. Sharp-eyed, expensive suit. I'd met him once before and knew instantly he'd be bringing trouble."

"And do you have any idea what he and your husband talked about?" Mac asked. She hesitated again.

"As you know, Inspector, I'm obliged to act as a waitress in my own home. In the process of serving their drinks, I took the opportunity to leave my phone, in recording mode, discreetly positioned behind a vase of flowers on the dresser. Then I left them to what they thought was a confidential discussion. It's a huge decision for me to take, but I'm going to let you listen to it."

"I really appreciate that," Mac said.

It was both fascinating and chilling to hear Baxter's disembodied voice.

"*... and there were some miscalculations with Kilcline. Like her not getting the insulin.*"

"*That was down to your lot. You should have left the detail to us!*"

"*OK, OK. But before she lost consciousness, we got confirmation of just how much they know. Even more than we thought. First an active link to some very well informed nutjobs in our home town, people who hate our guts. Kilcline eventually told us that Hofmann is about to fly out there. But even worse, the German has found out about something creative we're developing with a new piece of software. You don't need to know the details but it was kinda top secret. You'll appreciate that we can't allow him to continue causing such problems. So, the job's been changed. You need to pick him and his friend up today, pump them for information and get hold of their phones and laptops. Once that's done, get rid of them both. Understood?*"

"*Understood*"

"And you'll add MacMahon to the list as agreed."

"Agreed. With all these changes, there will of course be an additional cost."

"Of course. How much more?"

"The price will triple."

"Jesus!"

"It's a totally new spec. Do you want the job done or not?"

"We don't have a choice. You've got us over a fucking barrel."

"Good. We'll get on with it straight away."

"And don't forget, speed's vital now!"

Mac looked directly at Isla Toner.

"I'll need a copy of that."

"I know."

"And the existence of the recording poses a problem for you."

"I know. I should have told the police about it straight away. But if I were to agree to give evidence… might that help?"

"It would definitely help, but it's a big ask."

Mrs Toner put down her phone and stared out of the window. The blackbird was still singing.

"Do you know? I think I've reached a stage in my life when continuing to run away from all this would be harder than facing up to it."

A brave woman, Mac thought.

He called Freya from the Jimny, so she could order the takeaway. There'd be a lot of hard work involved in getting the cases to trial. But that was for another day. Mac enjoyed the drive home. The traffic lights all seemed to be on green and there wasn't a single hold-up.

Freya had the Indian food ready to serve and bottles of lager ready chilled. Given the size of the helpings, he knew a morning run would be a necessity. After the meal, they walked down to The Dunvegan. It was good to know that Robbie Toner wouldn't be leaping out to attack him again en route. The landlord remembered Freya from previous visits and asked how the artwork was going.

"Well, even Calum doesn't know this yet, but I've just had a commission for a mural on the wall of a new arts building in Dundee, which is pretty exciting – and a bit daunting."

"You're a dark horse! That's great news. When will you start work on it?" Mac asked, as they sat at his regular window table.

"As soon as I can, while I can still get up the scaffold!"

Mac looked suddenly concerned.

"Surely you won't be…"

"Don't fret… I've already roped someone in to do the high bits. I'll concentrate on what I can reach from the ground."

"Well, that's a relief." He kissed her – a good, long kiss.

"Hey, you two! Less of the snogging in that window seat. You'll put off the other punters," the landlord shouted.

"Look, I've been thinking," Mac said, ignoring the interruption. "How about going away for a couple of days on Saturday, just you and me, up to one of the nearer islands? Looks like we'll all get locked down pretty soon, so it would be good to fit in a mini break – before they pull up the drawbridge."

"That would be great and a good test to see if we can stand it together for that length of time!" Her serious face gradually dissolved into laughter.

Mac rolled his eyes.

He was far too easy to tease.

ABOUT THE AUTHOR

Dave Rigby lives in West Yorkshire and started writing ten years ago following retirement. He has self-published four books through Troubador. *Darkstone* is a thriller set in an imagined security state in Scotland. The other three books – *Shoreline* (2016), *Redline* (2018) and *End of the Line* (2021) - are a trilogy featuring Harry Vos, a Belgian private investigator.

ACKNOWLEDGEMENTS

Thanks to Emma, my editor, to Gabrielle, Joanna, Owen, Jim and John, my readers and to Edinburgh for inspiring my story. And thanks to The Book Guild for publishing *Mac*.

For writing and publishing news, or
recommendations of new titles to read,
sign up to the Book Guild newsletter: